THE CALL

TO MAJOR LEAGUE BASEBALL

Doug Ernest

One Printers Way
Altona, MB R0G 0B0
Canada

www.friesenpress.com

First Edition — 2022

Numerous names and terms, including real and fictious names and quotes, statistics, and definitions are used in this novel as illustrations and to bring realism to this body of historical fiction, and may, or may not, be accurate or true.

ISBN
978-1-03-913992-3 (Hardcover)
978-1-03-913991-6 (Paperback)
978-1-03-913993-0 (eBook)

1. FICTION, HISTORICAL

Distributed to the trade by The Ingram Book Company

DEDICATION

To my six grandchildren, Asher, Brandon, Brayden, Bryce, Evelyn and Liam. Thank you for allowing your "G Daddy" to see the world once again through the eyes of a child. Every interaction with you reminds me of my youth. Baseball will always be a little boy's game to me. It's also the perfect game for us thoughtful and analytical adults. I love the mental side of baseball—especially that interlude between pitches, when ballplayers and coaches make a "what if" decision, and then the pitcher steps up and throws a high hard one towards home plate.

PREFACE

It's always interesting to learn where a novelist got their idea for a book. Who influenced them and how? I began writing The Call to Major League Baseball two years after I watched a Major League Baseball game on TV. The game was played on May 12, 2018, between the Baltimore Orioles and the Tampa Bay Rays. I felt compelled to write a story about the Orioles' starting pitcher.

David Hess, age twenty-four in 2018, a right-handed pitcher, was drafted in 2014 by Baltimore in the fifth round of the MLB draft following a successful college career at Tennessee Tech. David worked his way through the Orioles farm system where, on May 11, 2018, he had been a member of the Triple-A minor-league team, the Norfolk Tides. He and his family will never forget that spring day because David received The Call to Major League Baseball by the Baltimore Orioles. It was the moment every little boy playing in Little League dreams of—getting called up to the big leagues.

The next day, May 12th, the Orioles put David in their lineup as the starting pitcher. His debut as a major-league player couldn't have gone better. He earned the win, pitching six innings, allowing three runs on six hits and striking out three Tampa Bay batters.

I was fascinated watching their newest rookie's major-league debut, not because of his strong performance, but because of his family and friends who were cheering him on from the stands. They had attended David's first big-league game, sitting together in a couple rows of seats along the third-base line. The TV broadcasting crew kept turning to the herd of Hess family members and friends. Their reactions during the game seemed more personal and intense than the rest of the Orioles fans in the stands.

As I watched the game and David's folks soaking up every moment of his big day, a couple questions crossed my mind: What had he gone through during his young life to bring him to major-league baseball? And what does it take to become a professional baseball player at the game's highest level of competition?

For the next two years, the questions kept gnawing at my sensibilities; I couldn't get away from them. Over time, I realized I'd never seen a book on the subject. So I decided I would take up the torch for college baseball players and those in professional baseball's minor leagues and write about what they experience—their routines, practices, travel, ballgames, old ballparks, money pressures and competition for promotion. I also wanted to write about little boys and teenagers who play baseball below the collegiate level because that's where boys' dreams are formulated, and it's where the fundamentals of baseball are learned and competition is met head-on for the first time.

As is common with professional baseball players, David Hess has bounced around a bit from team to team and even faced a demotion of sorts back to the minor leagues. After pitching for the Baltimore Orioles for parts of three seasons, he played a partial season for the Miami Marlins. He then landed with the Tampa Bay Rays organization and was assigned to the Rays Triple-A team, Durham Bulls, for the end of the 2021 season.

In October 2021, the Associated Press announced that David had been diagnosed with a cancerous tumor in his chest and that he would be starting chemotherapy treatments. My prayers are for a complete healing, and positive thoughts go out to David and his family for the reestablishment of his baseball career.

TABLE OF CONTENTS

CAST OF CHARACTERS

Hunter Henry Austin—protagonist
Archie Austin—his father
Janet Austin—his mother
Joseph Johnson "Jo Jo" Austin—his brother
Anthony Austin—his grandfather
Mike London—University of Virginia head football coach
Billy "BB" Bonner—AA Construction Company general manager
Evelyn Applegate—his neighbor and lifelong friend
Karen Applegate—his neighbor and Evelyn's mother
Asher Brown—his neighborhood friend
Liam Thomason—his neighborhood friend
Eleanor Brooks—his middle school flame
Bryce Jennings—his high school friend
Brady Doolittle—his high school friend
Brandon Doolittle—Brady's younger brother
Savannah Montgomery—his girlfriend
Lt. Colonel Bill Montgomery—Savannah's father
Robin Montgomery—Savannah's mother

Linda Leon—Savannah's college roommate
Joe Smith—Kempsville Pony baseball league coach
Jose Gonzalez—Kempsville Middle School baseball coach
Kelly Collinsworth—Kempsville High School baseball coach
Bennie Barnard—Trevecca Nazarene University baseball coach
Hunter Newman—Trevecca Nazarene University baseball player
Stephen Collins—Trevecca Nazarene University resident counselor
Melvin Johnson—his college friend
Robert Lee—his college friend
Mike Elias—Baltimore Orioles' general manager
Brandon Hyde—Baltimore Orioles' manager
Don Long—Baltimore hitting coach
Doug Brocail —Baltimore pitching coach
David Jennings—Baltimore Orioles' SE region head scout
Willie Jackson—Baltimore Orioles' field scout
Ryan Mountcastle—his minor league teammate
Cedric Mullins—his minor league teammate
Mike Yastrzemski—his minor league teammate
BJ Stewart—his minor league teammate
Austin Hays—his minor league teammate
Tanner Scott—his minor league teammate
Luis Pujols—Aberdeen IronBirds' manager
Eddie and Sarah Jones—Aberdeen IronBirds' host family
Keith Bodie—Frederick Keys Manager
Randy and Karen Joseph—Frederick Keys' host family
Gary Kendall—Bowie Baysox and Norfolk Tides' manager
Jason Isringhausen—Norfolk Tides player

1

PLAY BALL! (1986–1998)

Every baseball player has a story to tell, but some stories are more compelling than others.

Chief Petty Officer Archie Austin walked with purpose off the USS Theodore Roosevelt CVN-71 on the Naval Station Norfolk, his eyes searching for his Ford Mustang convertible parked somewhere in the massive twenty-five-acre lot. He was on an important mission, headed to Virginia Beach for a blind date with a lady. His buddy's wife had set them up. Spotting his Mustang convertible, he lengthened his stride. Soon the engine was purring with the white ragtop rolled down so he could enjoy the seventy-degree autumn air. The Mustang's dual exhausts roared as he sped off, thinking about his date.

It was November 14, 1986. The new aircraft carrier CVN-71 had only been put into service three weeks ago. Archie had been busy onboard ever since and had done nothing fun since the ship's crew took control of the floating airport. The thought of a blind date excited him. Her name was Janet Johnson. He wondered what she looked like. All he'd heard was that she was sweet, smart and worked as a librarian. He tried to imagine what she looked like. Was she tall or short, skinny or curvy, brunette or blonde, short-haired or long-haired?

Since Archie became a Christian, most of the girls he met were too wild. He was not into the partying lifestyle anymore. Since he stopped drinking every night, he believed he was a better sailor and a better man. His duties onboard the aircraft carrier were demanding and important to the ship's mission. He enjoyed going to work each day with a clear head and not having a guilty conscience about the things he'd done the night before.

Archie pulled a scrap of paper out of his pocket to check the address again, took a fast left down a narrow road and pulled up in front of a small townhouse. She was standing on the front porch, her hourglass figure clad in a black dress, her long brunette hair swept to one side. He let out a low whistle of surprise.

All he could think to himself was, "Why isn't this lady married?" he murmured. He looked in the rear-view mirror and answered himself with a smirk, "Because she's never met me." He jumped out of his car, his chest full of self-confidence, and walked towards her with a smile.

Exactly six months later, they were married.

Archie was standing in her family's church in Virginia Beach, looking sharp in his navy-blue dress uniform as he watched Janet walk gracefully towards him wearing a soft lace-covered wedding gown and clutching the arm of her father. The bride, having changed her last name to Austin, had no idea of the adventures and challenges awaiting her, and she could have never imagined the pride and joy her two future sons would bring her.

Once pronounced man and wife, Archie and Janet rented an apartment across the street from Pembroke Mall. It was a convenient location. Janet liked to frequent the Sears department store nearby. Most Saturday mornings, they would walk to the Village Inn Restaurant for omelets and fluffy pancakes. They hoped living in an apartment was only temporary and that someday they would buy their own house.

March 1, 1994 was a beautiful spring-like day in Virginia Beach. As Archie passed by a city ball field on his way home from work, he saw a half-dozen boys practicing baseball.

"I can't wait until I can take my kids out to play sports," he said. By now, Archie was now the father of one little boy, and Janet was due any day now. Archie hoped it was another boy.

"I'm going to teach them everything I know about playing ball." He smacked the steering wheel for emphasis.

At the same time, Janet was at home with their two-year-old son, Jo Jo. The toddler's given name was Joseph, but he'd already been tagged with the nickname Jo Jo by his grandfather, Anthony Austin. Granddaddy had taken one look at his first grandchild and called him Jo Jo. The nickname had just kind of stuck ever since. The toddler's full name was Joseph Johnson Austin. Johnson was his mom's maiden name. Everyone knew him as Jo Jo Austin.

Jo Jo had been a big baby. At birth, he weighed in at 9.5 pounds and measured 21.5 inches long exactly. He remained big as he grew; his pediatrician said he was in the ninetieth percentile.

Archie, who was very competitive, replied, "Of course he is. Austin men are always bigger and better."

On this warm March day, as Archie imagined baseball with his kids, Janet was at home, very pregnant and not feeling right. She'd been having Braxton Hicks contractions for the last two weeks. The slightly painful contractions lasted about one to two minutes, but she didn't think childbirth was on the agenda that day.

After lunch and a long nap, Janet got out of bed and quietly peeked into Jo Jo's room. He was still sleeping in his little bed. She was on her way to the kitchen to make them a snack when her water broke. She gasped in surprise. The baby was only thirty-six weeks. Janet grabbed the phone and called her husband.

Picking up, Archie said, "How's my pretty lady?"

"It's time, Archie." When she heard the car engine rev, she added, "Try not to get in an accident, dear." Janet pulled out her little suitcase and, as the pains started again, checked the timing. She called her neighbor down the hall, Mrs. Melody Anderson, a lovely older woman who liked to dote on Jo Jo, and told her it was time.

"So exciting," Mrs. Anderson said on the phone. "I'll just pack up my knitting and be right over."

By the time Archie got home, the little suitcase was all packed up, Mrs. Anderson was fixing Jo Jo a snack, and Janet was sitting in the living room, experiencing strong contractions while Jo Jo patted her arm.

"You need to go to the hospital," Mrs. Anderson said in a cheery voice. "Second babies always come out faster."

It took some effort for Archie to get Janet and her suitcase into the car as she was having strong labor pains.

"You're not going to … you know," Archie asked white-faced, "give birth in the car?"

"Just drive, Archie," Janet answered with a cry from another contraction. Archie didn't remember her being in such pain the first time. He set a speed record getting from the Pembroke area to Virginia Beach General Hospital. He ran red lights in town and then passed everyone eastbound on I-264 like they were standing still.

"Slow down," Janet said. "If you get into an accident, I will have this baby in the car." But that only made Archie grip the wheel tighter and step down harder on the gas. There was no getting through to her hard-headed man. Soon he had screeched up to the emergency room, Janet was settled into a wheelchair and they were wheeling her off to the hospital's labor and delivery department.

But the second child did not come faster as Mrs. Anderson had predicted. To Archie, the birth seemed to take forever. How could Janet take that much pain? Because of the baby's position, the doctor decided to do a C-section. Archie was allowed to stay, but he paced along the edges of the operating room, afraid to look.

Despite the fear and pain, Hunter Henry Austin was born, weighing in at 6 pounds and 17.5 inches long. Though he was pronounced healthy by the hospital staff pediatrician, he looked tiny.

Mother and baby had to stay in the hospital for four days. When Archie was allowed to bring them Janet her first meal after her surgery, he bought Chinese take-out to celebrate. At the end of the meal, Janet cracked open her fortune cookie and read the message.

"'Perceived failure is oftentimes success trying to be born in a bigger way.' That sounds like it came straight from heaven."

"I'm not sure I like the mention of failure," Archie said.

Janet tucked the blanket more tightly around Hunter, who was asleep in a little bassinet next to her. "I think it means this baby boy will achieve great things. He already overcame his premature, difficult birth."

A crystal ball could not have foreshadowed his future any better.

Hunter had one distinctive characteristic that nearly everyone commented on. He had large dimples in his cheeks. When he smiled, it caused everyone to smile back. Just being around him made people smile. Except for his daddy. Archie would look at his baby and say to anyone who would listen, "Why isn't Hunter big like Jo Jo?" Comparisons to his older brother began early for Hunter.

Life with two children seemed very full. Before Hunter came along, Janet and Archie liked to stroll along the streets of Virginia Beach near the oceanfront. On 19th Street was the Virginia Beach Civic Center, best known by its unofficial name, the Dome, after its geodesic dome shape. For thirty-five years, it had been the premier spot for famous artists but then it was slated to close. One summer evening, June 30, 1993, with Mrs. Anderson babysitting Jo Jo, Janet and Archie went to the Dome to see its final performance by Three Dog Night. It had been a nostalgic night. One year later, on September 9, 1994, pushing Jo Jo and Hunter in a double stroller in the warm air, they came upon an excavator ripping off chunks of the Dome, piece by piece. They knew it had closed but to see it being torn apart was heartbreaking.

"Oh no," Janet cried out, putting a hand to her heart. "I can still hear them singing 'Joy to the world."

"Can you believe this?" Archie fumed. "The city's tearing down the only music venue in Virginia Beach. What a bunch of morons!"

Archie was starting to feel the pressure of too little money in the bank and too much credit card debt. It wasn't cheap raising a family. He hoped that someday he and Janet could buy their own house, and they needed a financial plan to do that.

Soon after Hunter was born in 1994, Austin got interested in selling real estate. At first, he was only thinking about buying, flipping and selling houses that he could buy for a steal and sell for a killing. After all, he had a growing family to take care of, and with two kids at home, he hated the idea of six or seven-month navy deployments. He began studying for the real estate license examination.

"This way," he told Janet, "I might not have to re-up in the navy again."

Just by showing houses on the weekends, Archie sold almost one house a month.

"Wow," he said to Janet, "imagine what I could do if I weren't in the navy?" Archie's time in the navy wasn't going as well as he would have liked. By 1995, he had been passed over twice during selection processes for senior chief, which left him with a bad taste in his mouth.

"I think I can make a career in real estate," he insisted.

Janet was scared about him making the jump out of the military. "Are you sure, Archie? The navy provides security for the family. There are things to think about, like health and dental care. And there's the housing allowance."

But her caution couldn't dim his excitement over successfully selling houses; it kept him contemplating not re-enlisting in the military. They began having frequent arguments about his wish to leave military service.

"You are only thinking of yourself!" Janet yelled one night. "We have two boys to support, and my salary at the library will not carry a family of four."

"Honey," Archie replied, dismissing her, "a man's got to do what a man's got to do." He continued studying for the real estate exam as his wife slammed their bedroom door and went to bed.

Over time, Archie managed to convince his wife to accept his conversion back to civilian life. While she still wasn't sure he'd make money working in real estate, she was tired of fighting.

On September 30, 1995, Chief Petty Officer Archie Austin was honorably discharged from the United States Navy. While the future for him and his family was unclear, he liked to say, "We're like a naval aircraft carrier cruising at thirty knots. It's full steam ahead for this family."

Archie hooked up with a large real estate company in Virginia Beach. As he looked for listings of houses for potential buyers, he started checking them out with an eye for himself. It didn't make sense to him and Janet to keep renting when he was helping others buy and sell houses. He managed to get Janet interested by telling her, "As a veteran, I qualify for a VA Home Loan. We don't need a down payment."

Because he was now a realtor, Archie would occasionally take Janet through a house for sale as soon as it went on the market. She liked the Kempsville neighborhood of Virginia Beach, where she worked in the community library. Kempsville was an established neighborhood with lots of big trees, a library, a recreation center and several schools.

Archie took his wife to see a house right where she wanted to look, off Kempsville Road. As they drove near the address they were going to check out, their excitement grew.

"Look, Archie," Janet cried, "an elementary school, middle school and high school plus a rec center within a mile of our home." She laughed. "If it becomes ours."

"There's even the library where you work, and a police station is just down the road," he added.

"Oh, Archie, I've always wanted to live in a subdivision where everything is within walking distance like this one." Their car turned into Manor Drive, and they searched for the correct address.

"I love that the high school baseball field backs up to this street." He nodded approvingly. "My boys can play ball there someday."

"There it is, Archie!" Janet shouted out as she spotted the house. "Oh, it's so cute. Look at the window flower boxes. Oh, and honey, there are rose bushes everywhere!"

The four-bedroom, two-bathroom, 1,675-square-foot rancher was painted white with black window shutters, and it had a black roof. It had a garage, front porch and rear deck. Archie messed with the lockbox on the door until he got the house key out. Soon they were inside walking from room to room.

"And here's the kitchen." As he turned to let his wife go by, he noticed she was crying. "What's wrong, dear? Don't you like it?"

"These are tears of joy." Janet threw her arms around him in a hug. "I love this place. Everything about it."

He gave her a squeeze. "I love how spacious the backyard is." Back and forth, they went about how much they liked that house.

"The backyard is so shady."

"The deck out back is awesome."

"Think of the cook-outs we can have out there."

"I think this is the one for us," Janet said.

Archie gave her a big kiss. "Let's go write up an offer on this place."

Janet paused a moment and took Archie's hand. "Let me just take this all in." She stood there smiling and thinking about the future. "When God chooses to bless you, He doesn't mess around." On January 15, 1996, Archie and Janet purchased the house on Manor Drive. By the end of February, with the moving van parked in front of the house, they each lifted a foot over the doorstep into their new home. The Austins were putting down roots.

In the fall of 1997, Jo Jo was enrolled in kindergarten at the Kempsville Elementary School. It was the beginning of thirteen years of learning and achievement in the Virginia Beach public schools for him.

One cold winter evening in 1998, when Jo Jo was six and Hunter was four, the Austin family was driving to Frankie's Place of Ribs for dinner. They passed the local police station and noticed a sign advertising the Kempsville Recreation Association's next sports season. The sign gave information on registration for spring baseball leagues.

"Man, it's only February," Archie murmured, "and they're ready for baseball sign-ups?" T-ball league would begin for four-year-olds. A Coach Pitch league would begin for six years old boys.

"Hmm," he pondered, "it's the right age ranges."

When they were seated at Frankie's, he turned to Janet and said, "This might be a good time to get the boys involved in sports. The sign-up for baseball begins this month."

As they all dove into Frankie's onion loaf appetizer, the family discussed the opportunity. The boys were excited about wearing ball uniforms and being on a team.

"This would be a good opportunity for Jo Jo and Hunter to learn about teamwork," Janet said.

"What's teamwork?" Hunter asked.

"Well," she replied, "waiting your turn. Rooting for your teammates."

"Following a coach's directions," Archie added.

"That doesn't sound fun," Jo Jo piped up.

"Does so," Hunter said.

"Does not."

"Boys," their mother broke in, "eat your onion rings."

One day, Hunter was hanging out with his new next-door neighbor, Evelyn Applegate. They were the same age, but he was two months older than she was, as he liked to point out.

"My daddy signed me up to play T-ball," he told her.

"Then I want to, too." Evelyn and Hunter were best buddies who lived on opposite sides of a six-foot-fence. After Evelyn begged her mother to play T-ball with Hunter, she too was signed up for T-ball at Kempsville Rec.

Both Jo Jo and Hunter threw and batted right-handed. Since Jo Jo was going to play Coach Pitch baseball, Archie not only let him hit off the tee, he threw balls for him to swing at. The more Jo Jo practiced, the better his eye-hand coordination became. Soon, Hunter wasn't satisfied with just hitting off the tee and started begging his dad to pitch to him too. He swung and missed most of the balls, but he wanted to try anything his big brother did.

In Kempsville Rec ball, Jo Jo played in the league for six-to-seven-year-olds called Junior Farm baseball, where the coaches pitched to the kids. Hunter played in Kempsville Rec T-ball with the four-to-five-year-olds. Jo Jo was taller than most of his teammates. Hunter, on the other hand, looked tiny out on the field compared to the other boys and girls. He was sad that Evelyn was assigned to a different team.

Given the ages of the T-ball kids, coaches had a difficult time getting them to understand directions. Practices were a challenge. The kids got bored quickly and ignored their coaches. Frequently, they could be seen playing in the dirt or picking dandelions out in the grass. In the middle of practice, kids would run off the field to find their parents only to have Mom or Dad send them back out onto the field. It was a revolving door that would continue until the practice was over.

But Hunter never left the ball field until the practice was over, and he would never lie on the grass picking dandelions. He'd chase batted balls and throw them as far as he could. Hunter also loved to run, whether it was going after balls or running around the bases. He was quicker than the other kids too. His coaches had to keep telling him not to run in front of his teammates to catch balls, so the others had a chance to catch some balls too.

Although Hunter was developing his baseball skills and was enthusiastic about the game, for some reason, his father didn't seem to notice. He also rarely spoke words of encouragement, and compliments were out of the question. On the other hand, when Jo Jo got a base hit or caught a batted ball, Archie would leap out of his lawn chair and cheer him on. He only had eyes for his firstborn.

The next year, during another mild winter in the mid-Atlantic region, Hunter couldn't wait for baseball season to roll around again. He kept begging his father to go out onto the backyard and play catch, but Archie would say, "Wait for the spring, buddy. I don't play ball when it's forty-five degrees."

Jo Jo, at seven years old, played basketball during the winter. He was tall and athletic and picked up hoops quickly.

When spring finally arrived, Archie surprised his sons with tickets to the Norfolk Tides 1999 opening game. It was the first professional game the boys would see in person. As they drove to the stadium, Archie explained what the minor leagues were and how they were used to develop young baseball players and get them ready to play for major-league teams.

As they waited in line to get into the stadium, he continued educating the boys.

"Now, the Norfolk Tides are a Triple-A team. They're only one rung on the ladder away from the big leagues."

"The big leagues!" the boys crowed.

"You know, guys," he added, "some of these players might get The Call any day to the New York Mets. They're the major-league team the Tides belong to."

The boys responded with oohs and aahs.

"Can you imagine playing baseball on TV and having your face on a Topps bubble gum baseball card?"

Both boys got excited, but Hunter just about lost it. He turned to the folks standing nearby and said, "I'm gonna play for the Tides someday." He bounced in excitement. "And I'm gonna get The Call to play in the major leagues—"

"You go, tiger," an old man cheered.

"—and I'm gonna have my face on a bubble gum baseball card!"

Archie had arrived with the boys at Harbor Park Stadium early so they could get autographs from the Tides players. Before they found their seats down the first-base line, he took his boys into the team store and bought each of them a new baseball so they could have it autographed.

Jo Jo smelled French fries and followed his nose to a nearby concession stand.

"Hey, Dad," he yelled, "let's get some food. I'm starving."

"I'm starving!" Hunter parroted, eyeballing the hot dogs.

Soon, the three Austins headed towards their seats, balancing baseballs, baskets of food and cups of soda. Hunter had not even taken a bite of his food, and he already had mustard stains on his shirt.

They sat so close to the field—only four rows away—they could smell the cut grass and see the baseball players warming up in front of them. Jo

Jo and Hunter were grinning from ear to ear. After chowing down their food, they ran up to the railing separating the stands and the ball field and started yelling at the players for autographs. They were ignored—the Tides players were warming up their arms. Then, out of the Tides dugout, a catcher and pitcher emerged and started their long walk to the bullpen to warm up before the game. Little Hunter, who was waving frantically, finally caught the pitcher's eye.

"Sir! Sir! Can I have your autograph?"

The pitcher walked over to the railing.

"How you doin', kid?" he asked, taking out a pen as Hunter handed him his ball.

"I spilled mustard on my shirt."

"I see that. What's your name, kid?"

"My name's Hunter Austin, and I'm five years old. What's your name?"

"Jason Isringhausen," the ballplayer said.

"And, sir, how old are you?"

"I'm twenty-six."

"I'm going to play for the Tides someday too," Hunter burst out.

"I'll keep an eye out for you, kid." Then, with a wave, he was on his way to the bullpen.

As they watched Jason Isringhausen pitch to batters during the game, Archie explained the types of pitches Jason was throwing and how hard it was to hit them.

"Pitchers try to mess up the batter's timing," he explained, "by throwing fastballs, changeups, curveballs and sliders"—the boys nodded dutifully—"all at different speeds and in different locations around home plate." He pointed to the pitcher. "Guys, watch Isringhausen throw his curveball. It looks like it falls off the table. It's a twelve to six breaker."

"What does that mean?" Hunter asked.

"If you roll a ball off of a table," his dad explained, "it falls straight down, just as his curveball does as soon as it gets to home plate. You see, it breaks downward instead of sideways. This one's called a twelve-to-six curveball as the break of the pitch is on a straight path downwards, like the hands of a clock at twelve and six." Hunter nodded, but he couldn't really tell time that well yet.

"Curveballs," his dad continued, warming to the subject, "have a variety of trajectories and breaks among pitchers. This mainly has to do with the arm slot and release point of a pitcher."

Jo Jo, by now, had stopped paying attention. He just wanted to watch the game. Hunter kept nodding dutifully, his eyes clouded with confusion. His dad was using a lot of big words, but they sounded important.

"There are several nicknames for the curveball," Archie added, "bender"—that got the boys' attention— "the hook, Uncle Charlie, Lord Charles and the yakker."

"Yakker!" Jo Jo crowed, laughing. "Hunter, you're a yakker."

"You're a yakker," Hunter fired right back.

"Throw an Uncle Charlie!" Hunter called to Isringhausen. "Throw a bender!"

When they got home from the game, Hunter went into his room and pulled out his cigar box of baseball cards. He carefully took out a half dozen cards and looked them over. Hunter read off the names on each card: Mark McGwire, Sammy Sosa, Ken Griffey, Jr., Roger Clemens, Randy Johnson and Derek Jeter. He held the last one longer than the others and imagined his name and picture on the card.

"That's what I want to be when I grow up," he whispered. Hunter prayed to God, "Please, help me be a professional baseball player. That's what I want to be when I grow up; a Baltimore Orioles' baseball player."

2

JUST LUCK (1999–2007)

After the Norfolk Tides opener, the Austin boys were fired up for the start of the 1999 spring rec ballgames. Hunter was in the last year of T-ball with his friend Evelyn. His little legs had grown some, and he ran faster than the previous season, but he still was a little squirt compared to his teammates. He still kept running after every ball hit, no matter how far away from him it was, despite his coaches trying to get him not to do it and even though it annoyed the other kids—Hunter would cut in front of them to scoop up the groundballs. He just loved the game of baseball. At home, he drove his dad crazy trying to get him to play catch. Most of the time, Archie would talk Jo Jo into going outside to throw with his little brother. But oftentimes, Jo Jo preferred to play basketball in the driveway. Jo Jo liked any game with a ball involved. Hunter was only obsessed with baseball.

As summer turned to fall, Hunter was enrolled in kindergarten at the Kempsville Elementary School. Since Jo Jo was in second grade, the boys would make the short walk together to and from school each day. On his first day of school, Hunter was so nervous that he just stopped inside the doorway of the entrance. Jo Jo plowed into him.

"What are you doing?" he demanded.

"It's so big," Hunter replied. His head turned to take in all the students and teachers wandering about. The hall seemed filled with classroom doors.

Noticing Hunter's anxiety, Jo Jo put an arm around him and said, "Don't worry, little bro, I'll take care of you." And he did, as much as possible.

As spring rolled around again, Hunter was signed up to play his first season of Coach Pitch baseball in the Junior Farm baseball league at Kempsville Rec. Jo Jo was in his last season in the same age group. The brothers were psyched about playing baseball together on the same team. Hunter's friend, Evelyn, had moved on to girls' fast pitch softball.

The boy's grandfather was intrigued that they were playing on the same team.

"Why, don't you each look sharp your unis," he said to the boys as they jumped around the kitchen in their new uniforms. Their granddaddy was a former minor-league baseball player who used to refer to a uniform as a "uni." It only took him coming out to one of the boys' ballgames to catch the Little League fever. Maybe it was seeing baseball through the little boys' eyes or experiencing their enthusiasm for the game. But he couldn't wait to come back and watch his grandsons play the game that had been so good to him four decades ago. Anthony had never made much money in the minor leagues, but he lived the dream for a few years. So, that spring of 2000, Mom, Dad and Granddaddy became regulars at their ballgames. It was a fun season for the Austin family.

It took three games before Hunter got his first base hit. The next batter hit a ball through the infield, and Hunter ran the bases as if his pants were on fire. He didn't stop running until he had crossed home plate. Meanwhile, the batter stopped at first base since the ball didn't go much past second base.

The third-base coach tried to hold Hunter at third base, but he ran through his stop sign.

"What did I tell you!" his father said in the car after the game. "Always watch your base coaches!" He continued to reinforce that point all the way home.

Jo Jo, on the other hand, was a natural at baseball, football and basketball. In the same game where Hunter got his first hit, Jo Jo hit a ball over the left fielder's head for the first home run of his life. Archie ran up and down the sidelines, high-fiving all the other parents.

All through the car ride home, Hunter waited for his family to mention his first-ever base hit.

"Daddy," Hunter asked as they pulled into their driveway, "did you see my first hit today?"

"Yeah," his dad replied absently, "but did you see Jo Jo's home run?"

When they got in the house, Hunter went right to his bedroom, closed the door and fell onto his bed. He lay there, not saying a word as tears streamed down his cheeks.

In the spring of 2001, Jo Jo moved up to baseball for nine-to-ten-year-olds in the Senior Farm baseball league. It was kid pitch baseball, where pitchers tried to strike out batters, and base on balls were part of the game. In six-to-eight-year-old baseball, a coach pitched to his own players and made it as easy as possible to hit the ball. There were no balls and strikes called by an umpire. Of course, in either league, when Jo Jo made clean contact with the ball, it always soared into the outfield.

Jo Jo liked the Senior Farm baseball league because it was competitive, and somebody kept score. He was learning to enjoy winning. Archie made sure not to have any business appointments during his games. He didn't have the same commitment for his younger son's games.

Hunter was playing his second season of Coach Pitch baseball. He had practiced many times with his dad and brother since the last season. For a seven-year-old, he'd developed a knack for getting the bat on the ball—it just didn't go very far when he hit it. He mainly played infield because, unlike a lot of the other kids, he actually had a clue what to do when a ball came his way, although he still went after balls that other kids should have caught. He was quick on his feet and had cat-like reflexes.

When Jo Jo turned ten years old, it meant spring 2002 was his last season in the Senior Farm baseball league. He was the tallest kid on his team; he ate up the competition. Kids tried to strike him out, and he tried to take them deep. Jo Jo was developing into a power hitter, and when he came to bat, the opponents would move out deep into the outfield.

That March, Hunter turned eight years old and was finally having a growth spurt. He was no longer the smallest kid in his league; now he was one of the oldest. Coach Pitch baseball bored him a little as the pitches were so easy to hit. He couldn't wait to play kid pitch baseball.

Hunter terrorized his opponents with his footspeed, running the bases. His little ball shoes threw up so much dirt and sand it appeared he was running through a cloud of dust. He finally learned to play only one position at a time on defense and not steal batted balls headed for his teammates' gloves.

The next year, 2003, when Jo Jo turned eleven, he was no longer eligible to play in Kempsville Rec's baseball leagues, so he figured it was a good time to learn to play football and improve at basketball. He played winter basketball in a Kempsville Rec league and spent spring and summer playing hoops and pickup tag football games with his buddies. Sometimes, Hunter would join in and try his best against the bigger boys—he was the fastest runner of the bunch. But no matter who showed up to play, Jo Jo was always the best athlete there.

At nine years old, Hunter's eye-hand coordination was pretty good, and during his baseball games, it was pretty hard to strike him out. He was finally playing kid pitch baseball in the Senior Farm baseball league at Kempsville Rec. Before the season began, he practiced batting at the Kempsville Elementary School field with Jo Jo and their friends—whoever was willing. Sometimes, he coaxed his dad out to pitch to him. Even his granddaddy practiced with him sometimes. Hunter nearly always got the bat on the ball, but his swing had no power and the balls didn't go far. Because he ran so fast, during ball games he would beat out most groundballs and reach base safely.

Since Hunter had developed a strong throwing arm, the coaches had him pitch as well as play defense in the field. One game that season, he struck out the side in the first inning, one, two, three.

His dad could not hold his joy. "Atta boy, Hunter!" he yelled at the time. But later, on the way home, he said nothing. The car rides home after Hunter's ballgames were silent ones.

As the calendar turned to September 2003, Jo Jo moved from elementary school to middle school. Luckily, Kempsville Middle School was also located in the Austins' neighborhood. Jo Jo didn't have to take a bus or catch a ride; he relied on his Air Jordans. Hunter also walked to his school, but his parents didn't invest a hundred dollars in a pair of Air Jordans for him. He did get to walk to school with Evelyn, who was still his best friend.

One night at dinner, Hunter asked if he could play baseball in the fall Kempsville Rec league.

"It's too much money," said his dad, diving into a steak dinner.

His mom put down her fork, "Now, Archie—"

Archie pointed his fork at her. "And takes up too much of our time."

"But—"

"Enough said." And he went back to eating his steak.

Later, in his room, Hunter brought out his cigar box of baseball cards and absently shuffled though them. "I bet if Jo Jo had asked to play fall sports," he said to himself, "Dad would have said yes."

Sure enough, a few days later, Jo Jo's request to play football at Kempsville Rec received an immediate, "That's my boy!" and a promise to register him.

When Hunter stomped around, saying, "That's not fair! Mom, he's playing favorites!" his dad quickly shut him down with, "What's done is done."

Hunter tried not to resent Jo Jo as he watched him put on his football pads and jersey plus his helmet and pose for Dad's camera.

"You look like a gladiator," Dad said.

"I feel like one!" Jo Jo replied.

Jo Jo played in the eleven and under (U11) rec league. It was tackle football for boys aged ten to eleven. He loved the physical contact that football provided. He used his height to catch twenty-five passes, five of them resulting in touchdowns, and was selected by his teammates as his team's MVP at the end of the season. This gave him enough experience that, when February 2004 came around, he played both basketball and baseball for the Kempsville Middle Braves' teams.

Now in seventh grade, Jo Jo was having a great year. His God-given talents had elevated him to starting spots at both tight end and free safety. Now more than six feet tall, he caught pass after pass that came his way. He also proved to be a ball-hawk on defense, intercepting six passes and defending fourteen others. There was such a stir around town about what Jo Jo could do on the gridiron that his future Kempsville High School coaches came out to see him play in middle school.

Fortunately, academics at school came as easily to him as athletics, and he frequently made the principal's list for his high marks. He was a child any parent would be proud of, as Archie often said. Jo Jo's parents set up a special Facebook site to post their son's sports and academic accomplishments. Anyone looking at the site might not realize they had another son as they never shared news about Hunter.

Hunter turned ten years old in March of 2004. He was in his second season of kid pitch baseball and continued playing in the Senior Farm baseball league. That proved to be Hunter's last year playing baseball in the Kempsville Recreation Association. With his ability to get the bat on the ball, Hunter rarely struck out, but he was still physically weak. He continued to be a menace on the bases since he ran so fast. He was catching more balls than he missed. Since, at this level, so few balls were hit to the outfield, he frequently asked to pitch.

"Otherwise," he explained to his granddaddy (who made a point of practicing with Hunter regularly once he saw Jo Jo's sports Facebook site), "I feel like a statue in the field."

While pitching, Hunter had improved a little over the previous year, but his control was all over the place. The little boys standing at the home plate waiting for him to pitch sometimes got scared; Hunter would hit a couple of batters each game with his pitched balls, no matter how hard he tried not to.

After one of his ball games, Hunter overheard his dad complimenting another parent.

"Your boy sure played well today," he said.

"Same with yours, Archie," the parent replied. "Hunter did a great job pitching." On hearing this, Hunter's chest expanded with pride.

"Just luck," Archie said with a wave of his hand. "But Mac's son, Johnny, now he's turning into a great little player." Hunter dropped his head and went to the car. He stood there waiting for his dad to finish complimenting the other players.

Once they were home, Hunter called his granddaddy.

"Hey, little buddy!" his granddaddy roared. "How was your game?"

"Okay, I guess," Hunter replied in a low voice. "Can you come to my next game?"

"Sure, buddy." His granddaddy paused a moment, then added, "Did something happen today?"

"Not really." And Hunter would have left it at that, but suddenly the words burst from his mouth, "I just can't seem to be able to please my dad. No matter what I do, no matter how well I pitch or run the bases. He never has anything good to say about me. I pitched today, and the other team only scored two runs."

"You pitched well," his granddaddy said kindly.

"That's what another guy's father told Dad, but all he said was it was just luck."

"Well … my son, your dad, is just—" Anthony broke off. Then he took a deep breath and continued in a softer tone, "I'll do my best to get to your games for the rest of the season. And remember my standing offer to practice baseball with you. I may be old, but there was a time when I got paid to play. I played three years of Single-A baseball in the minor leagues. Maybe I can pass on some of my baseball wisdom to you."

"Awesome, Granddaddy!" Hunter exclaimed. "I want to play for the Norfolk Tides someday. You can come watch me play at Harbor Park."

"I see you have your life completely mapped out. I hope and pray that all your dreams come true, buddy."

They said their goodbyes, but before hanging up, Anthony Hunter thought for a moment, then said, "All I need is someone to believe in me. I feel like everyone is judging me and comparing me to Jo Jo."

Anthony gave his grandson some wisdom.

"Hunter, my boy," he said, "you can only feel sad and judged if you allow it. The most important thing is for you to believe in yourself. Remember, the only person you need to please and impress is yourself."

In the winter of 2005, Hunter turned eleven years old. He was in the fifth grade, the last year of elementary school. He couldn't wait to attend middle school with his big brother. That year, his parents signed him up to play spring baseball in the Kempsville Pony Baseball League. The kids played at the Kempsville Landing Fields, which had two lighted baseball fields and a two-story concession stand. They'd been used for nearly half a century for baseball games.

This was the forty-seventh and final season of baseball being played there. To Hunter, it was an awesome place. He didn't notice that the dugouts were old and well-used, the infields were all dirt, the parking lot was too small and the ball fields were only a few feet from a busy road. The previous February, the City of Virginia Beach had purchased the old Davis farm property, and Kempsville Pony Baseball was preparing to relocate to the future Providence Park. Soon enough, the boys would be playing in brand spanking new digs over on Reon Drive.

Hunter's name was entered in a pool of eleven-to-twelve-year-old boys for a Pony-league draft following a day where players showcased their batting, fielding groundballs and fly balls, pitching, catching and base running in front of the league's coaches. Hunter was selected as the team's last draft pick by the Cubs' head coach. The pony league that Hunter's cubs team played in was called the Broncos.

"Someone had to take Hunter Austin," he overheard a coach say.

His dad elaborated in the car. "Your downfall," he said, not noticing how Hunter just looked steadily out the window, "is your lack of size and strength. You've got no power. And if you hit the ball in the air, your fly balls are always caught for outs. Now, take your brother …" But Hunter had stopped listening and was concentrating on the blur of the road as the car sped along.

The previous year, Hunter had mainly pitched and played the outfield in Kempsville Rec. He pitched about half of his team's games, not because of his skill or control but because he could throw hard. He always kept batters on their toes because he had a reputation for wounding hitters each game with misplaced pitches. This year, he was mostly playing outfield with the older boys. His father took him to the Kempsville Rec ball fields that spring to practice playing the outfield. Sometimes, Jo Jo would come along to help; sometimes, Hunter's friends did. His dad spent a lot of time drilling him on how to play all three outfield positions—his dad had played the outfield in high school.

Hunter tried to listen, but Archie was always hard on him.

"What're you doing?" he would yell. "Are you an idiot!"

On occasion, if Hunter made a nice running catch or threw an accurate ball to a base from the outfield, he'd say, "Atta boy." That was as good as compliments got from his dad.

"To play outfield," his father said, "you have to be able to see the ball off the bat and judge how hard the batter hit it. You can hear the crack of the bat. Run with your head down" —he demonstrated the move— "to where you think the ball will land and pick it up again with your eyes, then make the catch."

Another technique his dad drilled into him was to improve his jump on the ball.

"Start quick and run fast," he said. Then he had Hunter practice over and over again. His first steps were running to the ball, so he could learn to get a read on it. After one long practice session, where Hunter practiced being in the right place to get a glove on the flying ball, Archie gave him a compliment.

"Hunter," Archie said, wiping the sweat off his brow, "with your footspeed, you can outrun the ball if you get off to a quick start and read the ball correctly."

"Dang," Hunter said, smiling, "you think I'm fast?"

"Don't get ahead of yourself, buddy," his father replied. "Here, catch this."

During their practices, Hunter manned the outfield by himself and had to run like the wind to field his dad's balls. The better he learned to judge the batted balls and break on them, the quicker he ran, and the farther his father had to hit the balls so Hunter couldn't catch them. It was like a game of keep away. Hunter loved it and had more stamina than his dad.

"Come on, Dad," Hunter said at the end of one session, "hit me some more balls. I'm not tired yet."

"You're a glutton for punishment," his father said, exhausted from hitting fly balls for Hunter to catch. Archie was old-school. He made Hunter catch the ball with two hands and showed him how to position himself before he caught a ball to make a strong throw to the infield.

"The key," he said, "is to move forward as you catch the ball so you have momentum on your side as you throw the ball. If you're standing flat-footed or, worse, backing up as you catch the ball, you have to take a couple of crow-hop steps forward before you release the throw, which takes valuable time away from holding or throwing out runners."

The 2005 Spring Baseball Season Opening Day Ceremony was like a big family reunion. Every team and every player in Kempsville's Pony Baseball League was invited. Players wore their uniforms and joined all the other teams on the ball field for speeches, introductions and singing of the national anthem and "Take Me Out to the Ball Game." It was a special way to kick off another year of baseball in Kempsville.

Hunter enjoyed playing against the older competition because they hit more balls into the outfield, and he could get more action playing defense. He really liked his Cubs' coaches because they showed interest in his abilities and gave him one-on-one coaching to improve his skills. Of course, they did this for all the players. Head Coach Joe Smith worked with him to improve his control while pitching. Two pieces of advice he gave were, "Step towards your target" and "Use the same arm slot for every pitch." For the first time, Hunter was shown how to use the stitches on the baseball to throw different kinds of pitches.

"Select one way," Coach Smith said, "and stick to it with all your pitches." So, Hunter chose to throw four-seam fastballs to use the baseball's threads to really spin his curveballs.

"Not the curveball," his coach cautioned, "till you're twelve or thirteen, or you might injure your muscles and ligaments."

"But I just learned how to break off an Uncle Charlie. A quality bender," he added. He still remembered his dad teaching him curveball nicknames at the Tides game.

"Sorry, champ," his coach said, "you're going to have to wait a couple more years before you can throw that hook."

The Cubs' coaches tried to teach him how to change up his pitch speed.

"No matter how fast you throw," a coach said, "at some point, the batters will time the speed of your pitches and hit them. So, keep them off balance by varying the speed of your pitches."

They taught him how to grip the ball for various pitches and throw changeup pitches. They emphasized the importance of throwing his changeup with the same arm motion as his fastball.

"As hard as you throw," Coach Smith said, "the changeup will mess up a batter's timing."

But, just like his fastball, Hunter couldn't consistently get his changeup over the plate. He entered the 2005 season in the Bronco League with good stuff, but his pitches were still all over the place. He ended up pitching less but playing more outfield throughout the season.

That year, Jo Jo made the step to being a real teenager (as he liked to point out to his younger brother). He was a strong basketball player, scoring fourteen points a game and averaging eight rebounds. He also was one of the baseball team's best hitters. But it was in football that he stood out as a star player. At thirteen years old, he stood six-foot-two and weighed 210 pounds. He was a force as a tight end and free safety, scoring ten touchdowns and intercepting five passes. Football coaches at Kempsville High came to see him play; they watched him in the fall of 2005 in anticipation of him playing for the Chiefs the following season.

The following year was an exciting one for Hunter. He was now in sixth grade, which meant that, for the first time, he was attending Kempsville Middle School with his big brother, who was in the eighth grade. They walked to school together each day, chatting and giving each other grief the whole way.

Spring baseball brought Hunter back to the Cubs team in Kempsville Pony Baseball for his second and last season in the Bronco League. His coaches finally let him pitch curveballs, but mainly because he kept complaining about their curveball moratorium.

"Come on, Coach," Hunter begged. "I'm twelve years old after all." So, they gave in to his nagging and let him throw his Lord Charles from the pitching mound.

Hunter had fun breaking off some big "yakkers" —a curveball with a big break, swooping like a bird. Too many of them bounced in front of home plate and were uncatchable. The other kids couldn't hit his pitched balls, so his number of strikeouts increased, but so did the number of his base on balls or walks. As the season wound down, Hunter pitched less and less, spending more time in the outfield. The team just couldn't live with all his walks and wild pitches. They never criticized his outfield defense, but they didn't rave about it either. Other than his footspeed on bases, his coaches never got excited about his play. He was really struggling to stand out as a baseball player.

The Cubs team had many talented baseball players and knowledgeable coaches, and by the end of the season, they finished in first place. Hunter's championship trophy was the first one he'd ever earned. Mostly, he'd been on teams where each player got a participation trophy. Even as a young kid, he had never liked getting a trophy just for showing up.

By the winter of 2007, the Austins had two teenagers in the house—Hunter was thirteen and in the seventh grade; Jo Jo was fifteen and the ninth grade.

"How did this happen?" Janet exclaimed.

Archie grabbed her and spun her around, "Don't you remember?" Then he gave her a thorough kiss.

Hunter groaned, "Uh, don't do that," and shielded his eyes as he fled from the room. Teenagerhood brought with it puberty, acne, body odor and a lot of talk about girls. Jo Jo had already had several crushes in middle school, and now in high school he had plenty of dates. Hunter, on the other hand, was always a little shy around girls, and he was riddled with self-doubt. He had a friendly, comical personality, but around cute girls, he sort of clammed up.

The brothers were growing so fast that their mother took them clothes shopping four or five times a year. Their father started complaining about all the milk they drank and how expensive it had become to feed and clothe them.

Jo Jo had had several girlfriends so far in high school, so he was "the man" at school. Besides being a stud ballplayer, he was good-looking and smart. It was easy for him to be confident around the ladies—maybe too confident. Since he had dated so many girls, he was developing a reputation as a "player" on and off the field.

For Hunter, the second year of middle school was better, and he'd adjusted to the larger school. He was growing up and was trying to deal with a new version of himself. He had facial hair (though it was rather fuzzy) and some zits. His voice was cracking— "It's so embarrassing!" —and he was having sexual thoughts for the first time. There seemed to be a lot of pretty girls in the teen group he'd joined at church for spiritual events and social outings. So, he was always around girls.

His relationship with his dad was not improving; he acted like a drill sergeant with his younger son. Hunter had a loving relationship with his mom, but her voice was often drowned out by his father's. Archie took his family to church three times a week, was a church usher and was respected at church. But at home, he was a strict disciplinarian, demanding respect from his family and quick to point out other's failures and shortcomings. Archie expected perfection from everyone else but couldn't see his own shortcomings. To his sons, he didn't exhibit God's love or love of any kind—no forgiveness, no grace.

Once, Janet asked Archie to tell her more often that he loved her. He said, in front of the boys, "Janet, I've told you that I love you. If anything changes, I'll let you know."

In 2007, Jo Jo was the best junior varsity basketball player at Kempsville High; he also made the varsity baseball team as a freshman. Hunter, on the other hand, was growing up but not getting any stronger, and this was a detriment to hitting a baseball. At Hunter's family birthday party, he asked his grandfather to work with him on his hitting before the spring season started. It was obvious to everyone that batting was the weakest part of his game.

One windy Saturday, Jo Jo, Hunter and Granddaddy went to the baseball diamond to practice pitching and hitting. Every so often, Anthony would stop the action to give each of his grandson's tips on their style and approach to batting. But it was the three words he spoke to Hunter that changed everything for the thirteen-year-old.

"Try batting left-handed."

Hunter had been batting right-handed since he was four and was excited about trying something new. His grandfather started his left-handed batting lessons by getting Hunter to hit off a tee. Then he pitched to him. Anthony worked with him to keep his back elbow up, keep his weight back until the last possible second and then swing level at the ball. Soon, the sweetest line drives jumped off of Hunter's bat. His new swing felt natural and not forced.

"Are you sure you never hit left-handed before?" his granddaddy asked.

"No, sir. I never even thought about it before."

"You have a completely different swing left-handed." His granddaddy shook his head in amazement. "You're so direct to the ball that there's no wasted motion with your swing. When you bat right-handed, you have a loop in your swing that makes it difficult for you to square up the ball. Left-handed, you're using your strongest arm to snap the bat as you swing." He threw another ball to Hunter, who hit it squarely and sent it across the field. Granddaddy shaded his eyes and whistled as he watched it go.

Hunter held a broad smile on his face for hours.

3

BEST LAID-PLANS (2007–2008)

Several times a week, Granddaddy Austin and a couple of Hunter's friends went with Hunter to a ball field to pitch to him and shag his batted balls. They all supported his passion for becoming a better hitter. By the time the Kempsville Pony Baseball League spring draft showcase day arrived, Hunter had a newfound confidence in hitting baseballs. He no longer had to poke balls over the infield or beat out groundballs to get on base. Instead, he could rip line drives over the infield and even back the outfielders up with fly balls.

The first time his dad saw him bat left-handed that spring, Hunter lined two ropes into the outfield. Archie's only comment about his youngest son's new batting skills was, "Why didn't you try batting left-handed sooner?" On the other hand, his granddaddy grinned from ear to ear seeing Hunter hit line drives. "After batting left-handed for only a few weeks, it looks like you've been doing it forever," he said. He gave his grandson a fist bump.

"You know, there's one huge advantage for you batting left-handed," he added. "After you hit the ball, you're two steps closer to first base than when you bat right-handed. And as fast as you run, they may never get you out on groundballs." But Hunter had yet to bat left-handed in a real game against pitchers throwing heat and curve-handed balls or with umpires calling balls and strikes. In the spring season of 2007, Hunter once again played rec ball for the Cubs in the Kempsville Pony, but he moved up in the divisions from the Broncos League to the Pony League. His name had gone back into the pool of eligible players of thirteen-to-fourteen-year-old boys after the annual showcase day. This time, the Cubs selected him as their seventh draft pick. The Cubs coaches liked his new lefthanded swing. Hunter entered the season full of hope with a new sense of excitement.

"I'm batting from the other side of home plate, using a new batting stance and drag bunting for the first time," he said to himself as he sat on his bed, shuffling through his baseball cards. "What could go wrong?"

But the best-laid plans and all that; you know how the story goes. No matter how carefully a project is planned, something may still go wrong with it. Learning to bat left-handed took longer to perfect than he'd planned. Hunter had a natural swing from that side of the plate, but it was a challenge to learn the strike zone and get his timing down—his instinct was to pull every pitched ball—batting left-handed, and hit breaking balls curving into him instead of away from him. His baseball season was a mixed bag of successes and failures. He struck out too much and walked too infrequently. From the left side of home plate, he had not yet learned the strike zone with his eyes. He swung at too many bad pitches—or as his granddaddy would say, "Son, you got yourself out."

Hunter was too enamored with how good it felt to square up the ball while batting left-handed, so he got into a habit of pulling the ball to right field. All season, his grandfather told him to wait on the ball— "Let it travel to the back of the strike zone and hit it where it's pitched" —and tried to teach him to hit outside pitches to left field. But he wasn't listening. Instead, he tried to power the ball to his pull field (the right field). He'd drop his back shoulder and hit under the ball, which resulted in too many fly balls caught by right-fielders. He didn't have the strength, bat speed or power to hit the ball over the fielders' heads. His efforts to hit home runs were futile.

The one thing he quickly learned to do was bunt and run at the same time—what some called a "drag bunt." But what he really dreamt about was being a power hitter.

"I don't want to lay down bunts," he complained.

He needed a shot of reality, and his dad was always good for that.

"Son, you don't have a clue on how to hit," his dad said on the way home from one of the games, his voice rising with indignation. "You swing from your heels like you're Babe Ruth. Your brother is Babe Ruth. You," he scoffed, "are Mario Mendoza."

"Who in the world is Mario Mendoza?" Hunter mumbled.

When Hunter arrived home, still wearing his dirty uniform, he hurried to his laptop, sat on his bed and googled the name "Mario Mendoza."

"The Mendoza Line," he read aloud, "is an expression in baseball deriving from the name of shortstop Mario Mendoza, whose poor batting average is taken to define" —his eyes bugged as he read— "the threshold of incompetent hitting." He sat back, away from the screen. "Wow. I must be terrible."

Negative thoughts swirled in his mind. Am I only fooling myself? Am I really the Mendoza of Kempsville baseball?

"I hate messing up! I hate my dad!" He grabbed his pillow and fired it across the room, knocking a framed picture of Cal Ripken Jr. off the wall. Still in his dirty uniform and minus his pillow, he lay back on his bed and let the tears flow till he fell asleep.

As summer moved to fall, Jo Jo, who was now in tenth grade, started the 2007 football season on the junior varsity team for the Kempsville Chiefs. At six-foot-two and weighing 215 pounds, he was plenty big enough to play for the varsity. Halfway through the season, he was promoted to the varsity team and played tight end. He was good at blocking and had a knack for catching most balls thrown his way. Of the seventeen balls he caught, three resulted in touchdowns. The coaches also worked him at outside linebacker on defense as well as both safety positions. The Kempsville Chiefs ended the 2007 season, winning only two games. But they had some good, young players returning for 2008, including rising star Jo Jo Austin.

The 2008 spring Kempsville Pony Baseball season would be the final time baseball would be played in the half-century-old complex on Kempsville Road. Throughout the season, coaches, parents and kids got quite nostalgic and began counting down the number of games left before the whole league relocated to Reon Drive.

Hunter approached the new baseball season with the same goal as the previous year—to be a better hitter. There was still so much to learn if he wanted to be a left-handed hitter. He needed to train his eyes to see pitched balls from the other side of the home plate. He had to judge curving balls breaking in the opposite direction. He had to figure out if a thrown ball was a ball or a strike. Since February, Jo Jo had pitched him hundreds of balls at the middle school field. Hunter had talked his dad into taking him to Grand Slam USA, an indoor batting cage. He wore out a pair of batting gloves before his team even began spring practice.

Once he could judge balls and strikes batting left-handed, Hunter concentrated on waiting for the ball to get deeper over the plate before he hit it, a tip his granddaddy gave him. That gave him a bit longer to decide the question, "ball or strike?" But most importantly, waiting longer to swing helped Hunter not to pull every pitch to right field.

He entered the baseball season full of optimism. He was learning to believe in himself, to feel comfortable in his own skin and not depend on positive feedback from anyone, especially his father. His mother didn't care how well he or his brother played; she always was proud of both her boys.

Hunter got up the nerve to try out for the Kempsville Middle Baseball team. He was in the eighth grade now and felt more confident. His buddies from the neighborhood were also trying out, so he felt protected from rejection. Still, he didn't know how he would stack up against the rest of the team, but he did know he definitely was not going to tell his father that he was trying out.

On cut day, three dozen boys gathered around a sheet of paper pinned to the coach's bulletin board in the team's locker room. One kid called off the names of who had made the Kempsville Middle baseball team. As the names went on and on, Hunter was starting to feel deflated until "Hunter Austin" and "Bryce Jennings" were called out back-to-back. Hunter and his buddy Bryce found each other in the crowded room, shouted in triumph and shared a congratulatory hug. Bryce was stocky and strong, and his bear hug almost broke Hunter's ribs.

At team practice the next afternoon, the head coach, Jose Gonzalez, motioned Hunter and Bryce over. They ran over with excitement.

"Yes, Coach?"

"I want to tell you boys," Coach Gonzalez said, "you barely made the last cuts." The boys were visibly deflated. "I'm concerned with how small you are, Hunter. You've got no power hitting." Hunter nodded silently. "And you, Bryce, you hit the ball very well, but you need serious work on your fielding skills."

"Yes, Coach."

"I expect to see you boys working hard."

"Yes, Coach!"

Hunter was going to try to play both on the school team and rec ball for the Kempsville Pony League. His mom was proud of him for making the middle school team, but she was concerned that he was over-committing himself.

"You'll be playing on both teams at once," she said. "Don't you think your grades are going to suffer?"

"Shucks, Janet," his dad spoke up. "He's barely passing his classes now. He can't do much worse."

"Archie Austin," his wife huffed. "Putting Hunter down serves no purpose."

"I wasn't putting him down," Archie said in surprise. "Just calling it like it is."

"Archie! Do you know that children can learn to hate themselves from their parents? And they can learn to love themselves from their parents too.

Which do you want for Hunter? We already know where you stand with Jo Jo."

"What are you talking about, woman!" Archie stormed. "I treat these boys exactly as they need to be treated."

The 2008 baseball season was not exactly a good experience for Hunter. Since he was only a part-time starter on his middle school team, he had to "ride the pine," which meant he spent a lot of time on the wooden bench when he wasn't playing. This was a new experience for him—he wasn't very good at being a reserve player. In rec ball, he played full-time in most of the games. It was something he took for granted. As the season wore on, he became resentful and his attitude worsened. He stopped rooting for his teammates when he was on the bench.

One day, his coach caught him sulking on the bench and yelled, "Hunter, grow up!"

Sometimes, he had to play for the two teams on the same day and still do his homework and go to church. He had no time for a social life, but that was okay because, come summer, he would be hanging out at the Virginia Beach ocean front with Jo Jo.

"Maybe this year, I'll learn to surf," he said in a hopeful tone, "or pick up some girls from out of town."

Jo Jo laughed and punched his arm.

As Hunter sat on his bed, going through his baseball cards again, trying to imagine his future, he thought about how he viewed himself as a baseball player and how others saw him. There was an obvious disconnect.

"I know I can do it," he said to himself, "but the school coaches and others, especially Dad, don't think I have any ability." He sighed. "At some point, someone has to believe in me. I mean, really believe in me. Not like Mom, who thinks everything I do is acceptable."

Although middle school baseball was getting him down, Hunter's rec baseball was better than the previous year. He started to see his value as a contact hitter instead of a power-hitter wannabe. With his footspeed and his lack of power and strength, he could see the writing on the wall. In training, the coaches always put Hunter at the head of the batting line as the leadoff hitter. They spent extra time with him practicing bunting for base hits. His footspeed had reached a level by age fourteen that he beat out any decent bunted ball and many groundballs.

His middle school coaches were quick to criticize and rarely complimented any positive plays Hunter made. His rec league coaches kept encouraging him to work on his flaws and coached him one-on-one. Whenever Hunter made an outstanding play, they would complement him openly in front of the team.

"Way to go, Hunter!"

If his dad heard this, he'd turn away and pretend he didn't hear them.

But while Hunter saw real improvements in his game during the 2008 rec league season, the other players in his league were also getting bigger, stronger and better. He was closing the gap between him and the best rec league players, but it was slow going.

When his father would say, "You're the opposite of your brother," he'd answer stubbornly, "I'm not opposite, just different."

When his father would admonish, "Why can't you be more like your brother?" It hurt Hunter to his core. It's not that he resented his brother; he didn't. The world seemed to worship the ground that Jo Jo walked on, including Hunter. He loved him like everyone else did. But it was like living with a rock star. His brother was excellent at everything—off the charts as a ballplayer, tall and handsome with an ability to charm the girls speechless and had more than his fair share of intelligence.

One night, when Hunter was reading his Bible, he came across a scripture verse in Galatians 6:4. "Pay careful attention to your own work, for then you will get the satisfaction of a job well done, and you won't need to compare yourself to anyone else." That was a mission statement he could buy in to.

"I'm going to stop comparing myself to others and ignore it when Dad compares me to Jo Jo. I'm going to focus on my possibilities and not my limitations."

What he didn't realize was that Jo Jo pushed him to be a better ballplayer. His brother's criticism only motivated him to practice harder. When he played pickup games with Jo Jo and his buddies, all who were two or three years older, he took his knocks and defeats.

As his granddaddy once said, "You only get better by playing against guys who are older and better than you."

Jo Jo played both varsity basketball and baseball at Kempsville High that same year. He was the "sixth man" for the basketball team, meaning he was the first player off the bench as a substitute. His jump shot improved throughout the season, and he became a reliable three-point shooter. In baseball, he became a part-time starter at first base and right field. He was a strong fielder with sure hands.

Being an eighth-grader had its perks for Hunter. He was one of the oldest students and could pick on the incoming sixth graders. Also, the fourteen-year-old girls looked prettier and more grown-up than the previous year. There was a lot of checking-each-other-out going on in the hallways. A few kids had already paired up as couples, and they became the talk of the school. There was one girl at school who Hunter had his eyes on. Her name was Eleanor Brooks. He tried not to stare at her when she passed by, but once he ran into a support post and saw stars because his eyes were fixed on her.

One day, he got up his nerve and sat at Eleanor's cafeteria table. Although she was surrounded by her friends, he was able to sit across from her.

"Now, this is some good mac 'n' cheese," he said as an opener. The girls at the table giggled, and Eleanor gave him an assessing look.

"What if I'm lactose intolerant?" she asked.

"Uh," for a moment, he floundered, then he added, "this is really the worst dish ever."

Eleanor laughed and gave him a nice, friendly smile. "I was going to go for the mac 'n' cheese, myself," she said. "I'm Eleanor, by the way."

"I'm Hunter."

Eleanor was surprisingly easy to talk to. After that first encounter, Hunter made a point of running into her in the hallway and saying, "Hi." He asked around at school and found out where she lived and learned that she walked to school too. When the bell rang at the end of the day on that Friday, he made sure he was standing in what he hoped was a relaxed stance just outside where he assumed she would pass by. As she came out through the school door, his heart flipped as his eyes took in her long hair, pretty face, tight jeans and all.

"Hey, Hunter," Eleanor said. "Are you waiting on me?"

"Yep," he replied, smiling like a fool.

"What's up?"

With a little hesitation, he said, "I'd like to walk you home."

"Cool. Let's go."

They had hardly got off the school grounds when she took his hand, leaned in and whispered, "I wanted to get to know you better. You're cute."

When they got to her house, they dropped their book bags on the front porch and then continued walking down to the Kempsville rec center. For a while, they sat on the kiddie swings and chatted until Eleanor said, "Let's go for a stroll."

When they got to the corner of the rec building, she took his hand and pulled him around to the back.

"For privacy," she said. She looked at him with a smiled and tilted her chin up expectantly. When he did nothing, she giggled and said, "Well, aren't you going to kiss me?"

Hunter's heart swelled and kind of panicked. But then she leaned in, and he got his first real kiss ever … and his second, third and fourth ones too.

As exciting as this was, the thought went through Hunter's head that Eleanor was a little fast for him. He was the more cautious type and she had been all over him that day ever since they left school. He was confused, and since he hardly knew her, he did not know what to think.

That night, Hunter told his big brother about his new crush, Eleanor.

"When did you meet this girl?" Jo Jo asked.

"Wednesday."

"And today's Friday."

"Yeah, I can read a calendar, Jo Jo."

"Sounds like she's a bit too passionate and way too fast for you, bro."

"What do you mean?"

Jo Jo put his arm around Hunter's shoulders and gave him a squeeze. "I'm just trying to look out for my little brother." Then, before Hunter could hit him, he released him. "I'm just saying," he said in a serious voice, "it sounds to me like Eleanor just wants a make-out partner and not a boyfriend."

Hunter nodded. "She scares me a bit." After that, he began ducking out of the way whenever Eleanor came around.

At the end of June 2008, Hunter graduated from Kempsville Middle School. He looked forward to going to school again with his big brother, but thinking about Kempsville High caused occasional waves of anxiety. He worried about how he would do academically and socially, but he believed he'd be a stud on the Kempsville Chiefs baseball team and would be able to play very well. His boatload of self-confidence would spring a few leaks.

After the spring rec league season ended, the Kempsville Pony Baseball League sponsored a four-day baseball instruction camp at the ball fields on Kempsville Road. It was right after school let out for the summer, so the kids were available. Coaches divided the kids into two age groups and assigned them to two different ball fields for five to six hours a day of instruction.

Up to this point, Archie had never let Hunter attend the Kempsville Pony Instruction Camp.

"It's too expensive," he'd say.

"It's only $60 for four days," Hunter would counter. But his dad would just shake his head.

This year, Hunter knew that in nine months, he'd be trying out for the baseball team at Kempsville High—he knew he needed to step up his game. Instead of begging his dad again for the camp registration money, he went straight to his grandfather and hit him up for the $60.

"I'd be delighted to help out," his granddaddy said. Anthony signed up his youngest grandson for the instructional camp and even drove Hunter to and from the camp each day.

Hunter loved all the instruction the coaches gave him. He didn't mind how many times they worked on a drill because he loved to practice. The most significant thing he got out of the camp, besides a good suntan, was nearly perfecting how to wait on pitched balls and how to hit them to the opposite field.

After one sweaty practice, when he was happily exhausted from his efforts, he was standing on the baseball field, listening to other kids' parents offer words of support. His teammates were bragging about playing travel ball every other weekend, and suddenly he got wistful. He wished his parents could understand how much he wanted to grow up to be a professional baseball player. He was envious of the hugs and congratulations his teammates got after their ballgames. He so badly wanted to get extra opportunities to travel and play baseball, and he wanted to receive affection and appreciation from both his folks. He was tired of hearing negative remarks.

As he stood in the circle of warmth and appreciation that swirled around him, he just felt mad. He stood there, frowning, red-faced and bound up, like he could feel a chip being born on his shoulder.

"One day," he muttered to himself, "I'm going to prove to everyone that I'm not too small, too weak, too dumb or too bad."

September 2008 brought about a new school year, and both Austin boys were attending Kempsville High—Hunter as a freshman and Jo Jo as a junior. The year 2008 was a real learning experience and an eye-opener for the Austin family. One of their two boys would taste bitter rejection athletically, and the other would have a break-out athletic season and would be a magnet for local press reporters and college recruiters from all over America.

Just before the two boys set out in the morning for the first day of school, their mom pulled Hunter aside for a talk.

"There will be many distractions," she said earnestly, "but try to stay focused on learning the subjects being taught." Hunter tried not to roll his eyes. "Be friendly with everyone, but take your time making friends. You want to pick good ones."

"I know, Mama."

"And don't hang out with kids who will lead you into trouble."

He laughed and gave her a big hug. "No, Mama, that's Jo Jo's job." He ducked as his brother tried to whap him on the head.

As they approached the school, however, Hunter felt overwhelmed. The school was huge.

"There must be two thousand students here," he said.

Jo Jo shrugged and then went off with his own crowd. Left behind, Hunter felt lonely and isolated.

New students at Kempsville were surprised when they learned Hunter was Jo Jo's kid brother.

"You're so small," one girl drawled.

"Did something stunt your growth?" another asked.

Kempsville High was blessed with a transfer football player from Cincinnati named Boomer Butler. Boomer was a high school junior who had started two previous seasons in Ohio and earned all-league honors as a quarterback for the Kempsville Chiefs. Because of Boomer, during summer practices, the coaching staff put new and more complicated passing routes into the offensive playbook. There was a new emphasis on throwing more passes than running the ball. With a strong-armed quarterback on the team and Jo Jo's physical development, the oldest Austin boy blossomed into a once-in-a-generation receiver.

Jo Jo was not only bigger, he appeared to be quicker off the line of scrimmage, running pass routes. Even at sixteen years old, he was a complete high school tight end. He could run forty yards in 4.6 seconds and became the Chiefs' starting free safety who frequently covered the opponent's tight end. He understood the different pass routes run by tight ends—he covered them like a blanket.

That season, he intercepted six passes and defended a dozen more. Jo Jo broke team records for scoring touchdowns (12), number of receptions (80) and receiving yardage (920). He received various atta-boys and awards after the season, including first team All-City. What Jo Jo could not have seen coming was the flood of college recruiters attending his games. They came calling, texting and knocking on his parents' front door uninvited.

There was also the press constantly wanting a word or two from the Kempsville star tight end. Jo Jo had not given college football much serious thought when he entered his junior year of high school. But by the end of the football season, it was all he could think about and all anyone else wanted to discuss with him, including his classmates and his parents. He let Hunter know how he really felt.

"I can't wait for basketball season to begin," he admitted one day, "so I can once again be one of the boys and not some kind of a god to everyone. All this attention is crazy."

Hunter wouldn't have minded just a little bit of it.

4

SPEECHLESS (2009)

Jo Jo again played both varsity basketball and baseball in 2009 at Kempsville High School. He was the starting shooting guard for the basketball team and they relied on his 3-point shooting. Jo Jo average 14.5 points a game and 3.5 rebounds. He really enjoyed playing hoops that winter as it provided a temporary reprise from college football recruiting

In late February 2009, Hunter and three of his freshman neighborhood buddies were watching a Baltimore Orioles spring training baseball game on TV.

"Guys, I have an announcement to make," Hunter said as they ate chips on the couch. "I'm going to try out for Kempsville High's Varsity Baseball team. Not the JV, but the varsity."

At first the silence was deafening. Then the air filled with laughter. Not a word from any of them, just laughter. There was not a believer in the room. "Even my best friends don't believe in me," Hunter thought.

As it turned out, all four boys tried out for the Chiefs varsity baseball team, but after lengthy tryouts, none of them made the final cut. All of them agreed to play on the junior varsity baseball team, except for Hunter. He was too disappointed to think clearly. He threw a fit in the gym locker room and had to be calmed down by a coach and his friends.

"Hey, we didn't make it either," one of his friends said. "It's not such a big deal."

"You're just a freshman," another friend said.

But Hunter had his heart set on it. Part of his fury was always hearing about his brother's achievements and having to face his dad about his own shortcomings.

"I told you that you weren't good enough," his dad said later at dinner when Jo Jo related the story of what had happened.

That rejection became a landmark moment, and the chip on his shoulder grew larger. But Hunter determined then and there not to give up on baseball, but rather to get bigger, stronger and better. That evening he called his grandfather.

"Hi, Granddaddy. I didn't make the cut for the school's baseball team."

"That's too bad, son."

"You know, I really thought I could do it. I just get so sick and tired of hearing how great Jo Jo is, and how I'm not very good. I'm just sick of it! You know?"

"Don't let others' opinion of you become your reality," his granddaddy said. "The boy I know loves baseball. And he works hard and prepares tirelessly for what he wants to achieve." There was a pause on the phone. "Do you know what boy I'm talking about here?"

"Yes, Granddaddy," Hunter said in a low voice.

"Now, I think I'm a pretty smart old guy. Are you going to take my advice and run with it?"

"Yes, Granddaddy."

"And are you the fastest runner we know?"

Hunter laughed, "Yes, sir!"

For Hunter's fifteenth birthday in March, his grandfather surprised him with a golden retriever. Hunter named her Cinnamon because of the color of her fur.

Having Cinnamon at home certainly changed his disposition. Each day after school, he would run home to play with his growing puppy. He still didn't take academics in high school as seriously as sports. Though he almost failed some of his freshman classes, he scraped by to end the school year still eligible to play sports in the fall of 2009. All Hunter seemed to care about was sports and his dog. He needed to find something or someone to help motivate him to take his responsibilities more seriously. She entered his life in June of 2009.

During the school baseball season, Jo Jo finally became the starter at first base. As a big, strong young man, he had developed into a decent power hitter for the Kempsville Chiefs. He hit seven home runs and drove in twenty-two runs. He had work to do on his batting average, but with his ten stolen bases, he proved to be the team's biggest run producer.

Jo Jo's younger brother, as people liked to point out, was a short, skinny and underwhelming freshman. Everywhere Hunter looked, there were bigger and better athletes. But when he got down on himself, he'd take Cinnamon to the park and run with her as fast as he could. When he looked into her eyes, he felt like a winner.

Kempsville Pony Baseball moved to Providence Park that April. It was also the league's fiftieth anniversary season. The new ballpark was conveniently located next to Interstate 64. Every player, coach and parent was excited about the sparkling new fields and facilities. It had covered dugouts, plenty of bleachers for the fans and large parking lots. The scoreboards were high school field quality. The largest of two fields, where the teenagers played, had an outfield fence that averaged about 300 feet from home plate. A warning track was laid just in front of the fence, and all the fields were lighted so multiple ballgames could be played in the evenings. At the opening day ceremony, a new tradition started, with the fans and players singing "Take Me Out to the Ballgame."

Hunter continued to play rec ball for the Cubs in Kempsville. He moved up in the divisions from the pony league to the colt league, so his name went back into the pool of eligible players. The draft occurred after the annual showcase day in front of the league's coaches. This time, the Cubs selected Hunter as their fourth draft pick because Hunter had value as a complete ballplayer. He could not only play very good defense and steal bases, but he was becoming a dependable leadoff hitter.

"It seems so strange," he told his grandad that night, "that the coaches at middle and high school don't value my baseball skills as highly as the Kempsville Pony coaches do."

Hunter loved playing on the new ball diamonds at Providence Park. The outfield grass was perfect to run on, and balls didn't take funny bounces in the outfield. His favorite thing was the warning track in front of the outfield fence. It made him feel as if he was playing outfield in the major leagues in front of 50,000 fans instead of an audience of fifty family members.

The colt league's Cubs team crushed the competition that spring. They won every game but one. The Cubs had three outstanding pitchers while the other teams were lucky to have one stud pitcher on their roster. Hunter made a couple of sensational catches in center field to get his pitchers out of tight jams to help his team win games. In the first game of the season against the Dodgers, Hunter threw out two baserunners who were trying to take extra bases. He quickly developed a reputation for having a strong throwing arm. Players had to be cautious running the bases when balls were hit in Hunter's direction.

Hunter's coach called on him a half-dozen times that season to pitch in relief of starting pitchers who ran out of steam or were getting roughed up by the opposing team. As a fifteen-year-old boy, Hunter could really throw hard. His pitching control was still an issue, but he would strike out two-thirds of the batters he faced. He was also as likely to walk the bases loaded before getting the third out. Unfortunately for his coaches, putting Hunter on the bump was always an adventure.

That baseball season at Kempsville Pony was special for Hunter in many ways. First and foremost, they won the championship in the colt league! For him, nothing trumped winning. Second, his team played on the brand-new ball fields at Providence Park. Third and last, it meant so much to Hunter to play on a team where he was wanted and respected. It helped wash away the sting of being cut from the high school varsity baseball team.

In June, Kempsville Pony Baseball sponsored their annual four-day baseball instruction camp at Providence Park. At fifteen years old, Hunter was eligible to participate in the camp for one more year. He used that information as leverage when he asked his grandfather to sign him up for another instruction camp. Once again, Anthony came through for him.

Hunter was excited about getting to play ball on the new Kempsville Pony Baseball fields again. The grass always looked like it had just been mowed, and the infield dirt was always raked and free of pebbles. He was also highly motivated to improve his skills. He'd be trying out again for the school team the following spring, and there was work to be done to win a roster spot. He ate up all the individual instruction that June, as well at the team practices. There were even some practice baseball games. By the end of camp, Hunter felt ready to play high school ball.

When school let out for the summer, he was glad to put his freshman year behind him. It had been a dud for him personally, but finally, it was summer and time to have some fun. On a sunny Saturday in June at the Virginia Beach oceanfront, Hunter's luck changed.

Fifteen-year-old Hunter was standing behind a family waiting to be seated at the Dough Boy's Pizza located at 17th and Atlantic Avenue, right at the Virginia Beach ocean front. His brother was off somewhere feeding a parking meter but would join him soon for lunch. The boys had been playing in the ocean all morning and were starving. Oblivious to those around him, Hunter heard a sweet voice in a Southern accent say, "Hey, have you ever been here before?" He turned and stopped on a dime.

For a heartbeat or two, he couldn't answer her. He was stunned. She looked like a goddess, a blue-eyed, suntanned with long blonde hair. She was pretty as a peach and young like him.

When he finally found his voice, he barely replied under his breath, "Yeah, a bunch of times."

She was part of a family of three waiting in line ahead of him to get a table. Hunter tried to think of something to say to her—anything! But she was so far out of his league. He didn't want to strike out and embarrass himself in front of the most beautiful girl he'd ever seen.

She turned to look at him. "We're on vacation here this week."

Hunter managed to nod.

"My parents are looking to buy a house in Virginia Beach while we're here."

He nodded again.

"My dad's in the army. He's a lieutenant colonel, and he's being transferred from Alabama to the Joint Expeditionary Base Little Creek–Fort Story. That's a mouthful, isn't it?"

"Uh huh." Hunter could not seem to make his brain work.

"We need to find a place to live by Labor Day. Do you know where we should be looking?"

At last, his mouth connected with his brain, and he said in a rush, "There are nice homes and great schools in Kempsville. That's where I live. You should move to Kempsville."

The goddess laughed. "Where is Kempsville? I've never heard of it."

But at this point, their table was ready, and her mom was pulling her away. In desperation, Hunter yelled out, "What's your name?"

"Savannah!" she said with a smile. And off she went into the back of the restaurant. Hunter stood on his toes to watch her go. His heart was thumping. He could barely breathe. Was this love at first sight? Or was he going to be sick?

Just then, Jo Jo arrived by his side.

"Are you okay?" he asked.

"What?"

"You look all red-faced and weird." Jo Jo frowned down at Hunter's feet, which were still standing on tiptoe. "What are you doing?"

Hunter flushed further with embarrassment and dropped down onto his heels. "I just tried to talk to a pretty girl," he mumbled.

"What? I can't hear you." Jo Jo leaned in. "Can you say that louder?" But the smirk on his lips suggested he had heard correctly.

Hunter punched him in the arm. "I tried to talk to a pretty girl, but nothing would come out my mouth."

Jo Jo laughed. "She must be some looker."

The brothers were soon seated with their favorite pizza in front of them. They were chatting about baseball and football and random things when the new girl walked by. Both boys stopped, pizzas on the way to their mouths, and just stared.

"I see what you mean, man," Jo Jo said when she'd passed by. "She is gorgeous! Did she approach you?"

"Yeah, dude, she did," Hunter said, looking almost scared. His brother gave him a high-five.

"They're looking to buy a home in Virginia Beach," Hunter said.

"Did you give them Dad's phone number?"

Hunter shook his head.

"Man, I don't know what to do with you," his brother replied. He made Hunter write their father's name and phone number on a napkin. "Now put your name and phone number on this one." When Hunter looked up questioningly, his brother just gestured to keep writing.

"Okay, now," Jo Jo said, "go walk over to her table and introduce yourself to the family and offer Dad's real estate services. And talk up our area. This napkin's for the dad. This one's for the goddess." He gestured with his two fingers, pointing first to his own eyes and then Hunter's. "I'll be watching you."

With napkins in hand, Hunter walked over to the table and did what Jo Jo instructed. They were a friendly family, and once he got started, it was easy to brag a little about living in the northern end of the city, closer to town center and farther from all the vacation energy and out-of-town visitors at the oceanfront. "Your family excepted, of course," he added, blushing a little. Since Savannah looked like she was still in high school, he also talked up Kempsville High School. Then he handed Savannah's father the napkin with

Hunter's father's information, and he handed Savannah the second napkin with his contact information once her dad was back in his seat.

On their way out of the restaurant, Savannah and her family stopped by the boys' table.

"Thanks for your thoughtfulness, young man," the Colonel said to Hunter. "Your daddy might hear from me before we leave town." Savannah gave Hunter a special smile.

That night, sleep was impossible for Hunter. All he could think about was Savannah's southern accent, her long, flowing, blonde hair and her face, oh that face! The next morning at breakfast, even though his eyes were puffy from lack of sleep, he gave Jo Jo a silly smile.

"Was meeting Savannah just a dream?" he asked.

Jo Jo laughed. "No, it wasn't a dream lover boy. Savannah is real. You gave her your number, man." The stupidest grin crossed Hunter's face.

Two days later, Archie received a phone call from Lieutenant Colonel Bill Montgomery. He told Archie that he'd enjoyed meeting his son and that his boy was quite charming and persuasive.

"Oh, you must mean Jo Jo," Archie replied.

"Oh no, he said his name was Hunter."

The men discussed the Montgomerys' real estate needs and budget, and the conversation turned to possible neighborhoods. Bill mentioned Hunter highly recommended the Kempsville part of town and Kempsville High.

"It's important that my daughter, Savannah, attend a safe and challenging high school. She's an excellent student who needs to be pushed academically or she gets bored."

"I can assure you, Bill, that Kempsville High's highly-rated academically. Our neighborhood schools attract many homebuyers to the area."

Archie took Bill, his wife Robin and Savannah to look at a few homes in the area. Low and behold, the house on Rochelle Arch that the Montgomery's fell in love with was only a few blocks from the Austin family home on Manor Drive. When Savannah called Hunter to tell him "... and the house is within the Kempsville High zone ..." they were both ecstatic.

"We're going to be going to school together!" Hunter told Jo Jo. "And we'll practically be neighbors!"

Before Savannah's family vacation ended, Hunter got to hang out with the Montgomerys at the oceanfront one night as they listened to a local band, "The Hot Cakes," play on the 31st Street Stage in Neptune's Park. Savannah and Hunter sat close on a blanket and pretended to listen to the music. But as they held hands in the dark, they were making their own music. Eventually, they got up and went for a walk by themselves on the boardwalk. They paused in the dim light to admire the statue of Neptune that sat high up on the boardwalk. It was right under the turtle being held by Neptune's hand that Hunter pulled Savannah in close. He wanted to say how beautiful she was, but then his eyes dropped to her sweet, soft lips, and he couldn't stop himself from pulling her into his arms and leaning in. Her lips were soft and amazing. The kiss seemed to last forever. At least they wanted it to.

When they broke apart, their arms still around each other, Savannah said, "That was some kiss!"

"The first of many," Hunter promised, "once you move here." Soon he reluctantly walked her back to her parents.

During the six weeks of separation that followed, Savannah and Hunter texted and called each other throughout the day. They friended each other on Facebook and quickly became familiar with each other's family and friends and what each was into.

One thing Hunter quickly picked up from Savannah's posts was that she was deeply religious and not shy about proclaiming it. More so than Hunter. Nonetheless, the Austin boys attended Sunday School, Sunday morning and evening church services, and a Bible study/prayer meeting on Wednesday nights at a non-denominational church. There was also an occasional weekend social outing for the church's teenagers, such as bowling, roller skating, Christian concerts and pizza parties. Hunter and Jo Jo weren't allowed to miss any services or activities at church.

Between their school homework and playing sports, plus all their church attendance, the boys were incredibly busy. They rarely took the time to read their Bibles as there always seemed to be something more pressing to do. They were taught at church about God's plan for their salvation and to become Godly shepherds influencing others for Jesus Christ. But they hadn't accepted Christ as their Lord and Savior yet, and they didn't want things to get weird with their friends by getting saved and confessing they were Christians. Savannah was different. She didn't hesitate to reveal to the world that Jesus Christ was the Lord of her life. She also knew what she wanted in life.

"I want to attend a Christian college and train to be a secondary school teacher," she said on the phone one day. "Then I want to be a high school principal someday. I want to be married and have a couple of kids. First, I have to find a boy who's honest, trustworthy, funny and athletic —not a brainy, nerdy one like me."

Hunter was blown away. She seemed to have her whole life planned out, and she was only fifteen years old. He hadn't thought past making the school baseball team next spring.

"You talk like you're twenty-five years old," he told her. "I have not even considered some of the things that you have already planned for. My only plans for high school are to play baseball and graduate. My dad told me not to plan on going to college as he does not think that I am college material. I just know I want to be a great ballplayer."

Not deterred by Hunter's apparent lack of self-evaluation, Savannah asked him, "So, what kind of girls are you attracted to?"

"I like long hair," he said, "a lot. And blonde hair blows me away." Hunter felt his face burn red and was glad Jo Jo was not nearby. "I like girls who are sweet and friendly. Oh, and I'm best friends with my neighbor, Evelyn, who plays ball with us boys."

There was silence at the end of the line, so Hunter thought he ought to add more.

"And it would be cool to have a girlfriend who's athletic."

"Well, Hunter," Savannah answered, "I can't play sports, and I'm seriously uncoordinated."

"Oh, okay, well … at least she should understand sports. I think it would be neat to watch the NFL games in my den every Sunday with my girl."

There was another silence, then, just as Hunter was beginning to wonder if he'd said something wrong, Savannah laughed and said, "I'd like you to teach me all the games you love so we can watch them together. And I'll come to your ballgames and root for you." Hunter quickly got a big smile on his face.

By the beginning of August, the Montgomery family had moved to Virginia Beach with all their goods arriving in a military shipment. Savannah's dad insisted that the family open boxes, hang curtains and put their clothes away before they did any socializing with their new neighbors.

"Even Hunter," he said, raising one eyebrow and nodding towards the stack of boxes. "Your romance will have to wait a few more days."

"Daddy!"

While Hunter waited on his new lady to become available, he spent extra time practicing baseball with his neighborhood buddies. Hunter Austin, Asher Brown, Bryce Jennings, Liam Thomason and Evelyn Applegate liked to get together and play sports. Sometimes, someone would bring along a basketball, and they'd throw down their gloves and bats and shoot some hoops. The guys grew tired of playing H-O-R-S-E, a game on the basketball court that involved matching baskets, with Evelyn because she always beat them. Evelyn had played on Kempsville High's varsity softball and basketball teams as a freshman. The group would get together with a few other guys for batting practice and play pick-up basketball games with two-on-two or three-on-three half-court games. Hunter was very protective of Evelyn, not because she was a girl, but because they were neighbors and good friends and had grown up together on different sides of a six-foot fence.

When Savannah was free to hang out with Hunter for the first time, she knocked on the Austins' front door unannounced. Janet opened the door and was taken aback at the young woman in a cute dress with long, flowing blonde hair.

"Hi, I'm Savannah," the young woman said.

"You're here for Hunter?" Janet couldn't stop herself from asking in an amazed tone. Remembering her manners, she welcomed Savannah in, stopping to give her a spontaneous hug. "I'm so happy to meet you." Taking her hand, she added, "Let's go look for Hunter."

When they heard yelling out back, Janet led her into the backyard. There, Hunter and Jo Jo were playing cornhole.

"Loser!" Jo Jo crowed as Hunter's bag missed the hole.

"You were distracting me!" Hunter yelled back. They were just squaring off to wrestle each other when Savannah slowly strolled across the rear lawn towards them. They turned to look, and neither could say anything as their jaws dropped.

"Well, Hunter," she said, "aren't you going to give me a hug?"

Hunter dropped his cornhole bags at Jo Jo's feet and ran to her. Jo Jo looked green with jealously. Janet stood looking teary. It was hard for Hunter to kiss Savannah right in front of his mother and his brother, but he just couldn't help himself. He had six weeks of affection for his new lady built up.

"Just now, when I first saw you," he whispered in her ear, "my heart momentarily stopped, and then it hemorrhaged love."

August felt like the greatest month in Hunter and Savannah's life. School didn't start until the day after Labor Day, so they had four weeks together. Hunter introduced his friends to Savannah, took her to Virginia Beach's Town Center, spent days with her at the beach and Ocean Breeze Waterpark, and took her to an outdoor concert at the Virginia Beach amphitheater. There, they played air guitar along with the Dave Matthews Band as they sat on a blanket under the stars. They went on inexpensive dates such as playing Jungle Golf—a mini-golf course on Pacific Avenue—or walking around Mount Trashmore Lake. They were inseparable.

Hunter was relieved that Savannah and Evelyn seemed to like each other. Although Evelyn was attractive, she was a serious athlete and Hunter usually forgot she was even a girl, even when they hugged and laughed together, but he didn't realize what was simmering beneath the surface of the ladies' relationship until Jo Jo took him into the backyard to throw a ball and talk about the situation.

"You don't get it, do you?" Jo Jo asked.

"What are you talking about?"

"Evelyn and Savannah."

"They're friends."

"You're an idiot."

He had no idea until Jo Jo explained that Evelyn was genuinely happy for him and that she could see he was really in love. But she wasn't crazy about him spending most of his free time with his new girlfriend.

"Shoot," he said to Jo Jo as he tossed him the ball, "she plays ball with me and my buddies all the time."

"Has she lately?" he asked, tossing the ball back.

"She's my best friend. Not my best girlfriend."

"I don't know," Jo Jo answered, "she's pretty in a girl-next-door kind of way, and she's the girl next door."

"How do you know she feels like that?"

"I heard her talking on the phone in her backyard."

"You spied on her?" Hunter asked, incredulous.

"I was just trying to get some shut-eye out here in the hammock. I can't help it if she's on the phone on the other side of the fence."

"But they're totally different!" Hunter exclaimed. "Savannah's, like, my dream girl!"

Then Jo Jo explained that, unfortunately, Savannah only saw how pretty Evelyn was, and she wasn't down with how often Evelyn and Hunter hugged and laughed together.

"You can't possibly know that!" Hunter exclaimed.

"I've heard the two go at it," Jo Jo explained. "Most of the jealous snide remarks happen behind your back. I thought it was time to help you stop being so oblivious."

They both agreed that the female mind was something deep and mysterious.

After meeting Savannah just before school was about to start that fall, Hunter's grandfather advised him to work on building a friendship with her and not just a romance.

"You can have both with a gal, and you must if you want the relationship to last," he said. "Do things like listen to her. Learn what she likes and dislikes. Figure out what makes her tick. Learn to disagree agreeably. Cry with her and laugh with her."

Hunter repeatedly nodded, trying to take it all in.

"Maybe I should get a notebook and write this down," he said, dashing into the house to do just that.

The more Hunter learned about Savannah, the more he loved her. She clearly was not just a pretty face. He listed the things in his notebook. He liked how thoughtful, intelligent and mature she was.

"All qualities I'm lacking myself," he murmured as he filled in his notebook. "Maybe she could be my mentor on being a better person. She seems to have it all together."

He liked how Savannah appeared to have a purpose in her life. She knew where she wanted to go next and who she wanted to be in the future. She even knew where she was going to spend eternity, something that really rattled Hunter since he hadn't made any reservations yet for Heaven.

That fall, Jo Jo would enter his senior year of high school. In the summer, he was already being heavily recruited by Division I colleges to play football. In fact, at last count, he had more than a dozen full scholarship offers, some even from Ivy League schools due to his strong academic credentials. All summer, Jo Jo had felt pressure from his dad and college football coaches to make a decision and choose a university to play football at the following school year. Many of the coaches wanted Jo Jo to graduate from high school early and enter college in January 2010—halfway through his senior high school year.

As one college coach said, as he placed a shiny brochure on their living room table, "We prefer to get recruits into the college's football program early to work on their strength and conditioning, so the student is more advanced for football season the following fall."

That was a big sticking point for Jo Jo.

"I want to finish high school here," he admitted to Hunter, who was sworn to secrecy on pain of death. "I want to play basketball and baseball here and graduate with my friends. I want to go to senior prom."

"Do you think Mom and Dad will let you?" Hunter asked. He was sitting on Jo Jo's bed as his brother paced around the room. Their parents attended a Christian church that didn't believe it was proper for their members to dance, gamble, drink, smoke or curse. Because of that, Jo Jo and Hunter weren't allowed to attend school dances or go to parties where there would be dancing or drinking. No explanation from their father, mother or youth minister seemed to make sense to the boys. They just wanted to get dressed up, bring a pretty girl to a dance and hang out with their friends.

"I'll convince them," Jo Jo insisted. "After all, what could go wrong at a chaperoned school dance?"

Hunter was fascinated by all the attention Jo Jo was getting. But his brother was simply overwhelmed with the choices of colleges and the different things that college recruiters told him.

"Do you know where you want to go?" Hunter asked even though he knew Jo Jo had been asked it already, hundreds of times.

"I just don't know," he answered, grabbing his hair in frustration. "When a recruiter doesn't mention their school's academic program, it turns me off. Do they even care about academics? I'm a well-rounded young man. I'm prepared for college academically, athletically and socially."

"Is that something Mom said?"

Jo Jo ignored Hunter's remarks and continued his rant. "I feel like recruiters who only talk about how I would fit into their football team devalue me as a student. I'm much more than a jock."

"You're an idiot," Hunter said, throwing a pillow at him.

"And you're dead," Jo Jo replied, grabbing the end of the pillowcase and walloping Hunter with the pillow as he screamed and laughed.

"Now boys!" They heard their mom call from the kitchen, which sent them laughing once more. Jo Jo entered his senior year of high school without yet making a commitment to attend a particular college. He kept his options open through the 2009 fall football season, mainly because he could not make up his mind. One day, he wanted to go far away from home to play, and the next, he wanted to play at an in-state college so his family and buddies could come to his games. Jo Jo talked his younger brother into trying out for the Kempsville High School football team in August.

"Dude," he said, "no one on the team is as fast as you, and you're really good playing tag football with my friends, and they all play on the school football team."

Hunter loved his brother's confidence in him, but he was still hesitant about giving tackle football a try. And there was the issue with their mom and dad, who worried about Hunter getting hurt since he only weighed 160 pounds soaking wet with rocks in his pockets. But his brother was the team's star football player, and that had a lot of pull with Hunter. So, he agreed to try out for the Kempsville Chiefs football team on one condition.

"Mom and Dad have to let me play."

"Done," Jo Jo said with more confidence than he felt.

One evening, he forced Hunter into the living room and convinced their parents to turn off the TV.

"We need to discuss high school football," he said.

After Jo Jo pleaded Hunter's case, their mom was adamant that Hunter was not going to play tackle football.

"Maybe Hunter should take up golf," Archie said, "so that he doesn't get hurt."

Visibly stung, Hunter wanted to leave the room, but Jo Jo held onto his arm. After a lengthy discussion, they came up with a compromise. He could play football in high school, but he could only play defense, so he wouldn't be carrying the ball, and the other team wouldn't tackle him.

So in August, Hunter joined Jo Jo and his buddies at high school football camp. Hunter took one look at the big teenage boys he was with and didn't feel very confident.

"I shouldn't be here," he said to Jo Jo, a little panicked.

"Don't worry about it. You know how to cover receivers. Remember the neighborhood touch football games."

On the first day of summer tryouts, the team put on helmets, exercised, ran around and took turns running pass routes with the head coach throwing the passes. Guys who wanted to play defense huddled up with the defensive coaches, and the guys on the offensive team met with the offensive coaches.

Later in practice, Mr. Jackson, an assistant coach, said, "Austin, you look fast to me. What's your speed in the forty?"

Hunter shrugged. "I've never been timed running."

Coach Jackson gathered a dozen of the fastest guys on the team, picked up a stopwatch, and had them run forty-yard sprints on the school track. He had to teach Hunter and some of the guys the technique of short-distance running because they didn't have a clue. Two of the kids who looked fast to Hunter had a forty-yard time of 4.55 seconds.

"Great speed," Coach Jackson said with a smile. "Hunter, you're up!"

The coach had Hunter run a few sprints until he had the technique right.

"Okay, let's time you."

The first time Hunter posted was 4.45 seconds, and there were high-fives all around.

"Do it again," Coach Jackson said. The second time, he ran the forty in 4.4 seconds.

"Wait a minute, young man. Why didn't you come out for football your freshman year?" The coach wiped his brow and shook his head. "You're the fastest football player Kempsville has ever had."

"Does that mean I've made the team?" Hunter asked.

"You're Jo Jo Austin's brother, aren't you?"

"Yeah, he's my brother."

"And you just ran a 4.4 second forty-yard dash, right?"

"If you say so."

"You're a Kempsville Chief, young man!" the coach yelled. Mr. Dodge, the team's head coach, who had wandered over to the track to watch the kids be timed introduced himself to Hunter.

"Welcomed to the team," he said with a smile. "What's your best time?"

When Hunter told him 4.4, Coach Dodge answered, "No way. I have to see that for myself." He asked the assistant coach for the timing watch and told Hunter to line up and run the forty, one more time. With a "ready, set, go!" he was off and running.

This time, running felt different to Hunter, like he was floating on air. Coach Dodge was jumping up and down and waving the timer as if he had won the lottery. On that third and final run, Hunter's forty time was 4.3 seconds.

When they rejoined the rest of the team for more drills, Coach Dodge spoke to the team.

"A track star was born today," he said. "Hunter Austin ran the forty in 4.3. That's an almost unheard-of time for a high schooler."

Jo Jo ran up to Hunter and hugged the daylights out of him, lifting him right off the ground and swinging him around.

"That's my little brother!" he whooped.

Jo Jo was an all-city tight end and heavily recruited by colleges, but he only ran the forty in 4.6. Not slow, but not blazing fast like his kid brother. Of course, there was another distinctive difference between the two Austin brothers. Jo Jo was six-foot-four and weighed 230 pounds. Hunter was five-foot-nine and weighed 160 pounds.

However, Hunter struggled with how to tell his football coaches that he could only play defense. They quickly started talking about ways to get him the ball on offense, so he could use his speed to complement Jo Jo's powerful route running and catching medium-to-short passes. One day after practice, Hunter got Jo Jo to come with him to the coaches' office.

"Uh, Coach," he said nervously, "I can't run with the ball or catch the ball."

"What?" Coach Dodge asked with a frown.

"So I won't get hurt," Hunter added. To his surprise, the coaches all started laughing as if he'd told them a joke.

Jo Jo spoke up. "Stop laughing. It's not a joke. He can't run or catch the ball."

"You've got to be kidding me!" Coach Dodge yelled.

"No, sir," Hunter said. "My parents only agreed to let me play if I don't play offense."

The coach threw his clipboard across the locker room. "This is pure craziness!"

After a period of silence, Coach Jackson asked, "Can you play on the special teams?"

The brothers looked at each other, thought for a moment and tilted their heads.

"Mom and Dad didn't say anything about special teams, did they?" Hunter asked.

Jo Jo gave him a slow, wide smile. "No, they did not."

"I guess that might be okay," Hunter told the coaches, and there was laughter and high-fives all around. And that's how Hunter became the Chiefs' punt returner as well as one of their cornerbacks.

As summer's end approached, the steady stream of big-name college head coaches and assistant coaches visiting the Austins' home to persuade Jo Jo continued with no signs of stopping. Louisiana State University's Head Coach Les Miles and Penn State University's Head Coach Joe Paterno visited on the same day. All of the coaches left behind school t-shirts, ball caps, pennants, gym bags and a lot of literature. Archie and Janet got tired of the phone constantly ringing about college football. Sometimes, callers in the West Coast forgot about the time difference and woke up the whole family; Archie gave them, "What for" due to their lack of common sense. Jo Jo had to silence his cell phone, so he could get his homework done in the evenings. He was being hounded by mail, email, text and phone, and coaches would show up at school and nearly accost him in the halls.

Jo Jo was over the recruiting process before it had concluded. At the same time, Hunter was green with envy.

"I wish it would all stop," Jo Jo said in irritation one day.

Hunter shook his head in disbelief. "But just look at all this attention. You've got reporters, recruiters, neighbors, friends and high school students all chasing you. Dad's saved, like, two dozen newspaper articles about your football exploits. You've got your choice of college scholarships. You're like a rock star—"

Jo Jo raised an eyebrow.

"—only less attractive."

"That's it. Prepare to die, pipsqueak." And the boys ran out of the house shouting at each other.

Hunter kept his real jealousy to himself—the green envy that sometimes felt like it was burning inside of him. All of his comments, to anyone who would listen, was that his brother Jo Jo was the best. He would tell them that someday Jo Jo would be a pro and play on TV. And he really believed it.

As the new school year began, Hunter and his big brother suited up for the Kempsville Chiefs football team. Jo Jo ran past, over, through and around opponents. He was a talented tight end who had more than a dozen college athletic scholarship offers. A full NCAA football scholarship included free tuition, room and board, and books, plus an opportunity to play ball in front of tens of thousands of people and millions more on TV. Dozens of assistant coaches continued to attend his Friday night football games. Hunter just tried to fit in on the team, learn the game and contribute wherever possible. By the third game, he felt more confident that no receiver could run past him. He started to jam the receivers near the line of scrimmage and run with them stride for stride. He also started guessing where the throws would go and began jumping some of the quarterback throws.

He got his first interception in a game against Landstown High School and returned one punt forty-five yards before he was shoved out of bounds. In the fifth game, the Chiefs were playing at Tallwood High School, just a few miles down Kempsville Road. Hunter broke up two passes and intercepted a third pass. He was also starting to figure out how to fake out the would-be-tacklers on punt returns by using misdirection moves. Using his quickness and ability to change direction, he would take two steps one way and quickly cross over his feet to the opposite direction; his opponents would run right past him empty-handed.

By mid-season, he was averaging eighteen yards per punt return. Then came game number eight at First Colonial High School. The field on Mill Dam Road was a little wet from a pregame shower. When Hunter fielded a punt on his eighteen-yard line, he started left but quickly broke to his right, and three defenders slipped and missed him. He was off to the races. Down the right sideline, Hunter ran right into the end zone for an eighty-two-yard touchdown.

The Chiefs defense then held the Patriots offense on a three and out and Hunter, still out of breath, got in punt return position to receive another punt.

"Who said lightning doesn't strike twice in the same spot?" Coach Jackson later said.

Hunter fielded the punt back at the ten-yard line and headed straight up the field. He bounced off a tackler at the twenty and started to his left, but two tacklers stood in his way. Hunter stopped and reversed the field. With three Patriots players right on his heels, he got around the right side of the field and again outran everyone to the end zone. This time, the touchdown went for ninety yards.

But there would be no more end-zone celebrations between the two Austin brothers. Later in that game, while playing on defense, Hunter attempted to tackle a wide receiver during a bubble screen play. He was landed on by a pulling guard who outweighed him by a hundred pounds. The pain in his right leg told him his football season might be over.

While the paramedics put an air cast around Hunter's leg, he only had two thoughts rumbling through his mind. "Mom and Dad are going to kill me," and "If this keeps me from playing baseball, I'll just die."

As he said to Jo Jo before they lifted him away, "Either way, I figure I'm a dead man."

Later, when the emergency room doctor walked back into Hunter's room holding x-rays of his lower leg, his mother asked, "How bad is it?"

"Actually, it's not bad at all," the doctor said. "He has a clean fracture of the fibula. The fibula is the thinner, weaker bone in the lower leg. Nothing is displaced in Hunter's bone, and surgery's not necessary. With plenty of rest and staying off that leg for six to eight weeks, it should heal up as good as new. I would say he can start running in about three months."

Despite creating some football highlights for his team, Hunter never played tackle football again. That's not to say there wasn't pressure. In his future high school years, the pressure from the football coaches and teammates to play football again was severe. Even Kempsville High's track coaches bugged him to death about running track. But Hunter was focused on baseball, more obsessed than ever really, ever since he lay there in the emergency room, thinking he might not be able to play baseball again because of his broken leg.

At that moment, his mind was filled with baseball names and trivia. It would float through his dreams. Abner Doubleday; Cy Young; Walter Johnson; Babe Ruth; Ty Cobb; Ted Williams; Mickey Mantle; Harmon Killebrew; Johnny Bench; Cal Ripken Jr.; Hank Aaron; Willie Mays; Ozzie Smith; Yogi Berra; Brooks Robinson; Sandy Koufax; Juan Marichal; Tony Gwynn; Ryan Zimmerman; Mike Trout; 60 feet, 6 inches; foul poles; bullpens; radar guns; batboys; on-deck circles; rosin bags; umpires; hit and runs; pickoff plays; diving catches; and walk-off home runs. When Hunter dreamed, he frequently heard his name called over the baseball stadium's loudspeaker, "Leading off and playing center field, Hunter Austin."

One good thing about playing for the high school football team was that Hunter found out just how blazing fast he was. He was determined to tailor his baseball skills to take advantage of his 4.3 speed. He thought of previous base stealers who had a lot of speed—Maury Wills, Lou Brock and Rickey Henderson.

"Maybe I can learn to steal bases like those dudes."

Hunter set out to dedicate his time and energy to baseball. He hit the weight room to get stronger and improve his conditioning. He'd heard about an ex-major-league player who prepped for professional baseball by swinging a bat in a swimming pool, so whenever Hunter could get rides over to his grandfather's house, he'd work out in his swimming pool with the water creating resistance, making Hunter use more effort to get the bat through the hitting zone.

Kempsville High football experienced its best season yet. They won nine regular-season games and lost only one. They won the state regional tournament and qualified for the state championship tournament. In the first round, the Chiefs played at home against TC Williams High School from Alexandria, the school featured in the movie *Remember the Titans*. Kempsville won, 21–7, and advanced to the semifinals against George Wythe

High School in Richmond. The weather was horrible with light snow falling and windy conditions. Kempsville High's passing game was grounded by the weather, and the Chiefs couldn't match their opponents' running game. Kempsville High was taken to the woodshed and beaten to the tune of 33–6. It would prove to be Jo Jo's last high school football game.

5

WHEN THINGS GET TOUGH (2009–2010)

October 3, 2009, marked the day the head coach of the University of Florida Gators and his tight end assistant coach came to Virginia Beach to scout Jo Jo's Friday ballgame. They stayed overnight and visited the Austins at their home on Saturday. Head coach Urban Meyer tried to convince Jo Jo to play football for the Florida Gators.

"First of all," Meyer said, "you'll get to play alongside Percy Harvin. You know who he is, son, don't you?"

"Just the jet-fast wide receiver and running back who played his high school ball at Virginia Beach's Landstown High School!" the assistant coach added.

"And if that's not enough of a drawing card," Meyer said, "you'll be catching passes from Florida's All-American quarterback, Tim Tebow."

Jo Jo was so excited that he wanted to sign a letter of intent right then and there, but his father grabbed his arm and interrupted.

"My family has to think about this decision. And more importantly, we will pray for God's will and direction for Jo Jo."

The football season ended in November. Jo Jo took a week off to rest and then started practicing with the Kempsville High basketball team, which had already started its season. Soon, he took his place as the starting shooting guard for the Chiefs. But his playing suffered because his mind was elsewhere. The pressure of being recruited by colleges for so long caused him to miss sleep and lose his appetite; it also led to arguments at home. Even his energy level seemed low. His long-range shooting was off, and in some games, he struggled to score in double figures. His high school basketball coach started to sub him out of basketball games more frequently to give him some rest.

Delaying Jo Jo's college commitment was a moment of wisdom for Archie on behalf of his oldest son because, on December 26, 2009, Coach Meyers resigned from his coaching position at the University of Florida for health reasons. And around the same time, Percy Harvin entered the 2010 NFL football draft following his junior season at Florida. By signing with an agent, Harvin gave up his amateur status and could no longer play college sports. The situation took another turn of uncertainty for the Florida football program on December 27, 2009. Urban then changed his mind about resigning, but instead, he took an indefinite leave of absence to address his health issues.

Sitting around their backyard firepit on New Year's Eve, feeling a little exhausted by the whole process, the Austin family decided to drop the University of Florida from Jo Jo's list of schools. The next day, Archie called the university to tell them Jo Jo wouldn't be attending Florida due to the uncertainty of Coach Meyer's health.

As news travels fast, especially on the sports recruiting trail, the University of Virginia's new head football coach, Mike London, called three days later on January 4. The previous head coach, Mike Groh, had been fired on November 29 following a season where the football team only won three games. Groh and his staff had been recruiting Jo Jo to play ball at Virginia, and he was fairly interested until the coaching staff was let go.

Coach London and an assistant to the academic dean visited the Austins' home on January 6. It was the first time that any of the colleges had sent someone to specifically discuss Jo Jo's academic interests and the school's degree programs.

Coach London looked earnestly at Archie and Janet and said, "I will treat Jo Jo like he is my own son." Archie nodded. That sold him on Virginia.

Then the coach put his arm around Jo Jo's shoulder. "I need you at Virginia to help me change the culture of losing and to be a leader on the team." Jo Jo nodded. That did it for him. He loved Coach London's approach to recruiting and his obvious sincerity. He said "yes" right then and there to Virginia.

Coach London pulled out some paperwork to show the Austins what an NCAA athletic scholarship included, and the assistant to the academic dean showed what academic majors and classes were available to Jo Jo.

"Let's join hands and pray about this decision," Archie said.

The family of four, Coach London and the assistant to the academic dean joined hands and asked for God's blessings on this decision for Jo Jo to accept a scholarship to the University of Virginia. Archie also said a short prayer seeking God's will in his son's life decisions.

After the "amens" were spoken, the coach brought out a letter of intent to attend the University of Virginia and handed Jo Jo a pen. He instantly signed it. Soon the ink was dry, but not everyone's eyes. It was an important moment for everyone in the Austin's living room.

Jo Jo would be playing football at the school Thomas Jefferson built in the foothills of Virginia. The Austin family would be able to make the three-hour drive to Charlottesville for all of Virginia's home games and return home the same night. Hopefully, the competition found in the Atlantic Coast Conference would prepare Jo Jo for professional football. And a degree from a strong academic university such as Virginia would look good on Jo Jo's resume. It was a win on multiple fronts for him and a big win for Virginia, as Jo Jo became their first football recruit in the Mike London era. The future was looking bright for everyone.

Well before Coach London had handed Jo Jo the letter of intent, the teenager had been tagged as a four-star recruit. Before his fall 2009 season had even begun, he was rated as the number three senior in Virginia by 247Sports and ESPN and number four by Rivals.

Following his senior year Jo Jo Hunter was first-team All-Tidewater after he led Hampton Roads in receptions for tight ends. He caught sixty-five passes for 1,100 yards and fifteen touchdowns. As a safety on defense, he intercepted six passes, defended twelve others and was involved in sixty tackles.

In January 2010, Jo Jo seemed to bring new inspiration to the basketball court that January. He got his shooting stroke back and seemed to enjoy playing basketball again. With their star player back in the lineup full-time and firing on all cylinders, the Chiefs developed a terrific offense and finished the season in third place for Virginia Beach high schools.

As spring rolled around, it signaled once again the start of baseball season. Hunter, now sixteen years old, tried out for Kempsville High's varsity baseball team with his three neighborhood buddies. During the team tryouts, Hunter proved he had improved by leaps and bounds. He felt extra pressure because Jo Jo was one of the team's best players, and he didn't want to embarrass himself or his brother. This time, all four of the friends made the final cut.

When Hunter found out he'd made the school team, the first thing he did was run to Savannah's house to tell her the good news. He was so excited that he hugged and kissed her repeatedly until he saw her mom, Robin, standing in the doorway. He jumped away from her daughter as if he'd been burned.

"We were only celebrating Hunter making the school's baseball team," Savannah quickly explained to her mother. "I'm so proud of him!"

"Well done, Hunter!" Robin said brightly. With a chuckle, she went back into the house.

That night at the Austin family dinner, Jo Jo was the first to tell his parents that he and Hunter would be playing together for Kempsville High's baseball team.

Archie looked right at Hunter and asked, "You made the team?"

"Yep," Hunter replied with a huge grin. "Jo Jo and I are teammates, just like we were in football."

"And you know how that turned out," his father said in an ugly tone. "You got carted off the field and ended up with your leg in a cast."

"I doubt that anyone weighing 260 pounds will fall on me on a baseball field, Dad."

"Give him a break, Dad," Jo Jo said angrily, defending his brother. "Hunter has worked extremely hard improving himself, and it paid off. Coach Collinsworth feels Hunter can help the team this year. He's so fast that no one will be able to throw him out when attempting to steal bases."

"I know Kelly Collinsworth," Archie replied. "I thought he was a good man, but now I think that he's lost his mind."

"What do you mean, dear?" Janet asked.

Her husband just got up and walked out of the room, yelling from the kitchen, "I'll just keep my mouth shut. Obviously, I've already said too much."

"Ain't that the truth!" Hunter yelled after his father.

Jo Jo patted his shoulder. "It's okay."

"I'm so tired of him putting me down. What he thinks of me no longer matters to me."

"What did you say, boy?" Archie yelled, coming into the doorway.

"I said what you think of me no longer matters to me."

"Don't talk to me that way!"

Janet jumped between them. "No!" she said. "I won't have this. I won't. You both just clam yourselves up until you're ready to apologize to each other." When it looked like they were going to start again, she put out her arms. "I mean it."

While Archie stalked back to the kitchen, Jo Jo swung his arm around Hunter's shoulders and said, "Let's go to the park." He turned to his mom and mouthed, "Thank you."

"So much for celebrating," Hunter muttered as they went out the door.

After Archie's latest outburst, Jo Jo took on the responsibility of supporting Hunter. Every day, he encouraged his kid brother and told him he was a good ballplayer and that he was good enough to be on the team—all the things Hunter wished he had heard from his dad. Savannah was his daily voice of reason and optimism, telling him that he was special and had

God-given gifts. The encouraging words worked. Hunter played ball like he belonged with the older boys. And he could do some things better than the other players. He could throw balls farther and more accurately from the outfield, and he could run faster. The coaches were excited about his potential as a basestealer. Now, if only they could help him get on base often enough to boost the team's speed.

People were no longer telling Hunter that he wasn't good enough, big enough or strong enough to play baseball—things he had heard his whole life. He had worked his butt off. His extraordinary efforts and dedication were starting to pay off.

He was also showing promise and improvement in his academic work. Savannah taught him studying techniques and test-taking tips. She even showed him how she took notes in class.

"Man," he said. "You're pretty smart for a sixteen-year-old." After he ducked from a pillow to his head, he added, "Seriously, how do you know all of that?"

"My mom's a high school English teacher, and both my parents have master's degrees. So, I've been taught by the best."

With Savannah's positive influence, Hunter improved a full letter grade From C to B in one year. He didn't mention this to his dad because he figured he'd just say something stupid and cutting. Instead, he got his mom to sign his report cards. She'd give him a tight hug and say, "Keep up the good work, son."

The Kempsville Chiefs began the 2010 baseball season on March 16 with a game against Cox High. Jo Jo had continued as the team's starting first baseman and provided the team with most of its power hitting. He was also a gifted defensive player and a good baserunner.

He was attracting the interest of professional baseball teams. There was at least one team scout at each of his games, even though their interest was tempered with the knowledge that Jo Jo had already signed to play football at Virginia.

The Chiefs played a typical schedule of fourteen games against Virginia Beach conference schools and four games during spring break against non-conference teams. During April break around Easter, the team traveled south to play games in South Carolina, Florida and Tennessee. Sadly, the four out-of-state teams beat the Kempsville team, mainly because of superior pitching. It was a reality check for the team. Still, the kids had fun seeing places they'd never seen before and playing at ballparks with first-rate facilities. Also, staying in hotels, staying up late and eating together helped strengthen team unity. However, the Chiefs went into the spring break trip thinking they were a terrific team after winning the first four league games of the season; they came home with their heads down. Coach Collinsworth had his hands full with regrouping the team and getting them to refocus on the games ahead.

During the road trip down South, since the coach rotated the lineups every day to give everyone game experience, Hunter played in all four out-of-state games—two as a reserve and two as a starter. In the third game in Kingsport, Tennessee, he played the whole game and put on quite a show. He got two hits in three at-bats, one being an in-the-park home run. For anyone else, the hit would have only resulted in a triple, but with his foot-speed, he ran through a "stop sign" of sorts by the third-base coach and raced across home plate way ahead of the cutoff man's throw. Hunter's teammates celebrated his unconventional home run, but his coaches were as mad as the devil losing a fiddle contest down in Georgia.

"When I tell you to stop at third base," Coach Collinsworth yelled, "you stop at third base!"

Fortunately, all was forgiven in Hunter's next at-bat. He dragged a bunt down the first-base line and legged out a base hit. He beat the throw to first base by a stride and a half. Hunter proceeded to steal both second and third bases and then scored on an error by the third baseman. In two straight at-bats, his fast feet had generated two runs with virtually no one else's help.

Coach Collinsworth shook his head and said to his assistant coach, "That Hunter is so unique that we can't keep him on the bench. Us coaches have to think outside the box because he's so unique." He shook his head again. "Let's talk to the base coaches and tell them to turn him loose on the bases and let him take some chances on the base paths. His speed will unnerve opposing pitchers and make fielders rush their throws. Let's use that to our advantage."

The Kempsville Chiefs returned home to Virginia Beach and got right to practicing for the remainder of their city-league schedule. Coach Collinsworth had learned a lot about his team on their spring trip. Lesson number one was that his pitching staff needed to improve and pitch longer into games. Lesson number two was that there was no drop-off in talent when he played his bench players. He planned to rotate the players in and out of the games to give the younger guy's experience and confidence.

Kempsville High continued to win all of their league games, and their record grew to six wins and zero losses for the season. But their undefeated run ended at First Colonial High School. Hunter started in center field for the first time since the spring trip. Late in the game, he was on first base after getting his second single of the game. The next batter hit into a force play as Hunter slid into second base just as he was stepped on by the First Colonial shortstop. Hunter limped off the diamond, and the Chiefs medical staff put an ice pack on his ankle. As Hunter rode the pine the rest of the game, he looked over and saw the First Colonial football stadium. Immediately, he had flashbacks to the night he broke his leg making a tackle on that same football field.

He leaned over and said to a teammate, "I'm 2-for-2 here. I've played two games at First Colonial and left with two injuries."

Hunter had to sit out the next four baseball games while his sprained ankle healed. By the time he could dress out again for a game, the Chiefs were playing their twelfth game of the season, and their league record was eight wins and three losses. They were in the running for a first-place finish, but in game twelve, they needed to beat Princess Anne High School Cavaliers, who, up to that point, had only suffered two defeats.

The game with Princess Anne began with Hunter on the bench and not in the starting lineup. He was trying to fit in again with his teammates since he missed considerable time as his ankle healed. Jo Jo was having a big game against the Cavaliers. In the top of the seventh inning, with the score tied, he singled up the middle. He previously had homered and doubled. Coach sent his little brother out to pinch-run for him; the coach was obviously playing for one run to get the lead. As the next batter looked to sacrifice bunt Hunter to second base, the pitcher uncorked a wild pitch that went back to the backstop and bounced away from the catcher. As the catcher chased the ball, Hunter ran to second base, made a wide turn and hit the gas again, making it to third base standing up. After the batter struck out, the catcher lobbed a throwback to the left-handed pitcher, who had his back to third base. The pitcher never saw Hunter running down the baseline towards home plate. He only reacted after hearing the fans screaming out a warning.

"He's stealing; he's stealing! He stole home!"

The Austin boys had produced the go-ahead run, which held up in the bottom of the seventh to secure the victory over Princess Anne and a tie for first place in the league.

The Chiefs bats came alive during the final two games of the 2010 season. They scored a total of twenty-two runs, beating Ocean Lakes and Landstown high schools to end the season with a league record of eleven wins and three defeats. Kempsville High School won the Virginia Beach City regular season title.

"We did it, little brother!" Jo Jo screamed, picking him up and chucking him about.

Going into the pending league tournament, the Chiefs were the top-seeded team. Kempsville High's baseball team looked fine-tuned during the City of Virginia Beach Tournament—the team played sweet music together. Coach Collinsworth orchestrated several rallies of three or more runs per inning, which took the pressure off their pitchers and allowed Hunter to play defense during the last few innings of the games. Kelly referred to Hunter as his security blanket due to his ability to roam the outfield, stealing base hits from opponents. Kempsville High won all their games in the city tournament, and they were awarded the championship trophy. "Up next," Jo Jo crowed, "the state championship tournament."

The tournament began for the Chiefs with two games in the Tidewater regionals and then, if they advanced, the quarter-finals, semifinals and finals in Richmond, Virginia.

Just as the Chiefs ballplayers had done in their city tournament, they rolled through the two regional games defeating Granby and Great Bridge high schools. They were playing their best ball of the year at just the right time. The Chiefs had six starting seniors on the team to provide internal leadership and experience. At this point, the team seemed to be willing itself to victories.

The whole Austin clan, including Granddaddy Anthony, made plans to travel to Richmond. No one wanted to miss seeing Jo Jo and Hunter play together for the last time and compete for a state championship to boot. Savannah begged her parents to take her to Richmond to root for her guy. They relented and made hotel reservations so all three of them could attend.

Kempsville High faced Mills E. Godwin High in the quarter-finals. Godwin had a star pitcher, Todd Hickman, that the pro scouts were drooling over. He'd already signed to attend Georgia Tech on an athletic scholarship but was considering skipping college and going straight to the pros.

The game between Kempsville and Godwin was tied, 1–1, after six innings. Figuring the game would be decided in the last inning, Coach Collinsworth inserted Hunter into the game in center field for the top of the seventh. He also inserted him into a spot in the lineup, so he would lead off the bottom of the inning. Godwin was put out 1-2-3 in the top of the seventh inning. This meant the Chiefs could win the game by scoring a single run in the home half of the inning.

Hunter walked to home plate with the game up for grabs. He worked the count full before hitting a line drive to the opposite field. The left fielder short-hopped the ball as Hunter rounded first base. The next Chiefs batter laid down a perfect sacrifice bunt, which moved Hunter to second base. Up to bat came Jo Jo Austin. As instructed, he was patient and worked the count to two balls and two strikes.

The Godwin's pitcher thought the Chiefs' number three hitter was maybe timing his fastball because he'd previously jumped two pitches, but he pulled them foul. So, when the catcher put down one finger to get another fastball, Hickman shook him off and finally got the fist, which meant to throw a changeup. The change of speed pitch came in twelve miles per hour slower than the previous pitch, and Jo Jo absolutely crushed a two-hopper towards third base. The Godwin third baseman backhanded the ball, but it popped out of his glove, and he had to load up twice to make a hard throw to first base. The ball sailed upward and pulled the first baseman off the base. Meanwhile, Hunter had taken a long secondary lead off second base before the ball was hit to third base. When the throw went across the diamond to first base, Hunter tore up the base path getting to third and, without hesitating, rounded third base in a flash and sped toward home plate. After leaping to catch the throw, the first baseman was in no position to make a strong throw to the catcher, so Hunter slid in way ahead of the ball from first base.

"SAFE!" the umpire yelled. "Ballgame is over!"

Complete bedlam broke out on the field with the Kempsville High's players, family and fans running onto the field to celebrate the victory. They had beat the best team in the state, 2–1.

"As I predicted," Coach Collinsworth pointed out, "two runs were enough to win the quarter final game. Now, on to the semi-finals!"

At dinner after the game, Archie walked his oldest son around the interior of the restaurant and introduced him to complete strangers. He told everyone that Jo Jo had gotten the winning hit in the state tournament that day. The first few times Jo Jo heard him say that, he corrected his dad.

"It was an error by the third baseman, Dad, not a hit."

But Archie wasn't going to let the facts get in the way of a good story.

"Hunter's the one who scored the winning run," Jo Jo tried to interject.

"Hunter was valuable to the team," his dad admitted in a low voice, "but only in a very limited role." Then he proceeded to brag about his oldest son to the crowd.

Fortunately, Savannah and her parents were also sitting at the table with Hunter and his mom and grandfather. They kept reminding him that the team would not have won without his fast feet and base hit in the last inning.

"Hunter," Bill said, "you're amazing. You provide your coach with so much flexibility. He can use various lineups for different purposes."

"Thank you, Colonel," Hunter replied. "It's been fun to play on such a talented team with my brother and friends. Coach said I'll have an expanded role next year. I'll get to bat leadoff and play center field full-time." Savannah sat next to him, smiling proudly at her guy.

The next day, the Kempsville Chiefs baseball team squared off against Rappahannock High School in the semi-final game. The game couldn't have been more different from Kempsville's quarter-final victory. To start off with, Kempsville was behind by six runs before they'd even batted. But, by the fourth inning, the score was tied, 8–8. Then things got bizarre. In the fifth inning, Jo Jo hit a grand slam to put the Chiefs up 12–8. But after he scored, the home plate umpire leaned over to clean off home plate, passed out and fell across the eighteen inches of white rubber. He was revived and moved into the shade while he waited for an ambulance to arrive. Everyone was speculating that the summer heat had given him heat stroke.

After one of the base umpires put on the face mask and chest protector and got behind the plate, the game proceeded. After Rappahannock scored one more run in the top of the sixth and the third out was recorded, the sky opened up and rain poured onto the field. After about five minutes of pelting rain, the field was a mess, but the game proceeded in the bottom of the sixth inning. The Chiefs were already using their third pitcher of the game, and he couldn't get the ball over the plate due to the wet pitcher's mound. His front foot slipped each time he strode towards home plate. He was six-foot-five and his stride was extra-long, so his balance was challenged by the wet field. After four straight batters had walked and one run was scored, Coach Collinsworth went up to Hunter, who was sitting on the dugout bench, and asked him if he could pitch to a few batters.

Hunter gulped. "Gosh, Coach, I haven't pitched anywhere for a year. And never in high school."

"I know, but you've pitched before in the rec league games, so at least you have the technique down, and you understand what you're supposed to do."

"Okay, Coach," Hunter relented. "When I pitched, I threw hard, but I walked lots of guys."

"Hunter, you can't do any worse than what's going on the mound right now."

Hunter nodded and walked out to the mound. The situation found Kempsville leading by the score of 12–9, but the bases were loaded, and nobody was out. When Hunter was warming up on the mound, his arm felt lively. Probably because he hadn't been playing and throwing much lately.

"What pitches do you throw?" his catcher asked him.

"Mainly the heater and a curveball." They agreed on signs—one finger for fastballs and two for curves. It all felt so weird since Hunter and his catcher had never thrown together before, but the state championship was on the line. He remembered an old saying his grandfather would say, "When things get tough, the tough get going."

Rappahannock's first batter of the inning stepped into the batter's box, still slippery with mud. The first pitch from Hunter zipped up under his chin. "Chin music" was another of his grandfather's sayings. Although it was unintentional, the off-target baseball got the batter's attention. The next two fastballs caught the plate, so the batter was down to his last strike. Hunter shook off the catcher's sign for another fastball and instead he got the sign for a curveball. He uncorked an Uncle Charlie that broke twelve inches; the batter mistook the speed of the ball and was way out in front with the bat.

"Strike three!" the umpire called out.

After getting that first out of the inning, Hunter looked over and saw his dad pumping both his fists into the air imploring him to do the impossible—be the closer for his team, even though he hadn't pitched in a ballgame in a year.

At first, he thought sarcastically, "Boy, Dad really doesn't expect much of me." Then it hit him between the eyes that this was the first time his dad had shown hope and expectations for his success. It was the first time he'd witnessed his dad cheering him on. He had to step off the pitcher's rubber and compose himself. As he was messing with the rosin bag, Jo Jo walked over from first base.

"You okay, little bro?"

"Yeah," Hunter answered, head down. "I just saw Dad rooting for me and I wasn't prepared for it."

Jo Jo laughed. "Forget about Dad. Concentrate on each batter and tell yourself that you're better than they are. Then go out there and strike them out!" That was the focused energy Hunter needed to hear. He stepped back onto the mound.

Three swings and misses and the next batter walked back to the dugout. Hunter was bringing the heat now, and the Rappahannock players couldn't catch up with it. With two outs and the bases loaded, Hunter slipped on his follow-through and the ball hit the batter in the back. The runner from third base advanced across home plate to score his team's tenth run. With the bases still loaded, and trying to protect a shrinking lead, Hunter went back to his bender to strike out the final batter of the visitor's sixth inning. Hunter had come into the game and got three outs on three strikeouts and, most importantly, only allowed one more run to score.

As Hunter crossed the foul line and approached his dugout, his coaches and teammates mobbed him with hugs for putting out the fire and helping the Chiefs retain the lead. A couple of the kids were yelling, "Hunter is the fireman! Hunter is the fireman!"

In the dugout, Coach Collinsworth asked Hunter if he could pitch the last inning and try to close out the game. Hunter was in such a zone; someone would have had to tie him to the bench to keep him off the bump that last inning. To say the least, he was ready, able and willing.

With one out, in the bottom of the sixth, the Chiefs got three straight singles, the last by Hunter. He was credited with an RBI as one run scored. Kempsville High took the field for the seventh inning of that state championship semi-final baseball game leading Rappahannock by the score of 13–10. Kempsville only needed to record three outs before their opponents scored three runs to win and move on to the finals.

The first Rappahannock's batter hit the first pitch straight up in the air, and first baseman Jo Jo called off his smaller brother near the pitching mound and caught the ball for the first out. As Jo Jo handed him the ball, he put his hand on Hunter's shoulder and said, "You're doing great, Hunter, and the team really needs you to be a leader right now." Those unique words of encouragement sounded so wonderful to Hunter that he almost broke up in tears, right on the ball field. He snapped out of it when Jo Jo yelled at him, "Come on dude, you can do this!"

The second batter of the inning beat out a dribbler towards shortstop for a single. Hunter reminded the infielders to concentrate and not give the other team anything.

"Make them earn what they get. Don't help them!" he said. The leadership Jo Jo demanded of his little brother was on display.

There was one down and one on. Hunter threw a fastball past the next hitter on the first pitch, but on the second pitch, he timed his swing perfectly. The ball was hit on a line straight back towards Hunter on the pitcher's mound. As his heart momentarily stopped, he instinctively threw his glove up and snagged the ball in the webbing. He then glanced at the runner off first base and threw behind him to Jo Jo standing with his foot on first base. Jo Jo caught the ball for a game ending double play. The cheers were deafening. The Kempsville Chiefs had won again! They were on a roll, rolling right into the Virginia State Championship game.

Hunter was mobbed by his teammates onto the ground as the guys jumped on top of him in a dogpile.

"Hunter! You saved the day!" his teammates shouted, one after the other.

"That's showing fire in your belly, son," Coach said.

After his teammates finally allowed Hunter to get off the ground and off the ball field, his dad met him near the dugout with tears in his eyes.

"Hunter, my son," he said, barely able to get it out, "I have badly underestimated you. When I've said you can't do something or aren't good enough, you just went on proving me wrong. I've been ignoring your triumphs. But there's no denying what you accomplished today. You took the challenge from your coach to pitch without any practice pitching this year, and you went out on the mound, set your defense, threw strikes and fielded your position. You made me so proud today that you are my son. And I know that Jo Jo will forever be thankful to you for saving this game, and his last season like that. Now, because of you, he gets to play for a state championship tomorrow."

"And me too, Dad," Hunter added quietly. "I get that chance too." Hunter reminded his father. "*Perceived failure is often times success trying to be born in a bigger way.*"

His dad made a choking sound, then pulled him into a hug. Hunter and his dad embraced for what seemed like forever. A funny thing happened that night at dinner. Archie walked around the restaurant arm-in-arm with his youngest son, introducing him as the star pitcher on the Kempsville High School baseball team to anyone who would listen. Hunter tried to set the record straight that he'd only pitched two innings, but Archie would have none of that. Once again, his dad was not going to let the facts get in the way of a good story. Hunter kept pinching himself to be sure that it all wasn't just some good dream.

Savannah and her parents tried to spend time with Hunter that evening, but he was constantly surrounded by fans and teammates patting him on the back. When Hunter finally got a few moments alone with his girlfriend, he burst into tears as she held him tightly. All his emotions from the game, and his dad apologizing came busting out. When she told him, "You're my hero," he lost it again.

"No one's told me these things before, Savannah. It's just overwhelming."

He walked Savannah to her hotel where he kissed her goodnight.

"Get some rest, dear," she said. "Tomorrow's another big day for the Austin boys."

The Virginia State Championship final game was delayed by one day after twenty-four hours of rain. But the following day was perfect for baseball. The inclement weather passed overnight, bringing in cooler temperatures and a lot of sunshine. Kempsville High School faced Park View High School from Sterling, Virginia. Both teams had their number one starting pitcher on the mound so all anticipated a close, low-scoring game.

Kelly Blacksmith toed the rubber for Park View. Coach Collinsworth had a hunch he should start Hunter in center field, even if the player he normally started there was a senior and this would be his last game of high school baseball. That was not an easy decision to make. But the Coach had seen Hunter do extraordinary things lately, with very limited opportunities. He seemed to fire up his teammates with some of his contributions to recent team victories. So, the Coach wrote the name "Hunter Austin" in the leadoff batting spot for the Chiefs.

With Park View's defense playing Hunter shallow in the outfield to start the game, he caught up with a fastball from Blacksmith and sent it over the right fielder's head. By the time the ball rolled to the fence and was retrieved, Hunter was on his horse between second and third, watching the third-base coach. He never broke stride as the coach sent him home. The second baseman's relay throw was way off the mark as Hunter slid across home plate with his third inside-the-park home run of the year.

"Not bad for a part-time player," Hunter later said, high-fiving his brother.

The Kempsville High players called home runs hit over the fence "dingers." But they referred to Hunter's home runs, which were legged out around the bases, as "pingers" since, typically, they were not mighty blasts. As Hunter ran into the dugout, his buddies were chanting, "Pinger, pinger, pinger ..."

Hunter's first-inning run held up for a Kempsville lead of 1–0 going into the fourth. In the top of the fourth, Hunter attempted a sacrifice bunt, but with his speed, he beat out the throw to first base by Kelly Blacksmith. Hunter stood at first base with two base hits under his belt. Seconds later, he and the runner on second base executed a perfect double steal. Then the Chiefs' number two hitter hit a "seeing eye" groundball through the hole between the first and second basemen. Both baserunners scored to increase Kempsville High's lead to 3–0.

Kempsville's ace pitcher, George Browning, was throwing a no-hitter through five innings. The game was speeding along with only two innings left; the players on Kempsville High's bench started tasting victory—maybe a little too soon. In the top of the sixth, Hunter and the batter following him both walked. They both came around and scored on Jo Jo's long fly ball that landed just out of reach of the center fielder. Jo Jo made it to second safely with a slide and a pile of dust. Kempsville's lead had grown to 5–0, and the fans and players on the Chiefs' side of the diamond were giddy with glee over the prospect of being a state champion.

In the home half of the sixth inning, Browning seemed to lose his pinpoint control of his pitches. It appeared that he was grooving his pitches down the middle of the plate instead of on the corners, which had made him unhittable to that point. The first two Park View hitters ripped singles into the outfield. With two on and no one out, Browning walked the batter in the team's number-three spot. Up came Park View's big boy. His nickname was "Tiny" for some odd reason; Tiny's six-foot-five frame would indicate otherwise. As the cleanup hitter for his team, he frequently swung from his heels. Case in point, in one swing from Tiny's bat, a nasty sounding swing to the Chiefs' pitcher, Park View had four runs on the scoreboard and were back in the game. The grand slam had an amazing effect on both teams. Now the Park View sideline was jumping up and down, and the Kempsville side of the field acted like they were attending a wake.

Kempsville's head coach removed his star pitcher following Park View's "Grand Salami." Pat Jennings, the Chiefs closer, was brought in from the bullpen to try to get a two-inning save. He was able to prevent the Park View team from doing any more damage to the scoreboard during the sixth inning.

"Here we go!" Coach Collinsworth yelled to his players as they came off the field to bat in the top of the seventh. His Chiefs led the game by 5–4 with one inning left to determine the state championship.

Kempsville got nothing going in the seventh inning against Kelly Blacksmith, so the game rolled on into the bottom of the seventh ending. Park View, as the home team, had the last at-bats. The picture was clear—they had to score at least one run to force the game into extra innings. But if they scored two runs, Park View would win and become the state champs. If Park View failed to score, then Kempsville High would be bringing the championship trophy back to Virginia Beach.

Pat Jennings, the Chiefs closer, easily retired the first two Park View batters in the bottom of the seventh inning. The buzz on the Kempsville sideline and dug out had returned, and no one was sitting anymore. Everyone was on their feet and living every moment with their team. The tension in the air was real and strong. The Chiefs' head coach implored his guys to, "Just get one more out!"

Smack was the sound that the bat made as a line drive produced an inning-extending single to center field. *Dink* went the next batter's bat as it produced a little pop-up that landed on the grass behind Jo Jo at first base. The runner from first base made it to third safely. Now, runners were on the corners and a very strong hitter was coming to the plate for Park View High. He, along with Tiny, were the two power hitters for the Northern Virginia baseball team. But their team was down to its last out, and they were desperately trying to get in the potential tying run that was currently standing on third base.

Hunter was trying to calm himself down in center field because the situation at hand was so intense. He was a thinker and a planner and very analytical. He loved that baseball afforded each fielder time between pitches to make a "what if" decision. They have time to predetermine what they would do with the ball if it is hit right at them, to their left, to their right, in front of them or even over their heads. They have to consider who is on base, the footspeed of the runners, keeping in mind the score of the game and how many outs there were. Was all that too much for a fifteen-year-old who was only playing his fourth complete game of the season? No way! Hunter was eating this stuff up.

Hunter studied baseball on TV and while sitting in the Chiefs dugout as a role player who rarely started. He discussed baseball ad nauseum with his brother, father and grandfather. But his assessment of the state championship baseball game's final moment turned out to be flawed. He tried to read the mind of the last batter of the game and determine how and where he'd want to hit the ball. He knew that batter could drive the ball all the way to the fence or over it, but surely, he would not swing for the fences with the tying run on third base and two out. All the batter needed to do was make easy contact with the ball and hit a single, and the game would be tied. Otherwise, Hunter figured, the ballgame would be over. So, Hunter moved in towards the batter, not backwards as he had done earlier whenever that particular Park View batter came to bat.

The pitcher looked to his catcher for the pitch sign as first baseman Jo Jo waved at his little brother in center field to back up. Hunter could almost read Jo Jo's lips from more than 200 feet away. "What are you doing, little bro?" In response, Hunter just shrugged, like he didn't understand. Jo Jo had no way of knowing Hunter was making a calculated move to steal a single away from the batter.

The next moment, Hunter heard the sickening sound of a batter crushing a baseball with the barrel of the bat. It was the sound of a batter who had really "barreled up the ball," meaning he got the best part of the bat barrel on the ball—he hit the ball with the sweet spot. Hunter could see that the ball was quickly heading his way in center field. He knew by the sound the bat made that it was hit over his head. In one brief moment, all the abilities and skills Hunter possessed were put on display—his excellent eyesight, good reactions, good judgement of where batted balls would end up and "sick" footspeed. In less than two seconds, Hunter had turned around and was running full speed back towards the center field fence. It appeared to everyone in the ballpark that the ball was hit too hard and too far for him to run it down while it was still in the air. But Hunter didn't give up on his effort to track down the ball. As he approached the fence, he noticed the velocity of the ball was slowing down. The ball was rapidly falling downward. It had reached its maximum distance. But Hunter was still fifteen feet from the fence. He could feel the gravel texture of the outfield warning track under his spikes. Out of pure desperation, he took two more fast steps and laid out in a dive, as if diving into a swimming pool at the beginning of a race. His chest hit the gravel first; his left arm was stretched all the way out. At the moment of impact with the ground, he opened the face of his ball glove. When his body skidded to a halt, he glanced at his glove and saw, to his utter disbelief, the ball in his glove. Somehow it found its way into his glove! Hunter had completed a miraculous catch! His head was spinning with excitement.

Since Hunter was so far away from the umpires in the infield, and he had dived away from them, they might not have been able to determine if he had caught the ball cleanly or if it had hit the ground. Both baserunners had crossed home plate and the batter shortly after. So, if the umpires didn't give Kempsville High the out on Hunter's effort, the game would be over with Park View as champions. On the other hand, if the umpires determined that he had caught the ball cleanly, the game would be over and Kempsville would be the champs.

After seeing the ball in his glove, Hunter remained flat on the ground, 350 feet from home plate, and lifted his glove to show the umpires that the ball was firmly tucked into the webbing and that, yes, he had indeed made the catch. Seeing that, one of the umps raised his right arm with a closed fist to indicate a put out. It was the end of the inning, the end of the game and the end of the tournament. The Kempsville High School Chiefs were the 2010 Virginia State Champions!

As Hunter scrambled off the ground near the center field fence, he could already hear a party going on back in the infield as the Chiefs celebrated his catch and their victory. But at that moment, something caught his eye. On the other side of the chain link fence, just a few feet away from him, was a blonde in a blue blouse. It was Savannah, jumping up and down, screaming his name. Her fingers were gripping the fencing tightly, and she pressed her face against the fence. Hunter, smiling broadly, stepped to the fence, pressed his face to chain link and kissed his lady on the lips. Tears were streaming down Savannah's face. They stood there and put their heads together.

"Honey, why are you out here behind the outfield fence by yourself when all the other fans are near the dugout?"

Through her sobs, Savannah answered, "Because I wanted to be as close as possible to my ballplayer. I was so nervous sitting with everyone else, and I just had to come out here near you. Everything is always calmer when I'm near you."

By the time Hunter made it back to the infield, all the jumping, piling on and back slapping had ended. But when Jo Jo and his dad spotted Hunter in the infield, they ran to hug him tightly.

"Son," Archie asked, "did you really catch that ball? I mean, that ball was uncatchable when it was hit."

"I did catch it, Dad. I honestly thought I was toast when that guy hit it so far."

"Toast?"

"Toast is when you get burned. It's really a football term, Dad. Anyway, I didn't get burned after all."

"Yeah, but you almost did," Jo Jo chimed in. "I would have killed you if you hadn't caught up to that ball. I told you just before that pitch to back up. Thank God for your speed, Hunter. Nobody else could have caught that ball."

"Ha, ha, ha" was all that came out of Hunter's mouth. He was too happy to argue about why he'd given his family, fans and team cardiac arrest on the game's last play.

Coach Collinsworth and the team's assistant coaches caught up with Hunter and his dad as they collected his bat bag and equipment from the dugout. They smothered him with hugs and thanked him for his efforts and for personally saving victories in the last two ballgames. They said repeatedly that his was the greatest catch they'd ever seen.

"Hunter, the coaches have talked," Coach Collinsworth said, "and we all agree that no one provided more value to the Chiefs team here in Richmond than you did, even if you only started one game. So, buddy, you will receive the tournament's most valuable player trophy. Congratulations, Hunter! Because of you, we're all champions!"

Fifteen minutes later, at the tournament's award ceremony, the Kempsville High School Chiefs received the large team trophy, individual trophies plus watches with "2010 State Champions" engraved on them. Then it was time for the MVP Award presentation.

"This tournament's most valuable player," Coach Collinsworth said, "only started one game. He only came to bat five times. He only pitched two innings. But the Chiefs would not have won the last two games without his efforts. He scored the winning run in the quarter-final game. He closed the semi-final game when we ran out of arms to pitch, even though he hadn't pitched all year. Plus, he just made the most amazing catch any of us have ever witnessed to save the championship game. Since baseball is a stat-driven sport, here is the MVP's tournament stats. Hitting: four base hits in four official at-bats for a 1.000 batting average, one base on ball, three runs scored, two RBIs. Pitching: two innings pitched, one hit allowed, three strikeouts, no walks, one hit batter, no earned runs, ERA of 0.00, and one game saved.

Even in limited opportunities, to bat one thousand and have a zero ERA, plus playing extraordinary defense, he led the Kempsville Chiefs with his will to win. Hunter Austin, you are the 2010 State Championship Tournament MVP! Congratulations, son!"

There was thunderous applause and whistles filled the evening air as Coach Collinsworth shook Hunter's hand and presented him with the MVP trophy. Within seconds, Savannah was in Hunter's arms, and they did a little Texas two-step, celebrating such a special moment. Quickly, a dozen or more of the Chiefs' players, including his brother, lined up to shake Hunter's hand or give him a hug, followed by each of his coaches. Suddenly, the conga line filled up with parents, fans, the school principals and teachers, and even a few of the Park View players on the second-place team as they greeted and congratulated Hunter on his amazing seventh-inning catch.

One of them said, "Man, you robbed us of a championship. I will never forget two things about you. One is that catch, and the other is how fast you run the bases."

After watching from a distance, Hunter's family and Savannah's family joined the end of the line to greet their little ballplayer. He was the one who was always an afterthought when it came to athletics at the Austin home. He was the one who always breathed his brother's jet fumes as Jo Jo soared above and beyond anything that Hunter could do. Leading his team to victory in the state tournament might have been a little justice being sent Hunter's way.

The last to congratulate Hunter on his play and award was his father. At first, Archie couldn't say anything because the right words wouldn't come. He just hugged his youngest son tight and kind of held on to him. Tears streamed down Archie's face and onto Hunter's cheek.

Finally, Archie said, "Hunter, I can't tell you how proud you have made me of you. I never knew you could play ball like that. Then again, I didn't really pay enough attention to you while watching Jo Jo so intently. For that I apologize. Folks have been telling me this week that you got your motivation to play hard and to work hard to develop yourself into a good ballplayer because of me, because I haven't complimented you or encouraged you. If that's the case, then, you're welcome."

"Dad, I'm not going to thank you for treating me so poorly. I'm not going to thank you for disrespecting me for sixteen years. I became a good ballplayer despite you, not because of you. You never encouraged me or believed in me."

"Uh, wow," Archie stumbled on his words in response. "I guess I deserve that, Hunter. All I can do, son, is apologize."

"It's okay, Dad. Let's leave that stuff for another day. Let's just get out of here and go eat and rehash the game. I'd love to stop at the Cracker Barrel at the I-295 Tappahannock exit."

"Anywhere you want to go, Champ," his father said. "I'm treating."

6

LIFE LESSON (2010–2011)

The 2010 school year was winding down. For Jo Jo, it meant saying goodbye and taking stock of his accomplishments in high school. He was voted by his senior classmates as "most likely to succeed" and "athlete of the year." Following his school's senior prom—Jo Jo managed to talk his mom and dad into letting him go—he received his senior class ring, and at the school's athletic banquet, he received trophies for athlete of the year and football player of the year. He graduated with a 3.8 grade point average and earned a National Honor Society Award. He attended his Kempsville High School's graduation ceremony and graduated with academic honors in his hand and an athletic scholarship in his back pocket. An incredible student athlete was ready to fly out of his family's nest and become a University of Virginia Cavalier. Jo Jo was transitioning from being a "Chief" to a "Wahoo."

Hunter had less lofty, but—to him—equally important goals. He was going to learn to drive. The first thing both he and Savannah did when school let out for the summer was go to the DMV to get a learner's license and study for the licensing exams. Savannah practiced driving with her dad as her instructor; Hunter asked his grandfather to teach him how to handle a car. Archie felt slighted about not being asked to pass on his driving "expertise," but Hunter just carried on with his own plans. Jo Jo and Hunter were both getting old enough that their father's voice was losing its power and impact on their lives. They were developing independence in decision-making, and Archie had a difficult time accepting that reality.

After a few weeks, Hunter and Savannah felt they were ready for the DMV driving exam. Since they were both sixteen (sixteen and three months, to be exact), they were already eligible to be tested.

During the summer, Coach Collinsworth kept in touch with Hunter. After his heroic exploits, the Coach expected Hunter to have a larger role on the Kempsville baseball team in 2011. The Coach taught Hunter two especially important lessons. The first was that, if you are good enough, you are big enough. The second was that to deal with failure, you had to learn from it and turn it into motivation for self-improvement. Hunter loved talking to his coach because he had the best perspective on things that Hunter needed to learn to improve as a person and as a ballplayer.

Hunter hit the Kempsville rec center three times a week for strength, agility and cardio workouts. He realized from his gym activities that it wasn't just his upper body that was weak, so were his legs. It took a lot of reps and sets before he saw even minimal improvement in his strength. In addition to his time spent in the gym that summer, Hunter went by his grandfather's house once or twice a week to swing a bat under water in his pool. The water resisted his swing, and he had to power through the water to get the bat head through the imaginary strike zone. Of course, swimming laps was a great cardio workout too. If that wasn't enough physical activity for the sixteen-year-old, he also worked part-time on his grandfather's construction crew.

Jo Jo went off to Charlottesville to attend the University of Virginia's summer football camp and conditioning drills while Hunter and Savannah spent time at the beach. Savannah, while not naturally athletic, loved the beach scene and she would sit and watch the surfers catch waves for hours on end.

One day, she said to Hunter, "I want to learn to surf. It looks like fun."

"Cool," he replied. "Let's learn together. I've always wondered what it would be like."

The kids did some research and selected surfing classes at the WRV Surf Camp and Lessons at 5th Street. As students, they could use the surfboards and tethers at no cost. The training was thorough. The instructor taught the fundamentals in the sand and then followed it with lessons in the ocean water. Each student received coaching as their skills increased. Hunter and Savannah were standing up on the boards in no time, and their surfing skills advanced quickly. But they were missing one thing—a surfboard—and quickly bought their own used six-foot-long boards on Craigslist. Within a week of taking surfing lessons, they were on the water riding their slightly used boards.

Although Hunter and Savannah had been dating for a year, he found that he couldn't spend too much time with her or stop looking at her. She was the most beautiful creature he had ever seen, anywhere, in person, on TV or in movies. As she lay with her eyes closed on a towel, her skin bronzed from a summer tan, her long blonde hair sun-bleached, a dusting of sand sticking to her soft skin that was still wet from the surf, he realized that not only could he not stop staring at her, it seemed the other hundred men in the surf had the same obsession. Everywhere they went, on the boardwalk, in the water, walking on the shoreline, laying their towels on the beach, shopping in the gift shops or eating out, guys checked her out.

"It's annoying," Hunter complained. "I guess beauty has its price."

"Hunter, you'll never know how profound that statement is," Savannah replied, tilting her head as if considering him with new eyes. "I'm not blind. I know I'm pretty. But it's become more of a curse. Guys act so rude and try to pick me up all the time, even right in front of you. It's totally disrespectful."

During the summer, Savannah worked for her mother's new company, which cleaned houses after renters and summer vacationers left their rental houses in Sandbridge. It was a part of Virginia Beach located south of the busy resort area. Savannah worked four ten-hour days each week with three days off. Hunter had a similar summer work schedule. Granddaddy Anthony had offered Hunter a summer apprenticeship learning carpentry. He used his days off from work to practice baseball, work out, and swim or surf.

Savannah and Hunter surfed together as much as possible. When at the oceanfront, they frequented Dough Boy's Pizza where they'd first met. They loved to play miniature golf, walk out on the fishing pier—and kiss under it—and listen to the free music that was available each night. They also enjoyed going to the Ocean Breeze Waterpark with a gang of friends to spend a full day going down water slides and surviving the power of the wave pool. Some evenings, they drove go-karts on the tracks next to the waterpark. Life was good for Hunter and Savannah that summer.

They were both involved in their parents' churches. Though they both went to church their whole lives, they each took away different understandings and commitment from the worship experiences and the teachings they received. One of them only showed up at church because his parents made him go; the other was invested in her religious culture and beliefs. Up to this point in their lives, Savannah's relationship with God was personal; Hunter's was only corporate.

As September loomed, Hunter knew his junior year in high school would be a lot different than his sophomore year. For one thing, Jo Jo was off to college. But even more, Hunter was more confident about his place at Kempsville High since he was older than half the students, had been a key contributor to the previous year's baseball state championship win and was going out with the prettiest girl in school.

The 2010 University of Virginia football season was not a success for Mike London, the new head coach, as far as wins and losses were concerned. The Virginia record was four wins and eight losses. But by bringing in a new coaching staff and running a pro-style offense, London developed some exciting football concepts and hope for the future. Based on his high level of talent and maturity, Jo Jo was not redshirted as most freshman football players in college were. He got to play in games that year as a true freshman, mainly as a part of Virginia's special teams. That fall, the Austin family made a half-dozen Saturday trips to Charlottesville to watch Jo Jo get on the field during all kicking situations.

In the winter of 2011, Hunter and Savannah both turned seventeen. Other than a strange interlude on Hunter's birthday, the two kids were inseparable.

On his birthday, in English class, his friends Bryce and Brady made a big deal of singing "Happy Birthday" to Hunter and the other kids joined in. Partway through the class, a cute co-ed named Sharlene passed him a note that said, "Hunter, it is a teenage tradition for the birthday person to be kissed as a birthday gift. I would like to give you your gift after class." Sure enough, after the class bell had rung and everyone else filed out of the classroom, Sharlene put her arms around his neck, pressed up against him and nuzzled his face. It was more than a seventeen-year-old boy could stand and for a few seconds, he lost his mind, broke his commitment to Savannah and his lips met Sharlene's for a prolonged, heated kiss. After he came to his senses, he broke contact and stepped back.

"I've got a girlfriend," he said, his eyes wide.

Sharlene shrugged. "It's just a birthday kiss, silly." So, they laughed it off and left the room, going their separate ways.

Hunter stopped at the bathroom to look at himself in the mirror. He looked like he'd been kissing someone. He grabbed some soap and washed his face and doused his head under the tap water, trying to wash off his guilt. When he went outside, Savannah was waiting outside in her parents' car and flush crept up Hunter's neck.

"Hey handsome," she said as he got into the car. "Your head's wet."

"I was hot," he mumbled.

"You're so funny," Savannah laughed and stepped on the gas.

Her parents trusted her to drive the family's cars. Sometimes, her mom would let her take her car to school for the day and give Hunter a lift. Savannah liked that because they could stop for a Slurpee after school. Hunter's dad would only let Hunter drive the family car if he rode along with him. Trust was not yet a part of their relationship, but overall, they were getting along better since the previous June's state tournament.

Hunter's girlfriend Savannah had worked for the last year to help him restore his damaged self-esteem. She also helped him work on being a better student. The results were promising for Hunter as he, for the first time, took some college prep classes his junior year; the very classes that his dad warned him not to take since he did not believe that his youngest son was college material.

Hunter entered Kempsville High's 2011 spring baseball practice in tip-top physical shape. Although he was up to five-foot-nine and had gained five pounds of muscle, he was still small by anyone's size standard for a seventeen-year-old boy. So, he focused his left-handed batting stroke on contact, not power.

As Hunter was growing up, his father made fun of his lack of power by calling him "old school" and "Punch-and-Judy," derogatory terms in baseball. As Hunter worked out more, his power started to increase. Defenses in his 2011 year underestimated him at first and his opponents would yell, "Move up! Move up!" That's when he'd step into the batter's box and hit the ball over their heads. Over time, they learned to respect the pop in his bat, and they played him more honestly, which ultimately took away his power hitting. So, he adjusted back to waiting on pitches rather than jumping them, which resulted in many opposite field base hits.

Like their football team, the Kempsville baseball team had graduated some outstanding ballplayers from the previous championship season, and the 2011 team wasn't nearly as competitive. Still, people came to watch their games—the usual crowd who attended high school baseball games—the players' parents and friends, and an occasional pro or college scout.

The season kicked off for the Kempsville Chiefs on March 16 at home against the Bayside Marlins. As he anticipated, Hunter started in center field and batted leadoff. In four at-bats, he totaled one hit and one base on balls. Unfortunately, no one on his team scored and the Marlins shut out the Chiefs on that cold, blustery day.

Over the next three Kempsville High baseball games, Hunter led his team to two victories by getting two hits and two stolen bases in each game. After four games, he was batting .350 with four stolen bases. Hunter proved to be a spark plug at the top of the Chiefs' batting lineup. His enthusiasm and skill seemed to fire up his teammates.

On April 1, as Hunter was getting ready for school, he felt exhausted. Like he hadn't slept a wink even though he'd slept eight hours. Later that day, in the school cafeteria, Savannah touched his arm and he felt warm. She laid her hand across his forehead.

"Hunter, you're burning up!"

"I thought it was just warm in the school or something," he mumbled.

Savannah walked with him to the school nurse to get checked out. Sure enough, he had a fever of 102 degrees. Hunter told the nurse he had zero energy that day and just wanted to go home and go to bed.

Hunter was excused from afternoon classes and his mom picked him up from school. Even after a long nap, his fever spiked to 103 degrees and he had a sore throat. The next morning, Janet took him to an urgent care center.

"Well," the doctor said, "Hunter's symptoms led to a diagnosis of mononucleosis. The kids call it 'the kissing disease.'" The doctor turned Hunter. "Do you have a girlfriend?"

"Oh, yes. A pretty one," he said proudly.

"Then she needs to be tested. You probably got the virus from kissing. It's spread through direct contact with saliva from the mouth of an infected person, or other bodily fluids, such as blood."

"But Savannah doesn't have mono, and I haven't been kissing anyone else."

"Well," the doc said, "someone's been kissing somebody. Now, you need to stop kissing your girlfriend and anyone else for a while. Mono is contagious for a period of time. The infection is typically not serious and usually goes away on its own in one to two months."

"Two months?" Hunter's jaw dropped. "But it's baseball season. I can't be sick now."

"Tell your girlfriend to get tested," the doctor said. "Get some rest. No exercise. And no more kissing."

On the ride home, Hunter was scratching his head. How could this have happened? Then he remembered Sharlene's birthday kiss. How was he ever going to tell Savannah?

When Savannah called and found out it was mono, there was a long silence on the phone.

"The doctor says you need to get tested too," he said weakly.

Hunter never planned to admit to Savannah that he'd been kissing Sharlene. And at first, she didn't ask. But about a week following his diagnosis, Savannah couldn't hold her tongue any longer.

"Hunter," she said as he lay weakly in his bed, "I want you to know that I don't have mono. And I've been trying not to ask you how you caught the disease." She was mad but at the same time, there were tears in her eyes. "I know you're sick, and I don't want to make you feel guilty, and you might be deceiving your girlfriend, but you can't fool God." With that, she put his homework down on the end of his bed and stormed out of his room.

As Hunter lay in bed recuperating, it seemed to his mother that he was getting sicker, not better. One morning, when he looked terrible and complained that his stomach hurt, Janet had seen enough.

"Hunter," she said, "we're going to get you showered and dressed. I'm taking you to Kings Daughter's Emergency Room." The Children's Hospital of the King's Daughters was located in Norfolk and was the leading children's hospital in southeastern Virginia.

During examination and testing, an ER doctor determined that Hunter's liver had been affected by the mononucleosis. He was admitted to the hospital for further observation and treatment.

When Savannah found out Hunter was in the hospital, she started crying and praying. She visited him in the hospital, held his hand and spoke words of love and forgiveness. Four days later, Hunter's liver was no longer causing him pain and his temperature was under control. But his level of exhaustion was even higher, and he barely could get in and out of bed to use the bathroom. His hospital pediatrician discharged him to return home to recover, but he needed to be pushed in a wheelchair out of the hospital to his parents' waiting car.

Hunter convalesced at home for nearly two months. His teachers sent home assignments for him to work on and his mother and Savannah helped him with his studies. His high school made some accommodations to allow him to take tests through the internet. But what disappointed Hunter most of all was missing the baseball season.

What a life lesson Hunter had experienced—everything you love and cherish can be gone in a moment of time.

As he said to his bedroom walls, "One day you're playing ball with your buddies, and you've got your arm around your girlfriend. The next day you can hardly get out of bed, and you might have ruined your relationship with her." The illness gave Hunter a new perspective on life. "Live each and every day to its fullness because tomorrow is not promised to anyone."

Savannah had her own perspective. "Sometimes, a delay in your plan is God's protection."

The time in bed left Hunter depressed about his future. Three high school seasons had passed, and he had little to show for them. In his freshman year, he didn't make the varsity team, and he'd refused to play on the junior varsity team. His sophomore season found him to be a valuable reserve on a Kempsville Chiefs state championship team, but then his junior season ended after only four games because he went and got mono from being stupid and unfaithful.

"I can't get a break," he said aloud. "Except when I actually did break my leg."

One day, after Hunter was well, but his spirits still seemed to be down, Savannah looked him in the eyes and said, "There is no expiration date on your dreams, Hunter. It's not too late to achieve them." She grabbed onto his hand and squeezed. "Set your target high and shoot for the stars. The moon is too low a target for someone with your goals, ambitions and talent."

By the time school let out for the summer, Hunter was on the road to a full recovery. Since he entered summer in a weakened condition, he told his grandfather that he couldn't work with him on his construction crew. Instead, he spent his time swimming, surfing, running, exercising and recovering.

Jo Jo was home from college for the summer and joined Hunter in some of his workouts at the rec center. They even threw a football around so Jo Jo could keep his hand-eye coordination sharp. But the thing they enjoyed sharing the most was surfing. Jo Jo grabbed some lessons down at the oceanfront and bought an old board from a buddy. Most of their twelve-mile jaunts to the ocean from Kempsville included Savannah. Sometimes Evelyn would come too, but she was on a softball travel team, so many of her weekends were tied up playing ball.

Hunter's sole focus during that summer was to get into game shape again. Savannah constantly asked him to take breaks from training so vigorously, and when he did, the only place he found peace and tranquility was on his surfboard.

As summer turned to fall, Hunter began his senior year at Kempsville High School healthy, happy and in love. The only time he and Savannah were apart was when they attended church as their folks insisted that they attend their own family's church. To celebrate the start of the new school year, Archie bought both his boys' old cars to run around in. At last, Hunter could pick up his girl, for dates and to drive to school "Not the reverse for a change," he noted. It made him feel like he wasn't a kid anymore.

Hunter was excited to get back to Kempsville High and walk the halls as a senior. On the first day of school, he walked through the doors looking healthy and sun-tanned with a pretty blonde on his arm and feeling plenty of motivation to make this year, his last in high school, his best one yet. Savannah's skills as a student were rubbing off on him. He had learned from her how to be a better student and how to get more out of his classes. This year, he was focused on getting better grades and not only playing a full season of baseball, but posting solid statistics. His broad aspirations could be defined as "student athlete," not just athlete.

Jo Jo was starting his sophomore year at the University of Virginia. He had won the starting tight end position on the football team, so his family was dying to go see some Virginia football and watch their budding star player in jersey number 88 play.

In the fall of 2010, the Virginia Cavaliers (or 'Hoos as they were called, short for Wahoos) had a football renaissance of sorts. The 'Hoos were very competitive as their play improved, and they finished the season with a record of eight wins and five losses. They also played in the Chick-fil-A Bowl in Atlanta, Georgia. Jo Jo made a name for himself in the Atlantic Coast

Conference by catching "50/50 balls" when he was well-defended. He'd developed into a scoring threat in the red zone and finished the season with fifty-two catches, 500 yards and seven touchdowns. He was selected to the second team all-conference.

Even though, as a realtor, Archie normally worked every Saturday, he somehow made it to all of Virginia's home games and traveled to Atlanta for Jo Jo's bowl game. Jo Jo had all the potential in the world and a career in professional football seemed possible. On the other hand, Hunter's athletic future seemed bleak at best. No colleges were beating down his door or ringing his phone all hours of the day and night.

Savannah was still the prettiest girl in high school. When she walked gracefully down the hall, her long blonde hair softly swinging across her sun-kissed shoulders, all eyes would turn to her. When Hunter was not around, guys approached her in the school halls to make small talk. When she spoke, her soft Southern accent turned them on. It didn't matter that she'd been going out with Hunter for two years; if they saw her without Hunter, they pounced. Ever the Southern lady, Savannah tried not to be rude to the hormone-driven boys, but she didn't like all the unwanted attention. She also felt it was disrespecting her boyfriend. She learned to walk the school hallways quickly so she couldn't be easily cornered. Oh, the pain and suffering of the beautiful.

In October, no one was a bit surprised when Savannah Montgomery was announced as the 2011 Kempsville High School Homecoming Queen. Savannah and her court of lovely ladies were escorted to the middle of the school's football field at halftime of the annual homecoming football game.

The very next evening, Hunter got into the black tuxedo his mom had rented for him. She helped him put on his first-ever bowtie and pinned a white flower to his tux. Hunter was about to escort the homecoming queen to the homecoming dance. He couldn't keep the smile off his face.

Hunter and his family drove down the street to the Montgomery's home to participate in picture-taking before the kids left for the big dance. When Hunter saw his queen in her dance dress for the first time, his jaw dropped and he lost his ability to speak.

"Hunter, don't just stand there gawking," Savannah said, embarrassed. "Say something."

Everybody just cracked up. That broke the tension and Hunter found his voice.

"I've never seen anyone look so gorgeous," he said. "Savannah, if beauty is in the eyes of the beholder, your beauty has made me blind." Savannah smiled so shyly at his words that it encouraged more. "When I look at other girls, I look right through them. I only have images of you clouding my thoughts. I love you, baby."

Suddenly all the laughter had turned to tears and hugs. Hunter gave Savannah the corsage he'd bought her, and she made a fuss over it as her mother pinned it to her dress. They all hustled out into the backyard for a photo-op.

An hour later, the Kempsville High Homecoming Queen and her escort walked into the decked-out ballroom in the Norfolk Waterside Marriott.

"I feel like I'm escorting an actress to the Oscars," he murmured to her. Savannah made a soft little squeak. He laughed. It was a special night for a special couple.

One day in November, Coach Collinsworth called him into his office for a chat.

"How you doing, son?" he asked. "Feeling recovered?"

"I'm good, Coach," Hunter replied. "I worked out all summer, ran and surfed."

The coach was absently tapping a pen against a clipboard on his desk. "Even though baseball season is still four months away, I wanted to know where your head was at after such a disappointing junior ball season. It must have been tough."

"Yeah, well," Hunter shook his head, "I still haven't gotten over the disappointment of missing most of last season. And after I finally won a starting spot in center field. But I'm up to 170 pounds even if I haven't grown any taller."

"Yep," Coach said. "You're small in stature, but you know, son, you have such a big heart." He gave him a smile. "We could use more like you. You're so determined to be the best you can be that you practice long and hard. And you play every game like it's going to be the last time you put on a uniform." Do not ever forget this, Hunter. You are a champion. We won that Virginia State Championship because of your heroics."

"Uh, thanks, Coach. That means a lot."

The coach sat back in his chair and looked at Hunter with kind assessment. "Some people have easy successes, but I think it means more when you have to work for it."

Hunter nodded. "My mom believes that too. She always tells me about how, the day I was born, she cracked open a fortune cookie that said, 'Perceived failure is oftentimes success trying to be born in a bigger way.' She took that to mean I would achieve great things after overcoming many challenges." He shrugged. "Who knew a cookie could foreshadow my life?"

7

GRUDGE MATCH (2012)

Hunter and Savannah both turned eighteen in the winter of 2012. With her birthday on February 26 and his on March 1, he liked to tell his buddies that he was dating an older woman. She may not have been that much older, but she was definitely smart beyond her years.

Over the few years they'd been dating, Savannah had talked a lot about Hunter's relationship with his dad. She had a way of reaching his soul as well as his mind. One day on the way to school, she climbed into his car and it took only one look for her to ask, "Hunter, what's wrong, honey?"

"Oh, it's just my dad. You know. Some dumb put-down this morning. I think he just feels he needs to remind me that I'm worth less compared to everybody else."

"You know that's not true!" Savannah protested.

"Is it?"

"What are you talking about?" She was getting angry.

"I never just do things well. Not like Jo Jo. I couldn't even make the varsity team as a freshman like he did."

"Look," Savannah said, trying to get his attention, "you're carrying a lot on your shoulders. And one is a huge chip on your shoulder about getting cut from the school team. It was years ago Hunter. Isn't it time you let that go?"

"No," Hunter said sharply. "My 'chip' will carry me where I want to go in sports. It reminds me that I am underrated and undersized, so I have to work and play harder than everyone else."

"All right then," she said, crossing her arms, "but the other thing you're carrying on your shoulders is a grudge against your dad—"

"Hah, wouldn't you?"

"—and that serves no purpose but to drive a wedge between you and your family. I know your mom hates it when you and your father argue."

"I don't argue with him, he argues with me."

"Your father is responsible for his actions and attitudes, and you are responsible for yours."

Hunter swerved his car into a parking spot outside Kempsville High and turned off the ignition. When he tried to open his car door, Savannah stopped him.

"Hunter, don't go yet. Let's talk this out right now."

"We'll be late for class."

"Just tell your teacher you had to see your counselor before school," —he gave her a look of disbelief— "I'm going to charge you big bucks because I have some counseling to do now."

That broke the tension in the air and a laugh escaped from Hunter. He blew out a breath.

"Okay, let's go for it."

Savannah started off her little lecture with, "Now, let's deal with your grudge towards your dad. I'll let your baseball coaches deal with that sports chip on your shoulder." She took his hand and held it gently. "Baby, holding a grudge doesn't make you strong; it makes you bitter. Forgiving doesn't make you weak; it sets you free. You need to be set free from all this baggage you're carrying because of the years of being under your dad's unfair scrutiny." She pressed his hand against her cheek.

"Your dad's parenting skills, or faults really, won't determine the kind of man you will be. You will decide what kind of a man you will be. When you hold a grudge, it can remain with you throughout your life. Sometimes, it's the first thing you think of when you wake up and it robs you of sleep at night. If you can forgive and let it go, God will do the judging. God is a just judge. He judges everyone accordingly. How can you expect God to forgive you of things you've done wrong if you can't forgive someone else for wronging you?"

They stayed in the car a long time that day. They talked and talked and even cried some as they pursued a resolution. The fact that they got in some trouble in the admissions office at Kempsville High for strolling in two hours late seemed unimportant to them. Hunter felt lighter and more at ease with himself than he'd ever been. He'd been able to break through his grudge and come out the other side, all because of his girlfriend's leadership and insightful words. While in his car, Savannah came up with a symbolic act to help Hunter drop his grudge towards his dad. She had asked him if he had any money in his wallet, and he dug out a five-dollar bill and four one-dollar bills.

"Okay, take the biggest bill," she said, "the five, and write 'father' on it."

"It's real money, Savannah," he said, balking. She lifted an eyebrow, and he slowly took a pen and wrote in big letters "FATHER."

"Okay," she said, "now open your car window and drop it out."

"Are you crazy?"

"No, I'm not crazy, Hunter. If you throw that five-dollar bill away with 'FATHER' written on it, the weight of the world will fall off your shoulders. Drop it out and visualize yourself releasing your father and all he's ever said to you. Let God judge your father. Stop doing it yourself."

With wooden movements, Hunter slowly lowered his car window. And even slower, he raised his left hand with the money in it and finally the bill reached the threshold of the window seal. Gritting his teeth, he lifted his two fingers away from their grip on the five bucks, and as the money fell away, a jolt of electricity shot down his arm. He felt his life resonating through his nerve endings. He felt his life coming back to him. As he cried, Savannah held onto him.

"It's okay," she said. "You've let your dad live rent-free in your head for years."

"Thank you," he whispered.

This was the beginning of new independence. Maybe it had to do with Hunter's newfound confidence, but Archie started cutting him some slack as far as his curfew was concerned, at least if he was with Savannah. While that might have shown more trust in her than Hunter, at least his dad no longer stood by the door at midnight to be sure he came in on time. In fact, most of the time, when he got home late at night, all the lights were out and his folks had turned in. Independence felt so good.

Both Hunter and Savannah were planning to attend college the next year and preparations were underway. Savannah's grades were so good that she was being recruited from various state and private colleges. She had her heart set on attending a Christian or religious university, at least for her undergraduate degree. Her parents were helping her look at potential universities. She needed scholarship money, so she was going to have to really sell them on her achievements.

Hunter's parents, on the other hand, were not encouraging him to pursue a college education. His father still didn't think he could do it. His mother loved him just the way he was. He didn't understand why they didn't want more for him. Even when he exceeded their expectations, they never seemed to raise their standard of hope. Fortunately, he had a lot of talks with Savannah and her parents. They reassured him he could do well in college and insisted that the road to financial freedom was through a college degree.

"Even if you don't qualify to play baseball in college," the Colonel said, "take a leap of faith and go for a college degree."

"You can do it," his wife asserted.

Hunter had no idea where he would like to go to college after high school. Of course, he preferred to go to college with Savannah, but he couldn't shake his dream of playing baseball at a university. All he could concentrate on, besides raising his grades, was playing baseball so well that he turned the heads of college recruiters. He would accept scholarship money from any college, anywhere, that would put him on their baseball team. It was a simple goal.

Through winter of 2012, Hunter continued to work out in the weight room at the Kempsville rec center, and he occasionally played pickup basketball there too. And just so he wouldn't be away from baseball for too long, he found an indoor batting cage to practice baseball once or twice a week.

In mid-February, the Kempsville High School's baseball program started preparing for the new season with a week of practice sessions. By the second week of practice, players were getting cut from the roster, one by one. On the first day of March, the final roster of the team's eighteen baseball players was revealed on a computer printout that Coach Collinsworth taped to his gym office door. He would use the first two weeks of March to get his team ready to play official ballgames while at the same time make decisions about who his starting eight position players would be as well as his starting pitching rotation.

It came as no surprise to anyone that Hunter was again on the Kempsville varsity team. He was clearly the team's best defensive outfielder, and he had all the desired attributes of a leadoff hitter. But the surprise of the pre-season baseball camp was that the coaches were working with Hunter to be a relief pitcher. Coach Collinsworth was captivated with how hard Hunter could throw a baseball. So, he assigned his pitching coach, Dale Snider, to work with Hunter at every other practice. Hunter had not been on a pitching mound since the state championship games two years before. Other than that, he hadn't pitched since playing in the Kempsville Pony League.

Coach Snider mainly worked with Hunter's mechanics. He lowered Hunter's leg kick, so he could more easily step straight towards home plate. Velocity was not a concern, but two other things were—his control and learning to throw a changeup. Hunter had a natural curveball that broke ten inches, if he threw it hard, and fifteen inches if he threw it slower. Coach Snider thought that, if Hunter could add a third pitch, one that was a change-of-pace pitch, thrown at, say, eighty miles per hour, it would make his ninety-two-miles-per-hour fastball look even faster to the batters.

The Kempsville Chiefs played two pre-season practice games with out-of-conference teams. It quickly became apparent that this year's Kempsville roster was weak in a few spots and that the pitching, overall, was not up to snuff. The pitching staff was led by two freshman kids, and that alone provided a viewpoint on how inexperienced the team was. Hunter and a couple of his buddies were the only seniors on the team.

Just before the first baseball game of the season with Bayside, Coach Collinsworth passed out uniforms in the team locker room. One by one, he handed each player his uniform, accompanied by a nice comment about the player. When the coach got to Hunter, instead of giving him his uniform, he asked for the room's attention.

"Hunter is a natural leader," he said to the players, who gathered around. "Rather than lead with his voice, he leads with his actions. To me, that's what captain does. In honor of Hunter being your new team captain, he'll wear a C on his uniform as well as the number 1 on his back. He has been asking us for two years to be able to wear the number 1. Hunter, here is your uni."

The players applauded as Coach Collinsworth handed Hunter his baseball uniform in front of the whole team. Hunter couldn't get beyond stuttering, "Thank you coach," over and over again.

On the drive home from school, Hunter's smile was so wide it almost hurt; he couldn't stop smiling from ear to ear. Coach Collinsworth's speech to the team about Hunter's attributes as a leader and as a ballplayer jacked him up so much that he wasn't sure he would get to sleep that night. He drove past his home to Savannah's house to share his celebratory mood. He kept asking her to pinch him to see if he was awake.

"I'm not going to pinch you," she teased, "and you're not going to wake up and find out that this didn't happen. Hunter, you're a good baseball player, a great person and a positive influence on other people. You were picked as team captain because you deserve it, and for no other reason."

The next morning, Hunter's dad touched his son on the shoulder as he wolfed down a bowl of Apple Jacks. "I hear that congratulations are in store, young man. You'll be the team captain for the school ball team this year!"

"Yeah. Thanks, Dad," he said over the crunch of the cereal.

"Well, it's good for you, that's for sure, but what good will that do the team?"

"Excuse me?" Hunter looked up, his spoon slack in his hand. "What did you say?"

"I just mean that usually the team's best player gets picked as captain. And you haven't been on the field enough yet to be considered the team's best player, have you?"

"Dad, you have no idea what you're talking about. It's not just about being the best."

But his dad didn't look convinced. Hunter had to keep himself from yelling by gritting his teeth as he added, "The coaches selected me to lead the team because I have set an example to my teammates of never giving up and practicing hard every day to improve."

His appetite gone, Hunter got up from the table and left for school.

The 2012 baseball season began at the Bayside High School field on Haygood Road on a cold, cloudy day in March. The Chiefs' bats exploded against the Marlins. Hunter Austin and his buddy Brady Doolittle batted one and two in Kempsville's lineup, getting two hits and two walks each at the top of the lineup. Kempsville's number three and four batters each hit home runs.

Hunter and Brady pulled off the coolest double steal in the top of the first inning. As the Marlins' pitcher started his motion to home plate, Hunter broke towards third base and Brady towards second base. The catcher pumped a throw to third base. He realized he couldn't stop Hunter from stealing, so he reloaded the ball and fired it towards second base. But the ball airmailed the shortstop standing on second base. As the ball was bounding around the outfield, Hunter continued to run home and scored. Brady jumped to his feet at second base and ran towards third. When the Bayside outfielder bobbled the wildly thrown ball, the Chiefs third-base coach waved Brady to keep running. He ran as the outfielder hurriedly threw home. But Brady beat the throw to score the Chiefs' second run of the inning. The next two batters, Liam Thomason and Bryce Jennings, crushed home runs over the outfield fence to jump-start the Chiefs to a 4–0 lead before Bayside got anyone out.

Hunter was moved from center field to pitcher for the last two innings of the game. He loved walking up on the pitching mound—it made him feel tall. Other than walking a batter and hitting one of them in the butt, he got through the last two frames of the game unscathed, and Kempsville beat the Marlins, 13–2.

As Hunter walked off the Bayside ball field, his grandfather came up to hug and congratulate the Kempsville captain's impressive opening game.

"Thanks, Granddaddy," Hunter said, grinning and looking around for his father. "Did Dad make it?"

"He sure did." But his granddaddy was frowning. Hunter followed his gaze and spotted his dad congratulating Liam and Bryce on their home runs. When it was apparent that Archie wasn't going to find his son and greet him, his granddaddy squeezed his shoulder and added, "Good game."

Mumbling goodbye to his grandfather, Hunter trudged over to the school activity bus with his head down.

Savannah missed the Chiefs' first game because she was touring a college in Tennessee with her mother. Hunter really missed her presence at the ball field and especially after he returned home to an awkward dinner where his mother was trying to make up for his father's disinterest.

When Hunter's phone rang after dinner, he took it to his room and hopped on his bed.

"It is so exciting!" Savannah said after a quick greeting. She was in Nashville, Tennessee. He settled back on his pillows with a smile as she gave him a report about her college-search tour of Trevecca Nazarene University.

"Mom and I wandered around the university looking at the buildings and facilities, and I made a point of walking by the baseball stadium to take some pictures for you to see. There was a signed that said, 'Jackson Field.' It seemed so spacious and green considering it is only March. They must take really good care of the ballpark because the facilities looked so pristine and the grass looked like it could have been a golf course."

Hunter couldn't believe how much better he felt just hearing her chatter on about some college in Nashville.

"Then I got up the nerve and found the office for Trevecca's head baseball Coach, Bennie Barnard, and while my mom waited in the hallway, I entered his office unannounced."

Hunter sat up in bed. "You what!"

"I walked straight into his office."

"Savannah!"

"Mom was kind of bored so she walked around and checked out several trophy cases in the Trevecca's athletic facility, and she saw plaques on the walls for Trevecca's Athletic Hall of Fame inductees—"

"Savannah!"

"Hush, Hunter. Mom said she read some of the Hall of Fame names like Melvin Taylor for basketball and Carol Ernest Schneidmiller for basketball, volleyball, and tennis. I told Mom it's incredible Carol was so accomplished. Then there was Kenny Thomas for baseball; Brenda Steen Gray, volleyball; Mac Heaberlin, basketball; Dick Johansson, tennis—"

"How do you remember all these names?"

"I didn't, Mom was so impressed she wrote them all down. She insisted I tell you the whole list, so hush while I finish" —with a chuckle, Hunter laid back against his pillow— "Brandy Barnett Brown for softball, Tim Bell for basketball, and Mom said many more but her hand got tired of writing. And we couldn't help but wonder, Hunter, what if you could play baseball at Trevecca? Think of it. You could leave your mark on the university's baseball program, and maybe someday we would see your name on trophies and plaques. Wouldn't that be great?"

"Savannah," Hunter said with a sigh. He wasn't quite over the sting from his father earlier in the day. "Are you going to tell me what happened in the coach's office?"

"Right! Coach Barnard! Well, I opened his door and he was sitting at his desk. And I admit, he looked a little surprised, but I gave him a bright smile and introduced myself as a prospective student. I explained my very talented boyfriend back in Virginia was looking for a college to play baseball for. Of course, I talked you up and said amazing things about you as a ballplayer and as a person too. I said, 'He's one of the best players on his team. He's a self-starter who's always trying to improve, and he's a good academic student too." Oh, and I added that you'd fit in on a Christian campus because you go to church all the time, and you're pretty religious. What do you think?"

"I— I—"

"We must have talked about you for thirty minutes, and at one point, I just went and asked him to recruit you since your senior baseball season was just beginning, and you needed to decide soon where you'll go to college."

"And?"

"Well, I had to do some negotiation."

Things hadn't gone exactly as Savannah had imagined when she first walked into Coach Barnard's office. She was a bit shocked when he'd simply said, "I can't recruit Hunter." Then he elaborated. "First of all, I will never get to see him play high school ball due to the distance from Virginia Beach to Nashville. And, more significantly, I'm not allowed to recruit him."

"What?"

"Trevecca is a university supported by the Church of the Nazarene in the southeastern region of the United States. Virginia is not within Trevecca's educational zone. Virginia is in the northeastern educational zone of the denomination, and the Nazarene college in that area is Eastern Nazarene University, which is in Quincy, Massachusetts."

Savannah pouted a little. "Since I live in Virginia, does that mean I can't attend Trevecca either?"

"No, no, no," Coach Barnard said with a smile. "You both can attend Trevecca. I just can't recruit Hunter to play ball for us."

"Oh," Savannah said with a swing of her hair. "Could he recruit Trevecca?"

Barnard laughed, and Savannah joined in.

"That's not how it works in collegiate athletics," he said. "We recruit ballplayers; they don't recruit us. We only have a limited number of roster sports and scholarship money to give out, so we have to be selective about who we offer a roster spot to. It's based primarily on their talent, but also on their character and standing in their high school, such as their grades. We don't want to invest scholarship money and coaching time in people who are likely to flunk out of school or get suspended for breaking campus rules." He tapped his desk as he considered different options. "How would Hunter do with a lot of rules and restrictions on his behavior?"

"Great. His dad is extremely strict on him, and his baseball coaches have pushed him hard to get the best out of him. He's used to having boundaries and discipline."

"Okay, young lady. Would you ask Hunter's high school coach to send Trevecca a letter of recommendation on Hunter's behalf? It would go a long way to opening a door of opportunity if his current coach tells us he's ready for college athletically, academically and socially. The character of our athletes is a big deal to us. A letter like that would be a nice complement to his admissions application. I can't ask Hunter's high school coach for some video of his baseball playing because that would look like I was recruiting him. And I am not."

"Of course not." She shook her head.

"You've seen him play, right?" —she nodded— "What's he really good at?"

"Running."

"He's fast?"

"He's the fastest runner in his school. They wanted him to run track, but he wants to play baseball. He tried playing football once until he broke his leg. He even had the fastest time on the football team."

"Do you know how fast his time was?"

"I'm pretty sure it was 4.3 seconds."

Coach Barnard sat up in his chair. "In the forty?"

"Yeah, I believe so."

"Holy Toledo! Nobody runs that fast except in the NFL or the Olympics!"

"I'm pretty sure that's what Hunter told me," she said perkily. "I have a good memory."

"Okay, besides running extremely fast, how does Hunter play baseball? What position does he play?"

"Mainly center field. He can pitch if the team needs him too because he throws hard. He chases down lots of balls hit to the outfield, and he sometimes outruns the ball. He often gets on base and steals a lot of bases. To be honest, Hunter missed most of last season because he had mono really bad.

But he's been training since last summer to get back in shape, and to me, he looks as fast and stronger than ever. Coach, probably the reason that colleges haven't recruited Hunter yet is because he missed all but four games in 2011."

Coach Barnard nodded his head in agreement. "I'm glad Hunter is well again."

On the phone to Hunter, she abbreviated the negotiation and got to the main point. "He told me, 'You let me know how his spring season goes and see if you can get his coach to recommend him to Trevecca.'"

"He wants me to go to Trevecca?" Hunter asked excitedly.

"That's what I've been trying to tell you. He said you might be able to help Trevecca's baseball team in the future. So, the best he can do for you is to allow you, in the fall of your freshman year at Trevecca, to try out for a walk-on spot on the Trevecca's baseball team. They have fall practices and workouts for the team, and you could participate in them. Then Coach Barnard and the other coaches would evaluate your skills, attitude and commitment, and then decide if they'll give you a roster spot or not."

"This is incredible."

"Well, I got all excited and had to stop myself from throwing my arms around him then and there. But I yelled, 'That would be amazing, Coach!' He explained to me that a walk-on roster spot means you would be a regular, full-time member of the baseball team. You could play in games at the coach's discretion."

"This sounds wonderful," Hunter said.

"There is a catch, though."

"Of course, there is," he grumbled.

"You wouldn't receive any athletic financial assistance, and you'd have to pay for all of your college costs. Plus, you'd have to meet the university's academic entrance requirements, as any student would. Since Trevecca is an NCAA Division II athletic program—I think I got that right—it can only give out nine baseball scholarships. Most of the scholarships are partial, anyway, and a single scholarship might be divided between two or three players."

After spending an hour with Coach Barnard, Savannah, and her mother, had gone on an organized tour of the Trevecca campus. She met with an admissions counselor, a financial counselor (about college loans and scholarship opportunities) and an academic advisor. Based on Savannah's high school transcript, it was clear she had a good chance of becoming the valedictorian of her large high school class. She was a serious candidate for a full academic scholarship. Acceptance of her admissions application would just be a formality, it seemed.

"It makes me happy to know there's a way for us to attend Trevecca together and for you to play ball. But a lot has to happen first. We just have to remember what it says in Romans."

"Romans?"

"In the scripture. Romans 8:28. 'And we know that in all things God works for the good of those who love him, who have been called according to his purpose.' If it's God's plan for our lives, it will happen."

8

DOING THE DOUGIE (2012)

On March 20, 2012, the Kempsville High Chiefs played baseball at home against Cox High School. Before the game, team and individual pictures were taken of the Kempsville players and coaches. The team looked sharp in their royal blue, red and silver uniforms. Unfortunately, they didn't play very sharp in the game that followed. Cox won 8–3. Hunter had no hits in the game and drew an "oh fur" at the plate—when a batter goes hitless in a baseball game (i.e., 0-for-4) it is called an "oh fur."

The third game of the season was also played at Kempsville High, this one against Ocean Lakes. The March 23 game was played in less-than-desirable conditions, especially for the fans. It was both cold and windy, and the wind caused confusion and missteps in the outfield for both teams. Hunter misjudged a wind-blown fly ball and it glanced off his glove as he tried to get in front of it. The scorekeeper noted the misplayed ball as Hunter's first error of the season.

When Hunter, in disgust, threw his glove off the back wall of the Chiefs cinderblock dugout, Coach Collinsworth quickly reminded him, "Hunter, you're the team captain, and you have to live up to a certain decorum when it comes to your behavior in front of your teammates. Throwing your bat or glove will get you thrown out of the game—by me."

"Sorry, Coach," Hunter mumbled. "It won't happen again."

Two innings later, he crushed a pitched curveball down the right field line and the wind-aided fly ball fell over the outfield fence for a home run. There was such a shocked look on his face as he circled the bases as it was the first time in his life that he'd hit a baseball over an outfield fence.

Following the game, Savannah and his mom ran up to him and hugged him.

"Hey ladies," he said, smiling broadly, "what about my first and only home run?"

Savannah squeezed Hunter's bicep muscle in a flirtatious way and said, "Yeah, my stud stepped to the plate and knocked one out for me!"

"Oh, Hunter," his mom said, "I am so proud of you. Your dad is just not going to believe you hit a homerun."

At dinner that night, with his mom, dad and grandfather at the table, Hunter wanted to share his incredible milestone.

"Did you hear?" he asked his dad. "I hit a legitimate home run today. I knocked it out of the ballpark."

"I knew it was windy outside today," his father replied. "But if you hit one out, it must have been a hurricane behind your ball."

Anthony put his fork down forcefully onto the table. "Well, I think that's an amazing achievement. Congratulations, Hunter." He picked up his fork, but then put it down again and turned to his son with a look of profound disappointment. "Archie, when you keep criticizing your kids, they don't stop loving you. They stop loving themselves."

For a moment, the room was so quiet you could hear a pin drop. Then everyone continued to eat, but the conversation was subdued.

Through the Kempsville High baseball season's first six games, Hunter was batting at a .389 clip. Baseball was such a statistical sport. There were so many categories where individual stats were accumulated, evaluated and compared to other players; team stats were also compared to other teams' results. Since baseball was a game of frequent failure, at least in batting, the best batters got out about seventy percent of the time and a base hit about thirty percent of the time. If the best professional hitters make an out seven out of ten times, the result is a batting average of .300. In the major leagues, a .300 batting average would likely result in the player being selected into baseball's annual All-Star game. It was difficult to find consistent excellence in professional and amateur batting. Besides being a sport of statistics, baseball was a sport of batting slumps and hitting streaks—ups and downs, hot and cold.

Even though the 2012 season was young, Coach Collinsworth was pleased to see Hunter's development as a hitter. He proved to be quite the spark plug at the top of the Chiefs' batting order. But no one took his .389 batting average seriously, especially his father. When Hunter showed him the Chiefs team stat page after six games, Archie guffawed and asked, "Who's been pitching against the Kempsville team? Girls?"

Savannah was clearly Hunter's biggest fan. She attended most of his ballgames and always lifted his spirts after a team defeat or if he had a poor ballgame. She enjoyed listening to his teammates, coaches and Kempsville fans congratulating him after his games. She could tell that the kind words meant so much to him. She also knew how much he wanted to play college baseball, but so far, the college recruiters had shown no interest.

Even though Hunter had found success on the baseball diamond, he was not resting on his laurels. At least three times a week, he went to the Kempsville rec center for private workouts in the gym, sometimes immediately following baseball practices and team gym workouts. It was as if he could never get enough training in his life. Some thought he had set unattainable athletic goals.

After the first eight games of the Kempsville baseball season, city schools closed for spring break. The Chiefs team record was a disappointing three wins and five losses. At least it was disappointing to the players. The coaches had come into the season understanding that the team roster was heavily weighted with freshmen and sophomores. Even Hunter, who was a senior, had only started a handful of ballgames before 2012. So, the team was short on experience and player leadership coming into the season.

During spring break, the Kempsville baseball team traveled to Myrtle Beach, South Carolina, to play in a tournament called the Cal Ripken Experience. It was one of the premium high school baseball tournaments in the nation at one of the most incredible facilities for youth baseball. There were many ball fields where the games were played; a few of them were miniature duplicates of old-time Major League Baseball ballparks. Besides the Cal Ripken Experience baseball facilities, Myrtle Beach offered a lot of entertainment for families and ballplayers—waterparks, dinner shows, go-karts, golf, the beach and the most miniature golf courses in America. Hunter was stoked to play in the tournament, and Cal Ripken Jr. was his all-time favorite baseball player.

The whole Austin family, including Jo Jo, who was on spring break from college, made the seven-hour drive to Myrtle Beach and stayed in a hotel room for a full week. Savannah talked her mom into going to Myrtle Beach with her and getting their own hotel room, so she could spend her free time with Hunter at the South Carolina ocean front. As well, she wanted to root for her guy during his baseball games.

The Kempsville Chiefs were scheduled to play four baseball games in a span of three days against school teams from New York, New Jersey and Ohio. Kempsville High's first game was on April 9, Easter Monday, against Sutherland High School from Pittsford, New York. A few hours later, they played a second game against Lake Catholic High School from Mentor, Ohio. The Chiefs came up short on the scoreboard in both games, but the games were competitive, and the last game against Lake Catholic wasn't decided until an extra inning was played. The Chiefs' disappointment in losing was quickly forgotten after the guys showered and put on their t-shirts, cargo shorts and flip flops, and headed down to the Myrtle Beach oceanfront. The bright lights of the boardwalk and the pretty girls walking around flashing their smiles and tans quickly healed the egos of the high school boys from Virginia.

Following the Chiefs' doubleheader that Monday, Hunter and Savannah had a joint dinner with both their families at the Sea Captain's House restaurant. It was a cozy 1930s cottage overlooking the ocean. After the kids stuffed themselves with fried fish and hush puppies, they separated from their families to explore the boardwalk by themselves. Once they spotted the huge Sky Wheel, an oversized Ferris wheel, they grabbed hands and ran through the crowd to get in line to purchase tickets. The Sky Wheel operated smoothly and quickly, and soon they had reached the pinnacle of the ride at almost 200 feet above the ground. And there it stopped momentarily. Hunter realized that no cars were above them and no one could see into their Sky Wheel car, so he put his arm around Savannah and pulled her in close for a kiss.

She laid her head on his shoulder. "Hunter, I love you. This moment seems so magical."

"I love you too, baby," he said softly, indulging in more kisses until the Sky Wheel operator knocked on their car door and yelled, "Come on guys, your ride is over. Get out of the car!" Laughing, Hunter grabbed Savannah's hand and pulled her out of the car.

"We kissed all the way down and lost our minds for a moment," he told the Sky Wheel operator.

"Yeah," he replied, "first you lose your mind and then stuff just happens."

The next day, Kempsville High School played against St. Peter's High School from Staten Island, New York. Although the game started at 10:00 a.m., and the players and coaches had stayed up late enjoying the sights, sounds and food on the Myrtle Beach boardwalk, but the team started out the game on fire. The Chiefs' bats exploded in the first three innings, and Kempsville went on to win, 7–1.

Hunter and his teammate Brady both had big games. Brady hit a home run and a double, and knocked in four runs. Hunter could do no wrong. He got three hits, including a triple, stole three bases and scored two runs. He made a diving catch of a sinking line drive to rob St. Peter's of two runs in the third inning, and he pitched the last inning when the Chiefs' starting pitcher got tired and started walking batters. He stepped on the bump with the bases loaded and no one out. After throwing his warmup pitches, he reached down and fumbled with the rosin bag to lose the sweat on his hand. Then he started pitching like Mariano Rivera, the greatest relief pitcher of all time. The first batter he faced hit a "come-backer" groundball to Hunter who started a 1-2-3 double play, throwing it to the catcher, who put out the runner from third who then threw the ball to the first baseman, who put out the batter. Hunter blew away the second batter with two fastballs and fooled him for strike three with a changeup.

After playing an inspired brand of baseball that morning and killing a foot-long sub and chips at lunch, Hunter was ready for a nap. Instead, he, Jo Jo and Savannah strapped their boards on the roof of Jo Jo's SUV and went surfing. As soon as they hit the cool April waves of the Atlantic Ocean, Hunter's energy and spirit returned even as the water chilled him to the bone.

"Why didn't one of us remember to bring wetsuits!" Savannah yelled over the waves.

The Kempsville Chiefs played against Lenape High School from Medford, New Jersey, on Wednesday at 6:00 p.m. Though a baseball game was scheduled for the two teams, it almost looked like a slow pitch softball game—both teams were hitting the baseball as if the pitchers were lobbing balls up to the plate. It made for a fun, interesting game for the fans.

Coach Collinsworth played his reserve ballplayers as well as his starters in a rotating fashion to give the young guys playing experience. Hunter didn't start the game and only entered in the sixth inning to pitch the final two innings. He batted once in the game as he led off the top of the seventh and final inning with the score tied 7–7. Although he clocked a fastball off the right-field fence and got a triple, he failed to score as the Chiefs couldn't hit the ball out of the infield. So, Hunter took the mound for the last half of the seventh inning against Lenape High School. In three pitches, the game was over. Hunter threw two fastballs by the Lenape cleanup hitter and figured he could do it one more time. But third time's the charm. The batter timed his fastball perfectly and sent it flying over the left-field fence and way up on a grassy hill for a home run. Lenape won 8–7.

Walking off the ball field after giving up the winning walk-off home run was a gut punch to Hunter. He felt responsible for the team's loss even though he didn't play most of the game. The coach tried to console his team captain with a hug. His mom and girlfriend did the same. His dad was nowhere to be seen. As soon as Hunter gave up the winning home run, Archie had marched away from the baseball diamond in disgust. Later, his family found him sitting alone in his car, sulking.

"Hunter gave away the game," Archie said gruffly. That was his story, and he was sticking to it, no matter what anyone else in the family said to him.

No one was in a mood to do anything fun that evening, so the Austins and Montgomerys grabbed some fast food and headed to their hotel rooms. After Hunter had showered and changed into his cargo shorts and a fresh t-shirt, he and Savannah went out for a walk on the boardwalk. He just had to get away from his dad and his sour comments about the ballgame.

As they walked hand-in-hand, Hunter couldn't stop glancing at her. She looked ravishing in a new sundress.

"Have I told you how lucky I am that you put up with me?" he asked. She squeezed his hand and gave him a light kiss on the cheek.

On the boardwalk, the bright lights, sounds of laughter and scent of sweet cotton candy created a fun, uplifting atmosphere. Savannah stopped at a ball-throwing game and asked Hunter to win her the top prize, a stuffed teddy bear nearly as tall as she was. It was not an easy task. He had to knock over all five targets with a baseball. His arm was still loose from pitching two hours earlier, so he started throwing baseballs and targets kept falling. As the barker announced to one and all that the huge teddy bear had been won, Savannah jumped up and down and started doing the Dougie dance right on the boardwalk. She got her teddy bear, but Hunter had to carry it around all night, and it was five feet tall. There was no more holding hands for the young couple that night.

The next morning, as the family was getting ready to go for breakfast—waiting for Jo Jo who was still in the shower—a text notification beeped on Hunter's phone. At the same time, one went off on his dad's phone.

They both reached for their phones and started reading. It was a text from Hunter's coach.

Hunter started reading and suddenly he was yelling, "Dad, are you reading this? Can this be real?" His dad's eyes had bugged as he read his text.

"What it is it?" his mom asked, her eyes full of concern.

Hunter started reading, "Congratulations, Hunter, on being selected to the Cal Ripken Experience All-Tournament Team as an outfielder. Lord knows they didn't want you as a pitcher after yesterday's game. Ha ha!" Hunter added, "That was coach laughing, not me." He took a breath and continued reading. "Buddy, I am so proud of you. In three 1/3 games, you batted .456, scored three runs, drove in three runs, hit two triples, stole four bases and covered half the outfield for the Chiefs. I picked up your All-Tournament Trophy and t-shirt at the field late last night, and I will give them to you next week at school. Hunter, in your sophomore year, you were a state champion. In your senior year, you are not only the only Chiefs' Cal Ripken All-Star player, but you are the team captain. I know your high school baseball career hasn't gone as you planned, but in the little amount of playing time you have had, you have accomplished victories, awards and earned credentials that four-year ballplayers never achieve. Hunter, I have copied the whole ball team and your father on this text. I was sorry you couldn't have been awarded the trophy in the team huddle yesterday, so consider this to be your virtual team huddle."

"Oh my goodness!" he yelled.

"Oh my goodness," his father parroted, his jaw slack. Then he broke down and started crying.

"Honey?" his wife asked, running to him. He waved her off.

"No, it's okay. I got to say this." He wiped at his eyes. "Son, once again I have been wrong about you." He reached over to his youngest son and pulled him into a tight hug. His mom engulfed both of them with her arms. At that moment, Jo Jo came out of the bathroom along with a cloud of steam. He stopped abruptly and evaluated the scene in front of him.

"Uh, what's going on?"

"Coach Collinsworth just texted us," Archie said. "Hunter made the All-Tournament team as an outfielder." Jo Jo threw his arms around the group and nearly crushed them all with a bear hug.

"Jo Jo," his mom said, "you're going to kill us all."

As the family extricated themselves from the tangle of arms, Jo Jo said, "Man, Hunter, that's amazing! What was your batting average?"

"I think it was like .450. Here, bro, read Coach's text."

Jo Jo read every one of the Coach's words out loud all over again, and both their mom and dad started tearing up again, which made Hunter tear up. Then his dad hugged him again.

"I am proud of you, Hunter." And then he lost it completely.

Jo Jo looked around the room at everyone bawling and shook his head. "Shouldn't we be happy and laughing or something?" But that just set his parents off again.

Once they all got it together enough to leave the room and get breakfast, Jo Jo asked Hunter, "Hey, are you getting a trophy?"

"Yeah, next week at school, and an All-Tournament t-shirt too."

"The Cal Ripken All-Star player. Very cool."

That night at a celebratory dinner with the Montgomery family, Jo Jo made a toast to Hunter.

"I was always the one who was acclaimed as an athlete in the family, with college scholarship offers and my picture in the newspaper. Hunter, on the other hand, has had a lot of obstacles thrown in his path, rejection and injuries. I've watched him overcome every one of them and come out a leader, a winner and an all-star." He put his hand on his heart. "Little bro, I look up to you. You are an inspiration to me." He lifted his glass of sweet tea. "To Hunter."

"To Hunter!" everyone replied. It was an experience Hunter would never forget.

When high school reopened after spring break, there were personnel changes made to the Kempsville Chiefs baseball roster. Their starting catcher had injured his throwing arm in Myrtle Beach, and after having it examined by an orthopedic doctor, it was determined he would need Tommy John surgery on his elbow ligament. So, Coach Collinsworth called up a freshman catcher from the school's junior varsity baseball team and put him on the varsity squad. The boy's name was Brandon Doolittle; he was the younger brother of Brady Doolittle, one of the best hitters on the varsity team. Brandon was already, through six junior varsity games, knocking the cover off the ball; he really had a sweet left-handed swing.

The downside to adding another freshman to the varsity team was that the young team got even younger. Their two best starting pitchers were also freshmen and now their catcher would be a ninth grader also.

But, as Coach Collinsworth would tell them, "I'm excited about coaching up another young ballplayer. One day, all you freshmen will be talented seniors."

The baseball team played one of their best games all year on April 20 against the Tallwood Lions. The game was played a few miles down Kempsville Road at Tallwood High School. Ballgames between these two high schools were more like neighborhood squabbles. The pitching for both schools that day was outstanding. The only run for the Chiefs came in the top of the seventh and last inning when their newest catcher, Brandon Doolittle, hit a full-count, two-out home run to tie the game 1–1. As Brandon danced around the bases, ecstatic that he'd so quickly contributed to the varsity team, his mom jumped up and down so passionately that she almost fell out of the bleachers.

The game rolled into extra innings and remained tied through the ninth inning. But in the top of the tenth, Hunter, who'd been without a hit since his all-tourney award, took it upon himself to score a Chiefs go-ahead run. He dragged a perfect bunt past the pitcher but short of the second baseman. He was past first base before anyone fielded the ball. On the first pitch, he broke for second base as the pitch was delivered. The catcher's throw to second was right on the bag, but Hunter dove into the base headfirst and his hand touched the base just before he was tagged by the shortstop. Hunter got off the ground with wet dirt caked onto his sweaty jersey. He looked down at his dirty chest, and the thought crossed his mind, "Now it looks like I've played baseball today."

Hunter was in scoring position with no outs in the tenth inning. The new Tallwood pitcher, who had entered the game that inning, seemed rattled by his bunt and stolen base. The next batter, Brady Doolittle, hit a hard groundball right at the shortstop. Hunter didn't hesitate when he saw where the ball was hit even though two of the unwritten rules of baseball were telling him to hold his ground and stay on second base.

Unwritten rule number one was: "Do not make the first or third outs in an inning at third base." Unwritten rule number two was quite a bit longer: "When you're a runner on second base and there are less than two outs, and the batter grounds a ball to the shortstop, only run to third if you can run past the ball and it passes behind you. Otherwise, if the shortstop catches the groundball, and you're not past him yet, he can easily throw you out at third base. If you're past him, the shortstop will be forced to throw to first base to make a play on the batter."

Hunter lacked nothing when it came to running speed, and he also had nerve and hustle. As soon as Brady hit the ball on the ground towards the shortstop, Hunter broke like a rabbit towards third base. The ball was hit with such force that he couldn't pass in front of the shortstop before he caught the ball. So, he put on the speed, hot-footing it to third base, barely beating the throw to the third baseman. When the action was over, Hunter was safe on third base with no one out, and Brady had reached first base on the "fielder's choice play"—so called because the batter got to first safely as the fielder tried to get the other baserunner out.

Coach Collinsworth decided to pinch-hit Bryce Jennings for Asher Brown. Bryce struck out a lot, but he could also hit some long balls, sometimes home runs. Bryce swung aggressively at the first pitch and hit a pop-up high in the air. It landed just out of the infield, and the Tallwood second baseman had his back to home plate as he corralled the pop-up in the grass. Hunter had tagged up at third base just in case the ball reached one of the outfielders. When it was caught by an infielder, he figured his third base coach would tell him to stay at the base. But instead, all Hunter heard was his coach screaming, "Run! Run! Run!" so he broke for home plate, dirt exiting his spikes, grunts exploding from his mouth with determination written all over his face. The Lions second baseman turned all the way around and fired a throw to his catcher that bounced once and came into the catcher's glove hot. As Hunter was sliding, he could see that he was probably going to be tagged out if he slid at the plate. Consequently, he slid thirty inches to the right of the seventeen-inch-wide white rubber plate. As the catcher was swiping a tagging motion in Hunter's direction, Hunter slid past the plate, avoided the catcher's glove and, with his left hand, reached out and touched home plate.

"Safe!" the umpire yelled.

He got up, spitting dirt out of his mouth and brushing himself off as he headed towards his bench where his teammates mobbed him. His father ran to the backstop, the fence behind home plate, and yelled repeatedly, "That's my boy! That's my boy!" Father and son caught each other's eye as Hunter entered the dugout, and they pointed at each other.

Freshman pitcher Liam Thomason came into the game in the home half of the tenth inning to try to preserve the Kempsville Chiefs' 2–1 lead. Things got interesting for the young kid as the Lions loaded the bases with two outs. The tying run was on third base and the winning run was on second base. Liam threw a big bending curveball that jammed the Tallwood batter, and he popped up the ball, high into the early evening air. As the Kempsville catcher turned to locate the foul ball, Brandon ripped off his mask and dropped it on the ground. As he circled around under the ball, he stepped on his mask and started to stumble to the ground. The ball bounced off his catcher's mitt, and as Brandon grimaced in horror, Liam broke off the pitching mound and ran towards the pop-up, catching it on the rebound just before it hit the ground. For his hustle, Liam was rewarded with making the last out and gaining his first save as a pitcher. The Kempsville Chiefs were rewarded with a hard-fought victory against their neighbor and rival.

The next day, April 21, after viewing videos of Hunter playing high school baseball and looking over his school transcript, Trevecca's head coach, Bennie Barnard, called Hunter for a chat.

"Now, Hunter," Coach Barnard began, "remember, I'm not recruiting you to play for Trevecca Nazarene University. Your girlfriend contacted me. You are free to attend Trevecca and pay your own tuition, room, food and books.

But, here's the good news, buddy. I checked your high school grades, and I think you'll do well at Trevecca. I asked your girlfriend not to send me videos of you playing high school ball, but of course she didn't listen to me, so I watched them. You impressed me, Hunter. You play with so much heart and determination. I wouldn't like to be your opponent and try to deal with you on the ball field. I'd much rather you play on my team. Your footspeed just jumps off the screen. It looks like you cover half the outfield by yourself. At first glance, you might have enough talent to play DII baseball if you keep improving. Now, you're welcome to work out with the Trevecca's baseball team in the fall. Us coaches will evaluate you and give you a chance to earn a walk-on spot on the team. If you make the team, there's always a chance that, in the future, you could earn a partial or full scholarship based on your performance. So, son, the future looks bright for you, even if you weren't offered a scholarship in high school. A lot of ballplayers are overlooked or misinterpreted by college coaches. You're not very big, but the one thing I couldn't overlook watching you play is how big your heart is for the game of baseball. You must eat and drink baseball, sunup and sundown."

Hunter laughed. "Yes, sir, I sure do. I practice and play baseball as much as possible. I've also become a workout warrior, building up my little boy's body into a real man's. I hit my first two home runs over the fence this year."

"Good for you, Hunter. There's nothing like a baseball player hitting his first home run."

"Coach, thank you so much for giving me this opportunity. Savannah raved about Trevecca's ball field and facilities. I can't wait to see it."

"Get your college application paperwork submitted ASAP, son. And don't forget to apply for financial aid based on need, not baseball." They promised to stay in touch during the summer.

The Kempsville Chiefs next four games earned three wins and only one defeat. Their freshmen were now playing with confidence and many of the Chiefs were playing over their heads due to the hustle and inspiration of their captain, Hunter Austin.

"It's like being led into battle by a military captain," Liam said.

Hunter got hot with the bat during the four games and showed his teammates what was possible with the bat and feet. He hit at a clip of .545 over those four games and stole four bases.

With only two games left in his senior baseball season, plus the district tournament, it became crystal clear to Hunter that no college was going to offer him a baseball scholarship. It was disappointing to him, considering the kind of senior season he was having. But he realized that since he'd missed most of his junior season with mono, and he wasn't a starter during his sophomore season, he wasn't widely known to the college reporting services.

On May 10, Hunter's neighbor, Evelyn, got home from school at the same time he did, so they hung out in her driveway and got caught up on how their ball seasons had gone. With Evelyn playing on the school's softball team at the same time Hunter was playing on his baseball team, they rarely saw each other and never got to attend each other's games.

"Hunter, I've got some great news. Last night, a softball recruiter from Virginia Wesleyan College in Virginia Beach was at my house, and I've decided to attend that college and play softball for them."

"Wow, Evelyn. That's great! Congratulations. Virginia Wesleyan has a terrific girls' softball program." They were located in Virginia Beach and were an NCAA Division III school.

They hugged good night and were going to their separate houses, when Evelyn called out, "Hey, Hunter! Maybe we could double date for the senior prom. That way we can see each other at the annual sports banquet and graduation ceremony."

"It's a date!" he yelled back with a wave.

May 11 saw Princess Anne High School's baseball team visiting Kempsville High's ball field. Before the game began, there was a brief rain shower and the baseball field's grass was wet. The first batter of the game from Princess Anne hit a pop-up behind second base. Brady, the Chiefs' shortstop, charged out into the outfield grass and Hunter charged in towards the infield. The ball had the instincts of a seeing-eye dog and found a safe place to land, just out of their reach. When the ball bounced off the turf, it landed in a water puddle. As Hunter dug the ball out of the water, the Cavalier leadoff hitter never broke stride and raced for second base. Hunter quickly, with all the force he could muster, fired the ball towards second base. But the wet ball slipped as it came out of his hand, getting too much elevation and way too much velocity behind it. The ball flew over the pitcher's mound and the catcher's head. By the time Brandon retrieved the ball behind home plate, the batter was standing on third base and all the other players, coaches and fans were laughing and talking about the wacky play.

The rest of the Chiefs' defensive play was no laughing matter. They dropped two pop ups and two groundballs, giving Princess Anne too many extra outs. Hunter had another outstanding game with the bat in his hands and running the bases. In four at-bats, he got two hits, walked once and stole four bases. But, along with all the base on balls the Chiefs pitchers gave up, the Cavaliers eventually won the game, 8–7, and Hunter's personal achievements went unnoticed.

Kempsville's last regularly scheduled game of Virginia Beach School District's 2012 Baseball Season was played at Ocean Lakes High School on May 14. Liam and Bryce crushed home runs over the outfield fence to jump-start the Chiefs to a quick lead. Bryce's home run was his sixth of the year and the most by any Chiefs' batter. As Kempsville High's smallish leadoff hitter, Hunter hit his third home run of the season as he squared up an eighty-eight-miles-per-hour fastball that left the field faster than it arrived at home plate.

"That's my boy!" his father cried out, hugging his wife as she jumped up and down.

"That's our boy," his granddad said, wiping away tears.

After years of intensive personal workouts, Hunter was clearly a stronger young man. He was thrilled that his grandfather was present to witness his home run in person. Later in the game, Hunter was chilling on the dugout bench and the thought occurred to him that no one was telling him he was too small to play baseball anymore. Yet, he was still only five-foot-nine. He had reworked his body and had gained weight, mostly muscle.

He thought to himself, "Where are all my doubters and haters? Gosh, even my dad has accepted me as a ballplayer. At least, most of the time."

The Kempsville Chiefs finished the Beach District baseball regular season with a record of six wins and ten losses. Hunter stole thirty-two bases in thirty-two attempts.

On May 19, Kempsville High School's opening game of the 2012 Virginia Beach School District's baseball post-season was played on a neutral field against First Colonial High School. It was an electrifying baseball game with the lead going back and forth, and after the regular seven innings were played, the game was tied. It continued for three more innings.

Asher Brown and the Doolittle brothers, Brady and Brandon, were the hitting stars of the game. Every time Brandon got a hit, his big brother knocked him in. Brandon got three hits and scored all three of the Chiefs' runs. Brady also was credited with three hits and three RBIs. Asher got two singles and stole two bases. But it wasn't enough. The Patriots scored a run in the home half of the tenth inning to win the game 4–3. Hunter's last high school baseball game, and his team's season, didn't end as he had hoped. The Patriots advanced in the District Tournament; the Chiefs did not.

Although dejected by the stinging season-ending defeat, Hunter held his head high as he congratulated all of the other ball players. He knew he'd accomplished a lot that year. He listed them in his mind. "I was named the team captain. I played a full season as a starter without getting injured or sick. That's a big accomplishment. I turned eighteen! I've matured. I learned to be a leader to the younger players. And I was selected as the Cal Ripken All-Star player, an All-Beach District Baseball First Team All-Star, an All-Tidewater Baseball Second Team All-Star and the Chiefs' MVP. That's more than I could have ever dreamed up for myself."

Hunter's combined baseball batting statistics were twenty-three hits, twenty-one runs, ten RBIs, four doubles, four triples, three home runs, ten walks, thirty-two stolen bases and a .383 batting average. All things considered, it was a remarkable senior year.

Both Hunter and Savannah had received their Trevecca Nazarene University acceptance letters for admission in early spring. Hunter received a financial aid package, and Savannah received a full academic scholarship package. When her package arrived, Savannah's folks hugged her and told her they were enormously proud of her.

"We know you'll do great in college," her mother said proudly.

Hunter's parents, on the other hand, were surprised he'd been accepted into college even with a 3.0 grade point average.

"Why do you have to go so far away to college?" his mom asked. "We have Tidewater Community College right here in Virginia Beach and it doesn't cost much to attend. You know you have to pay back your student loan whether you graduate or not, right?"

His dad was actually biting his lips; he was trying so hard not to say something nasty.

"Why do you guys doubt me so much?" Hunter asked.

"It's not that," his dad said. "We just don't want you to bite off more than you can chew."

Hunter just had to shake his head and try not to let their lack of confidence slow him down. He had to stay laser-focused on his future.

Regardless, Hunter and Savannah made detailed plans for their move to Nashville. They would only take one car to cut down on transportation cost, and since her wheels were a lot newer than his, they decided to leave his old Chevy Malibu at home and take her 2009 Ford Explorer, which her dad bought her to reward all her hard work in high school. They could also pack more stuff in her SUV.

"I'm going to try to pick up a part-time job in Nashville," she said, "so we can have some spending money." Hunter hoped to make the baseball team in the fall, which would keep him too busy to work a job plus attend classes.

Soon, Savannah started dropping hints to Hunter about tickets for the senior prom. "May 24 deadline is coming up for you know what!" she texted. Tickets had been on sale all month, but Hunter had been pre-occupied with baseball. Suddenly, the deadline was upon them, and Hunter was broke. He told his parents it was going to be held at the Westin Hotel at Town Center. He asked them if they would pay for it. Of course, "it" included two prom tickets, the cost of prom pictures at the dance, tux rental and flowers for Savannah to wear.

"Ha, ha, ha," Archie laughed heartily. "Don't you want me to pay for your dinner too?"

"That would be great, Dad!" Hunter replied before he realized his dad thought it was all a joke. As he later explained to Savannah, "I swung for the fences with my parents, but I went down on strikes. I don't know where else I can get the kind of money I need for prom."

"I bet that my dad would give you the money."

But Hunter wouldn't hear of asking her dad. "No. It's tradition. The guy takes the girl to the prom. Not the other way around." Savannah shook her head and said something about "Men!" under her breath.

Hunter decided to ask his granddad. He sat there for quite a while before finally getting up the nerve to phone him to ask for a boatload of money for prom. Anthony sounded cooperative until he found out Hunter needed $370, and that didn't include dinner before the dance.

"Oh Hunter, my boy. That's a lot of money for one night of fun."

"It's more than one night of fun," Hunter said. "It's a night of memories that will last a lifetime for Savannah and me."

After a long pause, in which his grandfather cleared his throat a number of times, he said, "Ah … let me tell you what I would like to do for you guys. I was going to give you a graduation gift anyway, so let me do something meaningful that you can use now. I'll give you a gift of $500 for your prom night as your graduation gift. That will give you plenty money to take your girl out to a nice restaurant and still pay for all the other things that night."

"Oh my gosh, Granddaddy!" Hunter cried out. "Thank you so much." He became emotional as he continued to thank his grandfather for his generosity.

The next day, Savannah and Hunter walked over to Evelyn's house to ask her if she and her date would still like to double date with them for the senior prom.

"Yes!" Evelyn said. "We talked about that a few weeks ago, but honestly, I forgot all about it. I'll ask Riley and see if he's down with us going with you guys."

As Hunter walked his girl home from Evelyn's, he put his arm around her shoulder. "Hmm. You smell great. What are you wearing?"

"I bought a new perfume. It's called 'Nothing At All.' So, Hunter" —she batted her long eyelashes at him— "I'm wearing nothing at all."

"Ha, ha, ha," Hunter laughed, but at the same time, he blushed and tried to keep his mind on nothing at all.

When he was able to be normal again, he asked, "Baby, where would you like to go to dinner before prom?"

"Let me do some research and pick some place that's nice and, you know, romantic."

The next day at lunch, Savannah cuddled up to Hunter in the school cafeteria over chicken nuggets and mac 'n' cheese. "I've picked our prom dinner place."

"Really? Where are we going?"

"McCormick and Schmick's! It's right next to the Sadler Center concert hall in Town Center. I called, and they said it has some romantic tables that are private. I made reservations for four in case Evelyn and Riley can go with us."

June 2, the day of the prom, was soon upon them and all their plans were in place. Hunter was excited all through the day as he picked up his tuxedo and their flowers and cleaned out his car. Then he was getting dressed and ready to pick up his date. Evelyn and Riley were going to meet them at the restaurant and then walk to the prom with them. All done up in his tuxedo, Hunter spent time letting his parent's ooh and ahh over him and take pictures. He finally climbed into his now-spotless car with his flowers for Savannah and drove to her house. She looked so beautiful when she opened the door, with her shiny blonde hair loose and her body clothed in a clinging black dress. It took his breath away, and he lost all his poise, almost throwing the flowers he was holding at her. She laughed and pulled him into the house for her parents to make a fuss over him and take more pictures of the two of them. Finally, they were off.

McCormick and Schmick's was everything Savannah said it would be. Evelyn and Riley met them at the doors. Riley was also wearing a tux. Evelyn was wearing a rose-colored dress with a stunning heart-shaped necklace sparkling against it. She also wore her long hair down. It was brunette with streaks of blonde from being outside. The host led the four attractive teenagers to a table with privacy curtains around it. There were fresh cut flowers on the table and a glimmering candle. It was very romantic. The waiter was friendly and attentive, and he used their phones to take pictures as the couples cuddled, kissed and made silly faces.

After dinner, they enjoyed the evening air as they strolled down Commerce Street to the Westin. The couples looked up to admire the impressive building. At over 500 feet, the Westin was the tallest building in the State of Virginia.

The prom ballroom was decorated to the extreme, with radical lighting and colored streamers everywhere. Dozens of balloons swayed in every corner and strobe lights hung from the ceiling.

"The DJ's hot, but not as smoking as these girls in their prom dresses," Hunter said.

"I like that they're showing their assets," Riley said, "if you know what I mean."

"Riley!" Evelyn said and punched him in the arm—of course, being such a great athlete, it hurt. As Riley rubbed his arm, she had to admit that some of the young women were showing a bit too much skin.

The four of them went out on the dance floor, throwing themselves into the dancing with enthusiasm and a willingness to learn new moves. They shrieked with laughter as the Theater Arts teacher led them in the Creep, the Wobble, the Smurf and Gangnam Style.

"And I know you all know how to do this," she called, "the Dougie!" The kids cheered and more joined in.

Afterwards, they got refreshments and gathered with their school friends to admire each other's prom clothes and tell jokes. Each couple posed together for their official prom picture. Savannah and Evelyn looked so pretty in their flowing dresses and long, swinging hair that they turned heads all night.

Hunter noticed that couples were leaning over and writing something on a table in front of the DJ. When he saw a sign that read "Vote for your Prom Queen and Prom King!" curiosity got the best of him and he walked over to scan the list of candidates. When he found Hunter Austin and Savannah Montgomery on the list, he ran back to his group of friends.

"Savannah," he called out, "we're on the list for prom king and queen!" He picked her up and swung her around.

When he put her down, she patted his chest lightly. "I know, honey," she said with a grin, "I signed us up last week."

"Okay, guys," Hunter said to his friends, "let's all go over there and vote. You have to vote for me and Savannah."

"Only if you pay me," one of his friends joked.

Hunter endured the ribbing that followed them to the table with a grin. It was a lot of fun to put their names on the voting cards. Everyone laughed because none of them pictured Hunter winning.

"Now, Savannah," one of his teammates said, "I could see her winning, but paired with an ugly brute like you—" He broke off with a laugh as Hunter tried to wrestle him to the ground.

"Boys," a passing teacher cautioned.

They went back to dancing, enjoying refreshments and entertaining themselves.

At 10:00 p.m., the music stopped, and the DJ's voice came over the loudspeaker.

"It's time to reveal who our 2012 Prom King and Prom Queen are. May I have a drum roll, please."

As he set up his own drum roll—after all he was the only DJ there—and the crowd tapped on their legs, Savannah leaned over to Hunter and whispered, "Breathe, dude, we're not going to win."

Hunter hadn't realized he was holding his breath. He'd been praying silently in his mind for the last few minutes.

"I know," he said. "I can't help it. It's my competitive nature."

As Savannah laughed and hugged him, the DJ got back to the microphone.

"And the winners are … Savannah Montgomery and Hunter Austin!"

Pandemonium broke out as their friends and schoolmates they barely knew ran up to hug and congratulate them.

"I knew it," a girl shouted. "The longest running couple at Kempsville High School!"

Most everyone seemed thrilled. The previous year's king and queen came forward and placed a crown on the new king's and queen's head.

"Okay now," the DJ said, "it's time for your slow dance."

Hunter and Savannah stepped into the circle of light as their classmates hung back in the shadows.

"Grab her!" a guy's voice yelled, which made everyone laugh.

Hunter offered his hands and then pulled her in for their slow dance. Her blue eyes sparkled with excitement and reflection from the strobe lights above them. Hunter couldn't remove the stupid look on his face that spoke to all the other boys in the room, saying, "Ha, I got the girl and the crown."

It was late when Hunter got home, and he was still grinning. When he came in, happy, haired mussed up and wearing a crown, his parents couldn't believe he'd come home with yet another award.

Thinking back on the year, Hunter shook his head and said, "It seems like God has chosen to bless me with a senior year I could never have dreamed up."

The awards did not end there. Two nights later, at the Kempsville High School Spring Sports Night, he was chosen as the Kempsville High baseball team's MVP. Coach Collinsworth had a lot to say about Hunter after announcing his award.

"Hunter Austin is the most relentless player I've ever worked with." That got a lot of laughter from the crowd.

"It's true," Hunter said to those around him.

"Hunter doesn't compete with anybody but himself. Every day he is trying to be a better version of himself. No one I've ever coached was better prepared to play a game than Hunter Austin or had a dirtier ball uniform after the game. He gives his all between the lines, so he is always diving for balls or hitting the dirt sliding into bases."

Hunter's mom nodded and said to the other moms nearby, "It's true. I wash his uniform."

"Hunter, you have served your team well as its captain and as its most valuable player. Unlike many team captains, you didn't lead with your words. You led with your play and with your practice habits. Hunter, you have made your mark on Kempsville High School. Now go make your mark in college."

"Way to go, bro!" Jo Jo called out as he clapped and cheered.

Hunter's parents, brother and grandfather sat with him along with Savannah and her parents. They were all thrilled about Hunter's MVP Award. As people chattered and cheered and otherwise made a big deal over him, Archie sat quietly. He was feeling conflicted about all the attention and accolades his youngest son was receiving. On one hand, his heart was stirred when he saw Hunter race from first base to third when everyone else would have stopped at second, or when Hunter ran down a long fly ball on the warning track or threw out a baserunner trying to advance. His little boy had surpassed all his expectations on the ball field, in the classroom and in his love life. On the other hand, he didn't want to give the boy false hope about his future. He knew that the future didn't often give you what you wanted. It could fill you with regret.

He sat and watched his two sons handle Hunter's MVP plaque with big smiles on their faces. At that moment, he had a sense of pride for both his boys. He thought about how dedicated they were growing up, always trying to be their best. And about how much they hated losing. And it came to him in a point of clarity that Hunter had always had to work twice as hard as Jo Jo to make a ball team, to become a starter and to succeed. He'd had to overcome injury and illness. All Jo Jo had to do was show up and he was a star.

The feeling of admiration mixed with guilt for his youngest boy struck him like a burning heat. He bowed his head into his hands. Could the words spoken by him over the last eighteen years have propelled Jo Jo to greatness and slowed Hunter's development? A tear rolled down his cheek.

"Honey, are you okay?" Janet dropped a gentle hand on his shoulder. "You're crying."

"I can't help it," he said, his voice choked with sobs. "I'm feeling guilty about the way I've treated Hunter."

"Oh dear, you're being too hard on yourself."

"No. I should be hard on myself. I've been too hard on Hunter and it's hurt him and slowed his development. My God, Janet. How could I have been such a jerk?"

"Archie. It's okay to contemplate your failings. But it's time for you to be a supportive father. Go hug and congratulate your youngest son."

Archie, tears still streaming down his face, nodded and got up. Then he did just that.

9

GOD'S PLAN (2012)

Shortly before the June 13 graduation day, Savannah found out she would be the valedictorian of her high school class. A valedictorian had the highest academic achievements of the graduation class and delivered the commencement speech at the graduation ceremony. As soon as Savannah left the principal's office, where'd she'd heard the great news, she ran down the hallway to Hunter's locker. He was just closing the door when she leaped into his arms and then burst into tears.

"Are you okay?" he asked, horrified.

For a few minutes she couldn't speak. He just held her as his eyes tried to subtly look for cuts or broken bones. When she didn't seem to be physically hurt, he just held her and let her cry. Finally, she was able to mutter some words.

"I'm class va-va-valedictorian," she emotionally said.

"Oh my gosh, Savannah!" He was so relieved and proud that he whooped in her ear. Then he went nuts and ran down the school hallway yelling to hundreds of students, "Savannah Montgomery is the valedictorian! Savannah Montgomery is the valedictorian! Savannah Montgomery is the valedictorian!"

Hunter's excitement was more than just him being over the moon excited for his girlfriend's accomplishment. You see, Savannah had taught him the value of a good education and how to apply oneself in the classroom instead of treating school like a social club. But, most importantly, she taught Hunter to believe that he could make good grades and that he could get accepted into a college.

Since Savannah was his informal academic mentor, she was his role model for self-improvement and how to reach his goals. This proved to be invaluable to Hunter in baseball too. This was all so strange, coming just three years after Hunter's father told him, "Don't plan on going to college because you are not college material, in fact, you will be lucky to graduate from high school and get a job."

It was probably during Hunter's sophomore year that he had to choose which voice he was going to concentrate on. Would it be Savannah's who wanted nothing but the best for him? Or his father's, who seemed to disregard Hunter's potential, both academic and athletically. Hunter choose Savannah's positive voice and message for him. And it forever changed his life.

Savannah and her mom began putting down words on her laptop as they prepared her valedictory speech for the graduation ceremony. Hunter asked Savannah repeatedly to give him a hint about what she was going to say.

"My lips are sealed, Hunter. You're going to have to hear my speech for the first time at graduation along with everyone else."

"Either way, baby," he said, "I'm proud of you." He leaned forward to give her a kiss.

"Oh, you little devil," she said, pushing him away from the laptop screen. "You're just trying to get a peek at it." Then she shooed him out of the room.

Graduation was not a day of sadness for Hunter, Savannah and Evelyn. They were finishing high school and leaving all their classmates and teammates behind, but all three had college plans and other aspirations for the futures. And they couldn't wait to get started.

Savannah looked sharp standing behind the lectern in her dark blue cap and gown. But under her robe, her knees were shaking, and her mouth was dry. Fortunately, they had left a bottle of water for her. She smiled at the audience and took a sip of water. She had thought she didn't have any nerves. She had felt ready and confident. It's funny how standing behind a lectern getting ready to speak before a crowd can make your anxiety increase. Savannah took three settling breaths, cleared her throat and began. She started by challenging her fellow graduates.

"Fellow graduates, establish goals for yourself or else you will settle for anything. That goes for where you attend college, where you live, what you do for a living and even who you marry. Do not settle, guys. Set high standards for yourself and work until you have achieved them. It won't be easy, but nothing worthwhile ever comes easy. A wise person once told me if I do not stand for something, I will fall for anything. Do not fall for anything. Learn to say no. You may have to practice saying no so it comes easier later in life. Saying yes all the time will get you into trouble.

"Dr. Martin Luther King Jr. told us that 'The time is always right to do the right thing.' Do not fall for what the crowd is doing. Be an individual. Think for yourself. Choose for yourself. Do the right thing even if no one else is. Otherwise, if you go along with everything your friends want to do, even if you know it's wrong, illegal or immoral, you are practicing a concept called group think. Group think is a psychological phenomenon that occurs in a group of people when the desire for harmony or conformity results in an irrational or bad decision. The worst thing that can happen is when everyone agrees all the time. Remember, it's okay to dissent and not go along with the group. Dr. King was the very picture of peaceful dissent. Stand up for what is right even if it costs you to do it.

"I will be going to college to train as a teacher. As a teacher in a public school, I may have to dissent against group think which has creeped into many public school curriculums. Some teachers are being told by their administrators to challenge merit and individuality and instead to impress upon students the concept of using equal outcomes instead of equal opportunity. If teachers enable group think in schools, we will get rid of the concepts of merit and individuality which are characteristics that distinguish people from one another and it will reduce student motivation for greatness.

"I am a spiritual person. I have my own moral code. I will stand for some things, and I will not fall for others. When I lived in Alabama, it cost me a couple of boyfriends. No matter what they had in mind, they got the message on where I stood. But they didn't respect my moral code, so I stopped seeing them. It doesn't have to be a boyfriend or girlfriend. It can be the friends you eat lunch with at school, or maybe later in your life it might be your spouse or your boss.

"What is dangerous for you? It is dangerous not to think for yourself and let others tell you what you need to do, like what everyone else is doing, so you'll be cool or successful. It is dangerous for you to take advice from people you would never go to for advice. Do they really have your best interest at heart? Probably not.

"Class of 2012, we've graduated from high school! It's time for us to stand on our own two feet, to take our futures by the horn, and move the bull in the direction that we need to go. Believe me, there is plenty of bull out there getting in your way. Don't listen to it, guys. Learn to determine who is telling it to you straight, and who is trying to group think you. It's hard to trust others, isn't it? And trust is easily broken. You need to learn to trust yourself. As you make better decisions, you'll gain confidence and learn to trust yourself even more.

"The last thought I want to leave you with is this: Believe that you are enough, that you are adequate, that you are self-sufficient, and that sometimes, in order to succeed or stay out of trouble, you have to be an island, standing by yourself. If the waves of life are overwhelming, run. Run to the highest peak on your island and raise your hands victoriously like Sylvester Stallone did in the movie *Rocky* and then yell loudly, 'Yo, Adrian!'

"Class of 2012. We did it!"

The place was still roaring with laughter at the Rocky quote as Savannah left the lectern. The audience wildly clapped and cheered.

Next, the graduates lined up and marched across the stage to receive their high school diplomas. Soon the tassels were turned and caps were thrown in the air, and the Kempsville High School graduating class of 2012 walked out of the Virginia Beach Convention Center into a waiting future, where the sky was the limit.

Things slowed down for Hunter and Savannah after high school graduation and the end of the baseball season. They spent a lot of their time planning for college and finding ways to relax after working so hard their senior year. Even though they were out of school and eighteen years old, they still lived at home for the summer and were under their parents' roof and rules. For the first time, Hunter attended Savannah's Church of the Nazarene because he would be attending a Nazarene university in Nashville. His father no longer insisted he attend his family church, and it was a blessing to Hunter that his father was treating him more as a grown-up.

Over the summer, Savannah worked four days a week for her mother, cleaning vacation house rental property. Hunter worked three days a week in his grandfather's construction business. They both found time on their days off to surf in the ocean, hang out at the Ocean Breeze Waterpark, listen to free music near the boardwalk or play mini golf near the go-kart course. They were outside so much they built up bronze tans and always seemed to have sand between their toes and in their cars. Hunter also found time to work out and go to the batting cage. He wanted to keep in shape for college baseball.

When Hunter and Jo Jo were growing up, they weren't allowed to play on a travel sports team. It was expensive, they had to go to church on Sundays, and their dad worked weekends so he wouldn't be able to travel with them. Since Hunter was out of high school, eighteen and had his own wheels, he accepted an invitation from the American Legion Great Bridge Post 280 baseball program to play in the senior division that summer. The division included current and just-graduated high school players ages seventeen to nineteen, and they played ball from June to August.

Post 280 baseball teams played their games on weekends in different parts of Hampton Roads, Virginia. Hunter mainly drove by himself to the tournaments, although sometimes his grandfather tagged along, and a few times Jo

Jo went with him. There was more competition than Hunter was used to in high school baseball, and he had to step up his game. But trying to improve himself to answer a challenge was right up his alley.

Hunter's team placed first in the district but lost its first two games in the state-wide competition. Though his team was eliminated from championship play, he was selected to the all-tournament team after posting in five tournament games a .471 average, eight hits, one home run, seven runs, four RBIs and five stolen bases.

Jo Jo started classes in his junior and final year at Virginia in August of 2012. He was the starting tight end on the school's football team, and his mom and dad planned to attend all of his home games in Charlottesville. His father had even bought a football jersey to wear with Jo Jo's number 88 on it.

The Virginia Cavaliers football team had a challenging season and found themselves on the losing end twice as often as they won. They would end the season with a close loss to rival Virginia Tech, finishing 4–8.

Of course, with the Cavaliers being behind in so many of their ballgames, they threw a lot of passes in the second half of most games, so Jo Jo had plenty of opportunities to catch passes and score touchdowns. He finished the season with eighty catches, 750 yards and ten touchdowns. He was selected to the first team All-ACC and the second team All-American He flashed so much talent in college that the pro scouts were tracking his every move. He had enormous potential to play professional football.

When it was time to leave for college in August, Hunter and Savannah said their goodbyes to their families.

"With both you and Jo Jo away," his mother cried, grabbing Hunter into a fierce hug, "this house is sure going to be missing all that athletic testosterone. I'm going to miss you," she whispered.

His dad shook his hand and pulled him into a hug.

Then it was time to go. They gassed up Savannah's 2009 Ford Explorer, hit up an ATM machine and got on the road. They made the 650-mile trip from Virginia Beach to Nashville in one day. After a long full-day drive, they pulled up in front of the dorms and started unpacking their stuff.

It was late on August 20 when they arrived, and their classes at Trevecca didn't start until August 27. They had plenty of time to kill before academic work began. Hunter was situated in the Benson Hall dorm. He was assigned a small private room on the dorm's third floor in a suite with six other male students. The suite's other three rooms housed two students each. The third floor turned out to be a blessing to male students as there was a huge ramp leading from the parking lot to the third floor, so they didn't have to use the stairs to reach their rooms.

Savannah was assigned a room in the Georgia Hall dorm. She had a roommate named Linda Leon from Laurel, Mississippi. The girls thought it was funny that the school put Savannah in the Georgia Hall. After all, she was born in Georgia. Their room was on the first floor, so they didn't have to deal with stairs either.

The next morning, Hunter and Savannah went to the athletic offices to look up Coach Barnard.

"Coach Barnard, this is Hunter," she said, after knocking on his office door this time. "Hunter, this is Coach Bennie Barnard."

Coach shook Hunter's hand and said, "If you ever play pro ball, you need to hire your girlfriend to be your agent. She really has your back. Talks you up as if she's representing you."

Hunter smiled. "Savannah's the first person in my life to believe in me."

"Worth her weight in gold, young man. Well, now that you're here, let me tell you that, at Trevecca, being an athlete is about more than just winning ballgames." He pointed towards a plaque on the far wall of his office. "That plaque says, 'Christian, Scholar and Athlete.' That's our athletic motto. It states what we expect of our student athletes at Trevecca."

Coach Barnard told Hunter that baseball practice would start the following week, just after classes began. He gave his newest baseball prospect a schedule of team workout sessions and on-the-field practice sessions. Then he put his arms around both Hunter and Savannah and prayed for them to have a good year at Trevecca and to grow in Christ as they also grew as students and athlete. It was unexpected, yet meaningful.

As they left the building, Savannah said, "That was amazing! I never would have believed that a ball coach would care about his ballplayer's spiritual development."

"It's wonderful here, isn't it?" Then Hunter stopped in his tracks and shouted, "Oh man, I almost forgot to go see the baseball field!" So, still holding hands, they turned and ran down the street to peer through the fence at the baseball facility.

"Man," Hunter whistled. "This is first class. I can't wait to run in the outfield." He just gazed at the field a moment then blurted out, "The grass is so green it looks like a golf course! The outfield is as big as most major-league ballparks. Wow!"

It was a beautiful sunny day, and they enjoyed walking around the Trevecca campus, locating various buildings including the Waggoner library, Moore gymnasium, Boone Business building and Jernigan Student Center. The cafeteria was located on the main floor of the student center. They went inside and had lunch. Hunter was excited about all the choices of food. Savannah loved the salad and fruit bar. But what sent them to the moon and back was all the different flavors of ice cream. They explored the whole building and found another place downstairs to get food called the Hub.

Savannah and Hunter also checked out the school's bookstore on the lower level. In the Moore Gymnasium, they located the wellness center available to all Trevecca students to work out. Savannah was amazed by the use of the color purple in the basketball gym. They passed by the Boone Business building at first, but then decided to peek at the chapel hall inside. Finally, they wandered into the Waggoner library. Besides all the typical resources and thousands of books on shelves, the library had the 101 Coffee Shop.

"That'll be useful on study nights," Savannah said. Hunter just loved the smell of fresh coffee.

Next, they walked through the outdoor Quad and checked out the Bell Tower. The Quad was so open, green and relaxing. Hunter and Savannah found a huge rock near the Bell Tower to sit on and relax for a while, talking about what they'd just seen and enjoying the comings and goings of students and professors. It dawned on them that they were sitting in the heart of the college campus.

The next day, Hunter persuaded Savannah to go with him to the school gym.

"We can burn off all the ice cream we ate at the student center," he teased. For the past few years, he had been on a strict regimen of exercise that included lifting, resistance, isometrics, and running sprints and agility drills. He wanted to keep in shape.

Finally, the day Hunter was looking forward to rolled around, and the Trevecca Trojans baseball team gathered for the first time. Coach Barnard introduced the assistant coaches, training staff, incoming freshmen, transfers and returning players. Some of the players were on scholarship and some were walk-on players. The coach also welcomed the three guys who would try out to be walk-on athletes, which included Hunter Austin. Coach said he anticipated keeping only one of the three players.

Coach Barnard wrote a large word on his whiteboard: FAMILY.

"I want the Trevecca baseball team to be a family. A family that bonds and sticks together when things get difficult. Guys, look around you. Everyone in this baseball program is your brother … because we are a family."

As fall baseball practices and team workouts began in September, the three guys trying out to be walk-on athletes felt somewhat isolated. Even when "the three amigos," as the team labeled them, showed flashes of talent and promise, their teammates didn't encourage or compliment them. When Hunter complained about it to Savannah, she said it sounded like he was being initiated before he was accepted on the team. Whatever it was, Hunter kept grinding, hustling, throwing darts from the outfield and ripping line drives all over Trevecca's Jackson Field. Although the college pitching was far superior to what he'd faced in high school, he thought he was squaring up more balls than before because of the large green batter's eye in center field. That was something he didn't see in high school. Back home, the balls weren't as easy to pick up coming out of the pitcher's hand. Hunter kept reminding himself that pitch selection and timing were the keys to batting well. It took many at-bats to swing at just the precise time to square up baseballs.

"It's all about hitting the sweet spot on the bat," Hunter said to Savannah.

"Where is the bat's sweet spot?"

"It's really more of a region on the bat instead of just a spot," he said, warming to the topic. "It's approximately five to seven inches from the end of the barrel, where the batted-ball speed is the highest. Contact anywhere else will make your ball harmless. Hit the sweet spot, and you'll crush the ball. When that happens, someone in the dugout will yell out, 'He really barreled up the ball!'"

Hunter jumped into his individual workouts on top of the team practices and workouts. After everyone had left the gym, he'd sneak back into the weight room and go at it again. Day by day, he got stronger and more athletic. Coach Barnard told the team that besides hitting in team batting practices, he wanted every player to find a batting cage and hit on his own once every week. Hunter would hit twice a week in batting cages, sometimes quitting only when his hands hurt. Sometimes, he would lift and hit on his own after team practices. He had to drag himself back to his dorm room after a long day of exercising. Following a shower, he usually met up with Savannah for dinner in the dining hall.

"I'm a little worried about you, Hunter," she said one evening. "You're not thinking of keeping up this pace once classes start, are you?"

"I'm not sure if I can," he said, "but I'm determined to win a spot on the college baseball team the only way I know how. By always giving one hundred percent of myself and practicing until I get it right."

Savannah did some research online and came up with a regimen for his food intake and for periods of resting. She provided him with a list of high-energy foods to eat and others that were low-fat options. She also laid out how important sleep was so his body could regenerate and heal itself. Since students tend to stay up late at night studying or dating, Savannah suggested he set off thirty to sixty minutes a day for a cat nap.

Classes finally started for all the Trevecca students, and a few days later, Coach Barnard pulled the team around him during batting practice. He pointed out what was obvious to the team. Two of the three guys trying out were missing from practice because they hadn't made the team.

Then he yelled at the top of his lungs, "Congratulations, Hunter Austin!" All the Trojan players and coaches mobbed Hunter and patted his back and head, delivering congratulatory words of encouragement. For the first time, he felt accepted by his college baseball peers, and from then on, the team and coaches treated Hunter as an equal and as a teammate. Walk-on players and scholarship players were all united in one accord. They had bought into the concept that they were a family.

"We're going to be a formidable ball team for the approaching spring season," coach said proudly.

One evening, Hunter was studying with Savannah, taking notes in a spiral notebook, when he said, "I'm worried about how I'm going to do in my classes and in baseball games." He dropped his pen in disgust. "It's all so much harder. More challenging opponents and harder classes. I don't know. Maybe I'm setting myself up for failure."

Savannah touched his shoulder. "Baby, God is saying to you today, 'For I know the plans I have for you, declares the Lord, plans to prosper you and not harm you, plans to give you hope and a future.' That's Jeremiah 20:11." When he relaxed a little and nodded, she added, "Now pick up your pen and don't be lazy. We still have work to do," which made him snort with laughter.

Trevecca's baseball team used the fall months for conditioning. This included fun stuff like tug o' war with a rope, turning over a tractor tire, as well as the typical running and lifting of weights. The team played intra-squad baseball games to simulate a competitive environment. Coach divided the team into separate squads that played against each other. At the end of fall practice season, the team split into two teams and played an intrasquad World Series scrimmage for the best of five games. The scrimmage games were competitive and a lot of fun. It reminded Hunter of pickup basketball games in his driveway with his brother and a bunch of buddies. Everyone played hard, but there were plenty of laughs.

The fall semester flew by as Hunter and Savannah learned about college life. They were very busy between the higher academic demands of college, dorm life, attending chapel services, being far from home, being independent for the first time and missing their families.

"I don't know what I'd do without you," Hunter told her one evening.

"I'm so glad we have each other to lean on and confide in," she replied, giving him a kiss. "Let's go get some coffee!"

Just like in high school, Hunter had to endure jokes and jealously from other guys for dating such a beautiful lady. But everyone noticed how tight they were as a couple, and unlike in high school, there was no competition for Savannah's affection. Everyone respected their relationship.

Trevecca was a small, friendly campus. Even the professors and college administrators would make small talk with Hunter and Savannah when they passed outside the academic buildings or in the cafeteria.

Finding quiet time to study was often challenging in the dorm. Some of the guys never knew when to turn it off and go to sleep or hit the books. Nonetheless, Hunter enjoyed dorm life.

He bonded with two guys in his dorm and they became friends. Robin Lee was one of his suite mates and Martin Johnson was a Trevecca basketball player whose room was just across the hall from Hunter's. Robin wasn't an athlete, but he and Hunter had a lot in common. They bonded over studying late at night, ordering pizza delivery at midnight and listening to Robin's hundreds of Christian music CDs. Robin was the first guy at Trevecca who offered to pray with Hunter about school, the baseball team and his family. Those special quiet moments helped draw them closer together as friends. Martin was in a couple of Hunter's classes, and as they were both athletes, they'd chat about sports and sometimes eat meals together. They also enjoyed working out together in the weight room and shooting games of H-O-R-S-E basketball. Hunter made many acquaintances in his college classes, in the dorm and on the baseball team. But he felt satisfied with just two good buddies and one special lady to hang out with.

Once Hunter got to know his dorm resident counselor, Stephen Collins, he really bonded with him too. Stephen was one of the most caring men he'd ever met, and he quickly earned Hunter's trust and respect. Stephen always started a conversation with "How is your day going?" or "How is your girlfriend?" or "Hope your family back home is doing well."

When Hunter was sick, Stephen asked him, "Do you need anything for your cold? I've got some cold medicine in my apartment I can share. I'll add you to the list of people I'm praying for." Other than Savannah and his mother, Hunter had never had anyone in his life who showed such concern for him as a person.

There were many occasions when Hunter and Stephen found themselves hanging out in the dorm lobby, or in Stephen's apartment, discussing things such as "What is the meaning of life?", "What is salvation of our sins?", "How does the theology of various religions differ?", "Did our parents raise us right?" On and on it went. Once, after a detailed discussion, Stephen suggested Hunter might consider majoring in Philosophy. "You're a strong critical thinker."

Hunter laughed. "No way. I'm thinking about being a physical education teacher and a coach. I'd love to pass on all I've learned about sports to kids."

"That's true. Coaches use a lot of critical thinking before they reach their decisions. Think about all the in-game decisions a coach has to make."

One day, when they were chatting outside their dorm, Stephen asked Hunter a probing question. "Hunter, you seem to have a purpose for your pending professional life as a teacher and coach. And that's great. But, what about your spiritual life?"

Hunter frowned. "That's kind of personal."

"Yes, salvation of your soul is a very personal issue between you and Jesus Christ. I'd encourage you to have that talk with Him soon. You seem to believe that you're Godly because you've gone to church a thousand times in your life, and you give thanks to God before you eat a meal. Look, Hunter, you're a great guy. You are well behaved and you say all the right things. But being good won't earn you God's salvation, forgiveness of your sins and a place in Heaven for eternity. You cannot have Godliness without accepting Jesus Christ as your Lord and Savior. After you ask Jesus for forgiveness of your sins, then dive into the Bible. The word of God will develop you as a Christian. It will lead to true holiness. If you serve God, everything else in your life will find its place of importance."

Hunter was silent for a moment. "You're right, Stephen. I've been dragging my feet in making a commitment to God. I've had to learn to become self-sufficient and believe in myself, and not in anyone else. My faith in God is not extraordinarily strong. Just about everyone in my life has let me down in some way, except for Savannah, of course. She's perfect."

Stephen laughed. "She's a special gal, all right. I'm glad she's a faithful partner."

"I want to talk to her about salvation of my sins," Hunter said, "since she's been preaching to me about that for three years. I'm sure she'll be glad to pray with me, and she'll be thrilled if I finally take that important step."

"That's awesome, Hunter!" Stephen gave him a big man-hug. When Hunter was about to run off to class, he added, "Wait a minute, Hunter. I want to loan you a book. Let me just run into my apartment for a moment." When he came back out, he handed Hunter a book titled *The Purpose Driven Life*. "It's written by Reverend Rick Warren, a California pastor of a large church. This book is at least ten years old. I've lent it to so many people throughout the years so it's a little worn. But it's still relevant. I think it will help you understand why you're alive and God's amazing plan for you, both here and now, and for eternity. This book has been a bestseller for a long time. It will show you how to live a purpose-driven life."

As Hunter strolled across campus to his English class, book in-hand, he felt carefree, without any concern for his short-term future as his focus had been turned to a long-term purpose and finally putting God in charge of his life.

The next day off, on a glorious fall afternoon, Hunter and Savannah drove across the Cumberland River to the west end part of the city and spent a few hours at Centennial Park. It was a beautiful and quiet park away from the bright lights and loud music of Nashville's Lower Broadway, the Music City's Honky Tonk district. They brought along a bag of goodies to feed the ducks and a beach towel to sit on.

Hunter began telling Savannah about his recent conversation with Stephen. "I wanted to be with you when I gave my life to Christ."

With tears in her eyes, she asked, "Honey, is today that day?"

Hunter hesitated a bit. "Yes, I want to pray now." And he did. Hunter made Jesus Christ his Lord and Savior on a Saturday in October of 2012. His prayer was short and to the point, but Jesus heard his every word of repentance and regret for living a life of sin and disobedience to God. Through God's grace, Hunter was forgiven for his sins and set on a new path for eternity. Just then, off in the distance, chapel bells began ringing on the campus of Vanderbilt University.

"Is that for me?" he asked.

"Probably, honey," Savannah replied. "God works in mysterious ways. Maybe He is announcing your salvation to the city of Nashville as well as in Heaven."

Hunter couldn't wait to call his brother, parents and grandfather to tell them he'd become a born-again Christian. They were happy, enjoyable phone calls. Afterwards, Hunter called his youth minister back at his home church in Virginia Beach and told him the life-changing news. All those that he told promised to keep him in their prayers that he would be strong in his faith and a shining example of God's forgiving grace.

During the Thanksgiving break from school, Hunter and Savannah went home to Virginia Beach. The long separation from Hunter seemed to cause a change in his father. Archie asked Hunter how he liked Trevecca, and he wanted to know all about the baseball program there. It seemed to Hunter that this was their first conversation where he didn't feel as if he was under the microscope and on trial. The sense of judgement and the comparisons had seemed to disappear. Hunter suspected that this was a God thing, sort of like a God wink. Then Archie admitted that just before Thanksgiving, he prayed for God's forgiveness for his failures as a father. He asked for strength and direction on how to be a better dad.

Archie and Hunter had several talks over the Thanksgiving weekend. It was almost like they were trying to make up for lost time. What happened next caused Hunter to almost faint.

"Son, do you need any spending money?" his father asked, "You know, for gas or to take your girlfriend out on dates?"

Hunter could hardly answer because he was so moved. It was his father's first sign of generosity towards him.

"That's okay, Dad. Yes, Savannah and I are broke. Any money we have goes to putting gas in her car. We never go out on dates that cost money. But we're not upset about that because we have each other, and we love our college."

"There are no strings attached," his dad countered. "I want to give you $100 a week. Like an allowance. Just keep doing your best in school and on the ball field and you'll continue to make me proud." That last word—"proud" —was all Hunter had ever wanted to hear from his dad.

"I'm so grateful for your offer. It will be nice to spend something on Savannah and treat her special. There are hundreds of guys at our college who would gladly take her off my hands. Some of them have cool cars and plenty of money."

Archie laughed. "Son, that girl loves you. No one's going to steal her away from you. Take my money, Hunter, and treat her as she deserves. If you need a little extra cash, from time to time, don't hesitate to ask."

Hunter put his arm around his father. "Thanks, Dad. I mean it."

The fall semester whizzed on by and soon Savannah and Hunter returned home to celebrate Christmas with their families. Jo Jo was also home from the University of Virginia, and he and his father had several long, drawn-out conversations about the possibility of Jo Jo skipping his senior year of college and entering the NFL draft of collegiate ballplayers. Archie had paid a company to research, analyze and predict where Jo Jo would be drafted in the 2013 draft. They also predicted the kind of player contract he could expect if he were drafted—twentieth pick in the third round. Archie even called in his father to get his opinion on Jo Jo's decision because it needed to be made by January 15 in the new year. The NFL draft was four months later in April.

After praying about the decision, and a lot of discussion between Jo Jo, his parents, his grandfather, his little brother and Savannah, it was decided the time was right for Jo Jo to pursue his professional football career. A few days after Christmas, he signed the paperwork to declare his intentions to enter the 2013 NFL draft as a college junior and forego his senior year of football eligibility. The whole family held their collective breath, waiting to see what would happen at the NFL draft that was scheduled for April 25 to 27 at Radio City Music Hall in New York, New York, the Big Apple.

10

ENERGIZER BUNNY (2013)

After New Year's Day, Savannah and Hunter returned to Nashville early so she could look around the city for a part-time job. She'd adapted well to college life and was making straight A's, so she was ready to take on more responsibility and they needed additional money. A small allowance from her dad and Hunter's new allowance weren't really enough. Money was the major stress factor in her life.

Though quiet and studious around campus and focused on her studies, Savannah was a Southern girl who was brought up to be polite and friendly. Which meant she'd never met a "stranger," though she didn't talk their ears off either. She landed a part-time job just a few blocks from campus and only had to work on Saturdays. The perfect job for a college student. She would work as a dispatcher for a trucking company working 8:00 a.m. to 5:00 p.m.

When she told Hunter her good news, he smiled and said, "God's been good to us."

College classes and baseball team conditioning and practices were soon rolling along. On bitter cold winter days, after the basketball team finished practicing, the Trevecca ballplayers used the gym's basketball courts to throw and work on fielding groundballs. Hunter and his teammates also ran sprints, back and forth in the gym, and up and down the gym stairs from the main floor to the basement. On decent winter days, they used the Jackson Field to practice defense and, of course, take batting practice.

Hunter was shocked at how cold it got in Nashville. He thought he'd gone south to college. But any snow and ice only lasted a few days, and soon the temperature was back up in the fifties, even in January.

Shortly before baseball season began, the ball uniforms were passed out. Hunter was assigned jersey number 11. Each uniform was handed out with a note pinned to it with a message to the ballplayer: "Trojan, here before you lies more than a jersey. It is the foundation of our program and a tradition. The men that have worn this jersey before you have given their best, and it is now your honor to perform in it. Be the man that makes the difference today. Win a championship today."

Trevecca's baseball program was a member of the Great Midwest Athletic Conference, Western Division. It was called the G-MAC for short. Their 2013 schedule began on February 8 at the University of Alabama Huntsville. It would be the first baseball game played at Alabama Huntsville's new baseball stadium, Charger Park.

Hunter didn't think he'd likely play in the game, being far down the Trevecca baseball team's depth chart. In fact, he didn't think he'd likely play much all season. When the team filed into the dugout, he found a private place at the end of the pine bench to get settled at and take in the ballgame. As the ballplayers got ready to play, he thought about how things had been going for him. He couldn't really read Coach Barnard's assessment of him. Sometimes Coach was encouraging and complimentary; other times, he pushed Hunter awfully hard. Each time he was less than perfect, he sure heard about it. The bottom line was he was thrilled to be on a college baseball team and among such talented players. It drove him to keep up with them. But sitting on the bench, standing at the dugout railing, watching and rooting for his teammates on game day was just kind of depressing.

Hunter was not a particularly good bench player. He didn't root for his team while sitting on the bench with the same enthusiasm and energy that showed in his playing. He'd previously had many conversations with his brother about his disdain for riding the bench. Jo Jo had tried to get his little brother to be more team-oriented and less self-focused. Now almost nineteen years old, Hunter had spent most of his life trying to earn the respect, encouragement and appreciation of the adults in the room by improving himself, not by being a good teammate. He'd developed a "me against the world" mindset.

On the ball field and in the dugout, he had to find his own way of doing things. Apart from trusting his girlfriend and grandfather, he'd learned to only trust and believe in himself. So, sometimes he ran afoul of the team concept and sometimes he was thought to be aloof or uncaring.

As he sat in the dugout, never leaving the bench, watching the Alabama Huntsville Chargers win all three games and score a total of twenty-eight runs, one quote ran through his head like a mantra: "Perceived failure is oftentimes success trying to be born in a bigger way."

February 12 found Trevecca hosting Campbellsville at Jackson Field in Nashville. There were more than 200 fans in attendance for the Trojans' home opener. Not bad for a cold forty-five-degree day. Again, the Trojans came out on the short end of the score, being beaten 4–2. In the last inning, Hunter got off the bench for the first time that season to pinch-run in the ninth inning. He stole second base before the game ended with him there.

At the team practice the following day, Coach Barnard gathered the team around him.

"Our batters are not generating enough runs to be competitive. Only fourteen in the first four games. Our pitchers have been awful. They gave up thirty-two runs in four games." He paused to look at the individual faces around the room.

"Gentlemen, this is a formula for a terrible ball season. We have too much talent to be this bad. In fact, we have too much talent to be average. Something must change and it must change now, or we may not recover in time to reach our team goals. I'm going to make some changes to the batting lineup, and because of that, there will be changes to the defensive lineup. I want to try to inject some life into our offense." The players shifted around on their spot, not daring to actually grumble aloud.

"Yes, this is an experiment, and no, it may not be for the long term. It all depends on how it goes. But when we start the season 0-and-4 and have lofty team goals of winning the G-MAC Western Division, the G-MAC tournament, and playing in the NCAA World Series, we have to stop the bleeding now. I'm hoping that our four starting pitchers will bounce back in their second starts of the season. So, there will not be any changes yet to our pitching rotation."

He pointed to his team. "Guys, we have to win one ballgame before we can be great. We are zero for 2013. Losing tarnishes you. I would rather be shiny. I would rather be great. I want to challenge each of you to be great." He shook his head. "Greatness is a decision, not a right. Be your best today and everyday. Champions are made when no one is watching."

Hunter, himself, was big on messaging as a self-motivating tool and to help him focus. In his baseball locker, he'd hung a sign that read, "Energy and persistence conquer all things." It was a quote from Benjamin Franklin. He had another quote in his locker from his high school football coach who had told the football team, "The way you practice is how you will play the next game."

One of the changes Coach Barnard made to Trevecca's starting lineup for their fifth game was inserting Hunter Austin in center field on defense and in the leadoff spot of the batting lineup. The move shocked the other players. Hunter was an unrecruited, walk-on freshman. The player taken out of the lineup was visibly upset.

"He's inexperienced," Hunter heard a player complain in the locker room. "I was replaced by a walk-on with no talent."

The starting right fielder was benched and the starting center fielder was moved to right field to make room for Hunter to patrol the middle of the outfield. The player who was shifted to right field was a strong outfielder and hitter, but the Trevecca Coaching staff wanted to take advantage of Hunter's footspeed in center field. The right fielder who was benched took his displeasure out on Hunter by making snarly remarks to him and about him to his teammates. When Coach Barnard got wind of the dissenting attitudes, he got in a few of the guys' faces and tried to adjust their attitudes. It just ratcheted up the resentment towards Hunter and they mostly gave him the silent treatment.

Before the Trojans' fifth game of the season, which would be played in Nashville against Asbury University, Coach Barnard called Hunter into his office.

"Just a one-on-one chat," the Coach said. Hunter sat down nervously in the chair facing the Coach's desk.

"Son, we need you to jump-start our offense. I'm going to bat you today in the number one hole. With you there, we can play some small ball and maybe steal some runs whether we get extra base hits or not. Your ability to bunt and steal bases should shake up the opposing pitchers and it'll excite your teammates. We need you to light a fire under the rest of the team."

Hunter's jaw dropped open in surprise.

"Now, you don't have to do anything extraordinary. Just play your game. Your girlfriend told me a year ago that you have dreams of playing professional baseball. Big dreams start with small steps. Hunter, today can be the cornerstone that you build your future career on."

Then the Coach got up from his chair and came around the desk.

"I'm putting a lot on your young shoulders. Let's pray, Hunter." He bowed his head. "God, please give Hunter the strength and clarity to play baseball the way he knows how. Help him focus on the job at hand and not listen to voices around him who might be jealous of him for being in the starting lineup or those who doubt his abilities. We are grateful, almighty God, for sending Hunter to Trevecca. We are a better university and a better ball team with him here. We will give you all the praise and glory for all that is to come. Amen."

After practice, Hunter met Savannah in the Georgia dorm lobby. As she studied for one of her classes, he texted his family about his big break and called his big brother in Charlottesville.

"Jo Jo," he said, his voice trembling with excitement, "I'm going to start my first college baseball game." As he tried to tell him the details, he heard Jo Jo's voice yelling out to his roommates, "My kid brother's starting as a college freshman center fielder!"

Hunter's grandfather was thrilled to hear he'd made such huge strides in college in such a short amount of time. His father's reaction was less effusive.

"I've been tracking your team on the internet. Not doing well at all. I see Trevecca's lost all of its games. I can see Coach thinking starting you can't possibly hurt. Good job, son."

As he hung up, Hunter tried to focus on the encouragement, not the sting. It was even a compliment, really, considering it came from his dad. But it still stung. Then he remembered Coach Barnard's prayer. "Help Hunter focus on the job at hand and not listen to voices around him who might be jealous of him for starting ballgames or even those who doubt his abilities." That would be his dad. Hunter decided then and there he'd be laser-focused on what he had to do to help the Trojans turn around their baseball season. He'd leave his father's attitude for God to deal with.

February 15 found Trevecca hosting Asbury University on their home field in Nashville. There were only about eighty fans in attendance that Friday evening. There was not much enthusiasm on campus for the 0-and-4 Trojans and the weather was cold. Hunter got his first at-bat in the bottom of the first inning. After a nine pitch at-bat, the Eagles pitcher walked Hunter. The next pitch, he stole second base. His teammates leaned forward on their bench in the dugout to watch. The next pitch, he was sliding into third base and his teammates were up and screaming in support for their new leadoff hitter.

"His footspeed is incredible!" a teammate yelled.

"He's a terror!" another shouted, finishing it with a whoop.

Three base hits followed and Trevecca had a 3–0 lead in the first inning.

In the third inning, Hunter laced a line drive into right-center field that short-hopped the right fielder, whose glove slowed the ball down to a crawl. By the time he retrieved the ball, Hunter was on his way to third base with a triple. A sacrifice fly ball to the outfield drove him in for the Trojans' fourth run of the ballgame.

In the fourth inning, he put on his best Willie Mays imitation, a former San Francisco Giant who was a standout center fielder, as he cheated in on a small batter who proceeded to smack a fly ball over his head. Hunter got on his horse and ran the ball down, catching it over his shoulder with a basket catch as he streaked toward the warning track. The ease with which he made the difficult catch blew everyone away.

Coach Barnard turned to one of his assistant coaches. "The sign that a player is a great outfielder is when he can make hard plays look effortless."

After that, Asbury scored four runs in the sixth inning to tie the game. Hunter led off the home half of the sixth inning by laying down a push bunt along the third-base line. The Eagles third baseman was positioned well and made a nice play on the bunt, but Hunter just barely beat his throw to first base. After two pitchouts—with the Eagles trying to throw out Hunter if he tried to steal second base—the pitcher was in the hole with two balls and no strikes. He had to groove one over the plate. It was ripped into right-center field. Hunter broke for second base as soon as the pitcher made his move to the plate. He was already racing towards third base as the outfielder threw towards second base, keeping the batter from advancing past first. But Hunter never broke stride as he rounded third base. At the last second, the Trojans Coach waved him on to home plate. A hurried throw home by the Eagles second baseman was too late as Trevecca's leadoff hitter slid home.

"Safe!" the umpire called.

As Hunter got off the ground and wiped the dust off his uniform, his teammates mobbed him.

One of them yelled out to anyone who would listen, "That's the first time I've ever seen anyone score from first base on a single!"

The game ended with the Trojans winning, 10–4. In Hunter's first full college ballgame, he got two base hits, one base on balls, two stolen bases and scored three runs. Trevecca also played Asbury in the second game of a doubleheader that day. The Trojans won that game too by the score of 8–1. The team's pitching greatly improved in the doubleheader compared to their first four games, and their offense was electric, scoring eighteen runs in eighteen innings. Hunter had, in fact, set a fire in his teammates, and since hitting is contagious, it seemed the Trojans batters used the Eagles pitching staff for batting practice.

The next day, Trevecca and Asbury played another doubleheader at the Jackson Field. A crowd of at least 200 fans showed up, hoping to see a repeat of the offensive fireworks twenty-four hours earlier. They were not disappointed. The Trojans scored nine runs in seven innings in the third game and eight in the fourth game. In all four games, Trevecca averaged more than a run per inning and Hunter batted .600 and stole seven bases. By the end of that February weekend, he had won over his teammates.

The team was a lot different with him in the lineup. He energized his teammates. The players seemed to play with joy. They no longer felt the pressure to succeed after losing their first four games. They once again believed in themselves as a team and as a family. Coach Barnard was all smiles after Trevecca swept both doubleheaders. His gut feeling had paid off in a big way. With a new "Energizer Bunny" at the top of the batting order, the team's record was now 4-and-4.

The next morning, a Sunday, Hunter could barely get up to go to church. He had played four games in the previous two days and was beat. He and Savannah walked into the Trevecca Community Church ten minutes late, but the praise music filled his veins with energy and his heart with joy. During the preacher's sermon, he dozed off twice and Savannah had to nudge him in the ribs to wake him up.

In class Monday, a fellow baseball player pointed to him and said, "You're the man, Bunny."

Another waved and called out from across the class, "You're my hero, Bunny!"

Savannah frowned. "What's that all about?"

Hunter laughed and turned a light shade of red. "Oh, after Saturday's games, Coach told everyone I had energized the team. So, one of the guys said I was the Energizer Bunny."

Hunter couldn't shake the rabbit nickname all season. Even Savannah started calling him "Honey Bunny." At first, the look on his face showed he wasn't exactly thrilled. But after a while, he just got used to it.

A short time later, after turning in a term paper and acing an exam, Hunter hurried over to Jackson Field for a doubleheader with Trinity Christian College. It was late February and the weather was turning milder, which meant it no longer hurt to hit baseballs with aluminum bats. The Trinity Christian Trolls from Illinois must have thought the fifty-eight-degree weather was a heat wave. Trevecca split the doubleheader, losing the first game but winning the second game when Hunter provided unexpected power, hitting a laser down the right field line and over the outfield fence. It was his first collegiate home run. Savannah jumped up and down in the bleachers like a cheerleader as the ball disappeared into the darkness. The Trojans chanted, "Bunny, Bunny," repeatedly as Hunter circled the bases. Two previous times that game, that chant could be heard all over the ballpark when Hunter stole base hits in the outfield from Trinity Christian batters. His outfield play saved as many as four runs from scoring that game.

The next day, Trevecca and Trinity Christian played another doubleheader at the Jackson Field. Another large crowd of fans showed up to enjoy the sixty-degree Saturday afternoon and watch some DII level baseball. The Trojans scored eleven runs in each game to pick up two more victories, and Trevecca improved their overall record to seven wins and five losses. In the last two games played that Saturday, Hunter got four base hits, walked twice, stole two bases, scored five times and hit a home run. He was slowly but surely becoming a leader on the team. Even though he wasn't yet nineteen years old, his impact on the team's performance was becoming apparent to his fellow teammates as well as his coaches. Since Hunter had cracked the starting lineup, the Trojans had won seven out of eight baseball games.

On Hunter's nineteenth birthday, March 1, he learned he'd been named to the Trevecca Dean's List of students for the fall 2012 semester. To get on the list, the overall grade point average had to be at least 3.5. Hunter had come a long way from his first two years of high school where he was barely eligible to play school sports because of academic challenges. Savannah, of course, was also included on the Dean's List as she continued her streak of getting all A's.

One evening, when Hunter fell asleep on top of his bed's comforter, having just traveled back from Ohio following a doubleheader against Urbana University, Robert Lee, one of his school buddies, woke him up by throwing a pillow at his head.

"It's only eight o'clock, dude. What are you doing asleep?"

"Mmmph," Hunter muttered still half asleep.

"Look, I've scored some free Grand Ole Opry tickets for next weekend. You and Savannah want to go with me? I'll get myself a date."

"Okay, dude. Now get out of my room and let me sleep."

The Grand Ole Opry was a weekly country music concert in Nashville. On the evening of Saturday, April 13, Hunter and Savannah got dressed up and loaded into her SUV with Robert and Bobbie Jo Dole to make their way to the Grand Ole Opry. Hunter and Savannah had never attended the Opry before and were excited as they drove down Briley Parkway to the complex. A quick left turn into Opryland Drive, and they were at the Opry House.

"Be ready to get your country on," Robert said.

"Country music is simple," Hunter said. "It's just, 'Three cords and the truth.'"

Savannah let out a "Hee haw," as only a Southern girl can do. Bobbie Jo laughed and applauded her effort.

Of the musicians who performed that night, some were older heroes and some were younger, current stars. Among the performers were Connie Smith, Jim Ed Brown and Scotty McCreery.

Two weeks later, on April 27, Trevecca was playing their last two baseball games of the regular season. The Trojans had traveled 356 miles north, passing through Louisville and Cincinnati to get to Cedarville, Ohio, where Cedarville University was hosting four games with Trevecca. The two teams played a doubleheader on Friday, with each team winning one game. Hunter was totally distracted as the NFL draft was taking place in New York City at Radio City Music Hall. Round one of the draft had been held on the Thursday. Rounds two and three had been held on Friday. Rounds four to seven were happening that Saturday.

It was killing Hunter that he couldn't be at his family's three-day-long draft party at the Austin home in Virginia Beach. Family, friends and high school coaches were hanging out at the house on Manor Drive, watching the draft on TV and eating, eating, eating and eating some more. There were pool games being played on the family pool table as well as cornhole contests out in the backyard. There was a TV in the game room, and Archie had even rigged up a TV in the yard so no one would miss his son's big moment.

Jo Jo Austin was expected to get selected in the third round of the draft. But round three came and went, and he still had not been selected. So, the party was extended a third day to Saturday. Round four kicked off at noon, and Jo Jo wasn't picked for what seemed like an eternity.

Archie started yelling at the TV, "Would someone please pick my boy!"

And like clockwork, the announcer said, "With the last pick of the fourth round, and the 133rd overall pick, the Atlanta Falcons select, from the University of Virginia, tight end Jo Jo Austin."

Any disappointment over the delay in being drafted went right out the window. Complete craziness broke out inside and outside of the Austin's house. People were yelling, laughing, crying and slapping each other on the back. Everyone hugged Jo Jo and gave him their congratulations. Soon his cell phone blew up with calls and texts from his teammates in college and high school. Coach Mike London called and gave Jo Jo his love and excitement. Coach thanked him for taking a chance on the new coaching staff at Virginia and for being his first signee. London also shared some valuable information with the Austin family, giving Jo Jo a couple of names and phone numbers of professional sports agents.

"You'll need to pick one soon, son, and get to work on your first NFL contract!"

All this Hunter heard later. At the moment, the Austin house turned into pandemonium, and Hunter was in the middle of the Trojans' first game with Cedarville University in Ohio. He was in the on-deck circle, watching someone else's turn at bat, when he heard his name being called from behind home plate. He glanced through the backstop after someone yelled out, "Jo Jo got drafted by the Atlanta Falcons!"

Hunter lost it right there. It was the first time in his life he cried like a baby out on the ball field. Before he could bat, he had to walk back to the dugout and get a towel to dry his tears.

"Hunter, what's going on?" Coach Barnard asked, alarmed.

"Sorry, Coach. I just learned that my brother was drafted today by the Atlanta Falcons."

The Trojans dugout erupted in cheers and high-fives, and many of the players came out to hug Hunter, who couldn't stop crying, so the coach asked someone else to bat for him. Trevecca won the game, 5–0, and Hunter actually enjoyed riding the pine and talking to the other bench players about his big brother, Jo Jo Hunter. What an unforgettable way to finish the last day of the season.

As soon as the team was in the bus for the trip back to Nashville, Hunter called Jo Jo. By the end of the call, he must have told Jo Jo a hundred times how proud he was of him.

"Can you imagine," Hunter said. "Matt Ryan will be throwing passes to you. Matt Ryan! What do you think it will feel like to play in the Georgia Dome?"

They continued chatting about what it might be like to play on the Atlanta Falcons team for quite a bit longer. Aside for the phone call and a quick stop at McDonald's for dinner, Hunter slept all the way back to Nashville. The long baseball season was over and the playoffs were about to begin. The Trojans had finished their regular season by winning nine out of twelve baseball games and were entering the G-MAC playoffs on a roll.

The G-MAC Championship Tournament was hosted by Trevecca Nazarene University on the Jackson Field. May 6 marked the first game of the playoffs—the Cedarville University Yellow Jackets against the Trevecca Trojans in double elimination. Hunter's mother, father and grandfather made the drive from Virginia Beach to watch him play for the first time in college.

After the long ball season, Hunter was playing with a lot of confidence, but seeing his dad in the stands made him nervous. He'd stopped calling home to talk to his father about Trevecca baseball because, more likely than not, Hunter would hang up discouraged by his father's comments. Every compliment seemed to have a slap attached to it.

Savannah reminded him he was ultra-talented and had prepared for years for this moment.

"Honey Bunny, nothing your father says matters at all. You're a grown man now. You're finding your own way in life. On one hand, don't listen to your father, but on the other hand, don't disrespect him. He doesn't control you anymore, so don't let him." She gave him a tight hug. "You know, if you get nervous just because he's around, you're letting him control you. Tune him out if you need to, but focus on your ballplaying. Don't let your father dominate your thoughts."

She emailed Hunter a quote from Mark Twain. "Keep away from people who try to belittle your ambitions. Small people always do that, but the really great make you feel that you, too, can became great."

Hunter emailed back: "Thanks, Savannah. I could never live without you."

Her reply was "You will never have to sweetie. I believe this is our forever relationship."

That night, Hunter had trouble sleeping, not because his father was in town and not because of the playoffs, but because Savannah's words kept running in his head. "I believe this is our forever relationship." It sounded like a declaration of marriage.

Hunter actually overslept the next morning and missed his 7:30 a.m. class. When he walked into his 9:00 a.m. class, from across the classroom, Savannah gave him a look that said, "Where have you been?" He put his hands together against his face to indicate he'd been sleeping, then his eyes slid away. He didn't want her to see into his thoughts.

Later that day, Savannah and Hunter met his family at Shoney's on Donelson Pike for lunch. Then, as his girlfriend and family went off to kill some time before heading off to the bleachers, he went into the locker room to prepare for their G-MAC playoff game against Cedarville. He found a moment to be alone before warm up to say a prayer.

"God, help me clear my mind about what Savannah said about our forever relationship and about my parents being at today's game. Also, help me focus on the game, so I don't let my coaches or myself down. And bless my play that it might inspire my teammates to play their best. Amen."

During the game, Hunter found he was relaxed and playing well. He recited a scripture verse under his breath that he had memorized and at that very moment, he realized God was answering his recent prayer. Philippians 4:6 – "Instead, in every situation with prayer and petition with thanksgiving, tell your requests to God. And the peace that surpasses all understanding will guard your hearts and minds in Christ Jesus."

He glanced into the stands and saw his mother smiling her approval. His heart swelled.

Although Trevecca lost the May 6 baseball game, 6–5, Hunter had the game of his life. He accomplished a rare feat in a baseball game by hitting for the cycle. Hitting for the cycle is when one batter hits a single, a double, a triple and a home run in the same game. The home run was his second home run of the season. He also stole two bases and scored three runs. Defensively, he had two outfield assists as he threw out two Yellow Jackets baserunners on the bases, one at the home plate and one at second base. The Trojans played inspired baseball, but only after they were behind, 6–0.

When Hunter barreled up a fastball and sent it over the right-center-field fence, a distance of at least 400 feet, his father later said his jaw dropped. He'd never seen Hunter go deep before. He sat quietly as the fans in the stands roared with approval and applause. But later, when his youngest son legged out a triple, Archie was on his feet rooting Hunter around second all the way under the third baseman's tag.

"That's my boy!" he yelled.

After the game against Cedarville, Hunter introduced Coach Barnard to his mother and father. The Coach complimented them on raising such good young man.

"Thanks, Coach," Archie said. "I have another son who's an NFL player. He's even more talented than my fireball here."

"I wasn't talking about Hunter's level of talent," Coach said. "I was complimenting the kind of person and Christian he is. If I had a son" —he turned to smile at Hunter— "I'd like him to be like Hunter."

"Coach, that means the world to me to hear you say that," Janet said. "Hunter is very independent and does things his way. He's strong willed and it's apparent he's used his determination to improve as a ballplayer and as a student."

Coach Barnard laughed. "You're right about his strong will. We were struck by how much intensity Hunter plays with, how driven and focused he is on the ball diamond. But away from the game, he's the nicest, most caring guy."

Hunter just smiled at the compliment. All ability to speak had left him.

"Now, when it comes to baseball," Coach continued, "Hunter somehow maintains his intensity game after game, which is no small feat. He always seems to be on top of his game despite not being on scholarship, despite being disrespected by opponents and the lack of encouragement by his dad."

"Excuse me?" Archie said.

"Sorry about that, Mr. Austin, but I've heard how you compare Hunter to his older brother."

"Well, all that's in Hunter's past," Archie said, brushing it aside.

"Yes, I believe Savannah's support has helped him get over all of that. He's so determined to succeed; he seems to be able to have overcome all the speed bumps that pop up in his path."

"Well, I am so glad that Hunter recruited Trevecca because you sure didn't recruit him. In fact, no school recruited him to play baseball." Archie widened his stance and crossed his arms.

"In our defense, we didn't even know of him before Savannah walked into my office and told me about how talented he was and about her hopes for him to play college ball and attend a Christian college. Plus, we can't recruit in the State of Virginia since it is out of Trevecca's educational zone."

"Coach, I want to ask you," Archie said moving on to another point. "Are you aware that Hunter wants to play pro baseball? Do you think he'll ever develop into that kind of a baseball player?"

Hunter rolled his eyes and wished he were somewhere else.

Coach smiled at Hunter. "His dream of playing in the major leagues sounds far-fetched until you consider how far he's come already. It would be a huge undertaking for someone so raw, but Hunter's not the type of player to be counted out. Because of his drive and work ethic, he can become anything he wants to become. The sky's the limit for Hunter. After all, there is no expiration date on one's dreams."

Janet spoke up. "Coach, how did Hunter get so good so fast?"

"Mom—" Hunter was now officially embarrassed.

Coach Barnard laughed. "No, it's a fair question, Hunter." He paused to collect his thoughts. "Hunter may not have played hundreds of baseball games as a teenager, but he's told me how many hours a week he and his buddies practiced and of all the hours he's spent working out to build up his body. I'd say he's developed himself out of his sheer will to get better and to prove his doubters wrong. I've told Hunter many times to remember where his gifts come from. I teach him to tell others that his talents are God-given. He's talented and he's gifted. But his gifts and skills had to be developed. Hunter planted his seed of success by living and dreaming about baseball. Then he watered his seeds by practicing endlessly and learning from his mentors. Finally, God brought forth the harvest by blessing Hunter's talents beyond anyone's imagination."

The next day, May 7, the Trevecca Trojans had to fight their way out of the loser's bracket of the double elimination tournament. They played Urbana University from Ohio. It was another close baseball game with the lead going back and forth. Coming into the ninth inning with the game tied, Hunter only had a double to show for his three at-bats.

He led off the home half of the ninth by dragging a bunt about thirty-five feet towards first base. The pitcher fielded the bunt but threw to first base too late to get Hunter out. With the pitcher concerned about Hunter's speed as he led off the base, the pitcher committed a balk—intentionally or unintentionally deceiving the runner—which moved Hunter to second base. At that point, the pitcher was really rattled. Hunter danced off of second base and as soon as the ball was pitched, he darted to third base, his slide beating the catcher's throw as he stole the base. As he represented the possible winning run ninety feet from home plate, Hunter caused the defense to play up at the infield cut of grass to prevent him from scoring on a groundball. It didn't matter—the batter hit a fly ball to left field and Hunter tagged up, easily scoring the winning run. Trevecca won, 6–5, and staved off elimination from the tournament.

After they beat Urbana that day, the team immediately had to play Cedarville University, which had beat Trevecca the previous day. If the undefeated Cedarville team beat Trevecca, they would win the tournament. For the Trojans to win the tournament, they had to beat the Yellow Jackets twice.

Both teams came out with their bats blazing. Cedarville scored two runs in the first inning. Hunter led off the bottom of the first with a screaming line drive hit right back at the pitcher. It hit him in his pitching shoulder as he was still following through with his pitch. The pitcher was in obvious pain and after just three pitches, the Cedarville starting pitcher was out of the game. Trevecca went on to win, 12 –7, and advanced to the tournament championship game on May 8.

The championship game was played at Jackson Field between Cedarville and Trevecca. Again, the bats were rolling for both teams. The lead in the game went back and forth several times. Hunter walked his first two times at bat, and both times he attempted to steal second base. He was only successful once. In the third inning, with two outs and the bases loaded for the Yellow Jackets, he ran down a line drive in the gap between left and center fields. Only pure footspeed let him cut off the ball before it hit the outfield fence, which would have cleared the bases of three baserunners. When Hunter returned to the Trojans dugout, he received a big hug from his pitcher as thanks for saving three runs.

In Hunter's third at-bat that day, the left-handed batter went with a high outside fastball and Hunter hit it just over the third baseman's glove. The ball rolled into the left-field corner. Any other player would have stopped at second base and been satisfied with a double, but Hunter never broke stride around second base, heading for third as if his pants were on fire. He slid into a cloud of dirt and dust just as the throw arrived from left field. As the dust cleared, Hunter looked up at the umpire to see both hands out away from his body. "Safe!" It was Hunter's fifth triple of the season.

When the Trojans relief pitcher struck out the last batter at the top of the ninth inning, Trevecca won the game, 10–7, and they won the G-MAC championship! The Trevecca pitcher ended up under a dogpile of Trevecca ballplayers. By the time Hunter and the other two outfielders ran in to join them, they jumped on top and became the cherries on top of the celebration sundae.

There were group hugs in the stands as well. Savannah, Archie and Janet grabbed each other in a group and screamed. Afterwards, they went out to dinner with Hunter at the Red Lobster and celebrated with shrimp and scallops.

"When I came on board last fall," Hunter said, digging into the seafood, "I didn't realize Trevecca had a championship-caliber team. And I never expected to be a starter in my freshman year. I was just glad to make the team. It just feels all too good to be true."

"When God chooses to bless you," his mother said, "he doesn't mess around."

"I had that thought yesterday during the game."

"Yes," she said, pleased. "I taught it to you when you were little."

At dinner, Hunter reminded his family that the next day, the NCAA Mideast Regional Tournament would begin on the ball field.

"Who will you all be playing?" his father asked.

"Not sure, Dad. I've been too immersed in the G-MAC tournament. Coach just said to be at the field at 1:00 p.m., and the game would start at 2:00 p.m. He thinks we'll play two games tomorrow. If we lose both games, our season's over. If we win the tourney, we'll advance to the NCAA Championship Tournament in Mason on May 15. Even if we don't win the current tournament, there's an outside chance we could receive an at-large bid to the NCAA tourney based on how well we did all year."

Archie was torn between sticking around for a few more days of baseball games in Nashville or returning to Virginia Beach as planned.

"Oh, Archie," Janet said, jumping in, "what's a few more days? We haven't seen Hunter play ball since last summer. Let's stay here and support him and Savannah."

"Okay, okay," Archie relented. "We'll stay until the end of the regional tournament. But, Hunter, you're going to give me a heart attack the way you run the bases. You run like a guilty criminal through a neighborhood with the police chasing you."

"Coach Barnard told me that I need to get my brakes fixed."

As the family laughed, Archie continued with sincerity. "Seriously, Hunter, I've never seen anyone run as fast as you. You ran a ball down today in the outfield that I thought you had no chance of catching."

"Thanks, Dad. My speed is a gift from God."

The NCAA Mideast Regional Tournament games took place on Jackson Field May 9 to 11. Trevecca's first game was against the Union University Bulldogs from Jackson, Tennessee. Immediately, the bats were rolling for both teams. The Trojans' number four and five hitters both hit two home runs apiece over the mini-green monster in left field. There was a twenty-knot wind blowing out to left that helped two of the four homers barely get over the peak of the fence. Hunter beat out a bunt, hit a groundball through the infield and lined a rope over the shortstop's head, scoring three runs and catching six fly balls in the outfield. Trevecca held on to win, 14–12.

An hour later, the Trojans took the field against Hiwassee College from Madisonville, Tennessee. Hunter got only one hit in the game, but it was an in-the-park home run over the center fielder's head, which drove in one other baserunner. When Hunter slid across home plate in the bottom of the sixth inning, his run ended the game as it made the score 13–3. College baseball has a ten-run mercy rule that applies at any point after five innings have been completed. A team must forfeit the game when the opposing team has a ten-run lead after seven innings. If the game is already scheduled for seven innings, the mercy rule applies in the fifth inning. On the other hand, if the game is scheduled for nine innings, the mercy rule applies in the seventh inning.

As everyone was walking off the field following Hunter's in-the-park home run, one of the Trojan players pointed out, "Hey, Hunter ended the game with a walk-off home run. And look, we're walking off!"

"You're a genius," someone said.

Hunter was once again mobbed by his teammates and coaches. He even got a high-five later from his dad.

"Hunter, my boy," his dad said, "who would ever think you could hit three home runs in a season? And I got to see two of them this week." He shook his head in disbelief. "There was a time in Little League when you couldn't hit the ball out of the infield."

"I don't try to hit home runs at all," Hunter said with a shrug. "But sometimes, I hit the ball on the nose with just enough lift that it goes a long way. This all feels a bit like a dream."

If the first two games of the tournament were like a dream to Hunter, the third game was like a nightmare. Baseball is a fickle game. One game you can do no wrong and the next you can do nothing right.

Game number three for Trevecca was played on Friday, May 10, against Campbellsville University from Campbellsville, Kentucky. Both teams were undefeated so far in the tournament. They were the last two teams in the tournament's winner's bracket. Hunter took the first pitch of his first at-bat off his right hip. He was given first base, but he was in a lot of pain and wasn't sure if he could run. On the next batter's groundball, he limped towards second base and was put out on a fielder's choice. When he got back to the bench, one of the Trojans trainers got Hunter into a back corner of the team's dugout for privacy and applied Atomic Balm pain ointment to his hip area.

"From where the pain is coming from," the trainer told Hunter as a coach hovered nearby in concern, "it seems that the injured spot is the gluteus medius muscle and not the hip joint. That's good news for the long term, but it won't make you hurt any less."

After a while, Hunter felt a bit better and his hip area loosened up enough that his limp was barely noticeable. But what was noticeable was his inability to hit the Campbellsville's starting pitcher. Hunter struck out his second and third at-bats. Clearly, he wasn't himself.

"How ironic," he said in the dugout. "The pitcher could hit me, but I couldn't hit him."

With Campbellsville leading 8–4, Hunter batted with two outs in the ninth inning against a different pitcher. He flew out to left field, ending the game.

"In some weird way it fits," his dad later said at dinner. "Hunter walked off the last two games. First, his home run caused the opponent to walk off the field as losers, and today's game ended with the opponent walking off the field as winners after Hunter made the last out."

"What a stupid thing to say, Dad," Hunter replied, clearly annoyed.

Trevecca was scheduled to play Covenant College on Saturday, May 11, in the final game of the loser's bracket. There was no doubt that Hunter would play. The only question was how effective he would be.

Before the game, Hunter soaked in a hot tub to loosen up his muscles. The treatment seemed to do its job. He took center field to start the game feeling like a million bucks, and the Scots from Covenant weren't on their game that day. In the first inning alone they made two errors after the Covenant pitcher walked the bases loaded. The Trojans jumped out to a five-run lead going into the second inning. After walking in the first inning as the leadoff hitter, Hunter led off the second inning too. He dropped a bunt down the third-base line and beat the third baseman's throw to first base.

One of his teammates on the bench turned to the guy next to him, and said, "Looks like Hunter's glute is feeling better. He burned it to first base."

Hunter scored from first base on a double to left-center field. Then the number three hitter for the Trojans jacked one over the left-field fence for an eight-run lead.

Covenant finally got to the Trojans starting pitcher in the fourth inning by batting around the lineup and scoring five runs. But heading into the game's fifth inning, Trevecca had a commanding 15–5 lead. Since there was a ten-run mercy rule in play, the Trojans only needed to retire the Scots in their half of the fifth inning without them scoring any runs and the game would be over. Covenant went quietly in the game's last inning and were retired three up and three down. Trevecca was victorious again.

Up next, the winner of the loser's bracket, Trevecca, played against the winner of the winner's bracket, Campbellsville University. In double elimination tournaments, this particular game was referred to as the "if game." If the undefeated team loses that game, there would be one more game played to determine the tournament winner. But if they won the game, the tournament would be over, and no more games would need to be played.

About an hour after the Trojans defeated Covenant College, Trevecca took the field against Campbellsville, the only team so far to beat Trevecca in the tournament. Although the Trojans were able to scarf down a sandwich and some fruit between ballgames, the hour break did not help Hunter's glutes. He felt stiff and a little sore again before game time, so he had the team's trainer rub him down again with Atomic Balm pain ointment.

Since it was Trevecca's second game of the day, the game would only last seven innings instead of the traditional nine. NCAA has a complicated set of rules dealing with the length of college baseball games, and this was one of them.

In the top of the first inning, Campbellsville already had one run in, and the bases were loaded. Their number seven batter barreled up the baseball and hit a long fly ball to right-center field that brought the fans to their feet in anticipation of a grand slam. Hunter broke quickly to his left and backwards after the ball was struck. He too thought the ball might land at or even over the fence. So, he turned his back to home plate and sprinted towards the fence, crossing the warning track and praying he wouldn't run out of real estate before the ball came back to earth. As he felt the gravel of the warning track under his ball cleats, he looked up for the ball. And none too soon. The ball was about to pass him in the race to reach the outfield fence. With a quick reach with his left arm and his glove opened, he snagged the baseball one stride from the fence. His motion took him into the fence and he bounced off and fell back onto the ground. He raised his glove with the ball securely in the pocket to show what world-class speed, great instincts and quality training can do for an outfielder.

Hunter's outstanding catch in the first inning kept Trevecca close to Campbellsville in the score. He led off the bottom of the first inning with a solid single to right field. Two pitches later, he broke for second base and was thrown out for trying to steal. It was only the third time all year that he was caught stealing. On the other hand, he'd been successful thirty-five times.

The lead in the "if game" went back and forth throughout the ballgame. When Hunter, with one out, batted in the sixth inning, he already had two singles to his credit in his first two at-bats. The game was tied 4–4. He sliced a line drive down the left field line that hit chalk on the foul line before rolling into foul territory. Rounding second base, he took a chance for a triple instead of settling with a double. Hunter hotfooted it to third base, and he barely beat the left fielder's throw. With a runner on third and only one out and the score tied, the Campbellsville head coach brought his infield in so they could cut off the potential run at home plate. The plan almost worked. The Trojans' number two hitter hit a ball into the dirt in front of home plate, which bounced straight up in the air. In the old days, baseball people would have called it a "Baltimore Chop." The pitcher had to wait for the ball to return to earth. Meanwhile, Hunter had broken for home on contact (the instant the batter pounded the ball into the turf at Jackson Field). The pitcher's throw to home plate wasn't in time to get Hunter diving in from third base. His run put the Trojans up by one run 5–4.

Campbellsville came to bat in the top of the seventh inning, needing a run to tie and two to take the lead. An error by Trevecca's third baseman, two bases on balls and finally a single, scored two runs.

Trevecca had the final at-bats of the ballgame in the bottom of the seventh inning. But they were down by a run, 6–5. The fans held their breath. Would there be a rally in the home half of the last inning? Not this time. The Trojans could not get a baserunner on base before they made three outs. The Campbellsville University baseball team won the NCAA Mideast Regional Tournament, with Trevecca coming in second place.

It was hard for the Trevecca ballplayers to watch Campbellsville's players celebrate on Jackson Field. The Trojans' third baseman who booted a groundball in the last inning sat in the dugout crying. Hunter dropped down next to him on the bench and put his arm around his shoulder. No words had to be spoken. The message from Hunter was clear. "I'm with you, dude."

Trevecca's coaches and players were hoping to receive an at-large bid to the NCAA Championship Tournament scheduled for May 15 to 18 in Mason, Ohio, but the invitation never came. The 2013 baseball season came to an end for the Trevecca Trojans on May 10.

By any measure, they had an outstanding season. After playing fifty-six baseball games, they finished the season with a record of thirty-four wins and twenty-two losses, winning sixty-one percent of their games. The team batting average was .325. The on-base percentage was .403. The slugging percentage was .428. And they hit twenty-three home runs. They'd also won the G-MAC Championship Tournament to qualify for the NCAA Mideast Regional Tournament, which they hosted at Trevecca.

Hunter exceeded his own and his coach's expectations during his freshman year. With his .380 batting average and his thirty-five stolen bases, he'd ignited the Trojans' batting lineup as their leadoff hitter. His play in center field was sometimes routine, but other times it was spectacular. He had a way of making difficult catches look easy. He'd also made some heart-stopping plays in the outfield that no one else had seen made before in DII baseball. His throwing arm produced eight outfield assists and his fielding percentage was .991. Twice during the regular season, he was awarded the Great Midwest Athletic Conference Baseball Player of the Week. After the season was over, he was awarded a position on the All-Great Midwest Second Team.

At the family dinner following the Trojans' tournament loss, Hunter's grandfather talked about his declining health and business.

"Look, little man," his granddaddy said, "what you don't know is that I'm sick. And it doesn't look good. I have a tumor on my brain that's too dangerous to operate on."

"That's horrible, Granddaddy! I'll pray for you every day, I promise!" Hunter was very sad. What a day for bad news. "How much time do you have?"

"No one knows for sure, Hunter, but other than headaches, I'm doing okay so far. The neurologist thinks I'll make it a few more years at least. In the meantime, he advised me to come up with a transition plan for someone to take over my business because there will come a time when my decision-making skills erode. Look, I want both you and Jo Jo to come learn my business this summer. I'll pay you all a fair salary for your time. When I can no longer work, I'll hire a construction manager to handle the family business while you guys are playing ball."

The next day, Hunter's family drove back to Virginia Beach, and he and Savannah cleaned up their dorm rooms and got packed and ready for their drive home.

Hunter stopped by the baseball office to say goodbye to all the baseball coaches and to talk to his head coach.

"Hey, Coach."

"Hey, Hunter. How's my most-determined player?"

"I was wondering if you would put in a good word for me to get an invitation to play in a summer baseball league in Hampton, Virginia. I've heard the Coastal Plain League is a wood-bat collegiate summer league. I thought I'd like to play for the Peninsula Pilots. They play games at the War Memorial Stadium in Hampton. I've never hit with a wooden bat before. I thought it would give me a chance to see how I'd do in the pros since they don't use aluminum bats. Would you be able to call the Peninsula Pilots Coach and see if he'll give me a roster spot? I thought maybe if you told him how valuable I was for Trevecca and about my stats and stuff, he might, you know, give me a chance."

"Of course, Hunter," Coach Barnard boomed. "Just give me the name and number, and I'll make that call for you."

"Roger that, Coach. There's another thing I was wondering about." Hunter looked down at the ground for a moment, then he blurted out, "Do you believe I did enough this year to earn at least a partial scholarship for next year?"

"Hunter, me and the assistant coaches are about to sit down and go over the team roster for next season and talk about scholarship money. Then we have to discuss how we want to break up the scholarship money we're allowed to give out by the NCAA. I can't promise you anything before that meeting with my guys, but just know that I'm not blind to all you did to contribute to a great season for the Trojans. We were heading down a dark hole until I inserted you into the lineup in game five. That may have saved our season and my job. Now, before you leave on your long trip home, let me pray for you."

After a quick prayer for Savannah and Hunter's safety and a hug from all the coaches, Hunter left the building. He walked across campus with a big smile on his face as he remembered the great year he'd had. He shook his head. "Is this a dream or what?" Then he remembered where all of his family's blessings came from: "When God chooses to bless you, He doesn't mess around."

"Isn't that the truth," Hunter said aloud.

11

SUCCESS VIBES (2013–2014)

The Energizer Bunny and his lady were back in Virginia Beach just in time to witness Jo Jo sign his first NFL contract on the family's dining room table. The whole Austin family was there as well as Jo Jo's agent. As Hunter's dog, Cinnamon, barked and carried on (now that her owner was back home), Jo Jo put his name to a four-year deal with the Atlanta Falcons for $2 million dollars and a signing bonus of $400,000. Only the signing bonus was guaranteed.

"Four hundred thousand dollars," Hunter said in awe.

Late in May, Jo Jo joined his new teammates at the Falcons corporate headquarters and training facilities for the team's OTAs or the "organized team activities." The NFL let their football teams have off-season training sessions, and many teams used them to help develop players. The OTAs occurred in late May and early June and were the only practices between the end of the previous season and the start of training camps in July. Players new to the NFL like Jo Jo attended seminars planned by the NFL from mid-June to mid-July.

Now that he was home from his first year of college, the first thing Hunter wanted to do was love his dog, Cinnamon. The second thing was to buy a pickup truck to use in his construction job. His granddaddy insisted on paying for it. The third thing was to go surfing, even though the water was still cool. First things first, he flopped on his bed with his dog. With Cinnamon curled up next to him as he lay sprawled on his bed, her muzzle warming his leg, his surfboard in the corner of his room seemed to be calling out to him. "Wax me down! Get me in the water!" Any truck-buying would have to wait.

After a few days of surfing in wetsuits in the cool Virginia Beach surf, Hunter and Savannah were ready to get to work—Savannah at her mother's rental house cleaning business, and Hunter at his grandfather's construction business. That summer would be different for Hunter because he would be concentrating on learning all facets of AA Construction. Hunter interned there all summer, and Jo Jo came by whenever he didn't have duties as a professional football player.

Hunter also picked out his new pickup truck, a silver four-door 2012 GMC Sierra 1500 with a V-8 engine, towing package and a thin strip of red running along the exterior. It also had eight Bose speakers and a Sirius Satellite Radio. With four doors, he could easily carry up to five passengers, yet the truck bed was large enough to carry a large load. It was a beauty!

A couple evenings a week, he played baseball in the Coastal Plain League in Hampton at the War Memorial Stadium. Soon after the summer league started in June, Hunter received a call from Coach Barnard. They chatted about the Coastal Plain League and hitting with wooden bats, and Hunter thanked his coach for helping him get into the summer league.

"Coach, your support for me and confidence in me means more than I can tell you."

"You're welcome, Hunter," Coach Barnard replied. "I actually called to give you some good news. The Trevecca baseball coaches have assigned scholarship money for the spring 2014 season, and we decided to give you a one-half scholarship for your next three years at Trevecca."

"Wow, Coach! That's such great news."

"It's well-deserved, son. Well-deserved."

At first, at the summer league, it was hard to play with a wooden bat. The sound of the baseballs hitting the wood bats was different. The balls didn't carry as far. It was frustrating to break the bats when a ball hit it in the wrong place. They'd never been taught to hit with the trademark up with aluminum bats because they didn't crack. For the first time, Hunter played with ballplayers who used pine tar on the handles of their bats for improved grip. Personally, he didn't see the need to use pine tar since he felt his batting gloves provided sufficient grip.

Although it took Hunter a couple of weeks to adjust to the wooden bat and the high level of competition in the summer league, he enjoyed the challenge. It was a national league, and he enjoyed meeting baseball players from colleges across America. The Peninsula Pilots were a strong team. The head coach, Ken Miller, rotated his twenty-two baseball players in and out of games whenever possible so they had equal opportunity to play, learn and improve. Hunter got to play all three outfield positions and bat as the designated hitter. The league was competitive, but there was an instructional feeling to it. Hunter held his own against the NCAA DI players, who filled almost every roster spot in the league, even if his university only played at the Division II level. By the end of the summer season, Hunter had worked his way up to the top of the batting order where he became the table setter for the Pilots—his primary job was to get on base so other players could drive him in.

In early July, Trevecca Nazarene University officially released its Dean's List for the 2013 spring semester. Both Hunter and Savannah were named to the list. Savannah continued to earn all A's in her classes; Hunter continued to exceed his father's college expectations for him.

"See how far you've come," Savannah said. "A few years earlier, you were a thoughtful, analytical high school boy struggling with self-confidence about your academics. Now look at you; you're on the Dean's List!"

That summer, Hunter and Savannah had discussions about their future together. After all, they'd been together as a couple for four years, and they'd been living it one day at a time with no thought to the future. But with a year of college behind them, they considered themselves adults. Savannah was still motivated to get a teaching degree and teach in a high school. Hunter had a future in his grandfather's business if he chose. But now his dream of playing professional baseball was more of a possibility. Since someday he and Jo Jo would be handed the keys to his grandfather's construction business, he started thinking about getting a degree in business administration.

At some point in the summer, the m-word came up. Hunter had been obviously avoiding it, so Savannah had to ask.

"Honey, do you ever see us being married?"

They were sipping sodas at the beach, and Hunter nearly dropped his into the sand. "Of course, Savannah. I don't ever envision us being apart."

Savannah smiled broadly. "Well then, how long do you think we should wait?"

"I figured we'd wait until after college. Don't most couples?"

"Not really, Hunter. There are couples at our college who are already married or who are getting married this summer. When they return in the fall, they'll live in the college's apartments."

Hunter paled. "Wow, that's fast work."

"Too fast for you."

"Is that a question or a statement?"

"That's up to you, Hunter."

"You know, I've got a lot on my plate right now, like baseball, school and the construction business."

"Just try to fit me into your schedule, honey." Her voice was dripping with sarcasm. She stood and rolled up her towel, a signal that it was time to go home.

The discussion of marriage got tabled for the time being, and the next time Hunter saw her, he pulled out two concert tickets to the Veterans United Home Loans Amphitheater in Virginia Beach.

Savannah got excited. "Who are we going to see?"

"You were raised in the South, right?"

"Yeah."

"Okay then, country girl, I thought you'd like to get your red neck on for one night. We're going to see Blake Shelton, Easton Corbin and Jana Kramer."

"Hee haw!" Savannah grabbed the tickets out of his hand to get a closer look at them. "I love country music, Hunter. I'm going to wear my jeans and cowgirl boots."

The concert was July 19. Hunter and Savannah found themselves carried along with the big crowd of 12,000 country music fans streaming into the large outdoor concert amphitheater. They laid a blanket on the grassy hillside and staked their spot for four hours of country music. When it got dark, Savannah pointed out the full moon to her man, who, at first, only gave it a quick glance. But then she kissed him, taking his mind and eyes off of the concert. His eyes closed as their lips embraced. Then they looked up into the summer sky and stared at the earth's only natural satellite.

She broke the silence. "Hunter, I love you to moon and back."

"I love you too."

On the way home, in the middle of reliving the concert, Savannah said out of the blue, "Hunter, I love the ocean so much. It's such a special place for us. That's where we met there and learned to surf together. Oh, that reminds me. I need to go to the 17th Street Surf Shop and buy a new bathing suit. I don't like how tight my old ones fit me. I'm 20 years old now and my body is changing."

"I know," Hunter smiled. "I've noticed."

"Ha, ha, ha," the two of them laughed out loud.

As Hunter enjoyed time with his girl, surfing in the ocean and learning from his grandfather, Jo Jo was busy excelling at football. He caught five passes in the final Atlanta exhibition game and easily made the Falcons fifty-three-man roster as the backup tight end to Tony Gonzalez, who was about to play in his seventeenth and final NFL season.

At the end of the summer, Hunter parked his new truck in his grandfather's garage before returning to Nashville. After a full summer of job training with his grandfather and receiving practical education in business, he decided to change his major to business administration. He also chose communications as his minor. Before he left his grandfather's house, he thanked him for the hundredth time for training him in his business and buying him the truck. "The confidence you've shown in me humbles me, Granddaddy. Now, just stay happy and healthy."

"I love you, my boy," Anthony said, pulling him into a tight hug.

"I love you too, Granddaddy."

Then Hunter and Savannah were off. The Ford Explorer turned off of Murfreesboro Pike and into Trevecca Nazarene University on August 22. The long drive left them pretty much beat them up and they would feel the effects for a few days after.

Over a chef salad at lunch the following day, Hunter was talking about his new motivation to take the right college classes to prepare to be a businessman someday.

As she sipped her Diet Coke, Savannah said, "Hunter, you have such a keen mind for business. I'm glad you're switching majors. I can tell, when you're talking about buying, selling, evaluating bids, demolition, construction and all those things, that you really love business because your eyes light up."

"Yeah, I'm passionate about being a businessman like my grandfather. He's sort of like my hero. But it might have to wait if baseball takes me where I want to go."

"And where is that?" she asked teasingly. Savannah had heard it many times, but she loved how excited and determined he got when he talked about professional baseball.

Hunter smiled and warmed to the task. "After getting drafted out of college, I'll spend a few years learning the ropes in the minor leagues. I'll be lying in bed watching TV late one night, probably ESPN, when suddenly my cell phone rings, and I receive The Call." He paused for a moment with a dreamy look on his face. "It's the call that tells you to come right away to play baseball in the major leagues. And you have to drop everything and go to whatever city the big-league team is playing at."

She snuggled against him. "Your future's all mapped out."

He put his arm around her and pulled her close. "It's only mapped out in pencil. I can't wait until it's mapped out in non-erasable ink with a signed contract."

Hunter made an appointment with his academic advisor, who helped him switch his major. Next, he registered for his fall classes. He would miss being in the same classes as Savannah and especially getting her help with his homework. But, as Reverend Rick Warren wrote about in his book, Hunter was now living a purpose-driven life.

Classes began quickly, as did fall baseball practices. What a difference one year made for Hunter. He was finally a respected ball player, a player with unique skills, a developing leader and an example to his peers on how to get the most out of their God-given abilities. His position on the team entering the school year in 2013 was secured, and his spot as the team's leadoff hitter almost guaranteed.

Hunter kept up with his individual drills and workouts on top of the team's practices and workouts. Whether it was running sprints or doing agility drills, lifting weights or doing cardio work, he pushed his body to its limit.

One day in mid-September, the Trevecca baseball coaches had the team meet in an empty classroom. As the guys walked in, they saw a projector, a computer and a giant pull-down video screen. The players began chattering to each other about what it could be. Coach Barnard called for quiet and all the coaches went to the front of the classroom. He turned on the projector and the first slide came up. It was a photo of Jackson Field. Then he showed them a photo of the first-base foul line with red lines drawn in the shape of a large rectangle just off the field in foul territory. He asked the team to guess what would eventually go in that spot.

"A swimming pool for the fans?"

"No."

"A restaurant?"

The answers got more comical.

"A landing pad for Coach Barnard's helicopter!"

"Don't have one."

"Landing pad for a UFO?"

Finally, the coaching staff had teased the team enough so they put up a slide with an artist's rendition of a building sitting close to the Jackson Field foul line, just past first base.

"Gentlemen," Coach Barnard said, "that will be the Trevecca baseball program's own building. It will provide an indoor heated or air-conditioned space for us to throw and take batting practice. We might even be able set up some tables and chairs so you guyss can have a snack between doubleheaders. You guys like it?"

"Like it?" someone called out. "We love it!"

The baseball players whooped it up, jumped out of their chairs and applauded loudly. There were high-fives exchanged all over the room, even a few hugs too.

Coach Barnard told them more details about the construction schedule, the utility of the building, and when the team could start using the facilities.

"A construction contract was signed some months ago and the project should be completed by the end of 2013. Since the building will be close to the ball field, it might affect how we practice this fall. We'll figure all that out later. Maybe we'll practice under lights at night when the construction equipment is not in use."

"How close to the field will the building sit?" a player asked.

"Around twenty feet off the foul line," an assistant coach responded.

"Wow, that's close." the team's right fielder said.

"Yes," Coach Barnard said, "but we'll pad the lower part of that side of the building."

A giant TNU sign would be on the side of the building facing home plate.

"Guys," Coach Barnard said as he was winding down the meeting, "if you have a chance, thank Trevecca's president and the athletic director for signing off on this project. This will not only make our baseball lives easier and more effective; it will assist us in recruiting."

They began the same conditioning drills as the previous year, the tug o' wars, turning over giant tractor tires, running and lifting. The Trojans once again played intrasquad baseball games and ended the fall with an intrasquad

World Series. As they practiced and played, construction occurred on the baseball training building nearby.

The team wrapped up its autumn baseball practice time, optimistic about what kind of team they would field in the spring. Everywhere on the team, there was talent, and the guys were playing like a family. Coach Barnard frequently wrote "FAMILY" on his training whiteboard to remind the players to stick together.

"Guys, everyone in this room is your brother because we are family!"

He reminded the players about their team's history. "We have a rich baseball tradition at Trevecca dating back to 1971 when it was a college and not a university, and the original team was called the Trojans Boys. They may have only won a few ballgames that first season, but they became the foundation we stand on. They didn't even have a ball field here to practice on! The original Trojans Boys had to carpool over to Shelby Park in Nashville and practice on a field without fences. And every ballgame they played was an away game they had to travel to.

"The first Trevecca baseball team didn't receive any scholarship money. Just look at the baseball diamond we have to play and practice on. We have fences, warning tracks, dugouts, seating for fans and lights for nighttime ball. Shucks, soon we'll have a brand-new indoor practice facility. And today, Trevecca awards the equivalent of nine scholarships for the baseball team to share. I just thought that you all needed to be told where this program came from so you can help me take it into the future."

By the end of the fall semester, the exterior of the baseball building was complete, and interior work and landscaping continued until Christmas. The new facilities would be up and running when the team came back in the new year.

Thanksgiving, Christmas and New Year's Day blew by fast. During the Christmas break, Hunter noticed his grandfather seemed to be getting feeble, and his movements were slowing. His headaches were worse, and he was starting to miss work occasionally. Anthony, Hunter and Jo Jo discussed the situation and agreed that the following summer when the Austin boys were back home, they'd hire a general manager to take over the daily operations. Then Anthony could stay home and be as comfortable as possible.

Back at Trevecca Nazarene University in January 2014, the new baseball building was ready for use. The baseball team loved taking batting practice indoors during the cold days of winter. With all the netting hung in the baseball building, it allowed multiple players to safely hit side by side while other players played catch. It helped them get their arms back in shape after two months off.

Hunter put up a new message in his baseball locker, this one by John C. Maxwell: "Dreams do not work unless you do." He believed that the difference between winners and losers was often the perseverance that went into achieving their dream. He had been out working and out training his teammates since his sophomore year in high school. His motivation came from the chip on his shoulder from being cut during baseball tryouts his freshmen year. People may have gotten in his way of his goals and slowed down his progress, but not his effort or want to.

Hunter also started posting messages for Savannah, to express his love through songs, poems and famous quotes. He snuck over to her car and stuck a love note onto the center of the steering wheel.

The next morning, when Savannah and her roommate, Linda, got into the car to go to the mall, their eyes focused on the pink note. Savannah read the message aloud. "Tell me that I can hold you for the rest of my life."

Tears filled Linda's eyes. "Savannah, you have the sweetest boyfriend."

Later, Hunter explained to Savannah that the quote came to him one night when he was holding her for what seemed like an eternity because he didn't want to say good night.

"I loved it, honey," she replied. "It reminded me of how much I like to kiss you."

That evening, when she was back in her dorm room, she expressed her frustration to Linda.

"I've been waiting for Hunter to ask me to marry him. We aren't even engaged yet!"

"Oh, you don't have to worry, Savannah," Linda said as she closed up her books and stacked them for the morning. "Just remember his note. He's crazy about you."

"I know that, but we've been a couple for four years! I need to know where we're going. Hunter is so consumed with playing baseball, working out and taking classes that I feel like I've lost my place in his life. After God, I want to be the most important thing in his life."

"Why don't you pressure him to marry you? You know, give him an ultimatum?"

"No, I don't want to push him away." But after chatting for a while, Savannah felt empowered to confront her boyfriend over his lack of interest in getting married. Could this possibly end badly for them?

The next time Savannah was alone with him she said, "Tony, who works in the campus bookstore, flirted with me today. He told me I'm beautiful."

Hunter, who had been enjoying the music from the radio, looked up and frowned. "Did he? He knows we're a couple."

"Maybe he thinks I'm available since we're still not engaged."

Hunter's eyebrows shot up. "Uh—"

"Maybe he thinks you think I'm not pretty enough to marry."

"Uh—"

"You don't want to marry me, do you, Hunter?"

"Don't be silly. Of course I want to marry you. Where in the world is all this coming from? It's so out of character for you to say such a thing."

"Out of character?" Savannah was so mad; the car swerved a little as she drove.

"You might want to slow down a bit."

The car did not seem to slow down, if anything they seemed to go faster.

"I want to marry you, Hunter. I want to be your wife. But you don't seem to have time for romance anymore. You don't seem to be planning a life with me."

"Savannah! Pull over!" Hunter demanded. With a huff, she signaled, pulled into a store parking lot and slammed the transmission into park.

Hunter turned to her and cleared his throat. "Look, Savannah, I love you. Completely. My love and commitment to you should never be questioned by anyone, especially you. But right now … I'm trying to handle so many important and time-consuming activities at one time, and there's just so many hours in a day. You know what the commitment is to be a college athlete. I have to stay in shape and practice. And I have to keep up with my college courses, especially since I miss so many classes because of traveling to away to games. Between the pressure of playing NCAA games, taking a full load of classes and keeping my grades up, my brain is on overload most of the time. I even have to apologize to God sometimes for not praying and reading my Bible enough. After all that, there's very little left of me for anyone else to enjoy."

"So, that's it?"

"What do you mean?"

"There's little of you for me?"

"It's just that I'm so busy."

"What did you just say to me!"

He tried to pull her into a hug, but she put her hands up to ward him off.

"Savannah, you know that all along we've assumed that one day we'll get married."

"Have we?"

"Yes," he insisted. "And I still hope we do. But I feel it's too soon to make that commitment, especially with how busy we both are."

Savannah shifted into drive and drove them back to the college in silence. Then she jumped out of the car, slammed the door, and ran into her dorm. That was the last time Hunter saw her for days.

Soon, Valentine's Day came along, and Hunter's lady was still not speaking to him. It also was his team's first baseball game of the 2014 season. Some students had started asking him where Savannah was. Some asked if they'd broken up. All he could tell them was the truth.

"She isn't speaking to me right now, so I don't know where she is."

Hunter's sophomore baseball season began in February of 2014. Trevecca baseball program was optimist about the new season. But Hunter was carrying a burden about his relationship with his girlfriend. Every time someone would ask about her, it made it more painful for him. He was hoping that his girlfriend troubles didn't carry over to the ball field.

Trevecca's first game was at home against Maryville University in a three-game series. The Trojans were shut out in the third game and only won one of the three ballgames. Hunter's influence at the top of the Trojans lineup interjected "small ball" into Trevecca's offense. They did get ten extra base hits in the series, without any balls leaving the ballpark, but the team also managed to bunt five times to reach first base, and their baserunners stole six bases.

"Better defense and pitching during this series would have resulted in more success for the team," Coach Barnard told them.

At the first team batting practice following the less-than-impressive series against Maryville, several Trojans chatted as they waited their turn in the batting cage. They talked about how hard it was to hit DII pitching and shared advice from the Trevecca coaches about batting and hitting. It was an overload of technical information—look for this, know the strike zone, keep your weight on your back foot, don't guess what pitch is coming, and on and on.

"I can't relax at the plate because I'm always trying to think about all the things coach put in my head!" one player exclaimed.

"Hitting in college is too complex compared to when I was a kid in Little League," another lamented.

Hunter jumped into the conversation. "I think that hitting only provides the illusion of complexity." That got everyone's attention. "I practice a lot, working on all the technical points of hitting, but when I step into the batter's box in games, I clear my head of thoughts and just do what I have practiced. I let my natural hitting abilities take over, using the proper techniques I honed during practice. The only thoughts I allow into my head when I get ready to bat in a game are positive ones. I visualize myself succeeding."

"Yeah, visualization," a teammate said excitedly. "That's a useful tool."

Hunter continued, "I force a memory into my mind about when I previously crushed a ball so when I get ready to hit, I visualize hitting a ball again just like in my memory." There was a lot of nodding of agreement in the batting cage. "Have positive thoughts on the ball field. Try it, guys, and see if it works."

Universally, the Trevecca Trojans adopted a positive approach to batting versus one of fear and confusion. The result was a fourteen-game winning streak. They averaged more than seven runs a game, and four times during the streak, they scored at least eleven runs. As a team, they didn't hit many home runs, but they filled up the bases with singles, doubles and base on balls, and they ran the bases like rabbits. The Trojans became a confident bunch instead of a bunch of doubting Thomases.

During the first seventeen games of the season, Hunter continued to exceed his coach's expectations. His .410 batting average and his fifteen stolen bases ignited the Trojans' batting lineup. Hunter's play in center field was solid one game and sensational the next. He also accumulated four outfield assists as opponents hadn't yet learned to respect his throwing arm.

Savannah and Hunter gradually got over their tiff concerning marriage. Their love was too deep and strong for that disagreement to rock their relationship's foundation.

Hunter turned twenty on March 1, a few days after Savannah. The realization that they had left their teens played on their minds for a few days. But they had already turned the corner on gaining maturity and taking their responsibilities seriously for college, work, baseball, religion and love. Not many twenty-year-olds were that focused. Also, at the beginning of March, they heard they'd both once again been named to the Dean's List of students for the fall semester.

In mid-March, Coach Barnard pulled Hunter aside during practice.

"Son, a professional baseball scout was inquiring about you."

When Hunter found Savannah leaving the Waggoner Library, he grabbed her and held her tight.

"Hunter, what's gotten into you? Is everything okay?" She sounded a little panicked.

"Oh, Savannah, things are better than okay. Coach told me today that a professional baseball scout was asking about me. About me!"

"Hunter! That's incredible! I'm so happy for you."

The Trojans' winning streak ended on March 14, and during the same game, Hunter's season hit a temporary wall when he was beaned with a baseball from a Rockhurst University pitcher. He was removed from the game due to a headache, and following the game, a coach drove him to the Vanderbilt University Medical Center. The ER staff determined he had suffered a concussion. Hunter spent one night in the hospital for observation before being released. He spent the next few days just lying around his dorm room, foregoing classes and baseball activities before a doctor cleared him. He had missed six days and most of four ballgames. The Trojans lost three of the games in his absence. They clearly missed the spark and energy he brought to the top of the batting lineup.

Hunter returned to his usual spot as Trevecca's center fielder and leadoff hitter in a game against Kentucky Wesleyan on March 21. He hit the first pitch of the game over the right-field fence for a home run. So much for being afraid of the baseball following his beaning.

Trevecca won seven of their last nine regular season baseball games, sweeping the last four games against Anderson Broaddus University Battlers and outscoring them 33–16 over the four-game series. Hunter had nine base hits, including three bunt singles. He ran wild on the bases, succeeding on seven out of eight stolen base attempts. After these final games, Coach Barnard congratulated Hunter for his efforts in front of the team.

"I want you all to know that Hunter finished the 2014 regular season with a batting average of .500. And that's a stunning number when you consider how hard it is to hit a round ball moving at more than eighty miles per hour with a round bat and hit it squarely to where no defender can catch it."

The team was silent for a jaw-dropping moment as they processed the number.

"Did I hear right?" a teammate asked. ".500?"

Then they were clapping and cheering and whooping it up. Hunter's teammates really liked him. They liked how hard he worked on his craft and how much he got out of his little body. Coach Barnard liked to describe

Hunter as a silent leader because he didn't tell his teammates what to do, he just showed them with his play, practice and workouts.

When Hunter's batting average was published online in G-MAC and NCAA publications, professional baseball scouts took notice. He started getting phone calls and in-person interviews from major-league teams. Coach Barnard received numerous inquiries from scouts concerning Hunter's specific attributes, like his blazing footspeed, outstanding throwing arm and, of course, his high batting average. Coach told them that Hunter had improved by thirty percent over his previous year, which had been a good baseball season for him. The most exciting thing to Hunter was when major-league scouts told his coach that he was now on their radar for the 2015 MLB draft of eligible amateurs. Hunter wasn't eligible for the draft until after he completed his junior year of college (May 1, 2015) or after he turned twenty-one years old (March 1, 2015). Unlike the NFL, baseball players didn't declare for or enter the draft. Everyone meeting those requirements were eligible to be drafted.

Meanwhile, the playoffs were coming up. The 2014 G-MAC Championship Tournament was scheduled to be played in Mason, Ohio, beginning on May 7. The NCAA World Series was scheduled for the same location starting on May 14.

Hunter's parents and Savannah had plans to attend Trevecca's playoff games in Ohio. His grandfather couldn't make the trip because of his poor health.

Hunter and his dad hadn't spoken much the last five months, so Archie hadn't delivered any of his put-downs in quite some time. Hunter wasn't really looking forward to seeing him in Ohio, but he wasn't dreading it as much as he had before either.

Savannah had thoughts about the situation. "Hunter, I really think you changed your dad's opinion of you during the playoffs last year. I thought your dad would pass out when you hit a home run. Since then, he hasn't been so hard on you."

Cedarville University Yellow Jackets were the Trojans' opening-round opponent in double elimination. Trevecca came out swinging their aluminum bats, and they punished the ball for seven innings. The game ended after the seventh inning due to the NCAA mercy rule. The final score was Trevecca, 14, Cedarville, 4. Hunter only had one official at-bat. For his first two at-bats, he was walked by the Jacket pitchers. His patience at the plate was rewarded his third time up when he barreled up a slider and drove it over the right-center-field wall. It was Hunter's third out-of-the-ballpark home run that year. His increase in power hitting was in full display on that one swing against Cedarville. The ball cleared the wall by thirty feet.

After the Cedarville game, Coach Barnard stopped in the parking lot outside the Ohio ball field to chat with Hunter, who was standing with his parents and Savannah. Of course, Hunter's home run came up in discussion.

"I've got something to ask you, Coach," Archie Austin said. "Both times I've come to see Hunter play, he's gone deep. Has he changed his approach at the plate?"

"Not really," Coach replied, smiling at Hunter and then bringing his focus back to Archie. "Hunter's still a single hitter at heart, and he sprays line drives all over the ball field. But he's strong enough now to turn on a ball and hit it a long way. Hunter could care less how far he hits balls. And he completely rejects the 'in thing' to swing up at the ball to get it into the air, hoping it will go over the outfield fence. Hunter practices hard to be able to swing level, to square up the ball and hit line drives. Sometimes he squares up a ball with just enough lift and it clears the fence."

The conversation turned to Hunter's chances of playing pro ball someday. Hunter looked a little less confident about this change of topic. Savannah took hold of his hand and squeezed it.

Archie asked, "What do you think Hunter's odds are of getting drafted in another year?"

"So much better now after the season he's had," Coach replied. "We've got pro scouts asking about Hunter nearly every day, trying to get all the information about him as possible. His .500 batting average and ability to steal bases has him firmly on the scouts' radar screens. I know stealing bases isn't in vogue anymore in pro baseball, but they cannot overlook his 4.3 speed."

Archie frowned and pursed his kips.

"Mr. Austin," Coach continued, "I want to repeat something I told you last year about Hunter's future. Back then I said the sky is the limit for Hunter, and I told you there's no expiration date on one's dreams. There is nothing that would mean more to Hunter than for you to get behind his dreams and support them."

Archie crossed his arms and widened his stance. "Well, it's hard to wrap my arms around the fact that Hunter is so good at baseball—"

"Dad—"

"—or good at anything."

"Really?" Coach asked, his eyebrows lifting in shock.

"Just being honest, Coach. You know, man to man."

"Well, Archie, that's difficult to hear. Are you telling me you're shocked that your son is good at anything?"

"No, not shocked. I have a son who doesn't surprise me when he does well, but you know, it's just not Hunter. I'm always surprised by Hunter. He doesn't give off success vibes. I'm just trying to understand it."

Coach Barnard was so flabbergasted by Archie's comments and lack of confidence in his youngest son that he said, "Well, Mr. Austin, it's been real. I have to go … do things." He nodded to the ladies. "Mrs. Austin. Savannah. Hunter, follow me; it's time to go," and then he walked away. Hunter shook his head and followed his Coach, leaving his mother, father and girlfriend standing in the parking lot at the ball field. He used the bottom of his uniform shirt to wipe his eyes.

"You just ignore all that talk," Coach said quietly.

The next day, May 8, the Trojans played the tournament's second round against the Alderson Broaddus University Battlers. The West Virginian school's baseball team proved to be difficult to beat. As the game progressed, the lead kept changing back and forth, but only by a single run. Trevecca tied the game in the home half of the ninth inning when the Battlers relief pitcher walked a batter with the bases loaded. The game rolled into extra innings with the score tied 5–5. Alderson Broaddus was retired in order to begin the tenth inning. The top of the Trojan's batting order was up for the bottom of the tenth, which brought Hunter to the plate.

To this point, he was 0-for-3 batting, and as his coach reminded him as he swung his bat in the on-deck circle that he was due. With the third baseman creeping in towards him to take away a bunt attempt, Hunter received an outside pitch that he placed on the ground right down the third-base line past the third baseman's reach. He cruised into second base with a stand-up double. As the number two hitter took some pitches, Hunter and the shortstop played a cat-and-mouse game as the Battlers tried to keep the Trojans' speedster close to the base in case someone got a base hit. Preventing Hunter from scoring was paramount, as he was the potential winning run.

A crack of the bat was followed by the second baseman catching a hard-hit line drive. He quickly turned and flipped a throw to the shortstop at the second base bag as Hunter reversed his steps and dove back onto the base just ahead of the double-play attempt. Now, with one out, Hunter stood off second base remembering baseball's age-old unwritten rule: "Never make the first or third out at third base."

"I guess it's okay if I make the second out at third then," he thought. A big smile crossed his face as his lead off of second base lengthened. When the pitcher leaned back to pitch, Hunter was already off and running towards third base. He beat the catcher's hurried throw for a stolen base. Two pitches later, the catcher couldn't completely stop a pitch in the dirt and the ball bounced fifteen feet from home plate. Hunter, who had taken a long secondary lead off of third base, broke for home. In a cloud of dust and dirt at home plate, the home plate umpire put his arms out wide. Hunter was safe. Game over. Trojans win!

Besides a dozen slaps on the back, Hunter's reward for hot-footing it around the bases in the tenth inning was a sweet kiss from his lady. Savannah had her arms around Hunter's neck as soon as he walked off the field. "I'm proud of you," she whispered. Her words meant the world to him following his father's hurtful words the day before.

Two days later, Trevecca played the Cedarville University Yellow Jackets for a second time after Cedarville worked their way through the loser's bracket. Trevecca was the lone remaining undefeated team in the tourney. To win the championship, they only had to beat the Jackets once. For Cedarville to win, they had to beat Trevecca twice.

Both teams came out with their bats on fire. Cedarville scored a run in the top of the first inning. Hunter led off the home half of the first with a line-drive single to center field. Two batters later, he jogged home in front of a home run that went over the fence in right field. In the fifth inning, he stole an extra base hit from a Cedarville batter by running down a long fly ball in right-center field for the last out of the inning. He ran off the field with a big smile on his face, and as he approached the dugout, he received many atta-boy slaps on the back.

As Hunter headed down the stairs, he spotted Scotty, his outfield fielding coach.

"Coach, did you see that?"

"Did I see that?" Scotty asked as he jumped up and gave Hunter the biggest bear hug of his life. "That catch was not of this world, dude."

"Thanks, Scotty. I honestly didn't think I was going to catch that one. That might have been more improbable than me stealing Savannah from all the other boys."

Laugher roared from the dugout as Hunter counted his blessings.

In the seventh inning, Hunter threw out a Yellow Jackets' baserunner at home plate on a short fly ball to center field. In the eighth inning, the Trojans broke the tie by scoring three runs. Hunter was in the middle of the big inning as he got his fourth base hit of the game. This time it was a drag bunt just past the pitcher but in front of the second baseman. Trevecca's Coach Barnard brought in his closer for the top of the 9th inning with the Trojans leading by a score of 8–5. Three strike outs later, the game was over, and Trevecca had won their second consecutive G-MAC Championship and earned a spot in the NCAA Mid-East Regional Tournament. The Trojans' relief pitcher quickly found himself at the bottom of a dog pile of baseball players celebrating an important victory. The outfielders, including Hunter, had so far to run that they were late to the party, so they ended up on the top of the pile of humanity.

Later at dinner, Savannah blurted out, "Hunter, we are so proud of you and what a great ballplayer you have become."

"Oh yes," his mom added. "No one but you thought you could be a college player."

"Mom, my goals are a lot higher than that," Hunter replied. "I want to get paid to play baseball!"

"Ha, ha, ha," Hunter's father laughed.

"What's so funny, Archie?" Janet asked.

"I think that Hunter is delusional. No one's going to pay him good money to play baseball! It's just—" He broke off as he looked around the table, eyes wide as if he were surprised, as if he'd found himself in the presence of crazy people and nothing was making sense. "I just don't see it like you all do. I mean, college ball is one thing, but professional baseball?"

The dinner table got very quiet.

Archie looked around at everybody. "What? I'm not saying he isn't playing good college ball. He obviously is, isn't he?"

Hunter sat in stunned silence. For the rest of the evening, he hardly spoke at all but just smiled absently while eating his food as Savannah and Janet made overly cheerful conversation about nothing anyone cared about. Archie remained annoyed with everyone.

Finally, Hunter found the words to say to his father. "Dad, the reason I don't listen to your nonsense is because you have always put limitations on me and what I am capable of. If you don't recognize my talent and potential, I will show you that you are wrong."

Later, when Savannah and Hunter were by themselves, she reminded him that he had already risen far above his father's expectations for him.

"You've become your own man, a successful man, making good grades in college, and you're becoming a stud baseball player. Your dreams are your dreams, not your father's."

After the tense meal, Archie decided not to stick around in Ohio to watch Trevecca play in the NCAA tournament. Everyone, including Janet, was mad at Archie's stupidity and lack of sensitivity, and he insisted on going home.

Hunter's mother apologized for not staying and taking a side. "I have to live with the man," she said in a moment of unusual transparency. She gave Hunter a hug and a kiss and, with her arms still wrapped around him, said, "Remember, perceived failure is oftentimes success trying to be born in a bigger way. That was my message from heaven for you, and your success just keeps getting bigger and bigger. I believe in you and so does God." Though Hunter was sad to see his mother go, he was relieved that he wouldn't have to deal with any more of his father's negative narrative.

The NCAA Division II Baseball Committee had selected forty-eight teams to participate in the 2014 NCAA Division II Baseball Championship. The championship provided for eight regional sites, each of which hosted six teams. All regionals were double-elimination tournaments to be played May 14 to 17. Regional champions advanced to the double-elimination championship finals May 24 to 31 at the USA Baseball National Training Complex in Cary, North Carolina. The finals were hosted by the University of Mount Olive and the town of Cary.

The 2014 NCAA Mideast Regional Tournament was scheduled to begin in Mason, Ohio, on May 14. This was the second consecutive year Trevecca had qualified for the tournament. Having won the G-MAC championship in Ohio, the Trojans had a few days to hang out before the NCAA tourney games began. Every day, when there were no games to play in Mason, Hunter visited the hotel's exercise room to work out. He felt that any day he wasn't doing something physical was a day wasted and a day short of him reaching his goals. The night before Trevecca's first NCAA game, Coach Barnard caught him in the exercise room at midnight. The coach kicked him out and made him go to bed and get some rest. Barnard's parting words were, "It's not how big you are; it's how big you play. And you play HUGE young man. Now go to bed."

Trevecca's first game of the NCAA tournament was against Cedarville University Yellow Jackets, the team that beat the Trojans twice in the G-MAC tournament a few days before. The ballgames were played on the same field in Mason as the G-MAC tourney. The Trojans starting pitcher just did not have it that day. He kept giving up big fly balls that ended up in the parking lot beyond the outfield fence. The Trojans could not keep up with Cedarville on the scoreboard as the Yellow Jackets won 11–7. Trevecca was immediately moved to the tournament's losing bracket, and they faced elimination with only one more loss.

On May 15, Trevecca's baseball team played the Toccoa Falls College Eagles. The game resulted in quality pitching, very good defense and not a lot of hitting. It was a refreshing change for college baseball. Hunter ran down two fly balls hit over his head and turned two potential extra base hits into outs. He also earned an unusual outfield assist when he threw behind a runner at second base and got him out before he could retreat to the bag. The baserunner tagged up on a fly ball to center field, and when Hunter caught it, the runner faked like he was going to run to third base. Since Hunter wasn't very deep when he caught the ball, he didn't believe the runner would tag up and go all the way to third. So, after catching the ball, he threw a perfect throw to second base and got the runner out when he returned to second.

Hunter was congratulated by his teammates for his creative throw behind the runner, but his coaches were none too pleased. When he returned to the bench, he got an earful about never throwing behind a runner from the outfield.

The Trevecca coaches quickly forgot about Hunter's bad throwing decision at the bottom of the ninth. The score was tied, 2–2, after eight innings. Hunter scorched a line drive that the Eagles center field misplayed. The fielder's instinct was to break in when he judged the ball would land in front of him. But the speed of the batted ball took it over the outfielders' head, and it rolled to a stop against the fence. By the time the outfielder reversed his steps and retrieved the ball, Hunter was rounding third base like his pants were on fire, and he quickly crossed home plate with the winning run. This was Hunter's second game-winning walk-off home run in a NCAA regional tournament.

Hunter's teammates and coaches surrounded him in the biggest group hug imaginable. Savannah gave him another hug, crying and grinning at the same time as he walked off the field.

After the ballgame, several major-league scouts approached Coach Barnard with glowing comments about Hunter's throwing arm, fast feet and sweet swing. Several of them were seeing him play for the first time.

"He will be draft eligible in one year," Coach Barnard said, "and he batted .500 this season."

".500?" one of the scouts asked.

"You heard me right."

"Dang, that sounds like a slow softball batting average."

Everyone laughed, and the scouts told Barnard they'd continue to track Hunter Austin's college career.

Three hours after defeating Toccoa Falls and knocking them out of the tournament, Trevecca played the Lancaster Bible College Chargers. The Trojans punished the Chargers from Pennsylvania, 13–1, and the mercy rule ended the game after seven innings.

On May 16, they played the Lee University Flames, another Tennessee university. Both teams had already suffered a loss in the tournament, so this was an elimination game for both. Hunter led off the game with an opposite field double, a steal of third base and a run scored as a result of a sacrifice fly.

But the Flames' starting pitcher was dealing some nasty stuff up to the plate, and the Trojans hitters couldn't hit it. Through seven innings of baseball, Trevecca only had Hunter's double to show for base hits, and Lee led 4–1. The Flames' closer entered the game in the eighth inning after the first two Trojan batters walked to start the inning. Unfortunately for Trevecca, they couldn't hit him either, and they failed to score again after the first inning. As a result of this 4–1 defeat, Trevecca's 2014 baseball season came to an end.

Trevecca's baseball program had been hoping to receive an at-large bid to the NCAA Baseball Championship finals scheduled for May 24 to 31 in Cary, North Carolina, but the invitation never came. Still, the 2014 Trevecca's baseball season was a remarkable one. After playing fifty-seven baseball games, the Trojans finished the season with a record of forty-three wins and only fourteen losses, winning an amazing seventy-five percent of their games. The team batting average was .332. The on-base percentage was

.399. The slugging percentage was .467. And they hit twenty-six home runs. They also won the G-MAC Championship Tournament to qualify for the NCAA Mideast Regional Tournament.

Hunter had improved over his freshman year. His sophomore batting average of .500 far exceeded his freshman batting average of .380. His forty-five stolen bases in 2014 exceeded his total of thirty-five in 2013. His ability to reach base safely and steal bases continued to ignite the Trojans batting lineup. Hunter's defense in center field improved as he made an effort to learn his opponents' batting styles and power so he could properly position himself. His fielding percentage was .995. He occasionally made jaw-dropping catches and his throwing arm produced nine outfield assists. Three times during the regular season, he'd been awarded the Great Midwest Athletic Conference Baseball Player of the Week. After the season was over, he was awarded a position on the All-Great Midwest First Team.

Hunter's future looked bright, even if his father couldn't see the light.

12

MOONLIGHT (2014)

After returning to campus in Nashville, Hunter and Savannah packed up their dorm rooms and got their things ready for the drive home. Savannah also went by her work and turned in her keys, assuring them that she'd return to the trucking business in the fall.

Hunter made a point of stopping in the baseball office to chat with Coach Barnard and to say goodbye to all the baseball coaches.

"I've been invited to play in the same summer baseball league as last year," he told his coach.

"Do you need me to give them a call?" Coash asked.

"No. Not this year, thanks. The Peninsula Pilot's coach has been tracking my play this season and recruited me."

"Good. It's a great opportunity to play against outstanding competition. Iron sharpens iron. You'll improve this summer, just as you did last year."

Coach Barnard invited Hunter to sit for a bit. "Now, I want to have some serious talk about your prospects for getting drafted after your junior year in college. I've heard conflicting comments about you from the pro scouts" — that made Hunter sit up in alarm— "some of them love your game. But too many of them are looking for players who will hit lots of home runs in the major leagues. These home-run seekers, they're evaluating your exit velocity and the launch angle of the balls you hit, and for them, the numbers are not high enough. On the other hand, other scouts see the potential you have as a single and double hitter who steals lots of bases. The challenge you have is your game is old school, and the analytics trends used in professional baseball today are to find bigger guys who elevate the ball with plenty of bat speed. One of the scouts called your type of play 'small ball.' They said, 'Small ball is as antiquated as a Blockbuster card.' Don't worry, son. I feel if you have another outstanding season in 2015, someone will draft you." He nodded his head as he spoke. "But I believe that many teams will pass on you because you're small, and you don't hit many home runs. If enough teams pass on you, you might drop to low in the MLB draft. But if one of the teams falls in love with you, they might pick you higher in the draft than anyone expects. Let's pray together now about your future."

Coach Barnard and Hunter bowed their heads and prayed together about Hunter and Savannah's future and safe travels home. Then, feeling less excited than when he came into the office, Hunter said goodbye to his college coaches.

Hunter and Savannah traveled east on Interstate 40 through Tennessee. Five hours after leaving Nashville, they saw the "Welcome to Virginia" road sign. They entered the town of Bristol on the Tennessee side and exited on the Virginia side of Bristol. Savannah said, "Only nine more hours to go."

"Only?" Hunter asked.

Hunter brought up the fact that he wasn't looking forward to being under his father's roof again. He and his father hadn't spoken the last few weeks.

"I'm just not feeling up to it."

They finally arrived back in Virginia Beach, road weary and sleepy. Hunter was thrilled to sleep with his dog, Cinnamon, again. Her thick golden coat was like snuggling with a blanket. He was equally excited to see his big brother, who was home for a bit. They got to spend a few days surfing in their wetsuits in the ocean and hanging out with their grandfather.

Jo Jo had got bigger over the year. His weight was up to 255 pounds of muscle and bone. The Falcons wanted him even larger, so he would be a more formidable blocker. In his turn, Jo Jo commented on Hunter's muscles.

"Yeah, dude," Hunter replied, "I'm a lot stronger than last summer, but I still only weigh 175 pounds soaking wet." The brothers fell over laughing at that comment.

With Tony Gonzalez retired, Jo Jo had a possible route to being the Falcon's starting tight end the next season. The team had signed two veteran tight ends to compete with Jo Jo for the position. He was in the second year of a four-year deal worth $2 million dollars—$500,000 per year. He had already banked most of his signing bonus of $400,000, only investing some of it on better wheels and furniture for his rented bachelor pad in Roswell, Georgia.

During the off-season, Jo Jo spent considerable time in Virginia Beach with his parents. In the Kempsville area, he worked with a personal trainer to increase his strength, and a nutritionist to help him with his diet.

A few days after Hunter had returned, Jo Jo drove him over to their grandfather's house to get his pickup truck for use that summer. The GMC Sierra had been kept in a garage and it still looked new.

"Bro, these wheels are sweet!" Jo Jo exclaimed.

Since returning from Nashville, Hunter and Archie only spoke to each other when they had to; otherwise, the house was pretty silent if Janet wasn't around. She tried to get them to talk to each other at the dinner table, but they both preferred checking their cell phones or watching TV. She was the referee between two strong-willed men.

Hunter and Savannah took a week to chill and hang out with family before they started their summer jobs. In late May, Jo Jo joined his teammates at the Atlanta Falcons corporate headquarters and training facilities for the team's OTAs. The team's training camp would begin in July, followed by four exhibition games in August.

Whenever he could, Anthony tried to include his grandsons in daily business decisions, so they could learn the ropes of running a business. But the boys were quite busy with sports.

At Granddad's business, the most significant objective that summer was to recruit and hire a general manager to run AA Construction. That would allow Anthony to retire. His health was slowly failing and it was tough for him to work eight-hour days.

Hunter, Jo Jo and Anthony all took different approaches to recruiting a general manager. Anthony used his contacts in the construction industry to ask around for recommendations. Hunter and Jo Jo went on LinkedIn and searched for possible candidates. In their separate searches, all three men selected the same candidate: Billy Bonner or BB to his friends. Billy had a lot of construction foreman experience, communicated well and had a real sense of humor. Hunter really liked him. After his references checked out, he was hired to start working July 1.

The Austins worked the rest of the summer, bringing Billy up to speed on company policies, facilities, construction equipment, projects, contracts, commercial customers, subcontractors, building part supplies, list of employees, payroll records and a thousand other things.

The transition of management controls at the construction company went smoothly and quickly. After his first month on the job, Billy was making many of the business decisions for the company, and Anthony was stepping away from the business he had founded thirty years before. By mid-August, he was able to limit his work to half days.

Besides helping out at his grandfather's business, Hunter again played baseball in the Coastal Plain League in Hampton. The summer wooden-bat league ran about two months, from mid-June to mid-August, and the teams played a few evening games each week at the War Memorial Stadium.

Like the previous summer, Coach Ken Miller rotated his twenty-two baseball players in and out of games whenever possible so they had equal opportunities to play, learn and improve. Hunter got to play all three outfield positions again. As the summer baseball league ended, he continued to build a reputation for himself, this time in the Hampton Roads area of Virginia. He had the highest batting average on his team at .400 and led the league with eighteen stolen bases and five triples.

The Coastal Plain League drew a crowd of major-league baseball scouts to each game. Some of them were quite high on Hunter's abilities; others still downgraded him due to his lack of power hitting. But on that final point, he did hit two home runs and six doubles that summer, with wood bats and in a limited number of games. Some evaluators detected an increase in power from the previous summer league.

In college, Hunter learned not to try to do too much at the plate. He focused on hitting pitches to all fields and hitting balls squarely—line drives—instead of jerking long balls to the outfield.

At a Coastal Plain League game, Hunter told a major-league scout, "Baseball has lost the art of putting the ball into play. Major-league hitters swing from their heels in an effort to hit home runs, and as a result, every year it seems we get a new record for strikeouts. My approach at the plate seems old school because it is. Small ball is a strategy built on doing all the little things well."

In early July, Trevecca released its Dean's List for the spring 2014 semester. Savannah was named to the Dean's List, but Hunter was not. His grades had slipped. All the team traveling and missed classes had made it difficult to keep up his grades. Savannah earned an A in all her classes except for two B's—one in statistics and the other in a killer math class. She hadn't earned less than an A since middle school and descended into a bit of a funk. Hunter just shook his head and said, "And you call me an overachiever."

Hunter and his father took in one of Jo Jo's NFL exhibition games in August. They drove to Atlanta to watch the Miami Dolphins play against the Atlanta Falcons. Jo Jo caught enough balls and made enough blocks in the exhibition games to earn a starting position at tight end on the Falcons roster. Rooting for Jo Jo seemed to unify Hunter and Archie, and they found they got along better when traveling. It was easy to be in agreement about Jo Jo's level of talent.

On each trip to Atlanta, Archie and Hunter stayed a couple of nights at Jo Jo's condo in Roswell. The football player treated his dad and brother to rounds of golf and dinners at fine restaurants. It was apparent that life in the NFL was good.

As Hunter dreamed of being a major-league baseball player, he watched and analyzed Jo Jo's life as a professional football player. There were no minor league NFL football teams. Instead, they relied on colleges to raise players right and prepare them for the pros. Major League Baseball drafted high school and college baseball players and always sent them for years of seasoning and training in the minor leagues. Most baseball players never made it to the major leagues, and in the minor leagues, they received very low salaries. Players had to be creative in their living expenses to be able to ride it out for three to six years before getting on a big-league roster and finally making real money—if it ever happened at all. Watching Jo Jo play gave him a lot to dream about.

Hunter and Savannah spent time trying to locate copies of old baseball movies. They were on a mission to watch as many as possible before they went back to college in the fall. In baseball terminology, they hit it out of the park. They found nine baseball movies and enjoyed watching them all: *A League of Their Own*, *Brewster's Millions*, *Field of Dreams*, *For Love of the Game*, *Major League*, *Moneyball*, *The Bad News Bears*, *The Rookie*, and *The Sandlot*.

Hunter and Savannah had discussed the idea of getting married for some time now. They adored each other and couldn't imagine not spending their lives together. They both wanted a church wedding. But everything came down to timing. They were only twenty years old, but they both had adult plans for their professional lives. They were currently busy balancing classes, studying, work, church, baseball and their relationship, but they were doing it well. After much deliberation, they agreed that getting married in a year, the summer of 2015, would be a good target to shoot for.

Hunter began putting down a plan of action, but he needed advice. So, he asked his grandfather for some. Anthony gave Hunter advice on how to buy a ring, how to ask for the girl's father's blessing, how to pop the question, how to plan a wedding and a honeymoon, how to find a place to live and buy furniture, and even what to do about health insurance.

While listening to him, Hunter started to feel a little nervous. "Wow, Granddaddy. There are so many things to figure out before getting married." He frowned. "It might be easier to stay single."

Anthony laughed, "Savannah wouldn't approve of that."

Later, Hunter asked his grandfather to loan him some money to buy an engagement ring. He said, "I'll also need to borrow some money to buy us furniture for our first apartment." Anthony graciously agreed to pony up ten grand (as a loan) for a diamond for Savannah and furnishings for their first apartment. He also offered to help his youngest grandson select an engagement ring and a wedding ring for his future bride.

Since Hunter was on a mission to marry the prettiest girl he had ever seen, he didn't let any grass grow under his feet. The very next day, after Anthony had transferred the loan money into Hunter's credit union account, Hunter dragged his grandfather to four different jewelry stores to check out their inventories. It became clear to Hunter that he preferred a more simpler diamond setting and not ones with too much bling. He struck gold. It was white gold with a diamond attached at Jared's Jewelers. He found a ring for Savannah that set his heart on fire. It was a princess-cut engagement ring. The band was white gold with a solitaire diamond setting. The diamond was a ½ diamond carat. He also picked out a simple wedding band that complimented the diamond ring. Now all Hunter needed to do was find the right time and place to put the diamond on his ladies' finger.

Hunter called his brother Jo Jo and told him that he was going to proposed to Savannah. Hunter told Jo Jo that since he met Savannah at the ocean front, he was thinking about popping the question there.

"I love that idea, bro! She will find it very romantic, especially that you thought it all out and came up with that yourself. The ladies love stuff like that."

At first, Hunter thought it might be kind of corny to propose at the same place that he and Savannah had first met. But Jo Jo's reaction to Hunter's tentative engagement plan sealed the deal for him. Now, he just needed to set up the engagement date night. But first, he wanted to ask her father for his permission to marry his daughter. He wanted to do this right. Hunter had already returned to Jared's Jewelers and picked up her rings, and they were burning a hole in his pocket and wedding bells were ringing in his head.

Hunter set up a secretive Saturday morning breakfast date at Hardees with Savannah's father. After sitting down with their bacon, egg and cheese breakfast biscuits, Hunter cleared his throat. "Colonel, I have something important to ask you."

"Okay, Hunter. But please, call me Bill. You know I've retired from the military, so you don't have to acknowledge my former military rank. And I have a feeling we're going to be family soon."

Hunter nearly dropped his breakfast sandwich. "You figured all this out?"

Bill chuckled. "Yes, Hunter. Sometimes it's hard for guys to understand what's in their hearts without showing on their faces. I also knew that someday some young man would want to marry my daughter."

Hunter nodded. "We feel that the time is right because we've been together for five years. I might get drafted by a major-league team next summer—I hope I am—and that would separate us, at least by distance. But if we do get married, and I get a contract to play baseball, Savannah could come with me and finish her college degree somewhere else. Or she could stay in Nashville for her senior year. That might be weird for a married woman to live in the dorm." Even though he knew he was rambling, Hunter couldn't seem to stop it. "I guess there's still stuff to work out. I haven't been drafted yet, so I might be right back at Trevecca my senior year, with her. Another option if I do get drafted, Savannah could stay at home with you and Robin, and she could attend Old Dominion University in Norfolk. You know she wants to get her master's degree, so she still has a lot of college ahead of her. But really, I love her and want to spend the rest of my life with her." He paused to take a breath. "I wanted to ask you for your blessing." He nodded his head, and took a couple of breaths and gathered his energy as if he was going up to bat. "Sir … can I marry your daughter?"

Bill sat back in his seat, his lips twitching a little. "Robin and I really like you, Hunter. You have treated Savannah with respect and love. Even though she's so beautiful, you haven't treated her like a trophy to have on your arm. We have never heard the two of you argue or disagree. You guys are good for each other. You've formed a bond that makes you inseparable. Son, you have my blessing. And her mother's too."

"Thank you, Bill!" Hunter was so excited and, frankly, relieved, that he jumped up and leaned over to give the man a hug. "Your words mean so much to me. I will always take care of Savannah and make you proud of me."

After departing Hardees, Hunter got in his car and just drove instinctively, without any forethought. He suddenly realized he'd driven to Dough Boy's Pizza, where he'd first seen Savannah. He slowed down as he peered into the restaurant, imagining he could see her long blonde hair and sun-tanned skin, once again, for the very first time.

He parked his wheels around the corner, crossed Atlantic Avenue and slowly walked by the 17th Street Park to the boardwalk. His mind was racing, even if his feet were not. This area almost felt like holy ground as he reminisced about the young couple they had been at age fifteen. He looked around for the perfect spot to propose to his princess. To his right, there was the Dairy Queen. To his left, he saw the music stage and a small field of grass for sitting and listening to music. On both sides were tall hotels. Hunter didn't see the perfect spot. His movements slowed as he approached the bike path and the boardwalk. Vacationers and locals were enjoying the summer weather by walking, boarding, roller skating and bike riding 300 feet from the water's edge. As Hunter crossed the boardwalk and approached the football-field length of warm sand, his eyes landed on an object near the water's edge. It was a lifeguard stand.

"That's it!" he thought. "That's where I'm going to propose."

The next day, Hunter told Savannah he wanted to take her to Dough Boy's Pizza to celebrate their fifth anniversary. He knew this would be a special night for both of them, but she had no way of knowing that something would be circling her finger when it was over.

"How should we dress for the evening?" she asked.

"We're going for pizza, so nothing fancy. But I'd love it if you'd wear a sundress for me."

Savannah laughed. "You always ask me to wear sundresses, Hunter. What's up with that?"

"Apparently, you never look in the mirror when you're wearing a sundress. You are radiant, feminine, and my gosh, you just take my breath away."

"Oh, Hunter, you say the sweetest things."

When Hunter picked her up for dinner, Savannah was wearing a light-yellow sundress and all he could do was smile from ear to ear and try not to stare too much. He walked into Dough Boy's that evening with his arm tightly wrapped around the waist of the woman of his dreams. Savannah and Hunter ordered a BLT pizza, and Dough Boy's original cheesy bread sticks with marinara dipping sauce. They slowly ate as they reminisced about their first meeting there. The dinner produced plenty of "I love you" and "I love you, too" spoken between comments on how good the food was.

Hunter had planned the evening down to what time they should leave the restaurant to be sure it was dark outside. Dark equated to romance in moments like these. He wasn't leaving anything to chance. He wasn't nervous about whether she'd say yes or not, but he was nervous about the setting. Would someone else take his chosen spot on the beach? Would the weather cooperate for an outdoor wedding proposal? There were so many variables he didn't have control over.

Earlier in the evening, when he was getting dressed for his important date, Hunter had paused and prayed for God's blessings on the evening's events and for their future as a couple. So, as he walked Savannah across the street and onto the cool sands of Virginia Beach, he had peace that only God can give. At that moment, he remembered a Bible verse that said, "And the peace of God, which transcends all understanding, will guard your hearts and your minds in Christ Jesus."

Just before the water's edge, they paused and stood while holding hands, listening to the waves crash onto the beach. Hunter pulled Savannah to him and kissed her with feeling. Then unexpectedly, he said that he wanted them to climb up on the lifeguard stand nearby. At first, she laughed, thinking he was kidding.

"No, honey. I'm serious," he said. "Let's climb up on the stand. I'd like to sit and listen to the waves."

After some persuasion, she took off her shoes, put her foot on one of the slats on the side of the lifeguard stand and hoisted her body as she stepped up to the next slat. Soon, she was up on top and waiting for Hunter to join her. It was so dark that she couldn't see he had delayed his climb to put a hand inside his pants pocket to make sure the ring was still there. Touching the ring made him suddenly nervous and excited.

"You coming, Hunter?" she called into the dark.

When he reached the apex of the lifeguard stand, he could see the glow of the moon on his lady's face. Savannah looked radiant, like an angel. He climbed into the seat, and they sat close together with his arm around her. The ocean breeze wafted across their faces in harmony with the splashing of the waves below.

He tried to think of the words he had practiced over and over again at his home. But as Savannah rested her head on his shoulder, he blurted, "Baby, will you marry me?"

Savannah sat up like she'd been stung by a bee.

"What did you say?"

"Will you marry me?"

"Oh, Hunter! Of course, I will. Oh my, you're proposing to me, right?"

Hunter smiled and laughed, suddenly giddy. "Savannah, I love you more than life itself. Will you spend your life with me, baby?"

Savannah tried, but she couldn't speak. She just smiled and nodded as tears filled her eyes. Then she threw her arms around her man's neck and cried tears of joy. When she could finally form words, she said in a muffled voice, "Hunter, there's nothing in this world I want more than to be your bride, wife, lover and friend. Yes, yes, yes, I will marry you!" Then she stood up and screamed out to the ocean. "I'm getting married!"

By the time Savannah sat back down, Hunter had removed the diamond ring from his pocket. When, at last, she took her eyes off of the water and looked at her fiancé, he took her left hand.

"Baby, I have something to put on your finger." As Savannah held her breath, he slowly slipped on the engagement ring. He could barely see her hand in the darkness, so he hoped he slipped the ring on the correct finger. He hadn't realized in his planning how hard it would be to find a finger in the dark until he was actually doing it. Savannah lifted her hand up to the moon.

"Hunter, I can't see it. I can't see it. What does it look like, honey?" But before he could describe it, she exclaimed, "I have to see my ring now! I can't stand not seeing it." She stood up abruptly. "Hunter, we've got to get down off of this and run to the lights on the boardwalk. Come on, honey, let's jump."

They held hands and, as a newly-engaged couple, leaped off the lifeguard stand; it felt like a symbolic leap towards adulthood and marriage.

The rest of the summer was far less eventful. Hunter played baseball some nights and worked during the week at AA Construction. He and Savannah made sure to hang out with Evelyn, his friend next door. They'd hardly seen her since high school ended two years earlier. Evelyn attended Virginia Wesleyan University, a local university. They had fun sharing sports stories from college since she played collegiate softball, and Hunter played baseball. Of course, the first thing Savannah wanted to show Evelyn was her diamond ring. Evelyn actually teared up when she learned the details of how Hunter had planned his proposal. She said, "I didn't realize Hunter was so romantic."

Just before driving back to Nashville with Savannah for their junior year of college, Hunter dropped off his truck at his grandfather's house for storage.

This time, when he was on the verge of leaving, he had a strange feeling in his stomach. He didn't want to say goodbye because he didn't want to leave him.

"I just want to tell you, Granddaddy, that you've been an immense presence in my life and that your influence will stay with me for the rest of my life."

"Oh, I do so love you," his granddaddy said, pulling him into a hug.

"I love you too, Granddaddy," he said, choking with tears. He borrowed a few tissues from his grandfather on the way out the door, smiling and waving to him.

"We'll see you soon!" he called out the window. "I love you, Granddaddy."

But as Savannah wheeled her Ford out of Anthony's driveway, Hunter sobbed uncontrollably. He had a feeling this would be their final goodbye.

13

GREATNESS INSPIRES OTHERS (2014–2015)

When Savannah and Hunter returned to Nashville in August to attend their junior year at Trevecca Nazarene University, she checked into her college dorm with some new bling on her left hand.

"Oh my gosh!" yelled her suitemates when they spotted her diamond ring. They freaked out and smothered her with hugs and giggly laughter.

"Trevecca's prettiest bachelorette is finally engaged," one roommate said, receiving a good-natured whack on the arm from a number of the young women.

Savannah was bombarded by all the typical questions.

"Have you set a date?"

"What took Hunter so long to pop the question?"

"Where did he propose?"

Savannah answered, "No date yet. We were too young for marriage until now. On an oceanfront lifeguard stand under the moonlight." The last one caused a chorus of squeals.

"How romantic!"

The barrage of questions continued, questions about her love for Hunter, how they met, how long they'd dated and how she knew he was "the one." As the crowd in the dorm grew larger, parts of the story were repeated again and again.

Then someone asked, "Since you're beautiful, and you've probably dated a lot of guys, what made Hunter stand out compared to your exes?"

Savannah paused thoughtfully. "Well, I went out with a few duds in middle school, and a hunk in ninth grade. Then I moved to Virginia and met Hunter, and we immediately hit it off. You know, I broke up with my boyfriend in ninth grade for pressuring me for … intimacy. He really upset me. So, I wrote down a list of the qualities I wanted in a boyfriend. And you know, when I read the list afterwards, none of the items had anything to do with how he should look. There was no tall, dark and handsome on the list. I just wanted someone who was nice, genuine, honest and respectful of me. And that's Hunter Austin. I mean, he's also cute and athletic and funny."

"Aww …"

She stopped and held her hand out to look at her ring, as did everyone in the room.

"You know, on several occasions, he's asked me what I see in him. Since he's a guy, I make it easy for him and say it's his dimples."

Laughter filled the dorm room. Savannah said one more thing before she kicked everyone but her roommate out of their room for the night.

"Most guys are insecure and jealous of other guys when they're dating a beautiful girl. Hunter isn't. He's mostly insecure about himself, not our relationship. He doesn't really understand why a beautiful girl would love him. It's taken me a while, but I think I've finally convinced him he's a catch and that any girl would be lucky to have him. I feel lucky he chose me."

"You're making me cry," someone said.

"Go cry in your own room," Savannah said with a laugh, and everyone dispersed for the night.

Hunter told Coach Barnard and Stephen, his dorm director, that he and Savannah were engaged since both men had left an indelible impression on him. Otherwise, he kept the news to himself. But when the guys in his dorm started making comments to him about married life being boring, how you couldn't have fun anymore, that raising kids cost a lot of money and other silly things about settling down, he figured the engagement news had gone around campus.

The fall of 2014 was up and running, and baseball practices began shortly after classes began. With many older teammates having graduated, younger guys right out of high school and community college were recruited for the Trojans' team. Hunter's reputation on the team automatically gave him respect among his peers, and the new ballplayers sought him out for advice or just to gain his approval. One day, Coach Barnard found him running sprints with the freshman ballplayers behind the outfield fence.

"Hunter!" Coach called out. When Hunter ran over to the fence, he asked in a quieter voice, "Why are you running in secrecy?"

"Coach, I didn't want you to see how hard I'm pushing the freshman ballplayers. I'm teaching them to be prepared to play the Trojans way."

Coach Barnard laughed, "That is precisely why I want you to be the one and only team captain this coming baseball season. Hunter, good players inspire themselves. Great players inspire others. You, young man, inspire others, including me."

At the next team meeting, Coach Barnard announced, "For the 2015 spring baseball season, Hunter Austin will be the team's captain." The team broke out in cheering and clapping. "That designation starts today. When Hunter gives you advice, take it and run with it. When Hunter practices or plays games, watch him play and learn from him. Stay in shape as he does. Work out as hard as he does. Practice your craft with as much dedication as he does. Study hard in school like he does. Represent this university as well as he does."

Hunter couldn't believe his ears. It was such a contrast to the things he'd heard from his father over the years. It was like a disconnection in his brain. As his coach spoke, Hunter shook off any thoughts of his father and enjoyed the moment. Captain. He liked the sound of that.

Hunter Austin might have been appointed team captain, but entering the fall of 2014, he wasn't even the highest-rated baseball player on the Trojans team. Due to his history of baseball success at Trevecca and his potential for greatness, Hunter Newman was viewed by major-league scouts as the most likely Trojan to be drafted by the pros in June 2015. He was very productive on the baseball field his first two years of college baseball while playing the infield for Trevecca. Although the two Hunters' baseball abilities and styles were vastly different, they had several things in common. They had the same first name. They played the game the way it was meant to be played. They practiced and worked out hard and earned the respect of their teammates. And they were the two best clutch hitters on the Trevecca baseball roster.

Hunter Austin kept up with his individual drills and workouts beyond what was expected during practices and workouts with the baseball team. His intense summer workouts helped him return to campus in 2014 as a twenty-year-old man rather than the teenager who played center field in 2013. His chest was noticeably larger as were his arm muscles.

"You're an eye catcher," Savannah murmured to him one day as they walked through campus as women's heads turned.

When her girlfriends commented on that fact to her, she would tell them, "My man is looking so good that I have to work twice as hard to keep my hands off of his muscles."

Hunter continued his quest to prove others wrong about his abilities and prospects for the 2015 season. Too often he overheard comments around the batting cage or coming out of the baseball stands like "He's good but ..." or "If he could only do [such and such] a little better." When others assessed his skills, there always seemed to be "but" in the evaluation.

He taped up a new message inside his locker, this one from NFL Coach Vince Lombardi. "You defeat defeatism with confidence."

The fall baseball program carried on in the same systematic way, hard work and productive, yet fun. There was so much talent on the team in the fall of 2014, there was strong competition for many starting positions. This assured they'd had a strong bench of players. The guys seemed to really like each other, and they displayed teamwork every day. Coach Barnard continued to emphasize that the Trevecca baseball program was a family, frequently writing "FAMILY" on his training whiteboard.

During the fall intrasquad games, Hunter focused on fine-tuning his strike-zone discipline and working deeper into counts. If he was going to surpass his previous year's batting average, he needed to be very picky about the pitches he swung at and not swing at balls outside the strike zone. He'd been trying to lay off borderline pitches, whether the first pitch, last pitch or somewhere in-between. He also valued base on balls as they gave him opportunities to steal bases and score more runs.

Savannah and Hunter were eating lunch in the cafeteria in early October when their friend, Robert Lee, came running in all excited, approaching their table with a big smile like he was Santa Claus.

"Guys! I've been hunting for you everywhere," he said, all out of breath. "I've got two gifts to give you all."

"Gifts?" Hunter asked.

"You won't believe it. I can hardly believe it. I have two extremely-hard-to-come-by tickets to give away to the 2014 Dove Awards" —Savannah gasped— "and you all are the first people I thought of to give them to."

"Oh my!" Savannah exclaimed. "That's a first-class show! It's like the Grammys for Christian music!"

Gushing with thanks, Hunter and Savannah gratefully accepted the tickets, and on the evening of December 7, they were dressed up in their Sunday best, standing in line, ready to file into the Allen Arena on the Lipscomb University campus to watch the 45th Annual GMA Dove Awards. The newly-engaged couple thoroughly enjoyed the singing, production and awards. Hillsong UNITED took home five Dove awards, including the coveted artist of the year and song of the year. Hunter's favorite praise song,

"Every Praise" by Hezekiah Walker, won a Dove award for contemporary gospel/urban recorded song of the year.

Soon after the show, they were off for Christmas at home. During the break, Hunter visited his grandfather and was happy to see he was no worse than he'd been the last summer. Still, his movements were slow, and sometimes, his speech was less than perfect. His headaches continued, but since he was retired, he could lie down when he felt poorly. Both Anthony and Hunter visited AA Construction to check in with BB, who reported that business was going well. Both Austins were relieved to see they'd left the business in good hands.

One evening, Hunter and Savannah joined Anthony for dinner at Rockafeller's Restaurant at the Rudee Inlet in Virginia Beach. The breaded crab cakes were to die for as was the view of small boats moving in and out of the inlet. As the three of them sipped iced tea and pushed away their plates, they discussed Hunter and Savannah's engagement and pending marriage. Anthony couldn't resist kidding them.

"Are you sure you kids really want to get married?" he asked. When Hunter and Savannah looked at him blankly, he added, "If love is blind, then marriage is an eye-opener." Their laughter filled the restaurant.

Both the Montgomerys and Austins got together Christmas week to talk about marriage and start planning the wedding. A lot was discussed and agreed on except for the date. Everyone agreed the following summer would be an ideal time, but there was Hunter's commitment to baseball and the unknowns it brought.

"If Trevecca plays in the final game of the G-MAC baseball championship," Hunter explained, "then we'll play it on May 9. If we qualify for the NCAA baseball regionals, the championship game will be played on May 18. And if we qualify for the NCAA finals, we'll play that game on May 30. Then the MLB draft is going to be held June 8 to 10. If I'm drafted, they'll expect me to report to one of their minor-league teams soon after I signed the contract. If I—" he broke off when he noticed the exasperated faces looking his way, then finished weakly, "there are just so many variables."

After a few moments of silence, he slowly said, "I guess … I could commit … to a Saturday in the summer." The families continued to wait as he scrolled though a calendar on his phone. "How about … June 13!" He put down his smart phone and explained. "The wedding will be after the MLB draft, but before I have to report to play professional baseball. Savanna and I could take a one-week honeymoon and return home around June 21. Then I'll be available to travel to a professional baseball training site. A team would probably accept a late-June start. If I'm not drafted, we'll still get married June 13, and we'll both return to Trevecca for our senior year. Savannah, If I'm drafted and I signed a contract, you could either travel with me to wherever I'm going, go back to Trevecca by yourself or live at home with your parents and attend a college nearby. That's really your choice, not mine." Savannah squeezed his hand and sighed. Hunter's plan of action opened up a lot of discussion between the two families, but no one could come up with a better plan. That meant Savannah only had six months to plan her wedding in Virginia Beach while attending college classes in Nashville. So, the next day, she and her mom went shopping for a wedding dress. It took three days for her to Say Yes to the Dress. In fact, she fell in love with it. It was white and lacy, with three-quarter-length sleeves; the cut was feminine and modest.

"It's a dress fit for an angel," her mother said as she swiped her credit card. "Hunter won't be able to take his eyes off of you." Savannah gave her mom a hug and they both cried.

"I'm sorry," her mom said to the salesclerk.

"You just have yourself a good cry," the woman said. "It happens all the time here."

Over the holiday break, there were many discussions about the wedding. Hunter agreed to be married in Savannah's church by her minister. The church had a large gymnasium with a kitchen, which would provide ample space for their wedding reception. Because she was a church member, they could use the church and gym for free.

There was disagreement about the number of bride and groom attendants, and who they should or should not be. They finally agreed they'd each have five people stand with them in the wedding party. The size of the reception also proved problematic. Bill Montgomery finally set a limit of a hundred guests besides the wedding party and immediate families, and he persuaded them to use the church's gymnasium. He wanted to control the costs. But he gave his blessings on serving a full-blown, sit-down dinner and even suggested he hire a three-piece instrumental band to play music during dinner. He also gave Savannah a generous budget to buy a wedding cake and decorate the gym and tables for the reception.

For the wedding party, Savannah asked three girls from Trevecca, Hunter's neighbor Evelyn Applegate and another friend from Virginia Beach. Evelyn was chosen to be the maid of honor. Hunter asked his friend's Liam Thomason, Brady Doolittle, Bryce Jennings and Asher Brown. He asked Jo Jo to be his best man.

Granddaddy told Hunter and Savannah that it would be his privilege to pay for a nice honeymoon for them. "Get away from here," he said. "Go somewhere exciting or somewhere tropical and chill."

"Oh my," they both replied at the same moment.

"Honestly, Granddaddy," Hunter added, "tropical and chill sounds perfect for a honeymoon."

"Thank you," Savannah added. "It's so generous of you, granddaddy."

Anthony smiled when he heard her say "granddaddy." He winked and nodded. "We're family now."

The holidays flew by and soon Savannah and Hunter were back in Nashville getting ready for the spring semester. The Trojans' new baseball program building was now a year old and well broken-in by the team. The team loved hitting indoors in the winter or on rainy days. They played catch several times a week, sometimes indoors, to keep their arms in shape. They could work on their pitching more. To prepare for the baseball season, the players ran outdoors and lifted weights in the gym. To compete at the collegiate level, the players had to work on their craft all year-round.

Hunter continued his major course work in business administration, and Savannah continued with secondary education. But with marriage on the horizon, their minds kept traveling, and they were less focused than before on their classes, papers and tests.

In the Trevecca baseball program, there was a lot of optimism for another outstanding season. The Trojans now had, not one, but two players being seriously scouted by professional baseball organizations, and the team liked to refer to the players as "the Hunters." The baseball season began for everyone on February 6 in South Carolina against University of South Carolina Aiken.

Hunter put up a new message in his baseball locker by Ralph Waldo Emerson. "The only person you are destined to become is the person you decide to be."

The weather was cold in the South that February, and the Trojans were not hot during the first three weeks of the season. They lost six of their first eight games. But it wasn't just the team's offense that was still trying to break out of winter; Trevecca's pitchers gave up an average of twelve runs each game over the first six games.

Clearly concerned with the path they were on, Coach Barnard and his assistants held a "Come to Jesus" meeting with the team.

"I'm not going to keep writing the same names into the starting lineup," Coach Barnard said, "regardless of your press clippings. What I'm seeing out there is complacency! Complacency! After following two years of qualifying for the NCAA tournament. Your history and your reputation mean nothing to your opponents. You have to earn the right to be in our starting lineup." Coach looked pointedly at the players. "Are you picking up on what I'm putting down?"

The entire team nodded in agreement. They understood what was at stake—playing time.

Early in the spring, Hunter just wasn't his old self at the plate. For some reason, whether psychological or physical, he didn't hit well in cold weather. He started pressing to be more productive but with no results. He was batting only .290 and Coach Barnard found opportunities to sit him on the Trevecca bench. It was just like when he started at college. Only it wasn't. Days away from turning twenty-one years old, Hunter had grown up by leaps and bounds. He was nearly independent of his parents, engaged to be married and three-quarters of the way to a college degree. He had future plans to help lead his grandfather's business and, of course, one big dream to be a professional baseball player. It seemed that he had more plans on the drawing board than an architect.

Certainly, he felt pressure to play well since he was tabbed as the baseball team's captain and because the major leagues were scouting him. But he was no longer a kid who'd sulk on a bench. Instead, he did the only thing he knew how to do—work harder and grind through it. The heated baseball facility next to the Jackson baseball field provided the perfect spot for Hunter to hone his batting skills. After team practices and ballgames, he loaded the pitching machine over and over again and then he sprinted back to home plate to pick up his bat and take more hacks. Sometimes, he was lucky enough to have a teammate or two present to feed balls into the machine for him. Until he got it right, Hunter wore out two pairs of batting gloves in the month of February alone.

All those extra batting sessions didn't reduce Hunter's routine of working out every other day. He worked on building up his leg strength. He wanted his legs to be powerful when he batted, even without having to lift his front foot or using it to step as he swung. That way, he could keep his weight on his back foot without rocking up, down or forward in his swing. His goal was to hit balls squarely, not to knock them over the fence. He believed if he kept his body balanced and level throughout his swing, his bat would also be level at the point of contact with the baseball.

After a couple of games on the bench, Hunter was inserted back into the lineup in the second game of a doubleheader against Wayne State University. It was the last day of February, and the temperature in Nashville got up to sixty-five degrees—practically a heat wave compared to earlier in the season. Hunter led off the bottom of the first inning by hitting the first pitch on the nose to left-center field. As he charged towards first base, with extra bases on his mind, the baseball carried over the fence. Home run!

The familiar smile finally returned to Hunter's face, but the frown he put on the faces of the opposing pitchers stayed there all game long. He lit them up for four base hits.

After his big game, he received a lot of joshing and kidding from his teammates.

"Where have you been hiding?"

"Are you new here? I didn't recognize you based on your play today."

Hunter and Savannah celebrated their twenty-first birthdays together with some friends after their church service. They went out to a popular Mexican restaurant. Savannah secretly told their waitress that it was Hunter's birthday, which it was, being March 1; Savannah had turned twenty-one a few days before. So, during their meal, a group of waitresses showed up at his table, slammed a thirty-inch-wide sombrero on his head and held it down while they sang, "Happy birthday." Hunter's friends took enough pictures of him looking stupid in the huge sombrero to blackmail him for life.

A few days later, both Savannah and Hunter received word they'd both been named to the Dean's List of students for the fall semester.

"It's a belated birthday present," Savannah said brightly.

Trevecca's next two games were against the University of Indianapolis. They only managed to keep Hunter off the bases two times in eight at-bats. He was finally squaring up the ball again, causing fans and teammates alike to reminisce about what he'd done the year before. Every trip to first base was a springboard for stealing bases. A frequent occurrence this spring was Hunter reaching first base, stealing second and being knocked in by the other Hunter, Hunter Newman.

Hunter Austin's batting average quickly reached .400 as he regained his swing and his confidence; he was once again inspiring his teammates with his play. He was stealing bases at a record pace, which caused his buddies to bring back his old nickname, Energizer Bunny.

In a doubleheader against Hillsdale College on March 14, Hunter accumulated three outfield assists—two of the runners thrown out were at home plate! The handful of major-league scouts watching the game quickly took note of his cannon arm. Hunter also got six base hits during the same doubleheader.

At the conclusion of the ballgames that day, a major-league scout cornered Hunter for an introduction and a chat.

"Willie Jackson," he said. "I'm scouting for the Baltimore Orioles." It seemed Willie had played Minor League Baseball as a center field and base stealer back in his day. He recognized Hunter's skills as being similar to those he once possessed, with one exception. "Dude, I never threw like you throw. The two darts you threw to home plate today made my jaw drop. I'm going to tell you right now; I'm going to keep my eye on you the rest of the season, and tonight I'm going to send my boss a glowing preliminary scouting report on you. I report to David Jennings, who's the Orioles' head scout for the southeast region. Maybe someday I can get him to catch one of your games. He frequently scouts the Vanderbilt baseball games across town."

Hunter was nearly skipping as he walked over to Savannah, who had waited patiently for him to finish talking to the scout.

"What did he say?" she asked eagerly.

"Savannah, he's a scout for the Baltimore Orioles. He said he loves my game. He's going to do a preliminary report on me tonight to send to his boss and tell the Orioles what a stud I am."

She laughed off the "stud" comment and said, "Hunter, that's wonderful! And the Orioles are your favorite team."

One week later, Trevecca played in the strangest doubleheader anyone could remember witnessing. Their opponent that day was Kentucky Wesleyan College, and the game was played in Owensboro, Kentucky. Due to the scheduled doubleheader, the baseball games were each scheduled to be seven-inning affairs. Both games went into extra innings, although Trevecca outscored Kentucky Wesleyan, 23–4, that day. The Trojans scored eleven runs in the eighth inning of the opening game and eight runs in the tenth inning of the nightcap. During the two games, Hunter Newman hit three home runs while Hunter Austin hit two triples and stole five bases. Their play were dissimilar in every way, but the two Trevecca Hunters were equally a pain in their opponents' sides.

As Trevecca fans at the game chanted, "Hunt, Hunt, Hunt, Hunt," Hunter Newman continued to drive balls into the outfield gaps and over the fences. He was more than a solid fielder at both first and third base. Hunter Austin, on the other hand, kept stealing bases, bunting, hitting line drives everywhere, and protecting Trevecca's center field like a soccer goalie.

By mid-March, Hunter Newman had twelve home runs and Hunter Austin was batting .475 and still stealing bases at a record clip. In April, Trevecca's baseball team continued rolling down the track, winning nine out of ten ballgames. In early May, they slid off the track a bit by losing three of their last five games as the ball season concluded.

During the Trevecca baseball season, major-league scouts could be seen with their JUGS guns measuring ball speed and their note pads, electronic notebooks and tablets evaluating the Trojans' players. The Trevecca coaches were frequently asked about a select number of their players' abilities and attitudes. The scouts mainly kept their opinions of an athlete private. But Willie Jackson spent an unusual amount of time following and evaluating Hunter Austin.

One day, Willie brought his boss, David Jennings, to watch Hunter play. Following the game, the two scouts talked about him to the Trevecca coaches. Willie just lit up about what Hunter brought to a baseball team. Jennings played it a little closer to the vest.

"From what I saw today, have read in scouting reports and heard from your coaches," he said, "Hunter has many baseball tools and is a well-rounded player and person. I'll keep my eye on his progress until his college games end this year."

Later, Coach Barnard told Hunter and Savannah that the Orioles were really interested in him.

"I told their scouts that you're the hardest-working, most-dedicated baseball player I've ever coached, and that you still play and practice with a chip on your shoulder for being rejected and overlooked so many times. The Birds were happy to know that you'll work hard to improve and not enter pro ball thinking that you're already 'all that.'"

It was exciting to Hunter and Savannah to know that he was on the major-league scouting radar.

The 2015 Great Midwest Athletic Conference Championship was a four-day tournament scheduled to be played in Mason, Ohio, beginning May 6. There was nothing but warm, beautiful weather in Mason during the tourney played at Prasco Park on the artificial turf of Legacy Field.

Just as in 2014, Hunter's parents and Savannah attended the G-MAC playoff; his grandfather did not feel well enough to make the trip.

Hunter's reunion with his parents was warm enough, but Archie couldn't stop himself from complaining about how much it was costing them to see him play.

"The flight, the car rental and the hotel room all add up. I'll have to push off retirement a few years just to pay my bills."

At dinner, during their first night together, Hunter told his parents he'd made the college's honor roll during the fall semester.

"I always knew you had it in you, Hunter," his father said confidently.

Hunter sat still as heat began to build up in his face. He was suddenly so angry at his father that he thought he would blow. Savannah took one look at his face and said, "Excuse us for a minute, Janet and Archie. Hunter has to help me get something from the car." When Hunter didn't even look at her, she said a little sharply, "Hunter. Come help outside." She took his hand and led him out and around the corner of the building, just in time.

"He has a lot of nerve!" Hunter yelled, trembling, "a lot of nerve to say that now. Dad was the one—he was the one when I was in high school who told me not to plan on going to college because I couldn't make it. He was the one who said I wasn't college material. He was wrong!"

"I know, honey, I know."

"He was wrong." Hunter hit his forehead with the ball of his hand. "He was wrong, and he doesn't get to be right now."

When he'd calmed down, Savannah took his hand gently and said, "Hunter, we've prayed that your father would change. Maybe this isn't about him being right or wrong. Maybe this is God answering your prayer. And maybe you have to give your father a chance to do God's will."

They went back inside, and Savannah said, "Sorry. There was a rip in my dress that Hunter had to help me fix." She smiled brightly and sat down. Janet gave her a look of thanks, and the dinner proceeded with no more fireworks.

Salem International University Tigers were the Trojans' opening round opponent of the double elimination tournament. Trevecca came out playing both small ball and long ball. In the first inning, both their top two batters in the lineup laid down bunt singles. Hunter Newman followed the two thirty-five-foot singles with a 375-foot home run. The Trojans jumped out to a 3–0 lead, and they never gave up the lead. Their pitchers did their jobs, and Trevecca won the game 7–3.

Hunter Austin picked up his third hit of the game in the eighth inning by hitting a fastball on the nose. The Tigers center field made the mistake of taking two steps in when the ball came directly at him. Quickly he realized his mistake and retreated backwards towards the outfield fence. But the ball cleared his head by ten feet and bounced off the fence, more than 400 feet from home plate. The shortstop took the center fielder's relay throw in short center field, turned and threw the ball towards home plate after realizing Hunter had not stopped at third base. The throw was offline as the Trojans leadoff hitter slid across home plate. Hunter had completed his first in-the-park home run of 2015.

Archie sat in the stands, stunned that in each of the three G-MAC tournaments he'd seen Hunter play, he'd hit a home run.

"Hunter hit another home run," he said in disbelief to his wife.

"It's what he does now, Archie," she looked at him with a puzzled frown. "You should know that by now."

"He was always a Punch-and-Judy hitter." Punch-and-Judy was an old school description that meant a hitter who just tried to meet the ball to hit it out of the infield for base hits. They never tried for homers because they lacked the strength or power to hit balls over outfielder's heads. "A home run in every game. I'll be."

When Archie found out the guy sitting next to him was a baseball scout from the Arizona Diamondbacks, he asked him, "What do you think about Hunter Austin?"

The scout made a face. "Hunter's baseball skills don't play out anymore in professional baseball. He rarely drives the ball to the fence, and he can't hit enough home runs. The big leagues are looking for the big boppers now. Guys that can hit between twenty-five to forty home runs a year. Hunter's skills are as outdated as an 8-track tape."

Archie took those as fighting words, and a huge argument ensued in the baseball stands between him and the big-league scout. For once, Archie found himself defending Hunter rather than devaluing him. He was all up in the scout's face and gave him "what for" about his youngest son while Janet tugged his arm and yelled at him to stop. A third man had to separate the men before things got really ugly. When they were pulled apart, Archie's right hand was clenched into a fist, cocked and ready to swing. The scout screamed out a parting shot to Archie by yelling another put-down.

"Any team that drafts Hunter Austin will be hunting elephants with a derringer!"

Red-faced and vibrating with anger, Archie walked over and leaned against the outside of the Trojans dugout. As he concentrated on breathing in and out, he thought about his boy. He'd never been able to see Hunter's talent as the kids grew up because he was always standing in his big brother's vast shadow. Now that both boys were away playing sports, and Hunter was no longer in that shadow, it was becoming clearer just how talented his younger son was as a baseball player. He looked down at his fists, still clenched and ready to punch the scout in the face, ready to defend his boy's reputation, ready for any consequences, and marveled at his transformation.

"Wouldn't Janet have been so mad if they'd thrown me in jail," he said aloud. He chuckled. Then he giggled. Then he started laughing; he was laughing so hard there were tears in his eyes, and he had to bend over because he could barely stand up.

When he'd laughed it all out, he wiped away his tears and said with a huge grin, "Well, isn't this just an ironic kind of day."

14

A MOMENT LIKE THIS (2015)

After the game against Salem International, Coach Barnard got wind of the dust up between Archie and the Diamondbacks' baseball scout and went to talk to Hunter and his parents. Savannah was with them.

"Look, folks," he said, "there's no agreement among the major-league scouts on any of our ballplayers. Their opinions are all over the place on Hunter because he's an unusual talent and a little bit old school. Some of the organizations can't determine how he would fit in on their teams."

He then addressed Hunter directly. "You've got so much speed, Hunter, yet so little power that you don't fit the mold as the ideal professional baseball candidate. But I guarantee you there are a couple of teams who are in love with you. They just aren't admitting it yet."

He turned back to Hunter's parents. "You only hear from them when they don't like you. The one exception is the local scout for the Baltimore Orioles. He's told me some encouraging things about Hunter's game, and he said that he has been sending the O's positive scouting reports on your son."

"That's encouraging," Janet said. "All it takes is one team to draft Hunter and give him a chance. It's all he wants—a chance."

"I've never coached a player who works as hard as Hunter to improve."

Archie stood up straighter and spoke to the coach. "I asked you this last year and I'm asking you again. What are Hunter's odds of getting drafted?"

"I feel very confident that someone will take a chance on Hunter and draft him. Maybe it will be in a lower round, but that's okay. The only disadvantage to being drafted, say in the thirtieth round of the draft as opposed to the third, is a whole lot of money. The bonus money to sign a contract nearly disappears in the lower part of the draft. But you still get your opportunity to play, and if you play well and show potential, you move up in the organization to a higher level of Minor League Baseball. When you level off or do poorly, they release you from the team or trade you.

"I'm not going to sugar-coat it. It's a rough life playing in the minor leagues, and the pay is horrible. But for guys like you, Hunter, it's all you've dreamed about. Hustling every day. Playing ball in dumpy old ballparks. Very long bus rides, poverty-level pay, separation from family and girlfriend, and competing more with your teammates than with your baseball opponents. The emphasis in the minor leagues is not on winning ballgames and championships. The goal is to develop baseball players and support the needs of the organization's major-league team. If the big-league team tells its Triple-A team to teach its third baseman to learn to play the outfield, that's what they do. There isn't a lot of camaraderie among the players because they are in competition for playing time and promotions. If a teammate gets promoted to the next level, there are regrets and jealousy from the players left behind."

It was sobering information and gave Hunter and his family a lot to think about.

The next day, May 7, the Trevecca Trojans played the tournament's second round game against the Kentucky Wesleyan College Panthers. The Trojans starting pitcher dominated the Panthers bats, giving up only six hits and no runs, and Trevecca won 3–0. It was a weird game offensively for Trevecca, as neither of their Hunters reached base, yet their teammates put together enough hits and walks to produce three runs. So, Trevecca advanced to the semifinals of the G-MAC championship and would next play the Ohio Valley University, a team that the Trojans had swept earlier in the season in a four-game series.

The following day, Ohio Valley opened the first inning against Trevecca by scoring four runs. But the Trojans later tied the score at 5–5 and came to bat in the bottom of the ninth inning with the game even. Who led off the last inning? None other than Trevecca's leadoff batter, Hunter Austin. He laid down the prettiest drag bunt towards first base and easily beat the throw for a single. He was moved to second base by a line single to left field. At second base, Hunter was potentially the winning run for Trevecca.

Next up to bat was power hitter Hunter Newman. The temperature was a perfect eighty-two degrees, not a cloud in the sky, and the wind was still. There was tension in the air; it was eerily quiet until Hunter Newman swung at the first ball pitched to him. Then all that could be heard was the *crack* of the bat—the sound of a leather ball being crushed by the sweet spot on an aluminum bat. As the high-flying ball flew outwards from home plate, Hunter Austin went back to second base to tag up in case the ball was caught. He watched with a few hundred fans, and dozens of players and coaches as the ball not only cleared the Legacy Field left-field fence but kept going and going.

"Home run! Home run! Home run! The Trojans win!" screamed the PA announcer. Tournament officials would later estimate that Newman's home run had traveled 440 feet. Trevecca won the game, 8–5, and advanced to the finals of the championship tournament. The Trojans were the lone remaining undefeated team in the tourney.

At dinner that night, Archie surprised his son by complimenting him on his ninth inning drag bunt. He'd been finding it easier to say positive things about his son's ballplaying to other people, but not to Hunter's face. Archie had come to the conclusion, admitting as much to his wife, that change was difficult. On Janet's advice, he'd prayed about his faults and asked God for his forgiveness. He'd also come to the conclusion that it was time to try a bit harder with his youngest son.

Trevecca played Ohio Valley University for the second time the next day, after Ohio Valley won the loser's bracket. To win the championship, the Trojans only had to beat the Jackets once; for Ohio Valley to win, they had to beat Trevecca twice.

Since they'd already beat Ohio Valley five times that year, Trevecca played with confidence. In fact, it looked like they were using the Fighting Scots' pitchers for batting practice. Hunter Austin had his first five-hit ballgame of his life. Three of the base hits were triples, which gave him ten triples for the year.

Due to college baseball's "mercy rule," the home plate umpire stopped the game when the seventh inning was complete, with the Trojans ahead 19–2. Trevecca's celebration broke out at Prasco Park when the Trojans' baseball players dogpiled in the infield and doused each other with water bottles. This year Hunter Austin was on the bottom of the pile—afterwards, he was sore for days from all the knees in the back and elbows to the head. When he hugged Savannah later, he told her he felt as if he'd been mugged.

During a post-game team meeting, Coach Barnard singled out the two Hunters. "These two fine young men with the same name have known nothing but winning seasons and winning conference championships at Trevecca because they both are champions at heart, and they lead by example on the ball field."

Soon after the tournament ended, the Trojans boarded their bus and headed back to Nashville to wait their fate. They didn't know yet whether Trevecca had been selected to play in the NCAA Mideast Regional Tournament. Before the bus pulled out, Hunter said his goodbyes to his parents and Savannah. His dad hugged him for an unusually long time, and then he couldn't bring up the words he wanted to say, he was so choked up. Hunter climbed on the bus and sat at a window seat, his parents and girlfriend standing nearby chatting. Suddenly, Archie got out one of his business cards and an ink pen. Leaning the card on the side of the bus, he wrote a message on the blank side of the card. He knocked on the window to get Hunter's attention and then held the note up to the window where only Hunter could see it. After reading it, Hunter lowered his head for the longest time.

Archie put the business card into his pants pocket as he and Janet got into their rental car. No one asked him what he wrote on it, but the curiosity was killing Janet. That night in their hotel room, she waited for him to empty his pockets and go into the bathroom. Then she picked up the card. It read, "Hunter, I am proud of you, my son."

The Trevecca baseball team pulled into Nashville late at night on May 9, following a long drive home from Mason, Ohio, with an overall record in 2015 of thirty-five wins and eighteen losses, and going undefeated in the G-MAC Championship Tournament. The Trojans wouldn't have long to wait in Nashville to see if they would earn a bid for the NCAA Division II Regional Championship as an at large qualifier.

On May 10, the NCAA Selection Sunday, the Trevecca baseball coaches, staff and players gathered together in their practice facility to learn their fate. The NCAA Division II Baseball Committee selected forty-eight teams to participate in the 2015 NCAA Division II Baseball Championship, but the Trevecca Trojans were not one of them.

The hurt and anguish of the ballplayers was on full display at that moment. Even after a fantastic season and having two amazing players on their squad, they didn't make the cut. No one could understand why. It just didn't make sense to anyone. There were a few walls punched and some tears shed. They thought they had done enough and weren't ready for the rejection that no one, even the coaching staff, could explain.

That Sunday evening, Savannah comforted her guy with a warm meal and a chocolate sundae at a Nashville restaurant. They acknowledged it was time to get packed up and head home.

"The bright side is," Savannah said, "we get to make the final plans for our wedding and honeymoon." And they had to begin planning for the possibility that Hunter could get drafted by a major-league team. They also needed to figure out their living arrangements if Hunter did sign with a professional ball team and move out of town. There might be so much to do in so little time.

The 2015 Trevecca baseball season was another year of high achievement for their program. After playing fifty-six games, the Trojans finished with a record of thirty-six wins and only eighteen losses, winning sixty-four percent of their games. The team batting average was .328. The on-base percentage was .421. The slugging percentage was .484. Trevecca Trojans hit thirty-three home runs. They won the G-MAC Championship Tournament for the third straight year.

Hunter had just completed his most successful season of college baseball yet. He exceeded his previous year's batting average with .530, which was not far off the NCAA all-time season record batting average of .551 achieved by Keith Hagman of the University of New Mexico in 1980. Stealing fifty-six bases in fifty-six games, and 136 stolen bases in three seasons, Hunter became the all-time Trojans career leader in stolen bases. He led the Trojans with ten triples that season, and his defense in center field continued to be excellent as his instincts reacting to batted balls improved. He ran down balls that ordinarily would have resulted in doubles, and his throwing arm produced ten outfield assists. His fielding percentage was .997. Three times during the regular season, he was awarded the Great Midwest Athletic Conference Baseball Player of the Week. After the season was over, he was awarded a position on the All-Great Midwest First Team and was named as an NCAA Division II Second Team All-American.

Trojans' infielder Hunter Newman was also awarded a position on the All-Great Midwest First Team and named as an NCAA Division II Second Team All-American. But most impressive was his selection as the G-MAC Athlete of the Year for all sports. Newman hit eighteen home runs and twenty-one doubles, and drove in seventy-seven runs. His batting average of .451 was the second best on the team.

It was a remarkable honor for the Trevecca baseball program to have two All-Americans on the same team, and the two Hunters were tagged with nicknames by their teammates. Hunter Newman was called "Thunder" because of his power hitting. Hunter Austin was called "Lightning" because of his footspeed.

The Monday after the season ended, Hunter and Savannah packed up their belongings. She felt nostalgic as she took down posters and signs and boxed up her things before their long drive home. After lunch, they walked around campus and said their goodbyes to the few students, professors and coaches. They didn't know if they would be back in Nashville in the fall living as a married couple and attending their senior year at Trevecca or if they'd be living out an adventure with Hunter playing Minor League Baseball in small towns across America.

The two toughest goodbyes for Hunter were to Stephen Collins and Coach Barnard. These men had mentored him, developed him for his future and helped shape many of the important decisions he had made at Trevecca. Stephen led him to the Lord Jesus Christ, and Coach Barnard led him to the verge of being a professional baseball player. Three years ago, Hunter needed positive male role models in his life. At Trevecca, he found them. Now he was going home a grown, disciplined and focused young man. Trevecca Nazarene University and its Christian mentors had prepared him not only for success, but as a beacon of light for a world full of lost sinners.

After turning in the keys for their college dorm rooms, Hunter and Savannah climbed into her Ford Explorer and headed east on Interstate 40 through Knoxville and the Tri-Cities of Tennessee. They always got a thrill out of seeing the "Welcome to Virginia" road sign, even though they were still a long, long way from home. As they traveled north through Virginia, they read practically every sign for any town off of Route 81.

"Bristol, Floyd, Christiansburg, Roanoke, Lexington, New Market, Staunton."

They turned and traveled eastbound on Route 64 nearly all the way to the Atlantic Ocean. Hunter said, "just like the old song, 'East Bound and Down,' we are booking it to the east coast, just as if the Bandit was driving."

Savannah laughed. "Honey, Jerry Reed you will never be."

"Darling," he answered right back, "you can call me the Bandit because I steal so many bases." Laughter filled their vehicle.

They made it home from Nashville on May 12, and soon afterwards Savannah was back at work with her mother, cleaning vacation homes in Sandbridge. Hunter reconnected with his grandfather, Jo Jo and BB at the AA Construction Company. The business continued to thrive under BB's leadership and Anthony was turning a large profit. The best news was that Anthony felt stronger and had fewer headaches than the year before.

As Hunter prepared for his wedding and the MLB draft, he didn't have time to work in the construction business during the summer. But he did have time to hang out with his grandfather, brother and old neighborhood friends. Evelyn seemed to be at his house or at Savannah's house every day working on the wedding's final plans.

Hunter picked up his truck from his grandfather's garage and took Savannah out on a couple of dates each week. They seemed to be falling more in love with each other every day even as they were on the threshold of marriage. Neither of them had any doubts or hesitations about making promises to each other on June 13. They agreed they wanted to fly to the Bahamas for their honeymoon and stay on an island that wasn't touristy or busy. Tranquility and isolation appealed most to them.

They decided to stay on the small island of Treasure Cay, which was in the north of the Great Abaco Islands. They'd fly out of Norfolk, Virginia, to Miami, Florida, and take a connecting flight to the Treasure Cay International Airport, about 200 miles from Miami.

The Great Abaco Island was located about fifty-five miles north of Nassau, the capital of the Bahamas. Green Turtle Cay was one of the barrier islands off the Great Abaco mainland. It could only be reached by a ferry from the mainland or a private boat. Green Turtle Cay was tiny and was about as isolated an island as one could find but still had access to hotels and restaurants.

Hunter took his old high school baseball coach, Coach Collinsworth, out to lunch to bring him up to date on his college baseball, draft prospects and pending wedding.

Before he could talk about the wedding, Coach said, "Hunter, did I hear right? Are you marrying Savannah Montgomery? Could you be that lucky?"

"Yes, I am that lucky, coach!" Hunter said with a laugh. "I knew six years ago that I struck gold when Savannah became my girlfriend. We met down at the oceanfront right after my freshman year. When she started attending Kempsville High a few months later, I'd already locked her up."

Coach took a sip of soda and shook his head. "Man, it's hard to believe it's been six years."

"It's also has been six years since you cut me from the school baseball team."

"You'll never let me live that down! And now you might get drafted to the major leagues next month." They laughed together and they start eating enthusiastically.

"But the truth is," Coach said, "you weren't ready yet for the varsity team. You needed seasoning on the junior varsity level, though you disagreed with me at the time."

"Yeah," Hunter agreed. "I was young and stupid. But that rejection and the chip on my shoulder proved kind of useful. I worked my tail off for the last six years. As Frank Sinatra sang, 'I did it my way.'"

"You sure did, young man."

"It's still hard to believe. I went to college with no scholarship offers and tried out for the school baseball team. Not only did I make the team, but by the fifth game, I was put in the starting lineup. By my sophomore year, I earned a half-scholarship. The team won the G-MAC championship all three years I played there. And twice, we went to the NCAA Division II regionals. Oh, and twice I made the All-Great Midwest First Team, and I was named as an NCAA Division II Second Team All-American this past season. Did I tell you? In my junior season, I batted .530 and stole fifty-six bases?"

"No way! That sounds like you're making this stuff up!"

"No, coach. I promise all of this really happened."

"You mean I can say I coached an All-American baseball player?"

"Yes, sir. And, coach, you know the college accomplishment I'm most proud of? Making the Dean's List in five out of six semesters. I knew I could play baseball, but I never thought I could make A's and B's in college."

"I couldn't be prouder of you if you were my son. Just think, you might soon get paid to play baseball. Hunter, you're the best success story of any of the high school kids I've ever coached. Your achievements remind me of a quote someone sent me. 'The ladder of success is best climbed by stepping on the rungs of opportunity.' That's a quote by Ayn Rand. And now you're on the verge of getting drafted by the major leagues." Both of them sat back, shaking their heads in wonder.

"Are you nervous?" Coach asked. "Do you care which team drafts you?"

"Not really. I'm more excited than nervous. God's going to put me on a team where I need to be. So, wherever I play ball, I'll know I'm there for a purpose."

"That's good, Hunter," Coach said. "To be successful in sports, you can't be scared and or timid. You have to go out there and show everyone you're better than they are."

The 2015 Major League Baseball First-Year Player Draft was held from June 8 to 10. The draft order was the reverse order of the 2014 MLB season standings. The draft contained forty rounds of selections and 1,215 players were drafted by major-league teams. The first two rounds were held on Monday, June 8. Rounds three to ten were held the following day. Rounds eleven to forty followed next on the Wednesday, starting at noon. Only the first draft day had TV coverage, although the entire draft was livestreamed.

The MLB scouting reports tended to agree on how many baseball tools Hunter possessed. The most were five. Baseball officials thought of Hunter Austin as a four-tool player, with the one missing tool being power. The four tools he clearly possessed were speed, hitting for average, fielding and arm strength.

With most of the MLB draft not being on TV, and Hunter's prospects not assured, his father and brother decided not to have a draft party for Hunter. Instead, Archie, Janet and Jo Jo planned to have a fun dinner party for Hunter to celebrate his being an All-American athlete and regularly being on the university's Dean's List. It was held on the evening of the final day of the draft, whether Hunter had or had not been drafted. In a big turn in direction, his father seemed genuinely proud of his youngest son's college accomplishments.

Hunter's party was held during the evening just three days before his wedding. His grandfather, Savannah and her parents, and Evelyn also attended, as well as Coach Collinsworth and a dozen or more of his former high school teammates and neighborhood friends. Twenty people in all. But when the guests arrived at the Austins' house on Manor Drive, Archie wrenched open the door and greeted them with a shout. "Hunter did it! The Baltimore Orioles drafted him. The draft announcement sounded like this: 'The Baltimore Orioles draft Hunter Austin, an outfielder from Trevecca Nazarene University in the eighteenth round.' That's out of forty rounds. My boy did it!"

There was so much to celebrate that night. There were laughs, high-fives, hugs and lots of happy tears. One minute Hunter's mom was laughing, and the next minute she was wiping her eyes.

"My baby boy's success just exploded after high school in a way that no one could have seen coming. I knew that fortune cookie held a message for him the day he was born. 'Perceived failure is oftentimes success trying to be born in a bigger way.'" She continued, warming to the subject. "My boy never lost his childlike love of the game of baseball. Hunter is still excited about going to the ballpark every day. I'm so happy watching him live out his dream."

Hunter didn't know yet where the Orioles wanted him to report to play minor-league ball. But he figured he would start at the bottom of the Baltimore's organization and have to work his way up. If he stalled at any level of the organization, he would likely be released, and his baseball career probably would be over. It would not be an easy road.

Then his father addressed Hunter in front of the guests. "You turned out good, Hunter. Despite my best efforts to keep you from succeeding. My opinion of you, son … is evolving."

Everyone present laughed at that, especially Hunter, and Jo Jo let out a loud cheer. Archie continued, addressing the crowd. "I am very proud to say that I have two sons who are professional athletes. How many other fathers can say that? I seem to be the only one who is surprised by your achievements Hunter. I guess being a realist gets me in trouble sometimes. I hope you continue to exceed my expectations for you and blow through the minor leagues right into the big leagues. As your mom just said, I, too, will be happy to watch you live out your dreams."

Then Hunter received a phone call from Coach Barnard.

"I just got the word that both you and Hunter Newman have been drafted. You in the eighteenth round to the Orioles. Newman to the St. Louis Cardinals in the twenty-second round. It's—" He broke off for a moment, overcome with emotion. "It's such an unforgettable moment for me. Two of my ballplayers make the All-American team and get drafted together … this experience is off the chart."

"I think Newman will be a great pro," Hunter said.

"I think that you will too, Hunter. And I'm not at all surprised that it was the Baltimore Orioles. Their scout was so excited about your skills. But I think, when a coach gets to work with young men like you and Hunter Newman, men full of ability, character and commitment, this day was inevitable, even if it wasn't predictable for you."

The next day, Coach Barnard was interviewed by a Nashville reporter about his two Hunters being drafted by major-league teams. Coach Barnard seemed to enjoy being in front of the camera.

"Now, Hunter Austin," he said, "is a tough-minded, determined guy. He has earned everything that he's gotten or achieved. He plays with an edge that comes from being overlooked on every level of baseball since Little League. Personally, I love him like a son. I wish my kids would work that hard for something."

By Friday, Hunter and Savannah were packing for their honeymoon and he was picking up his wedding tuxedo, bow tie and dress shoes. The wedding rehearsal was held that evening at Savannah's church with friends and family. Following the rehearsal, Archie treated the whole gang to dinner at his favorite steakhouse, Black Angus Restaurant by the oceanfront. He had reserved an entire room so their moments of joy and laughter would not disturb the rest of the restaurant's patrons.

Hunter woke up the next day, his stomach in knots. Saturday, June 13, 2015, would end six years of dating and begin the marriage of Savannah

Montgomery and Hunter Austin. By the end of day, they would be united in the bonds of holy matrimony.

Later in the day, dressed in a charcoal tuxedo, Hunter stood at the altar between the minister and his best man, Jo Jo. Excitement was building as he waited to see his bride in her wedding dress for the first time. To Hunter, it almost felt like waiting for a changeup pitch to get to home plate. He waited, waited and waited. Finally, the door opened, and he connected with Savannah's eyes as she entered the back of the church's sanctuary. When she looked to the side to smile at the guests, for the first time, he noticed her wedding gown. He could only gaze with astonishment. It was like he was looking at an angel dressed all in white. The dress's lace and flirty features spread a big, steady smile on his face. As Savannah paused beside her father at the back of the church, Hunter's eyes traveled over her hair and back to her exquisite face. Processing all the beauty made him feel a bit faint, and he thought his knees were buckling. Jo Jo reached out and put his big hand on his little brother's back to steady him.

The organist began to play "Here Comes the Bride" and Savannah and her father began their well-paced stroll to the front of the church. The congregation all stood and gawked, oohing and aahing at Savannah and her wedding dress as she passed by them.

From then on, everything was a bit of a blur for Hunter. When the minister pronounced them man and wife and instructed him to kiss his bride, he snapped to and laid one on Savannah. He knew they'd exchanged their vows, but at the moment his brain was not in gear. As calm and under control as he appeared on a baseball field, he'd totally lost control of his mind during their nuptials.

As the bridal attendants and ushers marched down the aisle and exited the church, Hunter and Savannah waited their turn. He held on to his bride for dear life, afraid his wobbly legs would fail him. Savannah leaned over and whispered in his ear, "Take deep breaths and let them out." That seemed to help, as did smiling at family and friends as he exited the church.

The fresh June air outside helped clear his head of anxious thoughts, and the memories of what had just occurred came rushing back with clarity, especially when Savannah said, "I do." A silly grin spread over his face as he thought, "She is mine, and I am hers."

The sit-down dinner at the wedding reception was a big hit. Bill Montgomery spared no expense on the food. The wedding cake's icing contained fake seashells and surfboards, a tribute to Savannah and Hunter's love of the ocean, and a remembrance of where they first met and where they got engaged. The cake provided plenty of conversation when the bride and broom cut into it. Instead of the usual vanilla or chocolate cake, their wedding cake had three layers, with each layer a different kind of cake. The bottom layer was lemon cake, the middle layer was red velvet cake and the top layer was carrot cake. In spite of the crowd's urging, there were no shenanigans by the bride or groom as they fed each other a bite of their cake.

Bill, Savannah and Hunter were the only ones in on a little secret at the wedding reception. Dancing was not expected, or even appropriate, at the church, so a DJ wasn't hired to spin dance music after the reception dinner. But Savannah wanted desperately to dance at her wedding reception with her groom. Leading up to the wedding, she couldn't put the thought to bed or take no for an answer. So, Bill ignored the church's policies and made plans for one, and only one, dance after the reception dinner between husband and wife. He made arrangements with the three-piece instrumental band he had hired to play dinner mood music to play a pre-recorded song through their speakers.

Following the reception dinner and good-luck speeches by the wedding party, Hunter and Savannah got up and walked towards the band. She put her arms around Hunter's neck and as the pre-recorded music began, they kissed and then they started slow dancing to Leona Lewis' version of "A Moment Like This."

"Everything changes, but beauty remains. Something so tender I can't explain. Well, I may be dreaming but till I awake. Can we make this dream last forever? And I'll cherish all the love we share. A moment like this. Some people wait a lifetime for a moment like this. Some people search forever for that one special kiss. Oh, I can't believe it's happening to me. Some people wait a lifetime for a moment like this."

By the end of the song, there were not many dry eyes in the room.

15

FOR THE BIRDS (2015)

As Hunter and his bride road away from their well-wishers, they waved and waved. Anthony Austin drove them to the Hampton Inn near the airport and dropped them there for the night. A shuttle service would take them to the Norfolk airport the next day for their flight to Miami. For what seemed like the hundredth time, Hunter and Savannah thanked his grandfather for paying for their honeymoon trip.

"Now kids," Anthony said, "you know what they say, 'Be good.'" Then he leaned in and whispered, "But not too good." With a wink and a wave, he was off and their honeymoon had truly begun.

Once inside their room, the honeymooners hung a "Do Not Disturb" sign on the door handle and double-locked the door. On their first night of marriage, they never heard the busy street noises or the party revelers returning to their rooms nearby. They were lost in their love for each other.

The next day, the flight to the Bahamas was a full-day affair. It was many hours of hanging around airports, changing planes, flying and then boating to their destination. Landing at the small airport in the Bahamas, Hunter and Savannah were blown away by how small the islands looked and the rich turquoise color of the ocean water. A short ferry ride took them to Green Turtle Cay on the northern Great Abaco. Their hotel was called the Green Turtle Club Resort and Marina.

Green Turtle Cay was one of the barrier islands off the mainland of Great Abaco. It could only be reached via ferry from the mainland or by boat. Green Turtle Cay was only three miles long and a half mile wide. It was an isolated island that wasn't touristy or loud, just what Savannah had hoped for. The peace and tranquility during their honeymoon were like heaven to the newlyweds. They found the island beautiful and the houses, with their white picket fences, charming. Most people got around the narrow streets by golf carts, so Hunter rented one for the week.

He and his wife spent many lazy hours hanging out at the hotel pool and on the nearly deserted beaches. When they first stepped onto a Bahamas beach, they thought their eyes were fooling them because the white sand had a pink tint to it. One day, they paid for a three-hour ride on a catamaran sailboat and another day they rented stand up paddle boards to ride on the shallow water.

Savannah and her new husband feasted each day on scrumptious lunches and dinners. Nearly every meal they ate was seafood. The fresh seafood in the Bahamas tasted like food that existed only in someone's imagination.

The Green Turtle Club Resort and Marina had a delightful restaurant with a screened-in porch overlooking the marina. Hunter loved watching the sailboats coming in and heading out. The restaurant had one interior room where the walls were covered with dollar bills. It was a tradition for customers to leave a dollar bill with their name signed on it and pin it to the wall.

On Sunday, June 21, the newlyweds boarded a plane back to the United States. It had been a glorious, unforgettable trip. As they listened to the whine of the jet's engines, they both agreed to return to the Bahamas someday. They spent most of the trip north looking at pictures in their cell phones they'd taken on their honeymoon and reminiscing about the special moments.

As they approached Virginia at 10,000 feet and began descending, the sun was setting off to the west. Reality started to sink in that their honeymoon had come to an end, and there were huge question marks waiting for them when they got home. They had not rented somewhere to live because of the uncertainty of Hunter's future. He had not yet signed a professional contract with the Baltimore Orioles. Questions abounded for them: Should he sign with an agent to negotiate his first contract or go it alone? Where would his first ball team be located once he signed on the dotted line? Most of the Baltimore Orioles farm clubs were in Maryland. Wherever he went, Hunter had to find a place to live in some unknown town. They weren't sure if Savannah would go with him all summer on his baseball journey or if she would stay home, working with her mother to earn some money. If she went with Hunter, he'd have to get a short-term rental large enough for the two of them. There were so many questions and yet so little time to arrange for their immediate future.

When Hunter and Savannah walked into her parents' house, Robin and Bill were shocked at their tans.

"Look at you!" her dad said. "All rested and happy."

"Your wedding photographer dropped off your photo proofs yesterday," her mom told her daughter excitedly, "and, Savannah, they are stunning."

"Mom, I can't wait to see them, but we are exhausted from a boat ride and two plane trips today. I really want to get some sleep. We can go through the pictures tomorrow."

Hunter called his parents' house and spoke to his father, mainly to let them know they were home safe.

"Two packages arrived by FedEx from the Orioles," Archie told him.

"I'll come by tomorrow, Dad, and look at them. I bet one of them is a contract offer. I'm a little anxious about that."

The next morning, as they sipped their coffee, Savannah and Hunter looked at the wedding proofs along with Robin, which resulted in many laughs, sighs and a tear or two. Robin helped them pick the ones they wanted to get retouched and printed as the final pictures of their wedding day.

Hunter called his granddaddy to let him know how much they had enjoyed the honeymoon. Anthony mentioned the loan he had provided to Hunter to pay for Savannah's rings and to buy furniture to set up their first apartment was paid in full.

"But, Granddaddy, why would you do that?" Hunter asked in shock.

"Simply because I love you. I played Minor League Baseball for a few years, Hunter. You won't make much money in the minor leagues. Then in the off-season, which last about seven months, you'll likely have to find a job to pay your bills. I know Savannah wants to complete her college degrees, so she won't be in a position to contribute much until she graduates with her master's degree and lands a good job. You have earned the opportunity to play pro ball. I don't want you guys to worry about where your next meal is coming from or if you can pay your bills or not. Take the business pickup truck with you wherever you go, Hunter. It's yours to keep."

Hunter felt so blessed. Both he and Savannah knew how uncertain his future was as a ballplayer. They wondered how many years the team would give him to make it on the major-league roster before they cut him loose. Everyone had warned him that the pay was paltry compared to the big leagues. In the minors, they only paid for the few months players actually played.

After getting off the phone with his grandfather, Hunter jumped up.

"Savannah, let's go to my parents' house and read the baseball contract. I think I'm ready to see it." At that point, they had no idea how much the Orioles were willing to pay him for his inaugural baseball season or if they were offering him a bonus to sign a contract or not.

When Hunter and his family sat down at his family's dining room table, they took a moment to stare at the FedEx.

"Honey," Hunter said nervously, "come sit down with me. We'll need to read them thoroughly and make some notes."

Before he pulled the packages open, he asked everyone to bow their head and pray for God's will in that moment and in his future. "Jesus," he prayed, "I'm nervous about opening the packages and reading what's inside. I ask for Your will in my and Savannah's future. I ask for Your wisdom to help me make good decisions because every decision I make off of the ball field affects two people now, not just myself."

"Amen," Janet replied.

The first envelope was a welcome package from the Baltimore Orioles. It explained the MLB organization, the team's management hierarchy and the hierarchy of the minor-league system. There was jargon about doing things the Orioles way and it gave some hints on what they were. And there was a huge amount of information about each minor-league team's city, hotels, restaurants and bars. Most importantly, there was information about hooking up with each minor-league team's "host families" who opened up their homes each ball season to one or more Baltimore minor-league players.

Staying with a host family helped offset the low salaries that minor-league players received. They were not paid during spring training or the offseason. Those who did not receive lucrative signing bonuses often struggled to afford meals, rent and basic equipment like cleats, gloves and bats.

The second envelope from the Orioles contained a contract, an offer letter highlighting the terms and conditions of a minor-league contract, and specific instructions to report to a particular minor-league team ASAP once the contract was signed by both parties.

The Orioles offered Hunter a $100,000 signing bonus to sign his rookie contract and to give up his amateur athletic eligibility to play college baseball.

He stopped reading to say to his family, "It's a $100,000 signing bonus."

He was to be paid a weekly salary of $300 for the remaining of the summer. Since there were only about nine weeks left in the summer, he would be paid $2,700 for the season. His baseball equipment (glove, ball cleats, bats and batting gloves) had to be paid by the ballplayer, so Hunter didn't see himself earning much at all. But he and Savannah felt blessed that he'd been offered a $100,000 signing bonus. Putting that in the bank would give them something to fall back on in the current year and in future years while he played in the minor leagues.

"For 2015, I'm assigned to play in the Class A Short Season at Aberdeen, Maryland, for the IronBirds." Aberdeen was a small city of 15,000 residents located twenty-six miles northeast of Baltimore.

After reading everything the Baltimore Orioles sent him, Hunter woke his brother up and had him join the family discussion about the deal and team assignment he'd been offered. Jo Jo was appalled at the low salary.

"But your perspective is kind of flawed," Hunter said. "Professional football doesn't have developmental situations like baseball. What do you think, Dad?"

"Let's ask your grandfather to drop by. In fact, I'll go pick him up." And he grabbed his keys and left.

Hunter just wasn't sure. He didn't know if he should accept the offer or reject it, or if he should hire an agent to negotiate a better deal. He kept thinking that if he signed with an agent, the agent would get a cut of any deal he signed with Baltimore, and any improvement to the contract's bottom line might not be better than their original offer. Jo Jo quickly got his own agent for his professional football contract on the phone and asked for his opinion. Savannah called her parents to come over too.

Soon both families were together. Archie ordered pizza delivered by Pizza Hut, and they ate as they listened to each other's input.

Jo Jo said, "My agent told me that since the dollar amount of any initial Minor League Baseball contract you receive is minuscule, he recommends not paying an agent to negotiate for you."

"I think you should just nix the contract offer and return to college and get your degree," Bill said. Robin nodded in agreement. In other words, give up his dream of being a professional ballplayer. It seemed they were mainly worried about their daughter's financial future.

Archie pursed his lips and then said, "I think you should go for it." Janet and Savannah agreed. "You need to live out your dream of playing professional baseball," Savannah said. "I've spent six years telling you that you could be anything you wanted to be and do anything you put your mind to. I'm not about to change my tune now just because I've seen in black and white how little money you'd be paid to play baseball. In fact, I can give up completing college to get a full-time job to help support us."

"No way!" everyone yelled.

Hunter spoke up. "Honey, you have your dreams too, and you've earned the right to achieve them just as I have. I don't see why we can't both keep striving and working to make our dreams come true. Let's put our heads together later and figure this out."

After additional dialogue among the family, Hunter's grandfather spoke a word of wisdom about shooting for one's goals and dreams. Archie said, "A basketball player misses every shot that he doesn't take!"

He pushed his paper plate away and told the gathering, "My decision, if Savannah approves, is to accept the contract offered by Baltimore, take the signing bonus and put it in the bank."

Savannah nodded her head and gave him two thumbs up. His dad thumped him on the back. "Congratulations, son." His mom gave him a hug. His brother high-fived him.

"It's the right decision, my boy," his grandfather said. "Remember your passion."

With a big smile, Hunter said, "As soon as I return the contract to the Orioles, I can leave for Maryland to start my career. In the meantime, Savannah and I will talk and decide what's going to happen next. I just want to thank you all for coming over, and remember to keep us in your prayers."

Savannah asked her mother if there was any way she could work full-time for the cleaning business while attending college remotely.

"Of course, dear. But business really slows down at the beach from October until Memorial Day, so I wouldn't have many hours for you in the off season. But in the summer, you could ramp your hours back up."

"And I could still continue working for AA Construction when I'm not playing ball," Hunter said, jumping into their conversation, "could I, Grandaddy?" His question was answered affirmatively.

"See, we can make it work," Savannah said. She also had one more important question to ask her parents in front of everyone. "Mom, Dad, could Hunter and I stay with you in your house on a more long-term basis as he tries to make a go of it in baseball, and I try to finish college? If we don't have to rent a place, it would help us a lot, and it would make us more mobile in case Hunter gets promoted to another farm team or is traded to a team in another state."

"Of course," Robin said. "We have two guest rooms and there's plenty of space."

"I can't get over how uncertain the future is for you guys," Bill said, crossing his arms and frowning. "You don't know for sure if Hunter will stay with Baltimore for even a full season. His contract could get canceled or he could get traded to another team. You don't know what the Orioles will do with him next year, or even next month. I know it's all so exciting, but I'm worried."

"Daddy, we have to do this," Savannah said. "It's Hunter's dream."

"What about your dream, sweetie?"

"I have everything I want for now. Hunter has to strike while the iron is hot."

Hunter laid out the baseball contract on the dining room table and signed it in front of both families as they took pictures of the momentous occasion. Savannah wrapped her arms around him and laid her head on his shoulder.

"You did it, baby," she murmured. "You are finally a professional baseball player." She knew about all the work, sweat, victories, defeats, praise and criticism he'd experienced preparing for this moment. She could not possibly be prouder of her man for overcoming obstacles and taking control of his future.

There was a round of applause and then everyone was hugging each other.

"Buddy," Archie said, "I never thought it was possible for you to be a professional ballplayer. I've never been so happy to say I was wrong."

"I'm so proud of you, my stubborn boy," Janet said.

Hunter and Savannah got into his truck with the baseball contract in hand and made their way to a FedEx store to overnight his contract back to the Orioles. Then they celebrated with hot fudge sundaes at the Carvel ice cream store. Next, he called Coach Collinsworth and Coach Barnard to tell them he'd signed a contract with the Orioles and would be playing for the Aberdeen IronBirds in the Class A Short Season League. He thanked his coaches for all that they did to prepare him for this moment. Finally, Hunter and Savannah sat and discussed how she should finish her degree.

They decided he would go to Maryland by himself and spend the summer with one of the IronBirds host families, if there was a spot available, while Savannah lived at her parents' home. Since she was on a full academic scholarship at Trevecca, it made no sense to transfer to another college for senior year and pay tuition. The next day, she called her class advisor at Trevecca and got approval to complete her degree work online and apply for a student teaching position in Virginia Beach or Chesapeake, Virginia.

The Orioles front office confirmed with Hunter that his contract had been received and signed by the team. He was given two days to report to Aberdeen and find a place to stay for the season. His first official act with his new team was to take a physical exam. Thursday morning, June 25, Hunter loaded his pickup truck with baseball gear, a couple of suitcases of clothes, his pillow and a framed picture of his wife standing on the beach in the Bahamas wearing a sundress with her hair blowing in the wind.

Hunter had said goodbye to his parents, grandfather, brother and dog the night before. Just before he left for Maryland, he said goodbye to Bill and Robin. Then Savannah walked him outside to his truck. This was the toughest goodbye of his life. He'd no sooner married the girl than he was leaving her. They embraced for what seemed like an hour; he just couldn't let go of her.

"Honey," he said to his bride, "I have the two things I want the most, you and baseball, yet they can't coexist for the time being. This is so hard."

Savannah spoke words of wisdom to her husband. "You don't have to understand the plan to trust that God has a purpose for your life. And when destiny calls, don't let it go to voice mail."

That evening, driving into Aberdeen, Hunter checked into a cheap hotel that had "left the light on for him." He ordered Chinese for dinner. As he finished eating, he cracked open a fortune cookie and read its message. "A great pleasure in life is doing what others say you can't." He sat back against the bed's headboard and wondered to himself, "How many people really believed I could be a professional baseball player?" His wife did. But, despite the faith she had in him and how much she loved him, she didn't fully understand how difficult it was to get drafted and climb up through the levels of minor-league ball. And surely, she didn't understand how difficult the last hurdle would be to climb over to get the call to the major leagues. Before dropping off to sleep, he had one final thought about his new path.

"The next few years should be quite an adventure."

On Friday, Hunter checked into the Aberdeen IronBirds baseball facilities and was immediately put through his physical exam. With that out of the way, the team's administrative assistant helped him complete human resources documents, such as tax and insurance forms. She asked him if he had made any long-term housing arrangements for the remainder of the summer. When he shook his head, she offered to get him set up with a team host family. It seemed there was a family that already had one IronBirds player bunking in with them, and they had room for one more. The team's front office staff called their official "host nest coordinator" and arranged to have Hunter stay with Eddie and Sarah Jones. The Joneses had a lovely two-story home. Hunter would get his own bedroom with a TV and cable and would share a bathroom with DJ Stewart, the other IronBirds ballplayer. After playing baseball for Florida State University, DJ was one of the Baltimore Orioles' two first-round draft pick in the same draft Hunter Austin was in.

The IronBirds baseball team was away playing in Lowell, Massachusetts, for a few days, and their next home game wasn't for two more days. Hunter went to the team's locker room and found a locker with his name on it. He stuffed his baseball gear into it, sat a framed picture of Savannah on the top shelf and hung up a quote from Coach Vince Lombardi, "The price of success is hard work, dedication to the job and the determination that, whether we win or lose, we have applied the best of ourselves to the task at hand." Finally, he put on some practice clothes and found the indoor batting cages.

After hitting balls for an hour, he went out onto the Ripken Stadium field and ran sprints. He spotted the grounds crew mowing the grass. He loved the smell of a freshly mowed lawn. He stopped one the workers and talked him into playing catch with him. After a break for lunch, Hunter located the team's weight room and began an extended workout. The next day, he was back at the ballpark repeating the same activities from the day before. After dinner, he called his wife, said his prayers and hit the bed hard. The next day, he would meet his coaches and teammates and start his professional baseball career.

Hunter laid in bed but sleep wouldn't come. His mind rotated from his new team to his new wife. When he was away from Savannah, he could hear her voice in his ear, smell her scent and imagine her smile.

Sunday, June 28, 2015, Hunter arrived at the Ripken Stadium, got out of his truck, and fought back his nerves by holding his head up high as to say, "I belong in professional baseball." He walked confidently into the IronBirds' baseball locker room. There was already a dozen or so player milling around as Hunter opened his locker, all the while he was trying to pretend that this moment was no big deal to him. Inside he was freaking out while thinking that for the first time someone would pay him to play baseball, or in the case of today, sit on the bench. This tall, handsome ballplayer, already in his game uniform, walked up to Hunter and introduced himself. "Hi, I'm Tanner Scott. I'm the starting pitcher today."

Hunter replied, "Hey, I'm Hunter Austin, and I hope to catch all the fly balls you throw."

Another player joined the conversation. "Yo, I'm Cedric Mullins. I'm the team's center fielder and leadoff hitter." Hunter's heart sunk. Cedric played the same outfield spot as Hunter and most of the time Hunter had been his previous teams' leadoff hitter.

Hunter said, "Man, I thought I was going to be the smallest guy here. You're shorter than I am!"

As Hunter later sat by his locker, taking it all in, the point wasn't lost on him that the real competition in the minor leagues was among the players competing for playing time, positions and promotions to higher leagues. The focus in the minor leagues was on player development, not winning ball-games. A minor-league team's two goals were to meet its major-league team's needs and develop baseball players.

Hunter tried to pick the right time to go into the coaches' offices to meet them for the first time. After he'd put it off as long as he could, he dragged himself down the hall and into the manager's office where there were four or five older men having a planning meeting. When the manager spotted Hunter, he put out his hand and said, "You must be Hunter Austin. I'm Luis Pujols. I'm the skipper on this team." He and the other coaches shook Hunter's hand and welcomed him to the IronBirds.

"We've heard how fast you can run," Pujols said, "and what a strong throwing arm you have. We read the pre-draft scouting report on you and management thinks you can be developed into a good professional. We're excited about working with you this summer to refine your game."

Hunter was impressed with how welcoming they were and that they understood how nervous he would be playing pro ball for the first time. Pujols told him that he was going to break him in slowly, so he could get his feet wet and catch up to the pitching he would face.

"The teams already played ten games, so you're a little behind everyone else. You'll have to get use to wood bats, and I know you haven't played a game in weeks."

One of the assistant coaches helped Hunter fill out an order for half a dozen wooden bats with the specifications he wanted. He was told it would take a week or two to get his bats and that the team would deduct the cost from his paycheck.

"In the meantime," a coach said, "you'll have to ask around the clubhouse and find another player who uses a similar bat and borrow it for the time being."

When Hunter returned to his locker, a uniform had been hung up for him for that night's ballgame. He turned it around to see the back. "AUSTIN 11."

"Wow," Hunter said, "that was my number in college."

He thoroughly enjoyed batting practice and outfield practice before his first pro game against the Batavia Muckdogs. After a few weak swings, he warmed up with the wooden bat and drove some line drives to all fields. At first, he was nervous because he felt like all eyes were on him, checking out his swing. But success breeds more success, and soon Hunter wasn't nervous at all. Instead, he was having fun doing what he loved to do: play baseball.

Hunter and Cedric enjoyed shagging fly balls together, and they soon became friends. They were the two fastest baseball players on the IronBirds team. Cedric threw left-handed and Hunter threw right-handed. Hunter batted left-handed while Cedric was a switch hitter. After home games, they could be seen climbing into Hunter's pickup truck and heading off to grab a bite to eat. They were together so much, their teammates stuck them with the nickname "Salt 'n' Pepper."

Hunter rode the pine for his first three games. He was lucky to even dress for the games as the IronBirds had thirty ballplayers on their roster and could only dress twenty-five for each game. Since Hunter had missed all pre-season practices and the team's first ten games, the coaches spent a lot of time with him before the games, evaluating his play. They were immediately impressed with his instincts in the outfield, his big throwing arm and how fast he ran. Even though these were strengths, the coaches worked with him on his approach to stealing bases and gave him practice at all three outfield positions, not just center field. His outfield defensive coach told him that being proficient in left, right and center fields would make him more valuable to the Baltimore Orioles and increase his value as a major-league prospect.

After not getting on the field for the team's first thirteen baseball games, Hunter's name was finally written in the starting lineup on the chalkboard in the locker room for the July 1 game against Staten Island being played in Aberdeen. He was batting second and playing right field.

As he stood there, ready to play, for some reason the national anthem sounded better that night to him. The stadium lights looked brighter too. Hunter ran out to take his position in right field for the first time as a pro, but with the passion of a Little Leaguer. No matter what team Hunter played on at the high school level or higher, he always had three things: a locker, long odds and a little boy's love of the game.

In the bottom of the first inning, Hunter heard his name called by the stadium PA announcer.

"Batting second for the IronBirds, and playing right field, number 11, Hunter Austin."

Hunter was still in the "pinch me" phase of his game. Every first thing that occurred that evening made him smile like a three-year-old on Christmas morning. He was so nervous up at the plate, he let two balls go by that were called strikes. Behind in the count, he fought off a couple of borderline pitches to stay alive. Then he timed up an outside fastball and grounded a single between third and short. Since Hunter felt like he was under the spotlight by his new coaches, he was too scared to try to steal second base. Good thing too, as the IronBirds number three hitter, Ryan Mountcastle, hit the third pitch to him over the left-field fence for a two-run home run.

Hunter slowly got over his case of nerves as the game progressed, and he was having the time of his life. He kept repeating to himself during the game, "Can you imagine that they are paying me to play baseball? I would do this for nothing!"

Through the month of July, Hunter was a sometimes starter and other times a reserve, where he would pinch-run, pinch-hit or play defense during the last inning or two of the ballgames. Even though he wasn't getting full playing time, he put in long hours practicing with his coaches on the finer points of baseball. Hunter also opened and closed the weight room each day. He proved to be a workout warrior, who was turning his five-foot-nine body into a beast.

Hunter and Cedric shared center field playing opportunities. They had similar skill sets—Cedric hit for more power, but Hunter had the better throwing arm and more footspeed—and they were clearly competitors for those defensive and offensive positions. Their manager, Luis Pujols, shuffled them around in the outfield with Cedric primarily playing left field when he wasn't in center and Hunter in right field when he wasn't in center. Both players were considered "plus defensive center fielders."

While adjusting to the wood bats, new environment, coaches and teammates, Hunter found himself off to a slow start at the plate. After batting his weight (.175) for the first four weeks of his season, he went on a twelve-game hitting streak. He got eighteen hits and twelve bases on balls during the streak, showing he was being patient in the batter's box. Even in his limited amount of playing time, he stole eight bases.

"Austin looks like a leadoff hitter to me," manager Pujols kept pointing out to the bench coach.

By the end of July, Pujols swapped Hunter and Cedric in the batting order—one to the two-hole and two to the one-hole. Cedric was on an extra base binge with many doubles and triples, so moving him down a notch would create more RBI opportunities for him. Hunter was finding so many ways to reach first base by base on balls, bunting and spraying singles to every field.

Although Cedric and Hunter were good friends, there was an underlying current of wanting to do better than the other. It was a bit like sibling rivalry between two athletic brothers who were nearly the same age. They might ride around town together, but they'd beat each other up playing one-on-one basketball in the driveway. No one wants to lose to their brother. Cedric and Hunter were such good teammates and buddies that one of their coaches tabbed them "brothers from different mothers."

The most challenging thing for Hunter, though, was being away from Savannah. Sometimes, he tried to tell her on the phone how much he missed her, but he often couldn't find the words to describe his feelings. One time, though, he found the words for her.

"Savannah, it's like I've been separated from my heart. I've given you my heart and both you and my heart are in Virginia, and I'm in Maryland." She was his whole world.

Savannah had locked up a student teaching gig in the fall at Landstown High School in Virginia Beach. Consequently, she was set up to complete her senior year of college through Trevecca Nazarene University by May of 2016. In the second semester of her senior year, she would take classes remotely via the internet. Savannah would do her student teaching assignment during the first semester of 2015. She was busy working with her mother that summer, going to church and visiting Hunter's grandfather. She reported to Hunter that Granddaddy's health was steady but had not improved and that he seemed to enjoy her visits. She also told him that Jo Jo and his neighbor Evelyn had been good friends to her in his absence, taking her surfing and to Dave and Buster's to play arcade games.

Hunter headed for the ballpark around 2:00 p.m. each day to prepare for the night's game, and he left the ballpark around 11:00 p.m. following the games. He and some buddies would stop on the way home to eat a late meal. The Greene Turtle Sports Bar and Grille in Aberdeen stayed open until midnight and had killer food. It was a favorite of the IronBirds. The day after a home ballgame, Hunter would sleep late and grab brunch before heading off to Ripken Stadium. There was usually a spread of food for both teams in the ballpark's clubhouses and locker rooms provided by the home team's clubhouse manager. Although it was free to the players, they usually left tips for the clubhouse person. On the road, players would have to brown bag it.

There were other new challenges for Hunter. The environment in professional baseball was like nothing else he'd ever faced before. The players were more competitive and wasted time (it seemed to Hunter) throwing digs and criticism at each other. In high school and college, coaches had emphasized teamwork and respect for each other. There was no "we are a family" theme in pro ball, it seemed to Hunter. As well, the cursing and dirty jokes in the professional locker rooms and dugouts made him cringe at times. "You're not at a Christian university anymore," he would tell himself.

The biggest challenge proved to be the long bus rides to play against opponents. They traveled in the IronBirds charter buses to places like New York, Connecticut, Massachusetts, Ohio, Pennsylvania, West Virginia and even Vermont. The hotels they stayed in certainly didn't have five-star ratings, and the players had to lug all their bags on and off the buses.

"Traveling's for the birds," Cedric said. "Not the IronBirds or Baltimore Orioles, just birds in general."

Savannah, Archie and Janet traveled from Virginia Beach to Aberdeen to watch Hunter play three ballgames against the Hudson Valley Renegades over three days in August. Hunter's dad paid for two hotel rooms. For Hunter and Savannah, it was nearly honeymoon part two, as they hadn't seen each other for six weeks.

Hunter and the IronBirds played well while his family was in town. The team won two of their three games, and Hunter went yard with a 400-foot home run to right-center field. He also had four singles and two stolen bases. After six weeks of professional baseball, he was once again playing with confidence.

The highlight of his family's visit was when his dad told him he'd exceeded anyone's expectations for him as a baseball player.

"Who would have thought you could play ball like you did this week in professional baseball? I am truly blown away, Hunter."

Archie also enjoyed meeting a few of the IronBirds, but he couldn't get over how big Hunter's house buddy was. As was his style, Archie asked DJ Stewart a series of personal questions.

DJ laughed. "I'm six feet tall, and I weigh 230 pounds. I went to Florida State."

Archie asked Hunter to introduce him to the IronBirds manager, so he arranged a short meeting near the ballpark's entrance before one of the ballgames. Luis Pujols was cordial and complimentary about Hunter.

"About your son, the kid is just so alive and detailed-oriented. He wants to play baseball perfectly. The hardest thing to do in sports is to hit a round ball with a round bat and hit it squarely on a line. Hunter hits more balls on the nose than any other player on our team. He is very difficult for our opponents to get out, and with his ball selection abilities, he walks a lot, which sets up his base-stealing opportunities. There are just so many ways he can impact a game."

As the weekend trip wound down, and his family was loading Archie's car for their trip home, Hunter pulled Savannah around the other side of his truck to kiss her goodbye. She looked so amazing that morning. He stared at her for several heartbeats before any words could come out of his mouth. Savannah could leave any man speechless. They said "goodbye" and "I love you" and then she walked toward Archie's car. Hunter watched her walked away, mesmerized.

He finished the short season batting .290 with three triples, four home runs, forty-five bases on balls and twenty-two stolen bases. The IronBirds ended the season with a record of forty wins and thirty-six losses, second in the league's McNamara Division. After the IronBirds' last game on September

7, Hunter emptied his locker and loaded up his truck. Four-and-a-half hours later, he was rolling into his in-laws' driveway in Virginia Beach.

16

GRIT AND GRIND (2015–2016)

With his 2015 ball season ended, Hunter was sitting at his grandfather's kitchen table discussing how his baseball career was going.

"It sounds like you're on your way, Hunter. I played three years in the minor leagues' A level and could never improve enough to move up. They'll probably give you at least three years to make the Double-A level before they give up on you. The fact that you hit .290 is a feather in your hat. Not too many guys do well their first year in pro ball. There are so many new challenges, like using wooden bats for the first time, the long bus rides, low pay and playing ballgames every day instead of just a few games on the weekend like in college."

That fall, his grandfather paid for him to hire a personal trainer and dietitian that his brother used. Hunter met with his dietician twice a month and his trainer twice a week, and worked out by himself a couple days a week. He also ran up and down the steep hill of Mount Trashmore over and over again. He could tell it was really developing his quads. He wanted to get the most strength possible out of his five-foot-nine, 175-pound body. He also found time during his training regiments to run sprints on level ground and to do agility running drills. What he didn't do a lot of in the beginning of his off-season was hit or throw.

In the fall of 2015, Hunter was invited by the Baltimore Oriole organization to participate in their three-week fall instructional league at Sarasota, Florida. The list of baseball trainees included nearly sixty prospects (new draftees and free agent signees, recent international signings and players at the bottom rungs of their organizational ladder). The fall camp was scheduled to use the many baseball fields at the Ed Smith Stadium complex and Buck O'Neil Complex at Twin Lakes Park and was to have an instructional league type of feel. The fall program focused on specific individual development and provided playing practice games, which could have accelerated player's progress through the minor league system.

The Orioles gave him a player development plan to follow during the instructional league period. He was given exercises to do on the field to improve his footwork running the bases and to increase the efficiency of his movements in the outfield. And there were individual batting drills for him to work on in a batting cage, including hitting off of a tee and on the field, such as swinging at front flips.

On October 11, in Atlanta, Georgia, Savannah and his parents attended the Atlanta Falcons' football game against the Washington Redskins. The Redskins were the Austin family's favorite team but, as Jo Jo played for Atlanta who was the Redskins' opponent, they had to root for the Falcons. The game had an exciting finish. The Falcons won 25–19 in overtime on a fifty-nine-yard interception return.

While in Atlanta, Archie asked Hunter if he was ready to go out into the world and get a real job. An argument broke out when Archie insisted that he was just trying to be supportive.

"I'm just worried about you. Didn't Bill Montgomery say the exact same thing? He didn't even want you to sign the contract."

"This isn't about Bill," Hunter said with anger. "It's about your inability to be supportive."

"Why does everyone get down my throat?"

"Mr. Austin," Savannah said, "what is the matter with you? Hunter has exceeded everyone's expectations in baseball. Why can't you be a fan of his, like the rest of the family?"

"Can we all talk about something nice?" Janet asked, ever the peacemaker. "I just want us all to have a good time."

After the games, Hunter went straight back to Sarasota and rejoined the instructional league that was still in progress—he'd had such a successful season in Aberdeen that the Baltimore organization agreed to let him have a few days off to watch his brother play football.

Hunter was glad to be back in Florida and a thousand miles from his father. One day, Baltimore Orioles' executives, dressed in khakis and golf shirts, were on the field watching Hunter and his teammates practice. The Orioles brain trust—General Manager Dan Duquette, Farm Director Brian Graham and Scouting Director Gary Rajsich—were evaluating their recent draftees, free agents and international signees up close. Hunter was taking batting practice in his second set of three rounds. The three executives stood next to the batting cage as Hunter smoked baseballs all over the field. If a pitch was away from him, he hit the ball just over the shortstop's head. If it was inside, the ball was pulled over the second baseman's head. If a pitch was down the middle, the batted ball screamed past the pitcher and landed behind second base. If Hunter decided to not swing level, he jerked the ball against the outfield fence. Even though batting practice pitches weren't burning up JUGS guns, Dan Duquette was still impressed with Hunter's ability to square up nearly every pitched ball and how he used the whole field as his playground. While Hunter was batting, Duquette kept shaking him head and making comments to his cohorts. The look on their collective faces was pure joy.

The three men made a point to meet and chat with each player as soon as they were finished hitting. As Hunter was removing his batting gloves, Duquette motioned him over.

"You looked like you were having fun out there."

Hunter smiled. "I was having a semireligious experience doing the thing I love doing the most—barreling up baseballs."

The men laughed, and Brian Graham asked him, "If it was a religious experience, is the ball diamond your cathedral?" That cracked them up.

"Great round of batting, son," Duquette said. "Your last coaching staff in Aberdeen completed their end of the season evaluation reports. They had a lot of positive things to say about you, Hunter. The team really got into the weeds, so to speak, in breaking down who and what each ballplayer is. There are things you wouldn't even think about on your eval reports, like how special your lateral quickness and acceleration is, all which are great attributes for an outfielder.

"We knew coming into the 2015 Short A season that you were the fastest guy in the organization, and you had one of the biggest arms of the position players. Austin Hays also has a gun for an arm. So, even though the final report on you discussed those, it wasn't new information to us. But a couple new things caught our attention, like, your leadership skills and how hard you practice and grid every day to improve. The two things that jumped off the page for us were about how amazing your eye–hand coordination is and how low your swing and miss rate is. I would guess the two are related. By the way, Hunter, what are your vision numbers?"

"20/10."

"My gracious!" Graham said. "I bet you could hit a black-eyed pea coming at a hundred miles per hour."

"I only swing at black-eyed peas on New Year's Day," Hunter joked, which cracked everybody up again.

Duquette got serious for a moment and told Hunter that due to some of his advanced skills, the Orioles were considering having him skip one level of the minor leagues so he could face better pitching.

"That would mean, Hunter, you would skip Low-A ball, the Delmarva team in Salisbury, Maryland, and instead play Advanced-A ball in Frederick, Maryland. You should know by Thanksgiving because we like to tentatively roster our minor-league teams by then. Of course, in professional baseball, nothing's guaranteed, what with demotions, promotions, trades, injuries and guys just plain quitting the profession. The changes are constant, especially with spring training camps every February and March. A lot of the time we lose confidence in players if they get off to a slow start in spring training, or we fall in love with them if they kick butt early."

Hunter didn't know what to say so he just kept silent and smiled.

As the meet-and-greet ended, Duquette said to Hunter, "We're happy to have you in the Baltimore organization. Good luck to you in the future." Hunter couldn't wait to call Savannah.

Sure enough, in November, Hunter received word from the Orioles that he was tentatively scheduled to play Advanced-A ball in Frederick. It would be his first full season in the minor leagues. The full seasons began in early April and ended in mid- September. The Frederick Keys were scheduled to play 140 games in 2016.

Savannah was concerned about the toll playing a baseball game every day for five months might take on Hunter's body and mind. There was so much pressure on minor-league players to succeed. There was always the fear that they would get released or demoted to a lower league, and there was always the stress of competing with their teammates for playing time and promotions. With no guarantees in their baseball contracts, the players had to prove themselves worthy every single day. Anxiety and depression were real risks. As were physical injuries.

Both Savannah and Hunter had a lot of questions about the pressure of the approaching baseball season and too few answers. But they knew who had the answers already and loved them, so they held hands and prayed to God for Hunter's protection so that he would have a sound mind as well as a strong body. One thing that Hunter never prayed about was for success on the ball field or for victories. But he did pray for God's protection and help in playing to the best of his abilities. He had already learned baseball was a game of failure. Even the best teams lost about forty percent of the time. And the best hitters failed seventy percent of the time. What really mattered at the end of the day was that he played his best.

As the fall of 2015 turned into the winter of 2016, Hunter found opportunities to work on his baseball skills. Much of it was at indoor baseball facilities where players could throw and hit against batting machines. Mainly, he worked out, swam and played pickup basketball at the Kempsville rec center. He also used his old high school's track to run sprints. Although Savannah and Hunter had no income coming in during the fall and winter months, their needs were minimal since they were living at her parents' house rent-free. They contributed to buying groceries, but that was about all that the Montgomerys would take from them.

By Christmas, Savannah had completed her student teaching requirements for college. She had just one more semester to go to earn a degree in secondary education. In January, she began taking online classes through Trevecca Nazarene University while Hunter spent the winter improving his physical fitness, visiting his grandfather and working at AA Construction.

In February, Hunter reported to the minor-league spring training camp at Twin Lakes Park in Sarasota, Florida. This was his first spring training as a professional, so he reported there in tip-top physical shape, excited and his head full of wonder. Every day, even if there was an exhibition game to be played, the players ran through fundamental drills. Hunter was surprised by the detail of the instruction and the level of repetition. The outfielders practiced every phase of baseball—hitting the cut off man; backing up other outfielders; throwing directly to second, third and home; playing balls ricocheting off of outfield fences; charging bloop fly balls; and catching fly balls hit over the outfielder's head. The infielders, pitchers and catchers had their own fielding drills. And everyone practiced various batting drills, such as sacrifice bunts, push bunts, drag bunts and the dying art of hitting behind the runner. There was also baserunning practice, and one day there was even a fun home-run hitting contest on each of the minor-league fields.

The six weeks of spring training flew by for Hunter, with days full of working out, practicing and playing baseball games. On one of their two days off, Hunter drove up to Clearwater to see his former minister from Virginia Beach.

When the players broke spring training camp around the end of March, they said their goodbyes and headed to their assigned minor-league team locations—Norfolk Tides (Triple-A), Bowie Baysox (Double-A), Delmarva Shorebirds (Low A) and Frederick Keys (Advanced A). Hunter Austin was assigned to the Frederick Keys, as he anticipated he would. He also was aware that the level of play was high and challenging in the Advanced A level, but he believed that he was ready, both physically and mentally.

On his way north to Frederick, Maryland, Hunter stopped in Virginia Beach for two nights and stayed with Savannah. Every time he saw his wife, he was reminded that, because of her extraordinary beauty and brains, she was way out of his league.

Savannah was on track to graduate from Trevecca in May of 2016. She told Hunter, "Since you can't attend my graduation ceremonies due to your career, and since I am 650 miles from Nashville, I am not going to "walk the line" and get my diploma in person. I assume that the school will mail it to me."

Hunter and Savannah both dreaded the six-month separation that was staring them in the face. They agreed to use some of his bonus money to pay for hotel rooms that summer so she could travel a few times a month to wherever he was playing. Hunter also wanted her to sometimes bring along his grandfather to watch him play. He managed to hang out with his parents, grandfather, brother and dog for a bit before it was time to get back on the road.

Hunter arrived in Frederick, located in the middle of the State of Maryland, and checked in with the Frederick Keys front office staff. He confirmed that he wanted to stay with a team host family. For the five-month season, he would be paid $290 a week, an annual salary of $6,500. The poverty line that year was $11,880. In spite of the low pay, the minor-league players had to buy their own ball equipment, pay for their housing and meals and contribute to clubhouse dues. They also didn't get paid for spring training, the fall instructional league or during the off-season. On days that the team was traveling or playing at an opponent's ballpark, they received $25 of meal money for each day when fast food might be the only option on their budget.

The Keys staff couldn't find Hunter Austin a host family for him to stay with during the 2016 ball season. Instead, they managed to fit him into a two bedroom apartment with four other players. The five guys shared the rent and utilities as long as they were a part of the Frederick Keys team. Since there wasn't a bed for Hunter, he had to buy an air mattress and sleep on the kitchen floor.

Having a mobile bed, he could move his air mattress anywhere in the apartment to find a place to sleep, which turned out to be a blessing of sorts. When the summer weather in Maryland heated up the apartment, it became apparent that its HVAC system hardly put out cool air. Hunter found that the coolest place to move his air mattress to was to the bathtub. The fact that he was short worked to his advantage as he was able to stretched out in the tub.

One of Hunter's roommates was John Means, an aspiring left-handed starting pitcher from Olathe, Kansas. When the two young men first met, they spoke of their hometowns and the colleges they'd played ball for. "Fort Scott Community College and West Virginia University," John said.

"Virginia Beach," Hunter replied. "I played for Trevecca Nazarene University."

"Nazarene! There's a Nazarene college in Olathe. It's called MidAmerica Nazarene University. Was your college in the NAIA level of athletics?"

"No. We played in the NCAA DII level. I believe Trevecca use to be in the NAIA before they upsized the program."

The first time Hunter entered the Keys locker room in their home ballpark, Nymeo Field at Harry Grove Stadium, he found a locker with "Austin" posted on the top of it. Hanging in his locker were practice uniforms, t-shirts and a home uniform with the number 5 on it. He couldn't help but remember that former Baltimore Orioles great Brooks Robinson once wore the number 5. As he'd always done before a season, Hunter taped up a note inside his locker as a motivational tool to himself. It was a quote by Winston

Churchill. "Success is not final; failure is not fatal: it is the courage to continue that counts."

This particular quote seemed to apply to professional baseball, as, by its very nature, was very difficult and sometimes unfair. Most batters failed three-fourths of the time to get a hit. Starting pitchers were frequently out of the game before the fifth inning. Relief pitchers entered ballgames and immediately gave up a hit or two and were then sent to the showers before they had worked up a sweat. Managers argued bad calls by the umpire and got tossed out of ballgames.

Hunter had once told Savannah that if she looked up the word "grind" in the dictionary, his picture would be there. He remembered his grandfather telling him professional ball was a grind—doing the same things day after day and trying to get better until your abilities were buffed and polished. But the point his grandfather drove home many times was about "grit."

"No matter how tough things get in a baseball career," Anthony said, "don't quit, don't give up—play until they cut you. If one team releases you, maybe another team will pick you up. Second and third chances occur all the time in professional sports."

Frederick Keys didn't play their first game of the 2016 season until April 7, so they had several days of team and individual workouts before boarding a bus for the eight-hour ride to the coast of South Carolina. The Myrtle Beach Pelicans were their first opponent.

Hunter had played with some of the guys on the Keys the previous summer in Aberdeen, but he didn't know most of the guys in the locker room. He had a large number of Frederick Keys players to get to know going into the new season. He looked over the team roster and watched the players practice, and the thought crossed his mind that each guy there was representing themselves more than Frederick Keys. The better they played, the more they separated themselves from their teammates in the pecking order for promotions from one level of the minor leagues to the next.

They all knew the chance to make it to the major leagues was slim to none. About one in 200 or 0.5 percent of high school senior boys playing high school baseball were eventually drafted by a major-league team. Only about ten percent of minor leaguers ever played in the major leagues, and for some, it was only for a few days. Even so, the minor-league players got up each day and went to dingy, old ballparks with a couple thousand fans in the stands to keep their dreams alive, at least until the light burning on their personal candle was snuffed out.

The talent in Advanced-A level baseball was immense and conspicuous. Hunter realized he had to keep improving so he didn't lose ground in the club's internal competition. His grandfather had already taught him that the score on minor-league scoreboards was less important than the team's internal ranking of their prospects. Major League Baseball had its own rankings of all of the minor-league players, but most important was a team's list that showed how much they loved some players and others, not so much.

Hunter wasn't a high draft pick in the 2015 MLB draft, so, at that time, he wasn't thought of as a major-league prospect. But he had such a strong Short A ball season that he shot up the Baltimore Orioles rankings and became somewhat of a prospect—someone with a shot at the big leagues, but not an overwhelming one. There were a few players who also made the leap to High-A ball in Frederick, including DJ Stewart and Tanner Scott.

Keys manager Keith Bodie seemed quite serious to Hunter. He ran a tight ship during practices because he was looking for results from his players. If they seemed to be having too good a time during practice, he would yell out, "Come on, men, act like professionals!"

Hunter climbed aboard the Keys' charter bus with his ear buds, a tablet, a smart phone and a brown bag with chips and a ham and cheese sandwich. During the eight-hour trip to South Carolina, he texted with his wife, brother, mother and grandfather. He used the tablet to manage his fantasy baseball teams. He also had his Bible and a highlighter to note passages of scripture that spoke to him. Reading in the Old Testament, Hunter was reminded about God's love and faithfulness. He highlighted the verse Nehemiah 9:17: "But you are a God ready to forgive, gracious and merciful, slow to anger and abounding in steadfast love, and did not forsake them."

The next day, April 7, 2016, Hunter got to experience his first opening day ceremony and pageantry. Just before the game began, both teams' twenty-five-player roster and coaches were introduced to the fans, one at a time. An army band played and a sergeant sang the national anthem.

Hunter was in the Keys' starting lineup playing center field and batting at the top of the lineup. In the sixth inning, he came to bat for the third time, still looking for his first hit of 2016. The Keys were trailing the Pelicans 2–0, but there was one teammate on second base as Hunter stepped into the batter's box. Because darkness covered the ballpark, the stadium lights shone brightly on the action below. In a rare moment for Hunter, he aggressively swung at a high pitch on the outside corner of the strike zone. With the combination of his swinging up at the ball (not his normal swing) and the bat's barrel squarely meeting the ninety-three-miles-per-hour baseball, the ball exited at a hundred miles per hour through the night air, up and over the Wendy's sign to the left of the "batter's eye," a dark area beyond the center field wall that helped batters see pitched baseballs.

It was estimated Hunter's two-run homer traveled 420 feet from home plate. Not bad for someone who, as a kid, couldn't hit a ball out of the infield. Hunter's two runs batted in were the only runs the Keys scored that evening, and they lost the season's first game 5–2.

Hunter was a 22-year-old grown man. He had spent the last eight years reworking his body, building strength and creating power in his swing. He was an accomplished singles and doubles hitter in college, twice batting at least .500. He had outstanding vision and self-control not to swing at bad pitches. Hunter had a knack for keeping his weight back until the last possible fraction of a second before committing to swing or not to swing. The Frederick Keys' batting coach began working with Hunter to teach him how to use his lower half of his body to generate power. He learned to rotate his hips quickly.

Professional baseball was still newish to Hunter Austin. Just before each game began, Hunter would cozy up to the stands next to the Keys' dugout and sign baseballs, hats, visors, baseball jerseys, t-shirts and scorecards. He was still amazed when anyone wanted his autograph. Besides signing his name, he would add "John 3:16." If anyone was curious enough to look it up in the Bible, they would read, "For God so loved the world that he gave his one and only Son, that whoever believes in him shall not perish but have eternal life."

Most nights, the games didn't end until after 10:00 p.m. Back in Frederick, after the players showered, it would be pushing 11:00 p.m., and the young athletes would be starving for steak, ribs or a burger. John Means, Tanner Scott, Stevie Wilkerson and Hunter—or "the Streak" as his teammates began calling him—could frequently be seen eating past midnight at Jo Jo's Restaurant and Tap House. Baseball teams are big on giving each other nicknames. Hunter's Frederick Keys teammates quickly began calling him "The Streak" when he found his footing on the base paths and stole bases at a record pace. He had received a valuable base stealing tip from one of his Keys' coaches. Hunter was told not to watch for a pitcher's first move with their ball hand. Rather he was advised to watch a pitcher's front foot. As soon as it moved towards home plate, he should break for the next base.

On May 7, Trevecca Nazarene University held its 115th Commencement Convocation. Seven hundred and thirty-three graduates received their degrees, and thousands attended the outdoor ceremony on the Quad. But the day came and went with no fanfare for Savanah. Even though she crushed the classwork, graduating with a 3.9 grade point average, she chose not to attend her graduation celebration because her husband was away playing professional baseball, and she lived 650 miles from Nashville. Any family celebration would have to wait until the fall.

Savannah frequently drove to Frederick to spend weekends watching baseball games and being with her husband. They found a hotel that offered the Keys' personnel a nice discount. Savannah got to know most of the ballplayers' girlfriends and wives as they all sat together during the games. She also became known to some of the baseball players because she hung out with them at JoJo's Restaurant after the games.

"Is her love for you purely mercenary?" his teammates kidded Hunter.

"Can't be," he'd answer. "I only make $350 a week. She could go on unemployment and make more than that."

Most of the kidding was good-natured. But once he overheard inappropriate comments in the team locker room about how his wife looked. He wasn't sure who said it, but there was lust in their voice. He'd already learned that locker room talk wasn't for the faint of heart. So, he pretended not to hear the chatter about Savannah.

The diversity in the minor league teams was a new experience for Hunter. There were more African American players than he'd played with before, and the number of Latin ballplayers exceeded them. Hunter struggled to understand some of the thick accents. Baseball was a big melting pot of cultures, languages and dialects. There were country boys, city dudes, college educated, poorly educated, rich and poor. Many minor leaguers came from Latin countries including the Dominican Republic, Venezuela, Cuba, Puerto Rico, Mexico, Colombia, Panama, Curacao and Nicaragua. Baseball players also moved to the U.S.A. from Canada, Japan, South Korea and Taiwan.

There were differences in the music listened, the food consumed and the way people dressed. How different cultures celebrated individual and team achievements also varied. Some players from the Latin countries loved to flip their bats after hitting a home run and take a very slow trot around the bases. More "old school" players raised in North America didn't think you should show up the opponent with excessive celebrations. Archie had taught Hunter and Jo Jo at a young age to act like their achievements were no big deal when they scored a touchdown, hit a home run or struck out a batter. "Been there, done that before."

Hunter didn't enjoy some of the music blaring in the locker room before ballgames. From one moment to the next, he would hear rap, R&B, funk, jazz, pop, rock, country, gospel and reggae music. The inappropriate language of players and coaches and in the musical lyrics was a challenge for Hunter and other Christian ballplayers. It was hard to tune it out because it was offensive and often loud. But to be successful, no matter the background, upbringing or culture, the team had to form a cohesive unit that was ready to go to battle against a common enemy.

Despite adjusting to the new experiences, Hunter continued to improve and exceed expectations. On average, he was getting a base hit every three times he batted, and with his patience at the plate, he frequently walked. His on-base percentage of .410 was ideal for a leadoff hitter. His successes in the first half of the 2016 season allowed him to be selected to the Carolina league All-Star team, and he played in the June All-Star game.

In July, Savannah was hired to teach high school English at Great Bridge High School in Chesapeake, about a fourteen-mile drive from Kempsville. She felt blessed to find a teaching job so quickly after college graduation, and Great Bridge High had a strong reputation for academics. Although earning a master's degree was on Savannah's radar, she planned to focus only on her teaching career and new marriage for a few years so Hunter's baseball career could run its course. If it ended, he intended to work for his grandfather's construction business while slowly completing his college degree.

The calendar turned to September. The baseball season ended for the Frederick Keys with a record of sixty-eight wins and seventy-two losses; they were third in the league's North Division. September 6 was Savannah's first day teaching high school students. The day ended with her exhausted and a bit frazzled after trying to get 115 juniors and seniors interested in school again after three months of summer vacation.

Hunter was selected as the Keys' outstanding player of the year in 2016. He crushed, lined, slashed, grounded, blooped and bunted base hits all throughout the Carolina league. Besides swinging to a batting average of .325, he received sixty bases on balls and stole fifty bases. And thanks to some tips on power hitting without jumping at the ball from the Keys hitting coach, Erik Pappas, Hunter also hit ten home runs. He took a serious leap up the Baltimore Orioles' list of prospects.

After the Keys' last game in the 2016 season, Hunter emptied his locker, hugged his teammates and coaches, and loaded his pickup truck. He was in Virginia Beach by bedtime. His beautiful wife and his mother-in-law were sitting on the front porch swing, waiting for their tired ballplayer to get home. After greeting Hunter, Robin said goodnight and then he was alone with his wife. They sat on the swing talking past midnight. Since he looked so tired, she took his hand and led him to bed. Before the lights were out, Hunter was snoring. Nine hours later, he woke up to the smell of bacon frying and coffee percolating. He reached for his wife, but she was already up, showered and helping her mom make breakfast.

Later, as Hunter was finishing his last bite of grits, he told Savannah he wanted to host a graduation party for her, and he wanted to pay for everything out of his baseball bonus money. Even though Savannah said it wasn't necessary, he went ahead planning an event to honor his wife's achievements in college. Bill and Robin insisted on having the party in their home, and Saturday, September 17 was selected as the date of the party. It was to be an informal pig pickin' picnic.

"Say that three times fast," Savannah joked.

They invited a couple dozen family and friends. Many brought her tangible gifts, cash and gift cards. Savannah's dad had a special gift to give her because of all she'd put into her college work and all she'd achieved.

Bill said to the party goers, "We all have to walk down to the Austins' house as our gift for Savannah is hidden there." Soon, all of the party guests strolled down Rochelle Arch like a parade and made a right turn at Manor Drive. Hunter and Savannah led the parade, walking hand-in-hand. In the driveway was a new shiny bright red SUV.

"No way!" Savannah gasped.

"Bill, is that beauty Savannah's graduation gift?" Hunter asked, his jaw dropping open.

"It sure is."

Savannah took off running across the street, dragging Hunter by the hand, straight to her new Ford Explorer. Everyone else caught up as she hugged the hood of her new wheels.

"Did she just kiss that?" someone asked.

"I could afford to spend so much money on this new vehicle," he explained to the crowd, "because she saved me a bundle on her college costs. She was on a full-ride academic scholarship," he added proudly.

Several days later, a delivery truck dropped off a small package for Savannah. After she opened it, she kept the package's contents hidden from Hunter. Then one evening at the Montgomerys' dinner table, she handed him a t-shirt she'd had custom-made for him. It was orange with white and black lettering on the front and back. Hunter read the message on the shirt, he started to laugh. And because he was laughing, it set everyone else off, and soon they were all laughing too.

Hunter put on the shirt and modeled it for everyone. On the front it read "Baltimore." On the back, it read "You will only test my arm once." Hunter laughed and laughed when he read the message it conveyed. He thanked and hugged his wife, then he said, "I love this message to my opponents who run the bases when I'm playing the outfield. Once this last season, I threw out two baserunners at home plate in the same game. But I don't think that the same guy tried me twice."

17

UPS AND DOWNS (2016–2017)

In October of 2016, Hunter made a commitment to a ninety-day plan at a strength-and-conditioning facility in Virginia Beach. It was a chance to work one-on-one with a personal trainer twice a week for three months. He planned to do baseball drills on the days he wasn't in the gym with his trainer. Although baseball minor leaguers don't get paid in the off-season, Hunter approached his intense off-season workouts and training as if it was his job. Following the personal training sessions, he would continue to work out and exercise on his own, often concluding with about thirty minutes of running sprints or agility drills on one of the area school ball fields. On his baseball drills days, he'd get his father, brother or Evelyn to throw with him and load baseballs into the pitching machine at the indoor batting cage.

Hunter and Savannah felt blessed by the support they were receiving from their families. Bill and Robin had opened their home to them. They'd been given two very nice vehicles. Though they never seemed to have two dollars in their wallets, Hunter and Savannah had enough to meet their needs. They felt so blessed by God for having such a loving, strong support group known as family.

In the fall, they received the Treveccan, a quarterly publication from Trevecca Nazarene University. The Lord spoke to Hunter as he read about the positive effects Trevecca was having on lives on the campus in Nashville and online nationwide. He also read about how people have supported Trevecca for more than forty years with their donations of money to fund scholarships and building projects. At that point, a light bulb went off in his head. He had received a signing bonus of $100,000, and yet he hadn't thought to tithe the money. Ten percent would be $10,000. He remembered the many blessings the Trevecca community had provided to him and Savannah during their three-year stay. What a financial blessing it was when he earned a partial scholarship for his last two years of college, and Savannah was awarded a full academic scholarship for her full four years at school. That didn't even take into account the knowledge they acquired, the friendships they made and the spiritual impact of university. And of course, the Trevecca baseball program was the training ground for Hunter's professional career.

When Savannah got home from work, he told her he wanted to tithe $10,000 to Trevecca as a gift.

"Ten percent of my signing bonus."

After a thoughtful conversation about their financial situation, Savannah supported his decision.

"It's a good way to give back to an institution that had such a positive impact on our lives," she said.

They decided to give the gift with a condition on it. They wanted the $10,000 to be an endowment named for dorm director Stephen Collins, who had convinced Hunter to give his life to Jesus Christ.

Trevecca made the contribution process quick and simple, and agreed to name the endowment for Stephen Collins. After the funds were transferred,

Hunter received a wonderful telephone call from his former dorm director and friend. Stephen was touched that his name was chosen to honor his positive influence on Hunter's spiritual development.

In January of 2017, Hunter got his next projected minor-league assignment by the Baltimore Orioles. He was promoted to Class Double-A with the Bowie Baysox in the Eastern League. He would be moving to Bowie, Maryland.

Meanwhile, in Atlanta, Jo Jo's Falcons qualified to play in the Super Bowl. He provided tickets to the big event for his mother, father, brother, sister-in-law and grandfather. Jo Jo also comped hotel rooms and airplane tickets to Houston, Texas, for the family.

Super Bowl LI (fifty-one) was played on February 5 at the NRG Stadium in Houston in front of 70,807 fans. The Atlanta Falcons represented the National Football Conference, the NFC, and played against the New England Patriots from the American Football Conference, the AFC.

Tight end Jo Jo Austin snagged a twenty-yard touchdown pass from Matt "Matty Ice" Ryan in the first half of the game and caught a total of four passes during the big game. Matt, Julio Jones and Devonta Freeman also had productive games for the Falcons. At one point, they were in the lead 28–3. Unfortunately for Atlanta, their defense appeared to stay in the locker room at half time. And it didn't help that Tom "the GOAT" Brady was quarterbacking their opponent. The GOAT threw for 446 yards on sixty-two pass attempts and completed forty-three of them. The Patriots won, 34–28, in overtime, and Tom Brady won his fifth Super Bowl ring and his fourth Super Bowl MVP Award.

In February, Hunter reported to the Orioles minor-league spring training camp at Twin Lakes Park. The competition in the outfield for the Baysox team looked impressive to him. But he'd never backed down from competition before and wasn't about to start. He already knew some of the outfielders in camp, like his old buddies Cedric Mullins and DJ Stewart. Other outfielders in camp were Austin Hays, Anthony Santander and Mike Yastrzemski. Watching those baseball studs play reminded him of playing ball at home against Jo Jo and his friends.

Competition always brought out the best in Hunter. His batting was more productive than the other outfielders in camp. He was robbing hitters of balls in the outfield gaps. He was running wild on the bases with an almost reckless desire to score runs.

"You can tell Hunter that he isn't good enough to do something," one of his coaches said, "and he'll find a way to do it. His determination is unmatched. That chip on his shoulder has served him well. I think his aggressiveness and skill in center field has changed the attitudes of the corner outfielders. They seem to have a new bounce in their step."

"Hunter Austin is one relentless ballplayer," another coach said.

Hunter was thrilled to be reunited with Cedric. When he was playing with the Frederick Keys, Cedric was playing with the Low-A Delmarva Shorebirds. As in 2015, they were pitted head-to-head to be the team's center fielder and leadoff hitter, along with a third player, Austin Hays. When any two of them weren't playing center field, they were likely in left or right field—or riding the pine.

After spring training, the Baltimore Orioles' minor-league players headed north to their minor-league teams. After an overnight stay in Virginia Beach to see his wife and parents, Hunter arrived in Bowie to play for the Bowie Baysox at the Prince George's Stadium. He was twenty-three years old. When he walked into the Bowie Baysox locker room, it felt comfortable to look for his locker and find his practice uniforms, t-shirts and towels. This time, his home uniform had the number 3 on it. Continuing his tradition, he taped a note inside his locker. This was from the Bible, Luke 1:37. "For nothing is impossible with God."

The Baysox administrative staff arranged for Hunter to stay the season with Daniel and Stacy Winchester, a team host family in Fairwood. He got his own room with a bed, TV and a pretty view of the wooded lot out back. Hunter was thrilled to have his own bed to sleep in after using an air mattress the previous season.

Mike Yastrzemski was also assigned to the Winchester family home. He had an interesting life story. He was the grandson of Major League Baseball Hall of Famer Carl "Yaz" Yastrzemski. Carl played for the Boston Red Sox and won the American League Triple Crown and the MVP Award, both in 1967. In 2017, grandson Mike "Yaz" Yastrzemski was playing Double-A ball at the age of twenty-seven. That was the age most players have either reached the major leagues or washed out of professional baseball. For years, Mike had endured the ups and downs, good news and bad news, hitting streaks and batting slumps of professional baseball as the Baltimore Orioles tried to decide if he was a major-league prospect or not. The name "Yastrzemski" on the back of his uniform guaranteed him nothing.

Mike had played in the minor leagues for a total of seven years. The "winner takes all" results from minor league personnel decisions can appear to be brutal and cruel. He had been riding the rollercoaster from Double-A Bowie to Triple-A Norfolk, and back and forth. He was still trying to find his footing as an outfielder in the Baltimore Orioles organization. At least he had an emotional support person, his fiancée, who he met while playing college baseball at Vanderbilt University. Throughout his college ball and minor-league experiences, his fiancée was there for him, and they shared many midnight telephone calls together.

Mike and Hunter quickly figured they were the same height and weight, they'd both played college baseball in Nashville—Yaz for Vanderbilt and Hunter for Trevecca—they swung the bat left-handed, played the outfield and had loving, supportive ladies. After hearing Mike's tales and horror stories about his experiences in the minor leagues, Hunter admitted to his new buddy that, so far, his professional career trajectory was moving slowly upward.

"I haven't hit any snags or roadblocks in my development. I feel a little guilty after all you've been through. It doesn't seem fair."

"Now, stop right there," Yaz said. "Professional baseball is inherently competitive and unfair. Every day some players move up while others move down; still others are given their release. And no one outside of the team's management has a clue why. The daily turnover of personnel is so obvious. Just look around our locker room. Today there are two empty lockers but by tomorrow they likely will be filled again. It's the minor leagues. The changes never stop.

"Hunter, every day they're paying you a few bucks to play baseball. So go out there and play your heart out today, and try to impress somebody. Don't worry about tomorrow, which you can't control."

It certainly was hard to make ends meet in the minor leagues. For the five-month baseball season at the Double-A level, Hunter was paid $450 a week or about $64 a ballgame. As an annual salary, it would only amount to $9,000—quite a bit under the poverty line of $12,060 for 2017. In addition to Hunter's $9,000 minuscule salary, he received $25 a day meal money on days that the team was traveling or playing at an opponent's ballpark. Whatever the price of success, he was prepared and willing to pay for it.

As Hunter observed the ballplayers practice, some new acquaintances and other old teammates from previous leagues and training, he was reminded that Bowie was only two steps away from the big leagues. Only Triple-A Norfolk stood in the way. The thought crossed his mind, "Baseball is America's pastime." Making the major leagues was every baseball player's dream. The gold at the end of the rainbow. The fame and fortune that awaited the survivors of the minor leagues, which he called the "Demolition Derby."

The Bowie Baysox opened the 2017 season on April 6 in Akron, Ohio, against the Akron RubberDucks. The Baysox players endured a seven-hour bus ride through Maryland, Pennsylvania and Ohio to play a four-game series. Before they played at home in Bowie, the Baysox also played a series in Erie, Pennsylvania, against the SeaWolves. Finally, they rode the team bus most of the night back to Bowie to play three games against the Harrisburg Senators.

With the team playing in Bowie for the first time, the players started searching for late night restaurants where they could chow down after ballgames. From time to time, Hunter, Cedric, Yaz, Austin Hays, David Hess, John Means and Ryan Mountcastle could be seen eating past midnight at Old Bowie Town Grille.

Hunter, like most players new to Double-A baseball, struggled to hit against the advanced pitching. And batting in the cold April climate of Ohio and Pennsylvania was not conducive to a high batting average or hitting home runs. In the series against the Senators, Hunter resorted to laying down a couple of beautiful bunts, which at least got him on base. He also managed to draw a few bases on balls, so their opponents had to deal with a very fast baserunner numerous times in three days. Although he wasn't yet squaring up baseballs, he managed to steal three bases and score four runs.

In Hunter's last at-bat on April 15, he drew an eight-pitch walk. During his attempt to steal second base, he dove headfirst into the bag at second, injuring his left thumb. He was removed from the game and attended to by the team's trainer.

The next day, the Baysox arranged for Hunter to receive an x-ray and MRI of his swollen thumb at a local Bowie hospital. A day later, he followed up with a hand specialist doctor to evaluate the imaging pictures. He was diagnosed with a broken left thumb and an injured tendon. The doctor said the healing of the broken bone was predictable, but the healing of the tendon was not. He felt the damage to the extensor tendon could be treated without surgery, using a rigid splint worn around the hand. The break was in the first metacarpal near the hand. Hunter's thumb and hand were immobilized with the splint, with therapy on the hand beginning in four weeks.

After the Baysox trainer reported back to the team's manager, Hunter was put on the sixty-day disabled list as of April 15, the day he was injured. He was allowed to return home to Virginia until he was ready for physical therapy.

Dejected, Hunter went back to the Winchesters' home, gathered his belongings and loaded his truck.

"Can you hold the room for me for two months while I rehab my thumb?" he asked Daniel Winchester.

"It's up to the team," Daniel said.

"But we'd love to have you back," Stacy said kindly.

Hunter also stopped by the Baysox locker room to say goodbye to his teammates, who were preparing for a game that evening against the Richmond Flying Squirrels.

"It's just for the time being," he insisted.

He hugged his buddies Yaz and Cedric and shook some sweaty hands. The team's manager and coaches patted him on the back and wished him well as he healed up. As the Baysox players headed out for batting practice, Hunter headed out into the parking lot and climbed into his truck. He sat there alone for the longest time, contemplating his future.

He knew how it worked in professional baseball. There was always another player on a lower level waiting for an injury so they would get promoted; one step closer to the big leagues. He wasn't even sure he'd still have his spot on the Bowie team when he got off the disabled list. Before turning on the engine, he bowed his head down to the steering wheel and prayed. He prayed for his thumb to be healed and for a successful return to the Baysox.

"Lord, remember all that I've gone through in my life to get to where I am. I'm only two levels away from my life's dream."

He was moved to get out the small Bible he kept in his truck and flipped to the book of Proverbs until he located Proverbs 3:5-6.

"Trust in the Lord with all your heart and lean not on your own understanding; in all your ways submit to him, and he will make your paths straight."

"Okay then," Hunter thought, nodding. He looked at himself in the rear-view mirror and said, "The Lord promises to ensure that my future is straight. I hope it's straight to the major leagues." On the drive home, his heart felt lighter. His faith had been lifted by the words from the Bible.

Hunter pulled into his in-laws' driveway about 10:00 p.m. By then he was once again confident in his chosen professional path. There was a purpose for his baseball journey to the major leagues, even the ups and downs. God had a purpose for his life and He was in control. There were so many people watching the progress of Hunter Austin's career, many of them doubting him, others rooting hard for his success. He hoped he would be an inspiration for others to shoot for the moon in their careers.

While it was a bummer to miss half of the Double-A baseball season, there were blessings too. He got to spend quality time with his family and friends back home. He spent a few days in his grandfather's construction office getting caught up on current projects. He enjoyed attending church again, something that was impossible during the baseball season.

He spent several evenings with his father and Jo Jo watching the Baltimore Orioles play baseball on TV. He thought Archie was going to start in on him one evening when he leaned forward as if he was going to lecture him, but he noticed his father eyeing his splint, and then he just sat back and went back to watching the game. He felt God's protection at that moment and was grateful for it. It reminded him of Romans 8:31. "If God be for us, who can be against us?"

Hunter spent an hour nearly every day at the Kempsville rec center doing the exercises his team's trainer had said he could do. After two weeks, he was allowed to start running. He would walk the few blocks down to Kempsville High School's baseball field and watch the baseball team play. Coach Collinsworth had Hunter attend a team practice so he could address the high school players and inspire them with his story. Following Hunter's pep talk, he autographed ball caps for each high school baseball player.

After being away from the Bowie Baysox for a month, Hunter was sent to Baltimore for rehab and to work with the Orioles trainers on conditioning. It became clear to him that Baltimore was still invested in him and his baseball future.

The first time he walked into Oriole Park at Camden Yards, home field of the major leagues' Baltimore Orioles, he felt like he was walking on hallowed ground. Then, in quick succession, he ran into Adam Jones, Manny Machado, Jonathan Schoop, Kevin Gausman, Dylan Buddy and Zack Britton. Suddenly, he felt like a teenager looking for autographs, he was so star-struck. He was meeting guys he had just watched play on TV.

Hours before the Orioles game that night, Hunter walked slowly around the baseball field in Oriole Park with his eyes wide open, taking it all in. This is where he wanted to play ball someday. He walked the complete outfield warning track, noting how close the fences were in the power alleys to home plate. A monster wall in right field blocked his view of the famous warehouse across from Eutaw Street, the walkway located between Camden Yards and the B&O Warehouse. Over one hundred home-run balls had landed in Eutaw Street, and each one had a small plaque on the spot where the ball landed. The Orioles warehouse met the far side of Eutaw Street just across from the flag court. No one had yet hit the warehouse with a baseball during an official game.

Walking near the right-center-field fence, Hunter could smell the smoke wafting from Boog's Barbeque stand on Eutaw Street.

Besides doing drills with the Baltimore trainers, he got to play catch with some of the Orioles. His thumb was a little stiff, and it was somewhat difficult to squeeze his glove as he caught baseballs. But at least the thumb no longer pained him. He wasn't allowed to take batting practice in case his thumb got hit with a pitch, but one day he was allowed to shag fly balls during the team batting practice with the Orioles outfielders. Three mornings a week, Hunter went to a rehab center in Baltimore and was put through the ringer, pushing his thumb and hand to its limit of mobility and strength. After rehabbing for three weeks in Baltimore and easing back into baseball activities, the team sent him to Sarasota for an extended spring training to get him up to game speed.

During the two weeks Hunter was in Florida batting, throwing, fielding and running the bases, he started to hear the term "analytics" being used a lot by team officials. Apparently, some of the other major-league organizations, like the Houston Astros and Tampa Bay Rays, had adopted the concept. But not the Baltimore Orioles.

"There are already big changes to professional baseball," a coach told the players at a team meeting in Sarasota. "Analytics has won the hearts of the general managers. It's also called sabermetrics. It rules baseball front offices and on-field decision-making. And it's growing throughout the major leagues. It's used to find the real impact a player makes on a game or to help them make a bigger impact. You already hear a lot of the terms. 'The spin rate of pitched baseballs.' And for hitting, 'launch angles' and 'exit velocities.'"

The coach was building steam. "Analytics makes everyone think bunting, stealing bases and groundballs are a waste of time. Fly balls and home runs are all the rage. Catchers are framing pitched balls back into the strike zone even if the ball wasn't initially in the strike zone, basically deceiving the umpire. Defenses are shifting three infielders on one side of the infield where the batter has a propensity to hit groundballs to. And defenses are using four outfielders to defend an extra base hitting batter. Starting pitchers are being removed from the game before they can face an opponent's batting order for a third time. That has increased the need for bullpens with extra relief pitchers to take over in the fifth or sixth inning. The Tampa Bay Rays are using relief pitchers to begin ballgames to throw two or three innings only. They call them 'openers.' The openers are followed on the mound by a long line of relief pitchers until the game concludes. With all the pitching changes, it's no wonder that pro baseball games last well over three hours. So far, because of analytics in the major leagues, the number of home runs is way up as is the number of strikeouts. For the fans, the games are longer and there's less action than before. If a player strikes out three times in a game but hits a home run in his fourth at-bat, he becomes a hero for his team. There's no shame swinging and missing six times if you crush the seventh pitch over the fence. Baseball is becoming an all or nothing sport."

When asked by a player when the Orioles were going to start using analytics, the coach said, "Sooner than later. It looks like every team will use analytics to gain an advantage on their opponents."

When he heard this, Hunter was almost sick to his stomach. Bunting and stealing was his game. And he tried hard not to hit fly balls. Was he already a dinosaur before he'd even reached the major leagues? Would they think he didn't fit their future plans because he didn't hit twenty-five home runs a year? Analytics didn't sound very encouraging to him.

One of the team trainers suggested Hunter use an "oven mitt" over his hand when he was on base. It was a protective devise that looked like an oven mitt. It was supposed to protect a player's fingers, thumb and hand from injury when they slide headfirst into a base. Hunter immediately bought into the idea, knowing that if he'd been wearing one in April, he would not have broken his thumb. The trainer gave him one for his left hand since he usually tagged a base with that hand. He used it for the first time in a practice scrimmage on the back field in Sarasota.

"The oven mitt makes me feel more like a chef than a ballplayer," he told his wife.

Hunter rejoined the Bowie Baysox on June 29, but he was not activated from the disabled list until June 30. He arrived in time to hop the team bus for a series of games with the Akron RubberDucks in Ohio that same day.

It had been about ten weeks since he'd played in a minor-league game. His body had healed, and by the time he left Sarasota, he got his swing down pat and was spraying line drives all over Ed Smith Stadium. But his manager, Gary Kendall, sat Hunter on the bench for most of the games in Akron as the team was already in mid-season and other outfielders had made their mark on the Baysox starting lineup.

Hunter was happy and disappointed when he returned to Bowie to learned that his teammate and friend, Mike Yastrzemski, has been promoted to Triple-A Norfolk. He was pleased that Mike was given another shot to play at the Triple-A level, but he would miss him as a road roommate and teammate.

Hunter was given a start in the outfield when the team returned home to play against the Hartford Yard Goats on July 4. It was a good thing too, since his whole family came to Bowie to watch the ballgames. Following the game that night, fireworks were scheduled to be set off for the fans. Apparently, Hunter couldn't wait for the fireworks to begin, so he created some of his own by hitting home runs in his final two at-bats. The last homer was a walk-off in the bottom of the ninth inning. Five minutes after Hunter ended the ballgame, the real pyrotechnics exploded beyond the Baysox outfield fence.

"Every time I travel to see you play," his dad said the next day, looking at Hunter with suspicion in his eyes, "you hit a home run. And tonight, you hit two. Were you showing off for me?"

"No, Pop. But I hope you were impressed." Then he couldn't stop himself from adding, "I seem to have a hard time impressing you."

"Are you still on that story, son?"

"The story's been going on for a long time. My whole life you've been impressed by Jo Jo and not by me."

"Well, you haven't deserved praise your whole life. What's got into you today?"

Hunter was too tired to get into another fight. "I'm glad you and Mom came to watch me play," he said. "But if your heart is not in it, please don't come anymore."

The next few days were a bit icy between father and son. The worst thing was Archie never seemed to understand why Hunter did well, and he never denied that his support was mainly belonged to Jo Jo.

"It must have been awkward for him to watch me put on a show for the last four games," he pointed out to Savannah. Even batting in the seventh hole in the lineup for the whole series and playing right field, Hunter had led the team to four victories over the Yard Goats. He had six extra base hits, drove in eight runs and stole two bases. He also earned two outfield assists by throwing out runners at second base and third base.

At practice the next week, one of Hunter's coaches, Coach Davis, told him, "Your potential for our major-league team is as a table setter at the top of the lineup. Us coaches just got excited seeing you hit a couple homers the other night. Sacrifice bunting and hitting behind the runner will soon be a lost art. So, when we see a prospect with some power, we get excited."

"I may be batting in the seven hole right at the moment, coach," Hunter said, "but I have the right game to bat leadoff. I think my ability to get on base and create havoc on the bases would more likely get me to Baltimore than hitting home runs. But I'm worried about analytics. They'll make it even more challenging for guys like me and Cedric Mullins to get to the big leagues. I think the Orioles could use some Salt 'n' Pepper. We could really spice things up in Baltimore. Don't bet against me and Cedric, coach."

August rolled around. Savannah began her second-year teaching at Great Bridge High, but she was starting to think about looking for a teaching position in Virginia Beach, closer to home, or starting a master's degree in school administration.

That same month, Hunter was back as the leadoff batter in the Baysox lineup and holding his own against some outstanding pitchers in Double-A. His manager told him, "One of the ways the Orioles evaluate their prospects is how they deal with adversity. In the big leagues, you're going to go into slumps, you're going to miss the ball, strike out three times, but are you going to bounce back the next night and be able to produce? Hunter, we like how you've come back off the disabled list and played so well that you've forced me to put you back at the top of our lineup. That's how you get to the major leagues; you play yourself there. If a player can't deal with adversity, like getting benched, hurt, sent down, passed over or being in a slump, they won't make it. Baseball is a game of failure and adversity. There are so many ups and downs. If you can't bounce back one at-bat after hitting into a double play, then you're no good to the organization. To be successful, players have to have short memories and be mentally tough and resilient.

Hunter, you're a mentally strong individual. Keep up your productive play, and your dreams might come true."

"Skip, my faith keeps me focused," Hunter replied. "It helps me quickly shred and eliminate negative thoughts so I can keep my self-confidence. 'If God is for us, who can be against us?' Romans 8:31."

August soon turned into September. The Baysox lost the last four games of the season as the players seemed to be going through the motions. Unfortunately, the final three games were playoff games against the Altoona Curve. It seemed the Baysox team couldn't wait for the long baseball season to finally end. After all, they'd been practicing baseball and playing baseball games—140 in the season—since February.

The Bowie Baysox had a competitive record in 2017 of seventy-two wins and sixty-eight losses to finish in second place in the Western Division of the Eastern League. But the most important grades for the Orioles' Double-A team were how well they developed or did not develop players for their major-league affiliate, the Baltimore Orioles. Only time would tell if the players the Orioles brought up from Bowie were major-league ready or not. The final exam was still being written on them.

18

MAGNIFICENT OBSESSION (2017–2018)

Austin Hays and DJ Stewart hit at least twenty home runs, and David Hess won eleven games playing for the Bowie Baysox in 2017. Hunter, who was the "salt" in the team's dynamic duo, spent seventy of the team's 140 games on the disabled list. In what amounted to one half of the team's baseball season, he batted .280, hit seven home runs and stole thirty-two bases and a .750 OPS (combined on-base and slugging percentages). Cedric Mullins, the "pepper" in the Baysox's spice rack, batted .265 with thirteen home runs, thirty-seven RBIs and a .778 OPS in seventy-six games.

After the 2017 season was finished, both Cedric Mullins and Hunter Austin were still considered prospects by the Orioles' management team. There was very little separating the two as far as ability, production and potential were concerned. They had the same kind of game, were prototypical leadoff hitters and ideal center fielders. They worried out loud that the Orioles wouldn't find spots on the major-league team for both of them, at least not at the same time. Their best guess about what would happen in the future was that one of them would get traded to another team since a team only needs one center fielder. Of course, they both had been forced to play the two corner outfield positions too in the minor leagues. Although unlikely, they might play left or right fields in Baltimore too. They spent a lot of time discussing the "what-ifs" of their careers.

After the Baysox's last playoff game, Hunter emptied his locker and said goodbye to his teammates and coaches. Like all the other minor-league players, he couldn't wait to get home. As he drove south on Interstate 95 towards Richmond, all he could think about was his lovely wife, who was teaching school in Chesapeake at that moment. He wondered if she was thinking about him too.

A screaming siren woke Hunter from his passionate daydream, and he saw the flashing lights of a Virginia State police car behind him. He put on his flashers and pulled over to the shoulder of the road. After receiving a $100 speeding fine and three DMV driving points against his license, Hunter was back on the road to home. But just like James Bond's drink of choice, he was "shaken, but not stirred."

He spent the next few days at home catching up with his family and old neighborhood friends. Everybody asked about his career and what was next for him. He became very good at telling his story as it seemed he told it several times a day.

Hunter spent the first weekend home surfing in the Atlantic Ocean with Savannah. The Virginia water was warm in September, but the beaches were nearly empty. When she was off work, they spent all their time together. It seemed absence did make the heart grow fonder.

On September 17, Savannah, Hunter and his parents drove to Atlanta, Georgia, to watch the Atlanta Falcons football game against the Green Bay Packers. Jo Jo scored a touchdown and a two-point conversion against the Packers. The game had a lot of action with Aaron Rogers bringing his team back from a 20–0 deficit at half time, but Atlanta held on and won 34–23.

Archie did his usual hero worshipping of Jo Jo. After his son caught a touchdown pass, he ran around the stadium telling everyone he came in contact with that he was Jo Jo Austin's father. A prouder father never existed. Hunter sat quietly and sulked, and Savannah's attempts to lighten the mood did nothing for him.

When Archie returned to his seat, Savannah couldn't control her temper. "Don't you realize how foolish you look when you only celebrate one of your sons?"

Archie just shrugged it off and said, "I'm going to go snap some photos of Jo Jo in action," and off he went. Hunter turned to look at his mom to see how she felt about his dad's behavior. Seeing her eyes well with tears said enough.

Once back at home in Virginia Beach, Hunter began his annual fall physical fitness program, which included working with a personal trainer. He even talked his way onto his old high school baseball field to practice running the bases and take batting practice with a half a dozen of the current Kempsville High baseball players. Since the kids were helping Hunter stay sharp with his baseball skills, he offered them playing tips and even demonstrated particular skills. He also worked with a couple of the outfielders on how to approach a batted ball, so they could use their momentum to help them get off strong throws to bases. He even held class one day at home plate with the guys on the techniques of bunting.

Hunter stayed close to his wife most nights and took advantage of every moment they weren't working. He loved her company and continued to think she was the most beautiful women he'd ever seen. But sometimes their careers drew their attention away from each other. There were evenings, with Hunter sitting by her side, when Savannah sat on her parents' sofa grading her students' papers.

Towards the end of 2017, Hunter found out the Baltimore Orioles were projecting he'd be reassigned to the Bowie Baysox for the start of the 2018 minor-league season.

In February 2018, he reported to the Orioles spring training camp in Sarasota, Florida. He always entered spring training full of enthusiasm and optimism. He still had the little boy excitement of playing a game. And, occasionally, he had to pinch himself that someone was paying him to play baseball. It was in spring training that he had to make himself act like a professional and not a ten-year-old playing in the Little League.

Spring training that year was significantly different for Hunter. Soon after arriving in Sarasota and checking in with the Orioles officials, he was told that he wouldn't be training in the Twin Lakes Park minor-league camp. Instead, he was assigned to the major-league spring training camp to train with the Orioles' big-league players and the team's best minor-league prospects at the Ed Smith Stadium complex.

"It's about time!" he said to no one in particular.

Apparently, the Orioles decided not to renew the contracts of a few veteran players, which opened roster spots for prospects that spring. Hunter was not yet on the Orioles forty-man major-league roster, but that wasn't a prerequisite to train with the big-league team in spring training. If he was ever promoted to play in Baltimore, he would have to be added to the forty-man roster and someone on it would have to be removed.

In spring training, Hunter held his own, playing with and against some of the best baseball players in the world. He struggled a bit to feel like he belonged in the Orioles locker room and on the ball diamond. It wasn't really a lack of confidence, but rather he was in awe. He was playing ball with nationally known athletes who recorded TV commercials and earned six-to-eight-figure salaries.

Every day, Hunter had dreamed of playing Major League Baseball since he walked onto a T-ball field in the Virginia Beach Kempsville Recreation Association. Those were the days when the game didn't come easily to Hunter, and he was so small his ball cap covered his eyes and his ball shirt hung down past his knees. But competition over the years only brought out the best in him. Proverbs 27:17 states, "As iron sharpens iron, so one person sharpens another."

Hunter grew up being cut from his school baseball team, being the last kid chosen in the rec-league draft and listening to voices telling him that he wouldn't amount to much. His determination to make something of himself and to prove his father wrong developed a huge chip on his shoulder. That chip had been his rudder, helping him navigate through his challenges in school, at home and on the ball field. Nothing came easily to Hunter, except meeting and falling in love with Savannah. His achievements always seemed to be the result of extra hard work and an approach to challenges that no one else took. "Perceived failure is oftentimes success trying to be born in a bigger way."

At the 2018 spring training camp, Hunter got to be coached by Orioles manager Buck Showalter and his coaches, as well as Ron Johnson, the Norfolk Tides manager. Hunter also got to rub elbows with dozens of baseball players who had major-league experience. After a few days of spring training, he got over his little boy hero worshipping of stars such as Chris Davis, Jonathan Schoop, Manny Machado and Adam Jones. After all, they put their pants on one leg at a time just like he did (something his grandfather told him about major-league ballplayers). But the big-league stars had a presence about them, self-confidence, and they acted like they belonged in the majors. Probably the biggest difference between the major-league players and wannabe-major-league players was their difference in salary. Hunter couldn't imagine what it felt like to be a millionaire. He never desired wealth or fame in his baseball career. His focus was very narrow and specific. He wanted to receive the call to the major-leagues and to experience his dream of spending one day in the big-leagues. Anything after that would be gravy to him.

Hunter focused on self-improvement as well as conditioning. He received outstanding coaching and training from the Orioles' large support staff in Sarasota. He got into many of the Baltimore games played at the Ed Smith Stadium after the Orioles starting outfielders got in their five or six innings of work. Most days in spring training, the major-league teams played two baseball games, one at home and one on the road. Hunter was frequently on the travel squad, riding the bus to opponents' ball fields throughout the Florida Grapefruit League where he started and played six or seven innings per game. Many of the major-league stars didn't want to ride on a bus for a couple of hours, so they stayed behind and played in their team's home games. Those dual ballgames played on the same day were referred to as split squad games. This gave the major-league team's future baseball players plenty of playing time to get ready for their approaching minor-league season as they were taught how to do things "The Orioles way".

For the second time in his career, Hunter got to meet and chat with the Baltimore Orioles general manager, Dan Duquette.

"Hunter," he said, "we've been observing your steady development as a ballplayer since we drafted you three years ago." He nodded. "You've passed a lot of other players drafted in front of you to become a serious prospect for Baltimore. Which minor-league team were you assigned to for 2018?"

"Bowie, for a second season."

"Listen, Hunter, in Double-A, there's a lot of movement of the players. Guys frequently get promoted to Triple-A and some straight to the major leagues. Some don't stay long in the bigs and they're quickly returned to Double-A or Triple-A. They get injured. Or they stink up the joint. So, we occasionally demote big leaguers back to the minors. You have the opportunity to play your way to Norfolk or Baltimore. But no one will give you anything. You have to earn it."

"I'll earn it," Hunter said, his eyes steady and true. "It's my mission in life to play in the major leagues. I'm not going to let anyone distract me from it."

"That's good," Dan replied. "I've heard your story. I'm glad you didn't let your dad distract you."

Spring training broke for the more than one hundred Baltimore Orioles minor-league players. After an overnight stay in Virginia Beach to see his wife and family, Hunter arrived once again in Bowie to play for the Double-A Baysox.

The Baysox administrative staff made the arrangements for Hunter to stay the season with another team host family. This time, he was assigned to live with Randy and Karen Joseph, who lived right in Bowie. Ryan Mountcastle was staying in the Joseph's home as well. He was one of the Orioles' two first-round draft picks in the 2015 draft.

Cedric Mullins and DJ Stewart made brief appearances in Double-A Bowie in 2018 before moving up to Triple-A Norfolk. Dan Duquette was right about the player movement from Double-A. It truly was a rollercoaster.

The relationship that teammates dubbed "Salt 'n' Pepper" were only together for forty-some games before Cedric finally got The Call to the Big Show. He was going to the major leagues. Hunter was still waiting for the phone to ring. Players go up and down, down and up, and the movement never ends. Some baseball players move locations while others stay in place. Player transactions occur immediately without any warning. The consequence of player movements can be impactful for everyone involved. The reality of player movement was for every guy who got moved upward, someone else had to be moved downward or released by the team. Every minor league player will eventually be promoted, demoted, released or traded. Nearly all professional baseball dreams die below the major league level.

Hunter Austin and Cedric Mullins always seemed to be competing for the same roster spot, playing the same defense position and the same place in the batting order. Yet they had hit it off as friends. They and another outfielder, Austin Hays, could be seen practicing together in centerfield frequently, laughing at one another in dugouts and hanging out late at night at the Old Bowie Town Grille. But in the minor leagues, relationships come and go as players are moved upward and downward in the organization.

For the second straight baseball season, Hunter walked into the Bowie Baysox locker room and looked around for his locker. He still had the same uniform number, three. As was his custom, he taped up a note inside his locker. The latest was a quote from Walt Disney. "To succeed, work hard, never give up and above all cherish a magnificent obsession." Hunter felt like he had a magnificent obsession.

Due to his baseball obsession, Hunter had to work to show interest in other things in his life, with the exception of his wife, Savannah, and, of course, God. He was so focused on being a major-league ballplayer, he found ways to eliminate things from his mind and avoid people that distracted him. Hence, he would not talk to his father during the ball season if he didn't have to. He asked his father not to attend anymore of his baseball games so he could concentrate on his craft.

If Archie was hurt by that, he didn't show it. Instead, he just replied, "Don't worry about that. I don't plan to watch you play anymore."

"At least we understand each other dad."

Hunter was healthy and motivated for the 2018 minor-league season. He'd never really felt like he'd arrived as a ballplayer in high school, college or even professional baseball. He believed he had to improve continually to keep the negative things his father said about him from becoming a self-fulfilling prophecy. Some of his previous teammates and coaches had worried about the amount of time he spent working out and practicing. When one of his old coaches had suggested he take a break and get some rest, he replied, "I will rest when my playing days are over." No one was going to out-work him to take his spot on a major-league roster. They might beat him out based on talent, but it would not be on preparation and determination.

Hunter was fired up by his recent conversation with Dan Duquette. In his mind, he kept hearing him say, "Guys frequently get promoted from Double-A to Triple-A and some straight to the major leagues." During the first half of the ball season, Hunter saw it with his own eyes as some of his teammates got promoted while he stayed put in Bowie, Maryland.

The Bowie Baysox opening game was on April 5 at home against the Harrisburg Senators. Opening days were fun and contained a lot of ceremony at professional baseball parks across America. Typically, someone famous threw out the first pitch. There was also a huge American flag on the field, and a marching band played the national anthem. Both the home team and visiting team lined the two baselines and every player, manager and coach was introduced to the fans in attendance. All baseball teams started their ace pitcher on opening day. There was a different kind of excitement in the air, mainly because every team was undefeated on opening day.

The Baysox and Senators opening game quickly turned into a slow pitch softball scoring affair. Line drives and home runs flew all over and out of Prince George's Stadium, and the two starting pitchers were quickly removed from the pitching mound and sent to the showers. A total of twelve relief pitchers were sent to the bump from the two bullpens before each team could get twenty-seven outs. Bowie finished on the short side of the score of 10–9.

Although Bowie didn't win their first game of the season, the fans were thoroughly entertained. At most minor-league games, between innings is more fun and entertaining for the fans as there are different games and fan-participation contests on the grass as the defenses and pitchers warm up. But during the opening game, there was even more action occurring during the innings than between them. Hunter was one of four Baysox players who hit home runs. He also had a bunt single and a base-clearing double.

Just as he'd done in 2017, manager Gary Kendall rotated the Baysox outfielders, not only in and out of ballgames but from position to position. He had three quality center fielders in Austin Hays, Cedric Mullins and Hunter Austin, who were all plus defenders. Austin and Hunter also had plus throwing arms. All three were being trained to play the three outfield positions so they could meet any outfield needs of the Baltimore Orioles. Off the field, the three were almost inseparable.

In the team's second game, played on April 6, Hunter used his unusual quickness and speed to steal the first run of the game. After opening the bottom of the first inning with a double, he took his primary lead off second base, then lengthened it significantly after the pitch was thrown as a part of his secondary lead. Cedric Mullins hit a groundball right at Hunter, who busted it towards third base as the ball passed behind him. The shortstop backhanded the ball and hurried a throw to first base. The ball short-hopped the first baseman, hit his glove and popped into the air. As the baseman tried to reach the loose ball, Hunter rounded third base at full speed, and without slowing a step, the third-base coach sent him home. Hunter beat the throw from first base in a cloud of dust at home plate. Later, he laid down a perfect bunt near the third-base line that the defense didn't even try to defend. He also drew a walk and next stole both second and third base.

After his second base hit of the game, the Bowie batting coach, Keith Bodie, turned to manager Gary Kendall and said, "Hunter is absolutely racking right now!" The Baysox went on to a 7–1 victory.

But just like that, Hunter stopped racking, hitting and squaring up balls. He became stuck in his first slump of his four-year baseball career. No one associated with the team could remember him going three or four games without a base hit. Hunter's minor-league career was one of consistency. He hadn't experienced the batting slumps that most batters endure during the long professional seasons. It was typical for all players to grind through a slump for a couple of weeks then break out of it in a big way and be selected as the player of the week. The ups and downs of batting against outstanding pitching was one of the most frustrating aspects of baseball. One day, the baseball looked as big as a cantaloupe, and the next, it looked no larger than a pea. Most days, a ninety-five-miles-per-hour fastball looked like a ping pong ball slammed in your face by a paddle. But when a batter had his timing down at the plate, he could still square up a fastball and turn it around and hit a home run traveling over a hundred miles per hour off of the bat.

Slumps brought out the worst in a player. Baseball players became grouchy, unapproachable and frustrated, and they frequently showed their temper. Baseball helmets, water coolers, trash cans, dugout telephones and even dugout walls weren't safe from a wayward punch thrown by a batter who had just struck out for the third time in a game. And all it took was one or two good swings resulting in well-hit balls for the slumping player to be smiling, flipping bats and buying a round of drinks after the game.

Hunter endured a 0-for-18 streak over seven games. He was given a few days on the bench to clear his head during his slump. But one day in Pennsylvania against the Harrisburg Senators, Hunter hit the first pitch of the game 420 feet over the center field fence for a home run. His batting coach had been working with him during batting practice to improve the timing of his swings. When a player went into a slump, it was usually because their timing was off or they were swinging at bad pitches. Hunter never seemed to swing at anything other than strikes. His chase rate was very low.

Hunter's hitting philosophy was to be selectively aggressive at bat and to stay inside the strike zone when selecting pitches to swing at. He also didn't jump at balls to pull them. Rather, he let baseballs travel farther than most players before his bat contacted them. That way, he had more time to identify the speed and direction of the pitch and determine if it was a strike or ball. Consequently, Hunter hit balls to all fields and not just his pull field, right field. Because of his bunting abilities, foot speed and how easily he hit balls to left field, it was difficult for infielders to shift to his pull field when he batted and to play deep out in the grass.

Bowie batting coach, Keith Bodie, had been working for about a week with Hunter to improve his timing during his batting slump. He suggested Hunter hit pitched balls right back at the pitcher, which would require perfect timing of his swing. Even if he fouled balls straight back to the screen during batting practice, his coach encouraged him, saying his timing was perfect, just not his contact on the ball. Once Hunter got his timing down, he was a hard man to get out.

Hunter was thrilled to play again with his buddy Yaz, although it was unexpected. Mike had been promoted to the Triple-A Norfolk the previous season. But after the season, he was demoted back to Double-A Bowie. Yaz was still on the minor-league rollercoaster; up and down, up and down. Unfortunately, his story wasn't unique for minor-league ballplayers.

Hunter and Yaz often hung out on road trips. When they had home games, they joined Cedric Mullins and Austin Hays at Old Bowie Town Grille or IHOP for late dinners. It was like an outfielder's only fraternity. Hays had previously been promoted to the major leagues on September 5, 2017, making him the first 2016 draftee to reach the big leagues. In twenty games for Baltimore during that season, he had very little success as he batted just .217. But the beginning of the 2018 baseball season found him back in Double-A. With Hays, it was never a lack of talent that slowed his progress. Unfortunately, hardly a year went by that he didn't have an injury that took him off the field for weeks at a time. Mullins was elevated to Triple-A Norfolk on May 30, 2018. He received a promotion after putting together a solid .315 batting average with six home runs, twenty-eight RBI and eight stolen bases through forty-eight games at Double-A Bowie. Later that season, Cedric was promoted to the major leagues, and made his major league debut on August 10, 2018. He finished the 2018 season with a .235 batting average and four home runs in forty-five games played and was prepared to succeed Adam Jones as the Baltimore center fielder.

The 2018 ball season in Bowie was flying by for Hunter. April had quickly turned to May and then suddenly the calendar flipped to June. Life was made up of batting practices, ballgames, long bus rides, cheap hotels, fast food and midnight phone calls home. Then one day he woke up and it was July 3. He lay in bed realizing he'd been stuck in Double-A baseball for a year and a half while players all around him had moved up to the Triple-A team, the Norfolk Tides, and some had made it all the way to the major leagues. Short of being cut, the worst thing a baseball player dreaded was being stuck at one minor-league level. Self-doubt was creeping into his mind.

"Man, I'm twenty-three years old and still in Double-A," Hunter said. "If I get much older, the Orioles might give up on me for a younger outfielder." Self-doubt and insecurity were the norm for minor league baseball players.

On the long bus ride back to Bowie from Erie, Pennsylvania, manager Gary Kendall walked down the bus aisle to the back row where Hunter was sitting alone talking on his cell phone to Savannah. Hunter quickly ended the call when he saw the team's skipper waiting to speak to him.

"May I sit down, Hunter?" Gary asked.

"Sure, skip. What's up?"

The manager eased himself into the seat next to Hunter and asked, "Aren't you from Virginia?"

"Yes, sir. Why do you ask?"

"Because you're going home, son" —a horrified look crossed Hunter's face— "I spoke to Ron Johnson, the Norfolk Tides manager, and told him you've got mental toughness, nothing fazes you on the ball field, and you're the epitome of heart over hype. Your small-ball game may be old school, but you excel at it."

Hunter sat very still as he asked, "So, are you releasing me?"

"Releasing you? No, son, we're promoting you! Starting tomorrow, you'll be on the Norfolk Tides in Triple-A. Only one step from the majors." As the manager made his way back to the front of the bus, Hunter called Savannah right back. "Baby, I'm coming home. I'm coming home. I've been promoted to the Norfolk Tides." He could hear Savannah screaming to her parents at the other end of the phone. "Starting tomorrow night, I'll be able to live in Virginia Beach with you and your parents while I play ball in Norfolk."

There was suddenly silence on the other end of the phone. "Savannah?" he asked.

"Oh, Hunter," she said, her voice trembling, "that's amazing!" Then she was crying for real. After a while, as he sat quietly, feeling her love come through the phone, she managed to say, "Hurry home, slugger. I can't wait to watch you play ball again. And I can't wait to have you home again. Our big bed is so empty without you."

"Me too. I'm so lonely at night when I'm away from you." And Hunter ended the call by saying, "I should be back home tomorrow morning or afternoon. We are traveling all night to Bowie from Erie, and then I have to get my truck and my belongings in Maryland, then drive to Virginia."

The last thing Hunter heard before the cell phone cut out was "Hunter, I love you, and I'm so proud of you!" That was all he needed to hear.

As the Baysox players and coaches slept on the charter bus, Hunter was too excited to close his eyes. He didn't want to wake up and find out his promotion was only a dream. The humming of the bus tires kept him temporarily focused on what lay ahead of him in Triple-A baseball. That level of the minor leagues would be a unique environment for him with the rosters made up of not only young, hot prospects, but also ex-major-league players trying to return to the big leagues with big money, charter flights, first-class hotels and large, beautiful ballparks. The money wasn't great at the Triple-A level of the minor leagues—Hunter was scheduled to earn $11,200 for a full season—but it was better than at Double-A.

As Hunter pondered the situation, his mind went back to his years of playing college baseball at Trevecca Nazarene University. It dawned on him that, by making it to the Norfolk Tides team, he was one of only a few Trojan baseball players to ever play Triple-A level baseball. He also knew that no one from Trevecca had ever made it to the major leagues. A few ex-Trojans' baseball careers had expired in Triple-A. Most of them below that level of baseball. Hunter wondered if he would be the first one from Trevecca to break through the glass ceiling of the major leagues. At that moment, he felt a burden to do it not only for himself but for his little university on a hilltop in Nashville. In a way, he was symbolically carrying a torch for the Trevecca Trojans.

After being up all night riding the team bus from Pennsylvania to Bowie, Hunter jumped in his truck and sped home to Virginia. He got there just in time to have breakfast with his parents, his brother and his lovely wife in the house he grew up in. All they talked about throughout breakfast was the Norfolk Tides.

Hunter managed to take a three-hour nap before heading out after lunch to Harbor Park in downtown Norfolk. It was only a twenty-minute drive from the Austin's driveway to the parking lot at Harbor Park. The Tides home park was located on the Elizabeth River near the Waterside District. The Tides game against the Gwinnett Stripers wouldn't start until 7:05 p.m., but baseball players usually showed up in the locker room around 2:00 p.m. before night games.

Hunter's neighbor Evelyn was going to join Hunter's family at the park to witness his first baseball game played in Norfolk. What a blessing it was to Hunter that he would be playing ball so close to home.

But Archie wasn't planning on watching his youngest son play. "Not going where I'm not wanted," he sniffed.

But when Jo Jo stretched up to his full six-foot-four frame and said, "It's been a year since you've seen Hunter play. You're coming with us even if I have to carry you to the car," Archie's first thought was, "It can't have been a full year!"

Jo Jo purchased a block of tickets and practically dragged his dad out to the family SUV, stuffed him in the Chevy Tahoe with his mother, Granddaddy and Evelyn, and put his vehicle in drive.

Meanwhile, at the ballpark, Hunter had found the Tides locker room easily after giving his name to the security guard, who questioned whether Hunter was a ballplayer or not since he was smaller than most of the studs who enter there before every game. But the guard found the name "Hunter Austin" on the daily updated roster list that the team provided to security. The fact that it was updated every day spoke volumes about the number of daily roster moves made by Triple-A teams.

Only a handful of ballplayers were in the Tides locker room when Hunter Austin breezed in looking for his locker. A ball boy greeted him and asked for his name. Hunter was thrilled to say "Austin," though his voice almost came out in a squeak, and he had to clear his throat and try again. Then he was led to his locker in the back of the room. His locker looked much like all the other ones in minor-league clubhouses with his home uniform hung on a hanger with his name AUSTIN and the number 10 on the back of the green ball jersey. His locker was well stocked with a batting practice uniform and size 9 baseball cleats. Batting gloves, elbow pad and shin pad were also provided by the team. The only equipment Hunter brought with him from Bowie was a couple of bats, his baseball glove and an old pair of ball cleats.

Once again, he taped up a note inside his locker, this one by adventurer Norman Vaughan. "Dream big and dare to fail." He had dreamed of being a professional baseball player since his first trip to a Tides game when he was five years old. Now he was about to play for the same Tides team. What goes around comes around!

Hunter was thrilled to see both Mike Yastrzemski and Cedric Mullins in the Tides locker room. After some hugs and back slapping, they got reacquainted, sharing their most recent lives moving around from one minor-league team to another. But they all acknowledged the same thing: "We're just one big step away from the big leagues."

Yaz showed some prophecy when he told his buddies that's it unlikely that all three of them, all being outfielders and all being small, will ever be in the Orioles' team at the same time. "It's more likely," he continued, "that one or two of us will get traded instead of being promoted to Baltimore."

It was quite the evening at Harbor Park that July 4. There were special patriotic pregame celebrations on the ball field, and a navy sailor sang the national anthem. Before the game, Hunter stood just past the Tides' first base dugout and signed autographs for kids and adults. For some time, he had added the Bible verse reference, "John 3:16," below his signature. But he felt compelled to change his message for the Norfolk Tides' games. That day he switched to Matthew 6:33: "But seek ye first the kingdom of God, and his righteousness; and all these things shall be added unto you." He signed his name to balls, ball caps, t-shirts, scorecards, girl's purses and even a broken arm cast. He followed his name with "Matthew 6:33" and always finished his twenty-second interactions with fans by saying, "God bless you."

That Independence Day, the Norfolk Tides and Gwinnett Stripers played America's game on the banks of the Elizabeth River. Following the game, there was a fireworks display behind the right-field fence. The exploding pyrotechnics reflected off the river as if it was a mirror. Most of the 10,000 fans had stayed glued to their seats after the last out was made on the field to watch the fireworks show. But it seems there were fireworks before the game—in Jo Jo's SUV.

Apparently on the ride to Harbor Park, Jo Jo chewed some butt and it belonged to his father. They had a "Come to Jesus" moment. It all started with a comment from Archie— "I just hope he doesn't embarrass us all" —and Jo Jo nearly drove off the road.

"What is wrong with you, old man?" he yelled, his hands pounding the steering wheel.

"You can't talk to me like that," Archie sputtered. "Janet? Anthony? Have you ever seen anything like it?" But his wife and father just looked straight ahead. Evelyn looked like she was going to cry.

"You are less than a real man," Jo Jo continued as Archie made indignant sounds. "And a lousy father—"

"I have been a great father!"

"—always discouraging Hunter's dreams while the poor kid works his butt off, always hoping you'll throw him some crumb of appreciation."

"It doesn't make sense to lead the kid on."

"Lead him on? He works harder than anyone I know. Anyone!"

"You've got to have talent too," Archie shot back.

"You're an idiot. Everyone thinks he's got talent. Everyone but you—"

"Not the major leagues, obviously."

"Your son is playing for the Norfolk Tides. Tonight! How can you say that?" —Archie crossed his arms stubbornly— "Let me tell you, old man, you will cheer for Hunter tonight, or I will make you."

"You will make me?"

"We will help," Janet said quietly.

Archie turned to her, shocked into silence. Anthony was nodding his head. "You're hurting your family, son."

For the rest of the ride, no one spoke. Archie sat quietly as thoughts swirled around in his head, feeling the sting of Jo Jo's comments. And somewhere between the family's SUV and the Tides stadium, he made a life-changing and family-saving decision. If it killed him, he was going to cheer for and support his youngest son. And then, in a flash of clarity that suggested God's presence, he came to the realization that if everyone else thought Hunter was a stud baseball player, then maybe he was the one with his head buried in the sand.

Jo Jo picked up the family's ball tickets at the stadium's Will Call window and handed each person a ticket, his eyes not meeting his father's. Then they walked through the turnstile, entered Harbor Park and climbed one flight of stairs. There, Archie grabbed Janet's hand, and they peeled away from the rest of the group, who continued walking down the stadium's concourse searching for their seats. He led Janet into the Tides team store located behind home plate on the concourse. He seemed to be on a mission. Archie bought both of them a Tides baseball uniform jersey and ball cap.

"Quick, put them on," he said, a little bossy.

When Archie saw Hunter signing autographs before the first pitch, he got up without saying a word to anyone other than his wife.

"Bring the phone to take some pictures," he told Janet. They managed to sneak past the fan host who was manning the prime seats closest to the field. Holding Janet's hand, Archie pushed his way through the teenagers and little boys hanging out near the railing until he was four feet from his youngest son. Only the three-foot wall and railing separated them. When Hunter looked up to see his dad wearing a Tides jersey and a huge smile, his face lit up with joy and surprise.

"Dad, you look amazing!" he yelled over all the little voices demanding his autograph.

"Son, I feel amazing! Can I have a hug?" A shocked Hunter stepped closer to the railing and hugged his dad while Janet snapped loving pictures of them. Then they looked at the camera and posed standing side by side, arms around each other.

"Dad, I'm sorry," Hunter said. "I've got to go. The games going to start."

Archie nodded, tears in his eyes. "Son, I love you. Have a great game."

Hunter barely made it into the dugout before he dropped onto the bench and covered his head with a towel as he tried to compose himself.

Too quickly for the new Norfolk Tides player, it was time for him to take the field with his teammates. As he ran out to his position in left field, he kept wiping his eyes with his jersey sleeve. He knew playing pro ball in his hometown area would present challenges, demands and benefits, but he couldn't have predicted he would pick up a new fan on day one; the fan who Hunter had auditioned for his whole life; the one he had looked up to as a child, a teen and a young adult; the one who had let him down over and over again. He had no idea what transformation had occurred in his father's life before that day's game. All he knew was that from left field, he could hardly see the pitcher throw the ball because of the tears in his eyes.

Fortunately for Hunter, no balls were hit his way the first inning, and he didn't bat until the second inning. By then, he had control of his emotions and could just concentrate on playing ball. Batting seventh in the batting order, he grounded out to shortstop in the second inning. In the fourth, he was walked after seeing nine pitches. He quickly stole second and third bases and scored a run as the result of a sacrifice fly. Old school, small ball had arrived in Norfolk, Virginia.

So had the long ball. In the sixth inning, Hunter hit a high, outside fastball over the fence in left field that first bounced off a picnic table in the hillside eating area and the baseball demolished someone's hot dog. That home run really had some mustard on it.

As soon as the ball cleared the left-field fence, Archie jumped out of his seat and started running down the aisle yelling, "That's my boy! That's my boy! Every time I see him play; he hits a home run!"

Tides manager Ron Johnson looked surprised that Hunter Austin had that much pop to the opposite field. For Hunter's whole life, he had surprised people. In his last at-bat in the eighth inning, he turned on a slider and crushed a line drive at 105 miles per hour. Unfortunately, the Stripers first baseman was standing in the right place, and he snagged the ball for a put out. Hunter contributed on defense by making a nice running catch of a fly ball in the left-center-field gap to end the game with the Tides victorious 10–5.

After the game, Hunter and a few other players sat in the dugout and watched the fireworks display. To Hunter, there was something childish about playing baseball and watching fireworks. Being at Harbor Park brought back so many childhood memories of seeing games there with his dad and brother and sometimes seeing fireworks on Saturday nights after the Tides games. For this one moment in time, he didn't feel like an adult or a professional baseball player. He was an eight-year-old boy eating cotton candy, asking for autographs, wrestling for foul balls, jumping in the bounce house on concourse, and being in awe at the late-night fireworks.

He was thrilled to be at home with Savannah. The separation they'd endured had been difficult. But quiet talks, long walks, and occasionally starting their day on the front porch sipping coffee reunited the couple's hearts.

Hunter played for the Norfolk Tides for the last two and a half months of the 2018 Triple-A International League schedule. Savannah attended nearly all of his games played that summer in Norfolk, and sometimes she sat with the ballplayers' wives and girlfriends. Occasionally, she pulled school papers out of her bag and proceeded to grade her students' papers. When she heard the sound of the crack of a bat hitting a ball, she'd quickly look up to see if Hunter was involved in the action.

She developed one friendship among the players' wives and girlfriends. At a previous minor-league game, she'd met Mike Yastrzemski's fiancée, but Mike had quickly moved on to another city to play ball. This time, the two women could spend some time together. When Savannah wasn't sitting with the family, she always tried to sit near her new friend and they'd talk about engagements, weddings, honeymoons, marriages and careers. Savannah was tickled to hear her refer to Mike as "Yaz."

Hunter started to make an effort to see his dad more often in his parents' house, and he bought his parents Tides baseball tickets whenever they wanted to see him play. Archie made an effort to keep track of Hunter's ballgames and his individual achievements. One day, he handed Hunter a baseball he'd snagged at Harbor Park.

"Son, will you autograph my baseball for me?"

Hunter signed it and hugged his dad. That baseball ended up on the fireplace mantel at Archie and Janet's house alongside a football signed by Jo Jo.

As the Norfolk Tides season progressed through July, Hunter's play in the field and at bat earned him more important positions in the lineup. He was splitting time evenly in center field and the corner outfield position with Cedric Mullins. There was some experimentation going on with the team's batting order too. Sometimes Cedric would leadoff with Hunter batting second; sometimes Hunter would lead off and Cedric would follow. The two outfielders, still affectionately called "Salt 'n' Pepper" by their teammates, seemed like interchangeable parts of the Tides Triple-A team. But in private chats, they both agreed that only one of them would likely be promoted to the Orioles.

Later that season, Cedric received The Call to the major leagues and made his major-league debut with the Baltimore Orioles on August 10. Hunter Austin finished the 2018 season with the Norfolk Tides following his promotion on July 4, 2018 from Double-A Bowie. When his buddy got The Call to the big leagues before he did, Hunter thought he could read the writing on the wall concerning his own future, and in his mind, they weren't positive words. Hunter knew the odds were low for any minor league player to make a major league roster. But when a player's competition, for playing time and opportunity, gets promoted before him, the writing on the wall gets more clearer for the overlooked ball player.

Both Savannah and Granddaddy counseled him.

"You have to stop comparing yourself to your teammates," Savannah said.

"She's right," Granddaddy added. "Just keep playing hard and grinding away. Unlike most of the guys in Triple-A, you've never been demoted."

Hunter had to nod in agreement.

"And your rise to Triple-A has been slow and steady," Savannah said. "So why wouldn't your rise to the Orioles be slow and steady too?"

"Yeah, that makes sense," Hunter conceded.

Anthony brought up another angle to think about. "Have you heard about the Norfolk Shuffle?"

"Yeah. Why?"

"There's a steady stream of player movement between the Orioles and the Tides," his grandfather pointed out. "Some players are promoted and only stay a few days in Baltimore before they're shuffled back to Norfolk. Hence the term, the Norfolk Shuffle," he added for Savannah's benefit. "Sometimes it seems the major leagues are playing a card game, and their baseball players are the cards. When the team doesn't like the hand they've been dealt, they throw away some cards and grab shiny new ones. "

"I don't get why this is important," Hunter said, a little impatient. He wanted to get on with his sulking.

Granddaddy shook his head as if Hunter had missed something obvious. "Because of all the player movement, you have a decent shot at the Orioles taking a look at you in Baltimore to see if you can help them."

Their wise counsel helped Hunter keep his focus through to the end of the Triple-A season.

Though he only played ball for Tides manager Ron Johnson for two and a half months, Hunter loved playing for his Triple-A skipper. Ron had the neatest sayings that always made the players think and reconsider their attitudes.

"If you don't like it here, do a better job," he would tell an unhappy baseball player who thought he was stuck in Triple-A. When players would be discouraged about their bad game or their hitting slump, Johnson would tell them, "Turn the page. The next day will be a new opportunity to succeed."

He had a way of putting a positive or hopeful spin on a bad experience. Hunter especially liked that Ron treated every one of his ballplayers the same, whether they were hot prospects or undrafted players. He understood that most players didn't want to be in Triple-A, where traveling was inferior and salaries were a fraction of those made in the big leagues.

After the 2018 baseball season, and following seven seasons as manager, Ron was fired as manager of the Norfolk Tides, even though he received the Orioles Cal Ripken Sr. Player Development Award at the end of the season.

Hunter's favorite memory of Ron Johnson was a time the Tides manager was exchanging lineup cards at home plate with an opposing manager who was complaining that his pitchers couldn't get Hunter Austin out. Ron's advice was to walk Hunter and get the next batter to hit into a double play.

Hunter cherished something that Ron had told the press about him. "His clutch hitting and willingness to bat behind in the count while waiting for a good pitch to hit are the products of having cold blood in his veins." Hunter liked that idea.

Johnson also said, "We like Hunter Austin. He's very analytical. He studies the game. He's able to figure stuff out for himself and make the appropriate adjustments. The thing that stands out to us in the dugout is that he is always trying to improve. He works out and practices skills longer and harder than any other two players combined. Hunter has worked for everything that he's achieved. Nothing has been given to him on a platter except for a bunch of rejections."

And that was true. Hunter finished the final two months at Triple-A Norfolk with a batting average of .300 and an OPS of .780 in fifty-five games, and hitting five home runs, stealing seventeen bases and achieving six outfield assists.

Everyone in professional baseball found the minor leagues to be more of a challenge than a reward. But it was the price each player had to pay, including enduring the all-night bus rides to another ballpark, eating a steady diet of fast food and staying nights on the road where they "leave the light on for you," all to have a chance to make their major league dream come true.

The challenges found in Triple-A were ratcheted up compared to that in Single-A and Double-A baseball. Triple-A was a pressure cooker. The pressure to impress and be promoted was constant. Dealing with the disappointment of not receiving The Call for another day was only topped by putting up with teammates who didn't want to be in the minor leagues at all. Each Triple-A team's roster had a handful of older ballplayers with major-league experience who thought they should still be in the big leagues and young guys who were unhappy they weren't there yet.

Players in Triple-A watched the box scores of their organization's major-league team to see if any of the players were doing poorly and might get demoted to the minors. They also read the disabled list. Anyone put on the DL was replaced, at least temporarily, from someone in the minor leagues. Any demotion resulted in an equal promotion. And any teammate's promotion to the big leagues further frustrated players because they had once again been passed over. Competition between teammates on the same team was hotter than that with opposing teams.

Hunter tried his best to stay above the fray and just play ball. He frequently called his grandfather late at night since Anthony had once played minor-league ball. He would unload his frustrations and disappointments with his play and his teammates' behavior. Granddaddy always knew just what to say. Someone once told Hunter that everyone needs a therapist now and then, and his therapist turned out to be his grandfather.

One day, when Hunter was visiting him at his house, Anthony said, "Hunter, I know you are big into quotes for inspiration. Well, young man, do I have a quote for you! This was attributed to Walter Elliot. 'Perseverance is not a long race; it is many short races, one after the other.' That's exactly how I view professional baseball. It's one level of baseball followed by another and then another, and at each level a player will find the challenge of playing well enough so that he gets promoted again."

After the last Tides game, Hunter cleaned out his locker, said his goodbyes to his teammates and coaches, loaded his pickup truck and headed home for the off-season. He only had a twenty minute ride to get there. Savannah was waiting for him outside her parents' house on their front porch swing, as she had done many times before. By now, all his adrenalin had worn off and tiredness had set in. They sat together on the swing, talking, sipping sweet iced tea, eating a midnight snack and getting caught up on their day before they went to bed. As always, they concluded their "us time" on the swing with prayer.

Savannah had already begun an online master's degree program through Regent University. Regent was a faith-based university located in Virginia Beach. This way, she could continue her course of study anywhere that had internet access.

They often talked about how their lives would change if Hunter made it to the major leagues and stayed there. His salary would increase at least fifty-fold and the team travel to away games would be first class in every way, including charter flights, nice hotels and a sizeable meal per diem. As wonderful as that sounded to a young man dealing with the hardships of playing in the minor leagues, Hunter didn't daydream about the lifestyle a career in the major leagues would bring. He couldn't dream past his first day, his first game playing for a major league team. At that current moment in time and for the last twenty years, receiving The Call for at least one day on a major-league roster was everything to Hunter. It was the light at the end of his tunnel.

19

ON THE THRESHOLD (2018–2019)

Following the 2018 baseball season, after a few weeks of relaxing, surfing, shooting hoops, playing golf and visiting old friends, Hunter recommitted to an intense ninety-day workout plan at the strength and conditioning facility in Virginia Beach he'd used in previous years. He did his usual off-season workout that included baseball drills, sprint and agility drills at the nearby rec center ball field, running up and down Mount Trashmore, and getting friends and family to load baseballs into the pitching machine for him to hit at an indoor batting cage.

The off-season following the 2018 season was a defining moment in the history of the Baltimore Orioles organization. "Change and redirect" were the buzzwords throughout the Orioles universe. And the organizational self-evaluation, changes and redirection were all brought about by one thing—losing.

The Baltimore Orioles finished their 2018 season with one of the team's worst records in MLB history. They lost 115 of the team's 162 games. First baseman Chris Davis posted a .168 batting average in his third year of a seven-year, $161-million contract, the worst batting average in Orioles history. At the trade deadline on July 31, 2018, Baltimore traded away many of their best players and acquired younger, unproven prospects who were, for the most part, still playing in the minor leagues. The O's traded Jonathan Schoop, Manny Machado, Kevin Gausman, Darren O'Day, Zack Britton and Brad Brach. The trade of Brach to the Atlanta Braves showed a new direction for the Baltimore team as they only received bonus slot space to sign international players in return for Brach. The international market for baseball players was one that the Orioles had rarely participated in.

After the end of the 2018 season, General Manager Dan Duquette's contract expired and wasn't renewed; it was the same for the team's manager, Buck Showalter. The changing of field leadership continued down into the team's minor leagues. Triple-A Manager Ron Johnson was released from his contract as manager of the Norfolk Tides, and Double-A Manager Gary Kendall was promoted to manage the Tides in 2019. The Baltimore Orioles underwent nearly a total transition of their organization following the 2018 season. They were also showing their intention to go after international amateur ballplayers and delve into the world of analytics.

Low-budget teams, such as the Tampa Bay Rays and the Oakland A's, relied heavily on the use of analytics to build a competitive team on a minimal budget. The concept of "sports analytics" was introduced to sports fans through the 2011 film, Moneyball.

Although throughout MLB, athletes, coaches and front office personnel were more receptive to using data to improve their performance, the 2018 Baltimore Orioles were one of the last teams to dive headfirst into the swimming pool of sports analytics. The Orioles ownership group felt they needed to hire team leaders who understood the value of analytics and recognized metrics and patterns that may not have been obvious to its previous team's manager and coaches.

After the 2018 season, the concept of analytics was about to be introduced to the Orioles organization, from the major league team down through their Low A minor league team. Terms like a batter's launch angle and exit velocity, pitcher's spin rate, defensive shifts using a short fielder or fourth outfielder based on a batter's count, and where he was likely to hit the ball would all become everyday jargon in Birdland. The first and most important step for the ownership group was to hire a general manager who could double as the team's executive vice president. They would be in charge of the team's rebuilding project and philosophical shift.

In November 2018, the Baltimore Orioles introduced Mike Elias as its executive vice president and general manager. Elias had previously served as the Houston Astros assistant general manager of scouting and player development. The Astros had become one of the most successful analytics-focused franchises in baseball.

Mike Elias quickly hired Brandon Hyde as manager of the Orioles and promoted Double-A Bowie manager Gary Kendall to manage the Norfolk Tides. Don Long was hired as the Orioles hitting coach and Doug Brocail as their pitching coach. The general manager's next task was to put in an analytics infrastructure in the organization from top to bottom.

The game of professional baseball in 2019 was hard for many traditionalists to recognize.

"Baseball has evolved too fast and gone too far," they said.

In the decade sometimes referred to as the "twenty-tens," the evolution, fueled by the use of sabermetrics, forced MLB out of traditionalists' comfort zones. Many of the changes to the old school ways involved a pitch count on starting pitchers to limit their number of pitches to about one hundred a game, over-valuing and overuse of relief pitchers, using "openers" instead of "starters," catchers "framing" pitches, balls being thrown away after they hit the dirt one time, swinging up at balls to hit more home runs, swinging from the heels in case the bat made contact with the ball so there was enough bat speed to hit a home run, and home-run hitters batting leadoff. There was a lack of emphasis on 1. hitting behind the runner to move him over and get him in, 2. on bunting and 3. less emphasis was on stealing bases.

This worried Hunter so much; his days were filled with anxiety. To his core, he was an old school ballplayer. The way he thought about and played the game had been strongly influenced by his grandfather's experience playing in the minor leagues fifty years ago. Anthony frequently complained while watching a baseball game on TV about all the modern changes to the sport.

"There's no action!" he would shout, frustrated by the many pitching changes, batter's stepping out of the batter's box after each pitch to reattach their batting gloves, and batter's swinging and missing and only occasionally hitting a home run. On the other hand, he loved Hunter's game of "hitting 'em where they ain't" and running like a deer around the bases.

Praying helped Hunter take a break from his anxiety. He enjoyed attending church again with Savannah and her folks now that he was back at home. He'd missed the preaching and praise music that he hadn't receive during the eight or nine months of baseball activities.

When he finally got a letter about his next assignment in the mail, he didn't really want to open it. He made Savannah do it. He was assigned back to the Triple-A Norfolk Tides with major-league spring training camp at the Ed Smith Stadium complex. In February of 2019, Hunter reported to the Baltimore Orioles spring training camp once again in Sarasota, Florida. Hunter knew he was ready to play in the major leagues if only he was given the opportunity. In his previous season, which was in Triple-A, he had played as well as his teammates during the two months he was in Norfolk, only to see some of them receive The Call to Baltimore while he toiled in the minors. It was frustrating. He had lived a life of being undervalued. But he also knew that "Perceived failure is oftentimes success trying to be born in a bigger way."

On his birthday, March 1, it hit him that, for a baseball player hoping to be promoted to the majors, he was getting old. Most players reached the majors within three years of starting in the minor leagues. He was about to begin his fifth year in the minors as a twenty-five-year-old. Other outfielders he'd played with in the minor leagues had already played for the Orioles including Austin Hays, Cedric Mullins, Anthony Santander and DJ Stewart.

He asked himself the same question everyone else in Triple-A was asking themselves, "Why not me?"

When Savannah called to wish him a happy birthday, she could tell that he needed some encouragement. She tried to talk some sense into her man, but first, they prayed for God's peace for him so that he could control his mental outlook on his career. She also gave her husband a word of wisdom from Biblical scripture.

"Philippians 4:6. 'And the peace that surpasses all understanding will guard your hearts and minds in Christ Jesus.'"

Spring training seemed a bit unorganized in 2019 since there had been such a turnover in management at the end of the previous season. Most of their team leaders in the front office were new. The new managers, coaches and ball players needed to get to know each other. From general manager Mike Elias and his top front office executive Sig Mejdal, through the team's hierarchy, everyone was trying to use analytics to help managers and coaches coach better and make better decisions about the players. The Orioles even had their own scouts evaluate and do scouting reports on the 150 to 200 baseball players in camp just as they would do on opponent players.

In spring training camp, Hunter got to be coached by the Baltimore Orioles' new manager, Brandon Hyde, and his coaches, as well as the Norfolk Tides' new manager, Gary Kendall, who Hunter already knew from his Baysox days. Hunter also got to play in big-league games with established major leaguers like Chris Davis, Jonathan Villar, Trey Mancini, Alex Cobb and Dylan Bundy. Of course, his buddies, Yaz, Cedric and Austin Hays were there too. But he felt a vacuum from all of the players who had been traded away the previous year.

Hunter began to doubt whether his skills and abilities would fit with the new changes the Orioles were implementing. Once again, he felt like he had to prove himself worthy of a roster spot. The chip on his shoulder from his childhood days resurrected itself in that moment.

"Why does nothing ever come easy for me?"

Day after day, year after year, he had to prove himself worthy. But his hard-headed approach would not allow him to quit working on his craft. He promised himself that, if he was going to get overlooked in spring training and/or in Triple-A Norfolk, he would give team leadership something to talk about in 2019. And boy did he.

The Baltimore Orioles' players, for the first time, who were expected to play in the minor leagues in 2019, were given cards with defensive positioning instructions on them for each opponent's batter. The "cheat sheets," as the players called them, slipped into their back pocket or inside their hat. It told defenders where to align themselves as each opposing hitter stepped in the batter's box. From the batter's perspective, it was a cat-and-mouse game. But no matter where the defense positioned their nine defenders, the goal for batters was the same; get a good pitch to hit and get the sweet spot of the bat on the ball.

Hunter enjoyed working with his new hitting coach, Don Long.

Coach Long told him, "I'm not going to try to mess with your pretty, level swing. I am impressed with your mental approach to hitting and your knowledge of the strike zone. I believe that you have a plan at the plate, and your baseball statistics prove that it is working for you." Coach Long talked to all of his players a lot about being ready to hit and believing that they can hit, maybe even more than about their hitting mechanics.

During the spring training batting practices, batters tried to elevate their bat's contact with pitched balls and hit them over the fence. At the same time, Hunter continued to fine-tune his level swing, not jump at the ball and hit balls to all fields. His ability to discern whether pitches were out of the strike zone and to wait until the last possible moment to swing at balls made him a tough out. Because of his base-stealing abilities, pitchers didn't want to walk him, so he frequently got good pitches to hit. And hit he did. Hunter batted .310, hit three home runs and stole ten bases during spring training games. He was turning some heads among the Baltimore leadership. But an immediate promotion to Baltimore, straight out of spring training, was not possible due to the glut of young outfielders on the Orioles roster. The reality was that his pathway to the major leagues was blocked. He had to wait for someone to get hurt, play poorly or get traded. And so, Hunter began the 2019 season as a member of his hometown Triple-A team, Norfolk Tides.

He was happy to be home after spring training, but he carried a burden with him that Savannah picked up on quickly. They were standing on the front porch in the quiet of the night, and she said simply, "Tell me what's concerning you."

"Savannah," he said, his frustration showing in his first word, "I'm on the threshold of getting to the major leagues, and I honestly believe I'm good enough, but I also believe that I won't get The Call. The Orioles don't need me, and they don't have room for me on their roster. Instead of promoting me, I'm staying in the minor leagues. I may die on the vine here in Norfolk waiting for a call that may never come."

Savannah wrapped her arms around her man and held him close.

"Hunter, you're the same man that the Orioles fell in love with four or five years ago. They gave you $100,000 not to go back to college for your senior year. You're the same man who earned a scholarship in college after you proved all the recruiters wrong. And you're the man who was the captain of his high school baseball team after only playing in a handful of games. You have stardom written all over you, honey, even if you can't see it. You are not only going to make it to the big leagues, but you will be a star someday. If you don't make it with Baltimore, you'll make it with another ballclub. I believe that, Hunter Austin. And I believe in you."

He dropped his chin onto his wife's shoulder and held her tight. Not a sound could be heard except for the croaking of a frog and Hunter's sniffles. Hunter's 2019 salary of $11,200, or $500 a week, during the six-month ball season, was the same salary he received playing Triple-A baseball in 2018. Professional baseball players are not paid during the two months of spring training or in the four months of off-season. They did receive an "allowance" during spring training.

The Norfolk Tides 2019 opening game was in Atlanta, Georgia, against the Gwinnett Stripers. The usual enthusiasm from the fans for the season's first game was on full display. The fan hosts were giving directions to seat seeking ticket holders. The concessionaires were walking the ballpark aisles selling peanuts, cotton candy, soda and beer. And during the seventh inning stretch, the baseball fans stood and sang, "Take Me Out to the Ball Game." Jo Jo attended the four-game series in Atlanta as he lived nearby.

Hunter led off the first inning of the season's first game with a line drive single past the pitcher's head. Someone on the Tides bench yelled out, "The pitcher is awake now!" In his next three at-bats, Hunter walked twice and grounded out. Even though he reached first base three times and stole two bases, he didn't score any runs. The Stripers walked away with a victory by the score of 3–1. The next day, Gwinnett could not keep Hunter off the bases or keep him from stealing. He reached base four times with three doubles and a base on balls. He stole third base once and second base another time. He scored three of the Tides' six runs and they shut out the Stripers 6–0.

Nonetheless, the Tides lost three of the four games with the Stripers, but not because of Hunter's play. After just four ballgames, he was batting .539, had three bases on balls, five stolen bases and one homer. He had provided the Gwinnett Stripers with "something to talk about," but he wasn't sure if the Baltimore Orioles had noticed.

Next, the Tides played a three-game series against the Charlotte Knights, the Triple-A affiliate of the Chicago White Sox, in Charlotte, North Carolina. Charlotte's pitchers dominated the first two games by throwing shutouts. Hunter managed to get one hit in each of the two games and stole another base. The Norfolk Tides also lost the third game of the series as Charlotte swept them. But the last game played on April 10 was a wild one. The lead changed five times as both teams' bats heated up during the warm Wednesday afternoon.

Hunter Austin couldn't be kept off of the bases as he bunted for a single, walked and hit two home runs. The last dinger traveled 430 feet into the right-center-field seats. The previous home run barely cleared the fence in the right-field corner, inches inside of the fair pole. Two Charlotte Knights were sorry they tried to score from second base during the three-game series. Hunter's throwing arm prevented both runners from scoring as his throws nailed each runner at home plate.

On April 11, the Tides home opener was played at Harbor Park. The security guard smiled and said hello as Hunter entered the Tides locker room;

he remembered him from the previous season. That alone made Hunter feel special.

Once he located his locker, he taped up a note inside it with a quote from American southern gospel singer and songwriter Dottie Rambo: "Defeat is one word I don't use … There's too much to gain to lose."

The Norfolk Tides home opener at Harbor Park was against the Toledo Mud Hens, the Triple-A affiliate of the Detroit Tigers. As usual, Hunter's family and friends attended and cheered on their hometown boy. Several of them spoke to Hunter before the game near the Tides dugout and a blue-eyed blonde, wearing a white blouse covered by a denim jacket, leaned over the railing separating the fans from the field and kissed him. Hunter was so relieved she was his wife. He even got a good luck hug from his mom and dad.

Love was in the air and the baseball was in the Tides starting pitcher's hand. "Play ball!" a fan yelled from just behind the Norfolk Tides dugout.

Earlier in that game when the Tides were scoring runs in a 30-minute half inning, Hunter was chilling on the bench waiting for his turn to bat. His mind wandered back to his previous season in Norfolk. Hunter remembered what the last Tides manager, Ron Johnson, told the 2018 team as it was underperforming, "If you don't like it here, do a better job." That saying and Hunter's promise to himself as he left spring training to give the Orioles' management something to talk about fueled his fire the first few weeks of the Tides season. Hunter never played better professional baseball than he did in April 2019.

The long home stand continued for the Norfolk Tides. Toledo Mud Hens left town only to be followed by the Durham Bulls. They were followed by the Charlotte Knights. None of the International League teams had much success getting Hunter Austin out that April. There wasn't anything that he couldn't do very well at that point in his career on a baseball field. His teammates joked with him, saying they wanted to take him to the ocean to see if he could walk on water. The biggest laugh his teammates got at Hunter's expense was when one of the guys found a used baseball with a couple threads loose. The teammate messed with the ball in the dugout during the game until he broke a bunch of threads and peeled back a piece of leather. He took a pen and wrote on the ball "Hunter Austin knocked the cover off of this ball." The next time Hunter got a base hit and scored a run, his teammate waited for him to enter the dugout.

"Hunter, the ball that you just hit has been thrown out of the game," he said, handing him the destroyed baseball. "You really knocked the cover off of the ball." Laughter filled the dugout followed by a bunch of back slaps from Hunter's teammates.

Symbolically, it did seem like Hunter had been knocking the cover off many baseballs in the first three weeks of the 2019 minor-league season. In the Tides' first nineteen games, he batted .400. His on-base percentage was .510. His on-base plus slugging percentage was .830. He went deep four times, had twelve extra base hits, stole eight bases and led the Tides outfield with three outfield assists. The Baltimore Orioles' management was indeed talking about the performance that Hunter was showing them. He practically demanded a promotion to the big leagues with his bat, legs and throwing arm.

The Baltimore Orioles major-league team was off to a slow start that April. Their pitching left a lot to be desired, and they were not getting any production out of their leadoff hitter, Cedric Mullins. Cedric took the place of long-time center fielder Adam Jones for the 2019 season. The Orioles thought they had found their centerfielder of the future, but in twenty-two games, Cedric was hitting just .094. On April 22, 2019, the Orioles sent him back to Triple-A Norfolk.

After his demotion, Cedric Mullins hit just .205 in Triple-A and consequently was further demoted to Double-A Bowie later in 2019. It was a humbling experience for Cedric, to say the least. But professional baseball was not for the faint of heart. Just ask Mike Yastrzemski.

The only other buddy of Hunter Austin's who hadn't yet made it to the big leagues before May 2019 was Mike Yastrzemski. Yaz had been knocking around the minor leagues for seven years, and it didn't look like he was being considered as a major league prospect.

Although Hunter was added to the Orioles forty-man roster before spring training of 2019, Mike was not. The team only invited him to spring training as a non-roster player.

During spring training, Yaz's minor-league roller-coaster ride took him from the east coast to the west coast. On March 22, 2019, the Baltimore Orioles traded Mike Yastrzemski to the San Francisco Giants. He was assigned to the Sacramento River Cats of the Class Triple-A Pacific Coast League to start the 2019 season, where he batted .316 and hit twelve home runs and twenty-five RBIs before he received The Call. The Giants promoted Yastrzemski to the Major Leagues on May 25, 2019 at the age of 29.

20

THE BIG SHOW (2019)

Professional baseball continued to be a heartbreaking dream killer for some, while dreams come true for others.

April 22, 2019, was an off day for the Norfolk Tides and the day was commonly referred to as Easter Monday. About 9:30 a.m., Hunter was fast asleep on the couch of his parents' house in Virginia Beach. He'd been visiting and had fallen asleep with Cinnamon on the couch while Savannah and his mom whipped up a brunch in the Austin's kitchen. When his phone rang, he was sound asleep. Since he didn't answer it, it rang again, and again. By the time he picked up and grunted, "Hello," the rest of his family had heard the ringing and had come into the room. Norfolk Tides Manager Kendall was on the phone.

"Boy, you better wake up and get in your car."

"What for, skip?"

"You are being promoted to the Orioles, effective today, that's what for. The O's are hurting at the top of their lineup and they need someone to jump-start their offense and raise a little havoc on the bases. So, I recommended you to Brandon Hyde in Baltimore. The Orioles manager asked me if you're ready for the big time and all I could say was that the pitchers in Triple-A cannot get you out and that no one has thrown you out stealing this season. So, Brandon will be your next manager, and you are now officially a Baltimore Oriole. Oh, the Orioles game tonight starts at 7:05 p.m. so be in uniform by 4:00 p.m. so you can take some batting practice, check out the outfield fences and the warning track. By the way, the ball really carries well in Camden Yards compared to Harbor Park in Norfolk. So … what do you think?"

For a moment, Hunter's mind was blank, then he blurted, "I always wanted to have my picture on the front of a bubble gum baseball card."

Hunter Austin hung up and then sat quietly for a moment holding his phone. His mind was spinning like a top.

Getting The Call was one of those things where, at first, you think you misheard what was told to you, but you know your manager would never lie to you about something like that. Hunter stared at the phone for what felt like an eternity before he could react to the great news. "I can't believe it," he said, his voice shaking. "I got the call to Major League Baseball." He looked up, his eyes wide. He could see identical looks of joy on everyone's faces. "They called me up to the big leagues folks!" The rest was lost in screams and cheers, hugs and kisses and two men sobbing into each other's arms with a dog jumping up between them. Savannah and Janet raced around to get him out the door.

"Savannah has to get him home and pack him up. He's going to the big leagues!" Savannah suddenly shouted, clearly losing her head as well. At that moment of exhilaration, Hunter believed that getting called up to the majors was the best moment of his life. It *only* took twenty years of playing baseball to reach the highest pinnacle of the sport. "*Perceived failure is often times success trying to be born in a bigger way.*"

The next few hours were a blur of craziness, as the Austin and Montgomery households tried to get Hunter packed up and on his way, while also celebrating his good news. Savannah took a moment of his time by pulling him aside to tell him how proud she was of him.

"You've reached the light at the end of your tunnel," she said, her arms around his neck. "You've accomplished your dream. And I'm so excited that I can finally see you play ball on TV." Laughing, he gave her a series of kisses.

When Hunter received The Call, it felt like his Red Sea had been parted. Surely God had a hand in this. Triple-A managers usually give the lucky ballplayer his call-up news face to face, typically right after a minor-league game was over. But since April 22, 2019, was an off day for the Norfolk Tides, a phone call was appropriate. When a player was called up to the major leagues for the first time, his teammates would give him a send-off in the clubhouse with everyone gathered around to offer congratulations. Most of the time the team's manager would call the ballplayer into his office and act like they were giving him bad news. Then with the ball player sweating bullets, he was finally told that he was going up to the show. Hunter missed out on those minor league traditions.

What the Norfolk Tides manager didn't tell Hunter was that Gary Kendall had closed his sales pitch early that morning for Hunter by saying to the Orioles' brass "Hunter exceeded everyone else's expectations for him, but not his own. He is exactly where he earned the right to be; right where he ought to be; and right where he deserves to be. Since the Orioles are beginning a serious rebuilding of their organization from the big leagues to the lowest minor leagues, Hunter Austin may just be the perfect guy to jump-start the Orioles' offense and defense."

Brandon Hyde, the Baltimore Orioles' manager paused for what seemed like an eternity before he said, "I tend to agree with you that we should bring up Austin today and send down our current centerfielder, who needs to find his hitting stroke."

Hunter posted the news on social media and then phoned his brother and grandfather. On the phone, Jo Jo couldn't stop laughing gleefully about his little brother's news. "That's so cool! That's so cool!" he kept saying. Jo Jo was between seasons while playing for the Atlanta Falcons. Then he started screaming, "Oh my God! Maybe we will both be on ESPN someday!"

Granddaddy broke down in tears on the phone, which made Hunter choke up again.

"I thought everyone would be smiling and laughing about my good news, but everyone's making me cry."

"You're my special boy," Anthony said. "You didn't let your many challenges defeat you."

"I want to thank you, Granddaddy, for taking over my baseball training and supporting me for the last ten years. I honestly would not have made it this far without you. I love you."

"And there I'm crying all over again. I love you too, Hunter."

Since Baltimore didn't promote Hunter until April 22, they retained another year of control of his baseball contract. For the first three major-league seasons, players started at a collectively bargained minimum salary with small increases in years two and three. Hunter's salary would start at $555,000. Even though the average salary of all MLB players that year was $4.4 million, he knew it wasn't until after the first three years that major-league players could start making some serious money, some getting paid more than $10 million in a year. After six years, they became free agents who were able to sell their services to the highest bidder. He was just happy to be going to the big show.

Cedric Mullins and Hunter Austin basically exchanged teams and locations, with Cedric moving back down to the Triple-A Norfolk Tides, and Hunter, for the first time ever, moving up to the major leagues to play for the Baltimore Orioles. As excited as Hunter was about getting called up to the big leagues, he hurt for his buddy, Cedric. For most of the years the two of them spent in the minor leagues, they were in competition to play center field and to bat leadoff. The head-to-head competition never seemed to divide those two small, fast rabbits.

Holding Hunter down in the minor leagues for the first 23 games of the Baltimore Orioles schedule prevented him from earning a full year of major league service time in his rookie season. Teams typically manipulate service-time by leaving their best prospects in the minor leagues through at least the first 16 days of a season. Doing so ensures that the team gains an extra year of contract control of their baseball players.

Hunter had learned that the salary for a player's first season in the major leagues was $555,000, prorated for the first 23 games he was not in the major leagues. Since a full season was 162 games, the proration salary amount would have likely been about $427,350. Besides their salaries, major league baseball players received meal money to spend when the team was playing games away from their home stadiums. The collective bargaining agreed upon meal rate was $105 a day in 2019.

The difference between Hunter's initial major league salary and his final minor league salary was astronomical. His final Triple-A salary was $11,200 a year. His major league salary in 2019 was to pay him what amounted to $3,426 a *day*. Speaking of a pay disparity, just four days in the big leagues would pay Hunter $13,703, more than he would have earned playing a full season of minor league baseball.

Before Hunter could contact the Baltimore Orioles about buying tickets for his family and friends to that night's baseball game, his phone started ringing off the hook from those reading his great news on social media. As he packed, he asked these folks if they could go to the Orioles game and see him play for the first time. His mom booked ten rooms at the Hilton next door to the Baltimore Harbor Park. But the best negotiated rate she could get was $300 a night per room. Janet promised to contact Hunter's list of those to invite to the April 22nd ball game and see who could make the drive or fly to Baltimore and stay at least one night.

Earlier that day, as Hunter was driving to Baltimore for his major-league debut, Coach Kendall called him again. This time he picked up right away.

"I wanted to tell you," Coach said. "Just block out all the noise playing in the major leagues. Stay mentally focused. There are so many distractions in the big leagues, like TV cameras, the press, fans, groupies, pretty girls, money, competition, teammates and the pressure to play well. None of that is important. Just keep your mouth shut, work hard and act like a professional because you never know when your opportunity to get in the lineup is going to come, and when it does come, take advantage of it."

As Hunter parked his truck in the players' parking lot next to Oriole Park at Camden Yards, he bowed his head and asked God for peace over his anxieties and to help him be able to play ball up to his abilities. He also thanked God for this opportunity to play in the major leagues. When he climbed out of his truck with his bag of bats, gloves and cleats, Hunter felt God's power and strength flowing through his veins.

When he walked into the Baltimore Orioles locker room for the first time as a part of a major-league roster, his name was already written in the starting lineup for the game. He was to bat in the number one hole and play center field. Opportunity was knocking. Hunter looked the room over for some clue to tell him which locker had been assigned to him. His eyes made contact with a huge sign hanging over one locker that read "Welcome to the show Rookie!"

"I guess that one's mine," he said as a big smile broke out over his face. He had to pull the sign down just to get to his baseball belongings in his locker.

In Hunter's locker, hung his white Baltimore uniform, trimmed in orange and black, with the name AUSTIN across the upper back and a huge number 3 below it. His thrill quickly turned to regret. It was the same number Cedric Mullins wore yesterday for the O's before Hunter Austin replaced him on the their roster. At that moment, Hunter understood how calculating and unforgiving professional baseball could be. He was only promoted at the expense of his friend. But he also knew he'd have to put Cedric out of his mind so he could enjoy his first day in the big leagues; the day Hunter Austin had dreamed about for twenty years.

Hunter was excited to see batting Coach Don Long again. Coach Long told him, "I'm not the least surprised to see that you have made it to the show, and I wasn't surprised that you were raking in Triple-A. I heard you were hitting .400 when you were called up. The Orioles desperately need someone to get on base twice a game to sit the table for the few big hitters that we have. You just might be that guy. Be patient, though. Failure in the major leagues is common, especially hotshot rookies who were previously tearing up the minor leagues. The pitchers here are the real deal, very talented and very smart. Do what you've always done and wait for a good pitch to hit. Pitchers will try hard to sit you up to swing at unhittable balls. Don't fall for their act. Be disciplined at the plate. If you see enough pitches, you'll get one that's hittable."

Hunter Austin got into his Orioles uniform and cleats, and located a sliding oven mitt, shin pad and elbow pad for his first big-league game. He grabbed a couple of his bats, a set of batting gloves and his ball glove, and headed up to the dugout. Batting practice at Oriole Park had already begun. Hunter was assigned to hit in a last group of players, so he grabbed his glove, hat and shades and ran out to the outfield to shag fly balls while he waiting to bat.

Hunter walked out to the warning track to size up how much area it covered and determine what the dirt-and-gravel mix felt like under his cleats. He noted that the power alleys in left center and right center were closer to home plate than in most minor-league ballparks. So, he expected to see more extra base hits, even home runs, in Baltimore than he was used to.

During his rounds of batting practice, Hunter laced line drives all over Oriole Park. He even jerked a couple balls up on the flag court overtop the scoreboard in right field. But mainly, he focused on hitting the balls where they were pitched and using the barrel of the bat to complete his level swings.

Later in the practice, Hunter saw some of his family and friends sitting in their seats along the first-base side of the park. They were close enough to the Orioles dugout for him to see their faces. It looked to him like his mom and dad had brought the whole neighborhood back home with them. He later learned that some of them came from as far as Nashville to watch his first big-league game and that a total of nineteen people came to see him play. Hunter went over to the wall railing to say hi to his gang of fans. But all too soon the big moment was upon them. After blowing kisses to his wife and mother, he stepped into the dugout and they disappeared from his view. It was time to put his game face on. It was time to earn his money. But mainly, it was time for Hunter to live out his childhood dream.

The crowd sitting in seats at Harbor Park specifically to cheer on Hunter that night was impressive, especially considering the short notice. Of course, all the Austins and Montgomerys were there. They wouldn't miss this day for anything. There were a bunch of his coaches from across the years, from his middle school and high school days, including Coach Collinsworth. Stephen Collins from Trevecca was there, as was his college buddy Robin Lee. Also, many of his neighborhood friends came including Liam Thomason, Brady and Brandon Doolittle, Bryce Jennings, Asher Brown, and Evelyn Applegate and her mom, Karen.

Later, some Orioles official speculated that the nineteen tickets sold to out-of-towners who came to support Hunter Austin's first major-league game might be the most family and friends ever to do so for a player. He said that the number to attend a player's first game was usually between two and ten people.

Manager Brandon Hyde put Hunter Austin at the top of the batting order and played him in center field for his first Orioles game. The weather was perfect for baseball that Monday evening in Baltimore, seventy degrees and hardly any wind. By the time the game began at 7:05 p.m., most of the 8,555 in attendance were in their seats ready to enjoy America's pastime.

About 7:00 p.m., the Orioles' starting nine players ran out of their dugout in Oriole Park and found their positions on the baseball field. After playing the national anthem, Hunter and right fielder Trey Mancini warmed up their arms by playing long toss. Baltimore starting pitcher, David Hess, threw his eight warm-up pitches off of the pitcher's mound. Catcher Pedro Severino rifled a throw to second base.

The white ball with red stiches was returned to Hess. Professional baseballs are made by hand at the Rawlings plant in Costa Rica.

David Hess spun the brand-new baseball around in his hand as he leaned in to get the sign from Severino on what pitch to throw. The catcher put down one finger. David nodded and griped the ball with his first two fingers squeezing the ball tightly across the ball's two seams. As David lifted his left leg and stepped towards home plate, his right arm followed with his hand releasing a fastball. As the ball soared towards the Chicago White Sox leadoff batter at ninety-two miles per hour, Hunter Austin's first big-deal, big-time, big-league game had begun. Now, he could exhale and try to shake off the butterflies bouncing around in his stomach. He tried to tell himself that it was just another ballgame, something he had participated in a zillion times before. But he wasn't good at lying to himself. This was different. This was for all the marbles. This was like standing on the summit of Mount Everest with both hands raised, like a Rocky pose, celebrating a mountain climb that took all the time, effort and money imaginable. He had arrived at the summit of his baseball career. What he didn't know was how long he would stay there and if he'd find success. But in this moment, he didn't care. He was living in the moment and living out his little boy dream.

After David Hess struck out the first two White Sox hitters in the top of the first inning, Chicago's stud hitter, José Abreu, smoked a ball to right-center field. The ball carried to the warning track and was sinking quickly. Hunter had been playing slightly on the left field side of center field since José was a right-handed power hitter. Trey Mancini in right field conceded that the ball was in the gap and would result in extra bases. Trey positioned himself to catch the ball as it bounced off the wall. But the Orioles center fielder conceded nothing, and he was on his horse as soon as bat met ball. Just as the baseball was about to contact the ground, it was snagged in Hunter's glove webbing as he landed chest first in the dirty gravel of the warning track.

In the stands, Jo Jo jumped up and down at his seat and high-fived strangers near him.

"That's my little bro!" he yelled.

Trey slapped Hunter twice on the back as they ran towards the O's dugout while the Orioles manager Brandon Hyde turned to Coach Long and yelled, "That was such an athletic play! Hunter really earned his Air Jordans."

After his amazing catch, Hunter was the birds' leadoff hitter in the bottom of the first inning. He was so excited after making that catch and out of breath after running the ball down and then jogging one-hundred-plus yards from the outfield wall to the dugout that he quickly lost all of his anxieties about playing his first big-league game. Now he was really into it.

As he took practice swings in the on-deck circle, Hunter noticed grass stains on his white Baltimore uniform. He remembered that his mom hated cleaning his ball pants when he played rec-league baseball. Apparently, dirt and mud are hard to get out of clothes, but grass stains are nearly impossible. What a crazy thing to have on his mind as he stepped into the batter's box for his first time at Oriole Park while his walk-up music played.

Just before the game that evening, someone from the Orioles organization asked Hunter what song he wanted to have played over the stadium sound system as he walked to home plate to hit. Officially, it was referred to as "walk-up music". Hunter told them that he hadn't thought about that yet. Then he had an idea. Since he'd paved his own path through baseball when so many others tried to discourage him, he knew what he wanted to hear.

"How about that old Frank Sinatra song. I think it goes, "I did it my way."

What Hunter didn't know was that Frank Sinatra's "My Way" was America's anthem of self-determination. Indeed, self-determination was what had propelled Hunter to this very moment. "My Way" became Hunter's first walk-up song in MLB.

The Chicago starting pitcher, Manny Bañuelos, delivered a curveball off the plate for ball one. He threw left-handed, and Hunter batted left-handed. Since he had the ability to cover the outer third of the plate better than the inner third, Hunter had very little difficulty hitting left-handed pitchers. He next received a fastball on the outside corner of the plate, which was perfect for his plan. He had noticed the White Sox third baseman didn't respect his ability to bunt, so the Orioles' newest leadoff hitter squared up and bunted the ball a total of forty feet down the third-base line. By the time the third baseman reached the ball, Hunter had passed first base.

It was the Baltimore's first hit of the game, and Hunter Austin's first base hit of his budding major-league career. The Baltimore Orioles dugout screamed at the umpires to throw Hunter's ball into the dugout. The trophy baseball rolled into the Orioles dugout as requested. It was a major-league tradition to keep baseballs for the player who'd just accomplished something important or memorial in their career, such as a first hit, first home run or for a pitcher, a first strikeout. The Orioles batboy secured the ball and later put in in Hunter's locker for safekeeping. Following a stolen base and a wild pitch, Hunter reached third base only to be stranded there as the third out was made.

In the third inning, Hunter ran the count to three balls and two strikes before not swinging at an outside fastball just off the plate's black. The fourth ball resulted in a base on balls. Again, Hunter died on the bases when the inning ended.

Through the first four innings, David Hess was wheeling and dealing from the bump for the O's with the White Sox only getting one base hit. The Chicago starting pitcher, Manny Bañuelos, was just as unhittable, so the game rolled into the fifth inning in the blink of an eye with the score 0–0.

But in the top of the fifth inning, the White Sox figured out Hess and knocked him around to the tune of four runs and four hits.

In the bottom of the fifth inning, Hunter came to bat with one out and no one on base. Ryan Burr, a right-handed relief pitcher was in the game facing the Orioles rookie who he thought, based on a scouting report, was a Punch-and-Judy hitter. Hunter turned on a changeup, hit it out front of the plate and lifted a fly ball to right field, which cleared the scoreboard and landed on the flag court, some 375 feet from home plate.

"Home run!" his father screamed from the stands.

It was Hunter's first jack as a big leaguer—his first "four-bagger," "big fly," "dinger," "long ball," "shot, "moon shot," "bomb," "blast," "homer" and just plain "home run." Some described it as "going deep" or "going yard." However you described it, Hunter's contact with the baseball resulted in a run being scored.

Jo Jo and Savannah got so excited about Hunter's home run that they ran up the stairs to the stadium concourse and made fools of themselves screaming and yelling in celebration. Hunter's father started bawling his eyes out with emotion. His mother just hugged her Orioles' program to her heart and smiled.

Someone from the Baltimore Orioles administrative staff went to the flag court in an effort to locate and retrieve Hunter's home-run ball. About a half hour later, she made her way to the Orioles dugout with the baseball and a big smile on her face. There was no telling what she offered the fan who caught Hunter's home-run ball, but it probably was another baseball plus a couple free tickets to a future ballgame. Again, it was an MLB tradition to return baseballs to the player who just accomplished a milestone like hitting his first home run. The batboy took the ball and put it in Hunter's locker next to the ball from his first base hit.

In the top of the seventh inning, the White Sox jumped all over Tanner Scott and scored another four runs to take an 8–1 lead in the game.

In the bottom of the seventh inning, Hunter managed the strike zone effectively and received another base on ball from the White Sox pitcher. He just refused to swing at borderline pitches. He never considered stealing second base with his team behind by seven runs.

In the top of the eighth inning, the White Sox feasted on Miguel Castro's pitches and scored another four runs to take a 12–1 lead in the game. When the score climbed past 10–1, it was like someone had pulled a fire alarm at the Oriole Park because the fans started heading towards the exits with one purpose in mind— "Get out of Dodge while the gettin' is good!"

By the time the Baltimore Orioles batted in the bottom of the ninth inning, only one tenth of the attendance of fans were left in the stands. But the nineteen devoted Hunter Austin fans near the first-base dugout stood and rooted for their guy as he batted in the last inning. Even as Hunter grounded out shortstop to first base to end the baseball game, his old fans, and the new ones he made that night, surged forward to congratulate him.

The final score for Hunter's major-league debut was the Chicago White Sox, 12, the Baltimore Orioles, 2. But the score didn't matter a bit to his family and friends. Their guy had reached The Show.

After reaching his locker after the game, Hunter received some fist bumps and pats on the back for his 2-for-3 game plus two walks, one stolen base, one home run and one diving catch.

Manager Brandon Hyde found Hunter and gave him a big hug for his play that night.

"I see what Gary Kendall meant about you influencing a baseball game in so many positive ways," he said. "Oh, by the way, I just talked to him on the phone about how you played tonight. Kendall told me to ask you if you've got your picture on the front of a bubble gum card yet."

Hunter laughed. "Not yet, skip. I just got to the big leagues today."

His family and friends were waiting for him when he exited Oriole Park in the players' parking lot. Many laughs and tears were shared as the Hunter Austin fan club celebrated in a well-lit but nearly empty parking lot at Camden Yards. Robin Lee and Stephen Collins were wearing Trevecca's purple jerseys.

"Did you know," they asked him, "that you're the first Trevecca Trojan baseball player to make it to the major leagues?"—that message humbled him—"We're already spreading the news around the Trevecca campus. Everybody's so excited and praising God."

At that moment, how Hunter felt led him to kneel in the ball stadium parking lot with his clan of loved ones, and he thank God almighty for blessing him with abilities and perseverance to fulfill his lifelong dream of playing major-league baseball. Thanksgiving had come early in Baltimore.

Not only was Hunter representing his former college in professional baseball, he was representing all the little boys who had ever played baseball in Little Leagues and rec leagues, and the bigger boys who played in Pony Leagues and the Babe Ruth Leagues. Of course, he was representing his middle school and high school too. But Hunter also took a lot of pride to be representing the city of his birth, Virginia Beach, Virginia. It made him just want to reach out to all of them and embrace them in a great big hug and say, "Never give up and your dreams can come true."

Hunter Austin joined the impressively long list of men from the city of Virginia Beach who played in professional baseball's major leagues during the 2019 season. The list included: **Mark Reynolds**, First Colonial HS, UVA. Colorado Rockies, **Ryan Zimmerman**, Kellam HS, UVA, Washington Nationals; **Neil Ramirez**, Kempsville HS, drafted in 2007 by Texas in round #1 (out of high school), Toronto Blue Jays; **Daniel Hudson**, Princess Anne HS, ODU, Washington Nationals; **Chris Taylor**, Cox HS, UVA, LA Dodgers; **Sean Poppen**, Cape Henry Collegiate HS, Harvard University,

Toronto Blue Jays; and **Hunter Austin**, Kempsville HS, Trevecca Nazarene University, Baltimore Orioles.

After all the excitement of the day had settled down, Hunter realized he'd forgotten to put up a motivational note inside his locker. The next day, he went in and taped up a note just below his two special baseballs. It was a quote from Rocky Balboa: "Every champion was once a contender that refused to give up."

AFTERWORD

It has been fifty-one years since I played my last baseball game or was in a baseball dugout or locker room. But I've never stopped loving America's pastime, as baseball was once known.

I miss seeing green grass stains on my baseball pants from diving for balls in the outfield, and I'll never dirty another pair of baseball stirrup socks from sliding into bases. The thing I miss the most about playing amateur baseball and softball is the camaraderie between teammates. The victories for me were sweet and the losses were bitter, but most of the memories that have lasted for decades are the relationships—of ballplayers rooting for and supporting each other and picking up their teammate who had made an error or hit into a double play.

Numerous names and terms were used in this novel. They include real and fictitious names, real and fictitious quotes, real and fictitious statistics and definitions. They are meant to bring realism to this piece of historical fiction. Not everything written is accurate or true. Historical fiction provides the author great latitude in presenting a story that may seem real but is mainly the author's imagination set in a real-world setting. It transports readers to another time and place, either real or imagined. It offers a fiction writer many opportunities to tell their wholly unique story.

I would like to honor the memory of Ron Johnson, the winningest manager in the Norfolk Tides franchise, who passed away in January 2021 as a result of the effects of the COVID-19 virus. Rest in peace skipper!

I'd also like to tie up a couple of loose strings for avid baseball fans. After being on the baseball rollercoaster, Cedric Mullins made his way back to the big leagues in 2020 and played like he never wanted to see the minor leagues again. As for Mike Yastrzemski, he also showed that "every champion was once a contender that refused to give up." Yaz finally received The Call on May 25, 2019, and put on the San Francisco Giants uniform. Now, I could give you both their stats, but you can read them yourself on their "bubble gum" baseball cards.

The spirit of this novel was to create a realistic story that was fairly factual and accurate and yet full of imagination and fantasy. I hope you enjoyed reading it. It was fun to write.

Printed in the USA
CPSIA information can be obtained
at www.ICGtesting.com
LVHW051252061123
762867LV00021B/112/J